THE LANGUAGE OF OTHERS

For Jessica Fontaine, the world is a puzzling, sometimes frightening place. As a child she is only content playing the piano, or wandering alone in the empty spaces of Audlands Hall, the dilapidated country house owned by her parents.

Twenty-five years later, divorced, and with a son still living at home, Jessica remains preoccupied by her need for physical and emotional space. Then her volatile ex-husband reappears, the first in a series of surprises that transform Jessica's present and her perspective on the past.

Related with wry humour, verve and compassion, this absorbing story of a woman negotiating life's ups and downs without quite grasping the rules of the game gives a fresh, illuminating insight into what it means to be 'normal'.

THE LANGUAGE OF OTHERS

OF OTHERS

Clare Morrall

WINDSOR

PARAGON

First published 2008
by
Sceptre
This Large Print edition published 2008
by
BBC Audiobooks Ltd by arrangement with
Hodder & Stoughton Ltd

Hardcover ISBN: 978 1 405 68676 1
Softcover   ISBN: 978 1 405 68677 8

British Library Cataloguing in Publication Data available

Printed and bound in Great Britain by
Antony Rowe Ltd., Chippenham, Wiltshire

For Alex and Heather

CHAPTER ONE

Jessica stood alone in the silent space, contemplating the Long Gallery in front of her—a beguiling, empty corridor of oak floorboards. She started to move, her roller-skates stiff and uneasy as they rumbled across the uneven wood. The growl of creaking ball-bearings drifted upwards, dissipating on its way to the arched ceiling until it was absorbed into the crumbling plasterwork.

Patches of sunlight illuminated her progress as she swept past the tall windows, her fat black plaits flying out behind her. Doric columns framed the windows, their white marble grubby and chipped, while busts of assorted Caesars stood guard at regular intervals, looking down their imperial noses with disapproval. The walls were powder blue. Gold-edged rectangles framed large areas of blankness where there had once been pictures.

Jessica Fontaine was seven years old, a sturdy, grounded-looking girl. Fat, according to her two boy cousins, bonny according to her distracted, unobservant mother. Her brown eyes, flickering with feverish excitement, were focused ahead of her for a change, shaken out of their normal downwards slant. Today she had to look where she was going.

She almost laughed out loud. This was joy. Air rushed past her, a wind in her ears that banished the outside world. She was exhilarated by the freedom of her solitude. Her feet were setting a rhythm, arms and body moving in harmony, as she sped past fireplaces, ornate silver-edged mirrors, a plaster frieze depicting the siege of Troy, everything as it had always been, but now fleeting, tenuous, inconsequential.

A few yards from the end, she realised that she didn't know how to stop. The vast panelled door loomed ahead, approaching faster than she had expected. She put her feet together, hoping this might slow her down, then stretched her arms out as a collision became inevitable.

Her hands slammed into the door but failed to stop the progress of the skates. Her feet kept moving until they could go no further, and she fell in a small heap, her bottom thumping heavily on to the floor and her hands stinging with pain.

She sat there for some time, coming to terms with the abrupt cessation of speed and her aching body. But none of it cancelled out the experience of flying, the weightlessness, the liberation. Inside, she was still moving.

'Jess!'

It was her sister, Harriet, from somewhere inside the house, searching for her, as always.

Jessica wished she could curl into an invisible hole, and remain separated. She wrapped her arms round her legs, dropped her head and rolled over on to one side. I'm tiny, she thought, non-existent. She pressed her eyes tightly together and saw kaleidoscope patterns in the darkness. Brilliant flecks of gold and red, swirling and throbbing inside her head.

She was disturbed by shrieks of laughter outside the window.

'It's by the fountain,' called a boy. ' "Ding dong bell, Pussy's in the well . . ." ' She recognised the voice of Philip, her cousin.

2

'No, it's in the clock tower,' shouted Colin, who always automatically argued with his brother.

There were three cousins, the two boys and Judy, racing through the garden with children from the village, following a treasure hunt organised by Jessica's mother.

Jessica uncurled herself and crept over to the nearest window seat to peer out. She rubbed with her sleeve at a small, grimy pane of glass until it came clear, and then she could see them all, bounding across the courtyard, heading for the distant clock tower. Jessica knew they were going the wrong way because she'd seen the clues earlier, but they were enjoying themselves so much that accuracy was irrelevant.

Her mother was with them, her miniskirt sliding up her legs, leading the crowd, laughing more than anyone else, not prepared to give anything away. She arranged a treasure hunt every Wednesday at two o'clock during the summer holidays for Harriet and Jessica, the cousins, their friends and anyone else who wanted to join in. They congregated by the lions on either side of the big wrought-iron gates. Jessica's mother was always there, on time whatever the weather, dividing them into groups, handing out the first clue on little strips of paper. Each clue had been copied out several times the day before. Harriet usually helped, forming slow but accurate letters. Jessica dashed off a few if compelled to, but her mother complained that she wrote them too fast and they were unreadable. The standard of the clues varied from simple to impossibly obscure—to give everyone a chance, her mother said.

The previous afternoon, they had prepared for

3

today's treasure hunt, sitting round the kitchen table with orange squash and flapjacks. Afternoon tea, their mother called it.

'What does this say?' said five-year-old Harriet, studying a list of clues.

'Hoop-la,' said Jessica.

'Oh yes,' said Harriet, as if she understood. She copied it on to a piece of paper in large wavering letters. 'But what does the "la" bit mean?'

'Nothing,' said Jessica. 'It's to do with fairs. Where you throw the hoop over the prize you want.'

'Oh,' said Harriet. 'So what does the clue mean? Where do you go?'

'Somewhere on the croquet lawn. Obviously.'

'Jess,' said their mother. 'Don't be patronising. You don't want Harriet to think she's stupid.'

'That's right,' said Harriet, and licked her pencil as she started on the next one.

Their mother leafed through the book of quotations in front of her and wrinkled her nose, shutting her eyes as if she was smelling something delicious. 'I love treasure hunts,' she said.

She had long, straight, honey-coloured hair down to her waist, which she tied into a single plait for most of the day. In the evening, after supper, when she and Jessica's father settled down in the drawing room to watch television, she let it out and it swayed sleekly, dense and shiny, enveloping her shoulders in a silken shawl.

Jessica watched her outside with the other children. Her mother liked to laugh a lot and wanted other people to laugh with her. The treasure was always a great disappointment to Jessica. It was usually only a few lollipops that had

4

to be shared by everyone, but no one else seemed to mind. It was as if the real treasure was the hunt, the running, the fun.

Jessica heard a noise behind her and turned round to see Harriet's shiny black shoes placed neatly in front of the window seat.

'There you are,' said Harriet, her delicate, elfin features lit up with satisfaction.

CHAPTER TWO

'Hi, Jess,' the email message reads, 'I really need to see you. Can we meet in Birmingham City Centre? By the bull? Friday. 12.30. Andrew.'

Why have I agreed to this?

I suppose I just want to reassure myself that he's still all right. Like checking up on a delinquent teenager who doesn't have the skills to look after himself properly.

His first email popped into my inbox a fortnight ago and caught me unawares. All casual and airy, like an old friend who'd lost touch.

'How's things? What are you doing with yourself now? Still driving the Mini, or have you advanced to more sophisticated levels? A Peugeot, perhaps? Or a Citroën? I saw in the *Evening Mail* that you and Mary are tickling the old ivories together. I hope they're paying you.'

It's been seven years since I last saw or spoke to Andrew. I used to deliver Joel to his flat on alternate Sundays, passing him over with a sigh of relief, my mind already ahead of myself as I anticipated a glorious day of silence. But once he reached sixteen, I told Joel he had to make his own arrangements. So there's been a good long recovery time. I've even taught myself not to think about him.

Where did he get my email address? I can't believe Mary would give it to him and I have the impression that he and Joel haven't been in contact with each other for some time. But he's devious. He can be very clever when he makes an effort.

Apparently, he has a new job. He gets up very early in the morning, takes the bus to Northfield and sweeps up rubbish. He has a cart and large broom and he likes it. I suspect it appeals to his sense of importance. 'Satisfying work,' he told me in one email. 'I'm a man of the people. None of your brain work needed. Just me and my broom.'

The really surprising thing is that he's been doing it for more than a month. There must have been hundreds of jobs since the last time I had contact with him, but I'm not tempted to ask for details. I prefer not to know.

I should have ignored him. I can't explain to myself why I replied, why we progressed into a light-hearted, witty repartee. It would be embarrassing to admit to anyone that I have any contact with him at all. My mother's voice is in my head. 'Are you mad?'

'What does he want?' my father would say. 'Is he offering you some belated maintenance?'

And Mary, even Mary would give me a look, although she wouldn't be prepared to put anything into words.

*   *   *

I recognise him immediately as I approach the Bull Ring. He's more seedy than he used to be. He looks like an expensive suit that's never been pressed, gradually losing its sharpness, the pockets dropping, a button missing, the shape of his knees imprinted in the trousers. He has one of those baby faces that won't age until he's at least sixty. Paul McCartney looks. He could be going on tour with a rock band and still pulling in the crowds if he put his mind to it. But he would never do that. Putting his mind to it was something he abandoned when he was twenty.

He's shifting impatiently from foot to foot because there are too many people round him and he doesn't want anyone to step on him. He doesn't know how to weave and blend, how to move with the flow, how to let things go.

He's always cultivated a neglected look. I can imagine him standing in front of a large mirror in the flat I've never been inside—he will have plenty of mirrors—and admiring his dishevelment. 'Yes,' he'd say. 'This would please my mother.' Which, of course, it wouldn't.

It's puzzling to me that I was ever drawn to Andrew. Those creases in his cheeks when he smiled played a significant part, I suppose, and his hair, which seemed so glamorous when I first met him. I don't believe in blond men now. I always imagine an arrogance lurking beneath those shining curls, a cold ruthlessness concealed behind the gold veneer. I'm not impressed by aging rock singers.

We don't kiss, embrace, or give any sign that we know each other except a nod of recognition. All is as it should be. We head directly for the BHS cafeteria because not wasting money on unnecessary luxury is an ingrained habit for both of us. Not that it really matters to Andrew, since I'm sure I will be the one who ends up paying.

*   *   *

Andrew argues with the lady dishing out. 'No liver with my bacon,' he says.

'It's liver and bacon, love. If you don't want liver, wouldn't it be better to have something else?'

He eyes her contemptuously. 'Why should I have liver if I don't like it? Why shouldn't I have bacon? Where's the logic in that?'

'You can have bacon and eggs, you know. We serve breakfast all day.'

He remains stationary in front of her, a look of steely determination on his face.

'Come on, Andrew,' I say. 'There's a queue behind us.'

This is a mistake. If you ask Andrew to be brief or understanding or polite, he will do the exact opposite on principle. He points at his mouth. 'Read my lips. No more liver.'

She purses her lips and a line of little wrinkles forms the shape of a temporary moustache. 'Bacon it is, then,' she says. 'Although don't hold me responsible if you meet the odd bit of liver.'

'Odd's the word,' he says and his face twists into an unexpected smile. 'That's what I've got against liver.'

The woman looks at the next customer. She will not be won over, which is good for Andrew. He has always believed he can charm people. He needs to

8

be outmanoeuvred by reality more often.

We shuffle along the rest of the counter, while Andrew debates the crispness of the lemon meringue, the freshness of the Danish pastries, the consistency of the cream on the fruit trifle. I don't argue. I take the same as him, not considering if I like it or not, ready to go for any option rather than spark an argument. How easy it is to fall back into our old roles.

We find a table and sit down, but not before Andrew has spotted some crumbs left by a previous customer and gone to find a waitress to wipe the table.

Life with Andrew. Exhausting, conciliatory, hard. It always was.

For fifteen years I've struggled to earn a living without him, bring up our son, who has not always cooperated in the experiment, and learnt to do all the things Andrew failed to do as a husband. I haven't exactly glided downhill with the wind behind me, but at least I haven't been doing it at the same time as fighting the Force Ten gale that was Andrew. I've made it. I've survived. And here he comes again. Like some giant black hole, manipulating events around him, feeding off his surroundings, sucking everything into his way of thinking.

I can walk away at any time. I'm free. So why do I feel sympathy for him? Why should I care about his state of mind? When I see him, I'm reminded of his endless frustration, his thwarted ambitions, and I know I'm looking at the unhappiest man in the world. There's no way for him to break away from himself.

'So how's Joel?' he says at last, sorting through

9

the gravy on his plate and pushing to one side all the bits of liver and onion he can find. The reject pile mounts up on the side. He eats by enclosing the fork with his teeth, but not his lips, then picking off the food. He doesn't close his mouth properly until he has removed the fork.

'You could ask him yourself,' I say.

'I would, but as I'm sure you know, he won't speak to me.'

So I was right. I wonder whose fault it was. Who made the decision to cut off communication? Which one took the first step and which one jumped in enthusiastically to take up the challenge? I can't ask Joel, who rarely answers personal questions. He either stares past me as if I'm not there, or changes the subject, or leaves the room.

'He's looking for a flat,' I say.

'He's not still living at home?'

I sigh. 'I'm afraid so.'

'Tell him to go. The boy shouldn't be sponging off you after all this time. He's twenty-four, for goodness' sake.'

'Twenty-three.' You'd think he would know the age of his only son.

'Whatever.'

'He's fine,' I say. 'His business is going really well.'

And as far as I can tell, it is. He goes off every day to his office, where he employs five people, and comes home at night looking pleased with himself. He has the intelligence and he has the application. He just doesn't want to leave home. He enjoys having his meals cooked, his laundry done, his bills paid without having to think about

10

it. I worry about him. Could he manage on his own, or is he another version of his father? Shinier on the outside, but just as incapable underneath.

Andrew and I eat in silence for a while. It's difficult to make conversation, and I wonder how we ever managed when we lived in the same house.

'Did you get a letter from the university?' I ask.

'Why would they write to me?'

'They want to compile an accurate record of all their ex-music students. Where they are, what they're doing. They call them alumni now, you know.'

He snorts. 'Alumni? Pretentious nonsense! What's wrong with graduates? They probably think that giving everyone a Latin title makes them more generous. They're after your money, Jess, that's what it's all about. Anyway, they're only interested in people who actually graduated.'

I should have thought of that. Not a good line of conversation.

'My mother turned up the other day.'

I stop eating and stare at him, convinced I've misheard. 'Your mother?'

He grins and he's that charming student all over again, a mischievous glint in his eye. 'You must learn to keep your mouth shut. It doesn't suit you to be gaping like that. Hold on—is that a gold crown I can see on the second molar, bottom right?'

I shut my mouth. 'Your mother?' I say again.

He nods and puts down his fork. 'My father's ill.'

I should know this, but I haven't spoken to them for ages. It's years since Joel and I were invited over for occasional visits. 'Is it serious?'

He nods. 'Apparently he's dying.'

11

'Oh.' I think about how to react. Shock? Pity? Sadness? I'm not sure which one to go for, so I keep my face neutral.

'Cancer of the liver.'

No wonder Andrew didn't want liver with his bacon. Should I feel sorry for him? After all, it is his father, even if they don't communicate. 'How's your mother coping?'

'I think she's enjoying the status. Nearly a widow.'

'You mean she actually came to your flat?'

He sighs. 'Yes. To tell me about my father, she said. To see how I live, she meant but didn't say, and to give me my violin.'

'She brought your violin?'

'Yes. All twenty thousand pounds of it. Although it must be worth a lot more now.'

'Did she leave it with you?'

'Yes.'

I can't believe this. 'Why?'

He pushes his plate to one side with a grand gesture. He's eaten all he intends to. 'She's been thinking.'

'Oh dear.'

'Quite. Anyway, she says it's mine, so I should have it. Apparently, once you're over forty, you're old enough to make your own decisions.'

Then she's six years late. 'It doesn't sound much like your mother.'

He frowns. 'I'm not sure what she's up to.'

'Did you invite her in?'

'No. Returning someone else's property doesn't give you the right to invade their privacy.'

I try to make sense of this violin business. Why would his mother give it to him? Isn't she worried

12

he'll destroy it, or sell it? 'Do you think she's expecting you to play it?'

His face sags. 'If she is, she can go on expecting,' he mutters into his coffee. 'She knows how I feel about that.'

'When was the last time you discussed it?'

'When was the last time she spoke to me?'

'So she knows what you thought about it when you were twenty, but she may not know if you still feel the same way.'

'Do I care?'

'Will you go and see your father?'

He hesitates. 'No.'

'But he might die without you ever seeing him again.'

'He should have thought of that. He knows where I am.'

'Andrew—he's your father.'

'Hmm.'

We don't discuss it any more. There have always been so many subjects that are best avoided with Andrew. Few things change.

We leave the cafeteria and emerge into the crowds of New Street. 'I must get back,' I say as we head towards the car park. 'I've arranged a last-minute practice with Mary.' I don't want to walk through the crowds with Andrew. It's difficult to stay side by side and he will get annoyed if I surge ahead without him or struggle along in his wake. I put my bag on my shoulder, trying to look businesslike. 'Lovely to see you. Let me know how your dad gets on.'

'Jess—' he says.

'Although I suppose with liver cancer it's all fairly inevitable, isn't it? Could he have a

13

transplant?'

'Jess—'

I look at him standing beside me, struggling to stay upright against the crowds that are rocking him backwards and forwards, a broken branch bobbing in a stream, buffeted by the force of the water, incapable of intelligent action to save himself. He looks crumpled, folding in on himself, lacking the strength to resist.

'What?' I say.

'I wanted to ask you—I've been meaning to ask you—'

'What?' I'm fighting my natural inclinations. I can feel myself being drawn along to save him, ready to dive in, even though I know I can't swim and I'll get caught up in the current—

'Couldn't we—?'

'What?'

'Couldn't we have another go? Try again?'

'Try what?' He can't mean what I think he means. Panic makes me talk faster. 'Another meal? Go to see your father?'

'Jess—' His eyes are urgent. A small child willing me to do what he wants. 'Couldn't we—you know—get back together again?'

I take deep breaths. I need to slow down and be logical. I won't allow him to switch on the pathos and expect us both to return to our student days. I know things now. He's not as he seems. He's a full-sized, authentic leopard. I've seen his spots and the colour can't possibly have faded.

'Jess?' he says.

'No!' I turn away from him fiercely and walk in the opposite direction, even though it's not where I want to go. I have to do this physically. It's the only

14

way. If I look at him too long, see past his bravado and glimpse the desperation beneath, I will start to waver.

'Jess!'

With relief, I realise that his voice is fading and he's not following me. I start to run. Up New Street, back towards the Bull Ring. When I reach the bull, I pause in the safety of its solid, shiny bulk and look back. I can't see him. The bull's tail arches above me, curled into a perpetual flick. I turn away and head for Next, up the escalators to Homeware where I can relax. He won't follow me here. He has no interest in curtains or coffee tables or sofas.

*   *   *

Joel is in the living room when I get home, sprawled over the sofa with his shoes off, watching *Bugs Bunny*. I love my son, but right now it seems as if there are too many people in my life, all pressing up against me, denying me the opportunity to breathe properly.

'Hi, Mum,' he calls as I disappear to the kitchen.

'Hello, Joel. You're back early.'

'Yes. We made a huge breakthrough, so I gave everyone the afternoon off.'

He formed his own company—ScarlattiSkills— at seventeen, and designs computer games. His ability must be an offshoot of his father's neglected talent. Patterns, new ideas, fast thinking, alternative ways of seeing things. He tells me he's making money. 'The world adores me,' he says every now and again, which I take to be an indicator of a successful business deal. He doesn't

15

lack confidence.

It saddens me that all those brains are employed in the pursuit of fun, rather than something more lasting and worthwhile, but I realise this is a narrow viewpoint. If people can't enjoy themselves, be happy, there's not a lot of point in anything. Happiness is only irrelevant if you don't have enough to eat.

'I'm not cooking tonight,' I call as I slip off my shoes and throw them to the side of the kitchen where I might or might not pick them up later. 'You'll have to fix something for yourself.'

'Oh . . .'

He has to learn. 'I told you this morning. I've got a last-minute practice with Mary before the concert tomorrow, and I'm staying for supper.'

He appears at the open door of the kitchen and I can feel his presence by the movement of air as it bounces towards me. The unrelenting whoosh of a real person, the suffocating sense of people where I want emptiness. 'You don't need to practise, Mum. You're already brilliant.'

I smile across the room at him. I'm grateful for the fact that he's not unemployed, an alcoholic, a drug addict, but I wish I didn't have to see him every day of my life. No breaks, no holidays, no time off for good conduct. He never goes away. He doesn't have any friends, only work colleagues. Something's not quite right. He couldn't get on with other children when he was younger, but why can't he do it now? Twenty-three years is a long time to have no social life.

He's tall like his father, careless with his body in the same casual, masculine way, but he dresses better. He buys his clothes on the internet and his

16

entire wardrobe arrives through the post, so I see each item before he decides to keep it.

'What do you think, Mum?' he will say, coming downstairs with the labels hanging out, creases still in the shirts, buttons only half done up.

'Lovely,' I say. 'Do you think perhaps the green is a little unsubtle?' Get a girlfriend, I think. Please get a girlfriend. Then you could ask her, and I would be saved this decision-making.

'But I like the green.'

'Have it then.'

'Not if you don't like it.'

The responsibility. It's flattering that my opinions matter to him, but what if I'm wrong? Why won't he go and ask his father? Why can't he consult someone at work?

I pick up some plates from the drainer and put them away in a cupboard. 'You could buy an *Evening Mail* and see if there are any flats available, since you've got some spare time this evening.'

He frowns. 'But I can't, can I? I have to cook my tea.'

'It doesn't take that long to prepare a meal. Most people can manage to produce something in half an hour.'

'What time are you going out?'

'In about an hour.'

'Then you could cook something. You'd still have plenty of time to get ready to go out.' He looks at me, his eyes soft and appealing. Small crinkles hover at the outer edges of his eyelids, almost an extension of his abundant lashes. They were there when he was a child, lurking innocently, uncertain of their purpose. Now he's worked out

17

how to use them, to charm me. I have a great desire to reach out and touch his cheek.

'You've got all evening.'

'But you're so much better at it than me.'

'That's because you don't get enough practice.'

I shouldn't give in. It doesn't help him and it doesn't help me. But it's tiring to fall out with people, easier to cook than engage in complicated debates. I've already used up today's spare supplies of energy.

'All right,' I sigh. 'But you'll have to eat it straightaway. It won't keep.'

'Brilliant,' he says, and flashes me a friendly, grateful grin before going back to *Bugs Bunny*.

'And you'll have to wash up.'

'No problem.'

I look out at the back garden. My large, comfortable white knickers are flapping on the clothes line in the sun, next to Joel's shirts, which I'll have to iron later.

CHAPTER THREE

I met Andrew when I was eighteen, on the first day of my first term at university. I stood in the deserted Barber Institute, where the Birmingham Music Department was located, at nine o'clock precisely and examined the high ceiling, the marble floor, the white steps at the far end that led to the art gallery upstairs. I liked the emptiness. It reminded me of our entrance hall at home, bigger, but with the same sense of space and grandeur. There weren't any shoes by the door, of course, no

18

croquet mallets or tennis rackets lying in a heap on the side. The floor was pale and gleaming, a testament to someone's dedicated cleaning, and there were no posters of Battenberg cake or chocolate Swiss roll on the walls.

I couldn't understand why there were no people around. I'd realised almost immediately that I'd made a mistake with the time, but I hadn't expected this total lack of activity.

Someone started to tune a violin. The dark, sonorous tones of D and G played together, the sliding up of the G string, the hollow satisfaction of a perfect fifth. The sound was coming from behind one of the large doors on my left, so I went over and listened.

The violin player started to play sections of concertos—Tchaikovsky, Sibelius, Beethoven—carelessly, tossing them off into the air like quick flurries of rain. Each one swirled around in the wind for a few seconds, sharp but brilliant, uncertain whether to settle for a serious downpour or move away and give up.

It took me a long time to summon the courage to ease the door open and peer inside. When I did, I discovered a small concert hall, half-lit, with seats sloping down towards the stage. The violinist was on the stage with his back to me, so I stepped in, not wanting to reveal my presence, letting the door close itself.

He was electrifying. Tall and thin, dwarfing the violin with his long fingers and huge hands, yet somehow completely in control. He didn't look as if he should be able to play it, he seemed far too clumsy—and yet he wasn't. The intonation was almost inhumanly accurate, rhythms neat and

19

detailed, the spiccato passages machine-precision fast, with the bow bouncing so tidily that every note sang. But it was the tone that affected me most profoundly. I was mesmerised by its richness, its vibrancy. My bones hummed with the overload of sensation. I struggled to breathe.

His back was long and drooping, and the messy blond hair which came down to his shoulders curled upwards at the ends. I liked the shape of him, the set of his shoulders, the way his body sagged and moved with the music. I fell in love with him before I'd even seen his face.

He was walking up and down as he played, mobile and easy, and it was only a matter of time before he saw me. I told myself to leave, but my legs refused to move.

He turned round and stopped. Just like that. The unfinished sound hung in the air, waiting for a cadence, painfully unresolved.

'Hi,' he said.

'Sorry.' My voice was so small, so insignificant after the power of his playing that it was little more than a whisper.

His face was angular and bony, the nose unusually large, and his eyes green, darker than I expected. He didn't seem annoyed, just curious. He peered at me through the dim lighting, his violin now tucked under his arm like a guitar, his yellow hair flopping over his forehead.

'Are you a first-year?' he said. His voice was very exact in its enunciation, but deep and husky, as if the rosin from the bow had coated his throat.

'Yes.' I nodded vigorously, conscious of the violin case in my hand, embarrassed that he might think I thought I could match his playing.

He jumped off the stage and came towards me. 'My name's Andrew Courtenay. What's yours?'

'Jessica Fontaine,' I said.

'A violin player?'

I hesitated. 'Not really . . . well . . . only a bit. Piano's my main instrument.' I shouldn't have said that. I didn't want to imply that I was anywhere near his level. 'I'm not that good. I loved your playing. I thought it was so—' I stopped, because there weren't any words that were remotely adequate, and I could feel heat radiating from my flushed face.

He nodded slowly. 'Good,' he said. 'Good.'

We looked at each other. Or I assumed he looked at me while I looked at the violin under his arm. I couldn't meet his eyes. I tried, but only got as far as his mouth.

'It's a lovely violin,' I said at last.

He grinned, and two creases appeared in each cheek, bringing an unexpected lightness to his face. 'It should be. It cost twenty thousand.'

I thought I had misheard him. 'Twenty thousand? Pounds?'

'No, buttons.'

It's a joke, I thought. I should laugh. But I couldn't. I stared at the violin, terrified that he would drop it, or that I'd somehow touch it and contaminate it. 'Crumbs,' I said.

'Quite.'

'Should you put it away, then?'

'Good idea. What are you doing here?'

'I'm an hour early. I thought I was meant to arrive at nine o'clock, but I made a mistake. The letter says I've got to go to the Elgar Room—I haven't worked out where it is yet.'

21

He nodded. 'They like everyone to meet up—the lecturers and the new students. I remember it well.' He smiled and I watched eagerly for the creases. 'I'm a second-year. We went through all this last year. Can't say I'd like to be new again.'

'Where is everyone?'

'Oh, no one comes in before ten. We don't have nine o'clock lectures here.'

'I could have had an hour's extra sleep.'

'Tell you what, why don't we go and have a coffee and then I'll take you over to the Elgar Room?'

*   *   *

Love changed me. Not slowly or imperceptibly, but with a violent jolt. An alarm clock had broken into my dream existence with a shattering shriek, forcing me awake. Up until then, for eighteen years, I'd been meandering along, imagining that I knew what I was doing, unaware that there was an alternative world moving parallel to my own.

I suddenly understood Chopin.

I played a nocturne to my piano teacher, Mrs Gulliver. When I'd finished, she remained motionless for a few seconds, looking down at her hands. Fading hands, showing their age with clusters of fine wrinkles, small raised brown spots, knuckles thickening and stiffening.

She raised her eyes and I was amazed to see tears in them. 'Yes,' she said and let out her breath in a long, satisfied sigh.

I smiled at her, uncertain how to react, but I knew she thought she had taught me to play like that. In reality, I'd discovered it all by myself.

I couldn't really understand what Andrew saw in me. It was as if a shaft of brilliant sunshine had decided to push its way into a dark corner of the house where it wouldn't naturally go, turning a corner to get there, penetrating walls that obstructed its progress, breaking all the laws of physics.

I think he enjoyed my adoration. He acted out the part of the gifted genius with passion and dedication, oblivious to the fact that I was his only admirer. I thought his mind soared above the rest of them, instinctively and intellectually, interpreting the world through his music.

So why did he spend so much time reading comics? He collected *Dandy* and *Beano* and accumulated piles of them in his room. He spent much of his spare time reading them, over and over again. Dennis the Menace, Desperate Dan, Beryl the Peril.

We would be sitting in his room at his house while I sweated over my harmony exercise. Should it modulate there? Can the bass line jump a seventh? Oh, parallel fifths again.

Andrew kept interrupting my thoughts.

'Why don't you read a comic, Jess? It'll relax you.'

'I prefer Thomas Hardy.'

'Desperate Dan is better. He can eat a dozen cow pies in one go, you know.'

It wasn't long before my last bus. My harmony had to be in by the next day, and I was struggling. 'There's no such thing as a cow pie. What's wrong with beef pies, or steak and kidney?'

He looked hurt. 'No, you're missing the point. It's a joke.' But he read the comics earnestly, without laughing.

'So how much of the cow goes into the pie? The head, the feet, the tail?'

He shrugged. 'Oh, all of it. That's the point.'

The point? There was no point to Desperate Dan. I couldn't understand Andrew's fascination with him. It was the same with cartoons. Every afternoon, we had to race back for children's television. *Wacky Races*, Dick Dastardly, Penelope Pitstop. If they weren't on, Andrew would give up on the television. If they were, he would watch obsessively, grunting at every bizarre disaster, every punchline. I tried to join in, I really did, but I couldn't understand them. There was nothing there that I could relate to.

This was the man who could transport you to another world with his music, who could lift you into another dimension, show you that there was a life beyond the mundane.

*　　*　　*

'I've got a friend who wants to come and see Audlands,' I announced one evening at supper. I was living at home while I did my degree, since my father thought we were close enough to the university and he didn't want to pay hall fees. I didn't mind. I had no desire to leave the safety of my familiar places.

'Wonderful,' said my mother with a vague smile. 'What's her name?'

'Andrew,' I said, looking at the pork chop on my plate and feeling a wave of heat rush into my cheeks.

There was a silence, during which I wondered if

24

they'd heard me, then a flurry of movement, as if everyone had dropped knives and forks on to their plates at the same time. Harriet and my mother started to talk together, raising their voices to be heard.

'Hey!' said Harriet. 'Jess has got a boyfriend.'

'How exciting,' said my mother. 'Why don't you invite him for lunch on Saturday?'

'All right,' I said.

'He can't come on Saturday,' said Harriet. 'I've got a match.'

I pushed my plate to one side. 'I'm not hungry,' I said, standing up.

'But it's apple crumble,' said my mother.

'Again?' said my father.

'That's not fair. You know we have to use up the apples.'

I left the dining room, anxious to escape to my room, but Harriet had followed me out. She grabbed me by the arm. 'What's he like?' she said.

I was confused.

'Andrew? What's he like?'

Like? I didn't know what she meant.

'Is he tall, dark and handsome?'

'Well,' I said, thinking. 'He's tall but not dark. He's blond. I don't know if he's handsome. How can you tell?'

'Harriet,' called my mother from the dining room. 'Can you fetch the custard? Your father's in a hurry.'

*   *   *

Next Saturday, my father and I drove over to Andrew's house to pick him up. He must have

25

been watching out for us because he came out immediately. I stared at him.

'What's the matter?' he said.

'Nothing. It's just—I've never seen those trousers before.'

Beige, smart, pressed. Where did they come from? I was accustomed to Andrew in the standard student uniform of jeans and baggy jumper, unless he was playing in a concert, when he had to wear a black suit and looked devastating. 'I bought them yesterday,' he said. 'C&A. I thought they were OK.'

'You look great,' I said, regretting my overreaction.

'Thought I should impress the parents.'

'Quite right too.' I tried to imagine my parents being impressed by anything and failed.

We drove out of Birmingham without speaking. It was difficult to hold a conversation in the presence of my father, who was not a talkative man. Or he might have been. Just not with me.

We left the main road and turned into the drive. The dark, empty branches of the horse chestnuts overlapped and tangled, forming an arch of lace against the dull grey of the sky. The road was littered with shattered conkers and the muddy brown of decomposing leaves. My father slowed down to ease the shock of the potholes and to give Andrew a chance to take in the view of the house. He pretended to be unmoved by Audlands Hall, but nevertheless liked to present it as a film director would. Opening up the scene with a shot of the avenue leading into the distance, drawing us along, approaching with self-conscious care, gradually bringing the Hall into focus. He knew that encountering the place for the first time was a breathtaking experience.

Andrew did not disappoint. I heard him gasp. 'Wow,' he said after a while. *'Brideshead Revisited.'*

'No,' I said. 'Audlands visited for the first time.'

The Hall is not as big as Blenheim or Chatsworth, but it's constructed from the same yellow stone, shimmering with a warm honeyed glow, even in the absence of bright sunlight. Four pillars frame the porch area—Ionic columns, according to my mother—adding height and dignity to the broad flight of steps that leads to the front door. As you come round the bend, the whole façade of the house opens up before you, solid and restful, growing out of the land into a perfectly proportioned Georgian country house. It's best seen in the early morning, when the rising sun creeps over the overgrown box hedges of the maze and transforms the windows into mirrors. The north-eastern sky is reflected back at itself with a clear, fresh light. Wisps of drifting mist linger, encouraged by the damp from the lake, and the Hall rises up through it all like a medieval castle.

The sun was missing on that morning when Andrew first arrived, but the mist was good enough.

'The outside is much more impressive than the inside,' I warned, terrified that he would think we were landed gentry and be disappointed when he encountered the spiders and the dust and the cold.

'So which bit do you live in?' he said.

I couldn't decide what he meant. Was he talking about me personally? My bedroom? Or which bit did we all live in? What did he mean by 'live'? The kitchen? Or the drawing room? I didn't know how to answer.

'We live in all of it,' said my father.

'Really?' said Andrew. 'Wow.'

'But there isn't an estate. The farmland was sold off years ago.'

Nobody had ever told me that. I'd just accepted the garden as it was, enormous and out of control. My father managed to cut the grass on the croquet lawn and the tennis court to please my mother, but the rest was abandoned and turned to waist-high hay as the summer wore on. It had never occurred to me that there used to be more.

My mother tells the story of how they bought the house. My father had inherited the family business—a chain of cake factories and shops which flourished in the late fifties after years of rationing and austerity. My newly wed parents were on their way to view a six-bedroomed executive house on the outskirts of Birmingham when my mother caught sight of a dilapidated For Sale sign on the main road. It was hanging round the head of a stone lion, which stared out from the side of a once grand entrance. Large wrought-iron gates were wedged open, distorted with age, sinking into their overgrown surroundings. The signpost had been placed there by a desperate estate agent who couldn't sell the house through the property pages of *The Times*.

'Stop!' shrieked my mother.

My father braked hard, believing he had run over a rabbit or a squirrel, and immediately reversed as instructed.

'Audlands Hall,' she read. 'Let's go and look.

My father was uncertain about the condition of

the drive, so they got out and walked. It was nine o'clock in the morning, a fatal time on a day when the sun was rising into a crystal blue sky and huge pink and white candles rose from the branches of the horse chestnuts. They turned the corner of the drive and stopped.

There was no contest. They didn't even need to look inside, although they probably should have done while there was still time to resist that first impression.

My father was cautious at first, but he was potty about my mother, whose romantic notions of having a country estate were much stronger than his common sense. There was also a pompous side to him, and the prestige associated with living in a real country house with a drawing room and a Long Gallery and disused stables appealed to him. He was, after all, a successful businessman and very rich. The whole world at that time adored his Crunchy Chocolate Brownies.

They must have been mad, really. Audlands had been neglected for so long that the decay was well established before they moved in, but my mother was full of wild enthusiasm. She hired carpenters, plumbers and electricians, who patched up and covered over. My father was generous at first, paying out vast sums of money for renovation, but as time went on and people grew weary of Crunchy Chocolate Brownies he became less willing to indulge my mother.

Now, two decades on, Andrew and I ran up the steps and straight past the pillars, which only looked good if you didn't go too close. Large chunks had been gouged out of them. My father always said that army vehicles had caused most of

29

the damage when the Hall was requisitioned during the war, but it was difficult to understand exactly how this occurred. I can only assume that motorcycles and jeeps drove up and down the steps for fun. Perhaps they were Americans.

I knew we'd be all right once we reached the entrance hall. There was a sweeping staircase with mahogany banisters, which had survived decades of sliding children, and a huge chandelier, swamped by dust and not connected to the electricity supply, but impressive nevertheless.

'Hey!' said Andrew, examining a fading poster that had been up on the wall for as long as I could remember. 'Crunchy Chocolate Brownies. I love them.'

'It is unfortunate,' said my father, 'that the rest of mankind no longer shares your enthusiasm.' He disappeared into the drawing room, where there was a small electric fire, to read his weekend papers.

I took Andrew to the kitchen. 'Let's have a coffee,' I said.

'I had no idea,' he said, settling into a wheel-backed chair and leaning over the pockmarked wooden table.

'Of what?' I filled the kettle and put it on the Aga.

'That you lived here.'

'Well, how could you, without coming and seeing it?'

'You might have told me.'

I wasn't sure what I should have told him. I knew the house was big, but it wasn't exactly clean and sparkling. 'People see things differently. I didn't know what you'd think.'

'Come on, Jess. Not many people live in a stately home.'

'It's not a stately home. It's a country house.'

'What's the difference?'

'I don't know. I think maybe you have to be a lord or something to be in a stately home.'

'And you're not?'

'Do I look like a lord?'

'No, but your father might be. Or your mother could be a lady.'

I laughed. 'You haven't met my mother.'

'Hi.' Harriet came into the kitchen and stood in front of Andrew. 'I'm Harriet, Jess's sister.'

She was not meant to be there. I'd chosen the day deliberately. At sixteen, Harriet was stunning. Tall, slim, long dark hair almost to her waist, almond-shaped eyes which were pale green, edged with a darker green. She was also good-natured. Everyone liked her. I didn't stand a chance with her around.

'Hi,' said Andrew.

'I thought you were playing hockey,' I said.

Harriet shrugged. 'They cancelled at the last minute. The other school's minibus broke down. If you're making coffee I'll have one, thanks.'

I turned away and poured the hot water, knowing that this was the end of my relationship with Andrew. Nobody noticed me when Harriet was there.

But when I turned back I found that Andrew was looking out of the window, ignoring Harriet, while she rummaged around in a cupboard looking for biscuits.

'You've got a lake,' he said with delight.

'I'm sure there were some ginger nuts in here,'

31

said Harriet.

It was puzzling that Andrew didn't show much interest in anyone else. He was a brilliant violinist, the best in the university. Why weren't all the girls queuing up to go out with him?

'I had plenty of admirers in my first year,' he said, whenever I asked. 'There were lots of people in hall to do things with.'

What things? Who? Where were they all now? He only ever had casual conversations with the other students—he wasn't part of any special group.

So when he ignored Harriet, I was thrilled. 'The biscuits were all used up yesterday,' I said. 'You shared them with Amy and Sarah.' Harriet had a huge circle of friends, many of whom seemed to spend half their lives at Audlands.

'Oh, yes,' she said with a giggle. 'Silly me.'

Harriet giggling? Her whole manner was different, her features sharper and more clearly defined, her movements more exaggerated than usual. What did this mean? Did she find Andrew attractive? Or was she like this with all men? I had never observed her before in this kind of context. I didn't like it. It made me feel uncomfortable, as if I were seeing a stranger who had been living in the same house as me for sixteen years, cleverly disguised.

'Sorry, Andrew,' she said, coming up close to him. 'No biscuits today.'

'No problem,' he said.

'Lovely to meet you,' she said, and brushed past him to the door. 'See you again.'

'Mmm,' he said, stirring sugar into his coffee.

At the door, she turned and looked at me over

his shoulder. She put both thumbs up and winked.

I didn't know how to react. People didn't have little intimate conspiracies with me about boyfriends. I had always been excluded from that world.

'Can we go on the lake?' asked Andrew.

'If you want to. There are a couple of rowing boats.'

I had spent much of my childhood pottering around in a boat, rowing between the islands, making little dens where I could sit in private and read. My cousins and Harriet had also liked the lake, but I'd avoided them, sneaking round the other side of an island, spying on them, wanting to be part of their Swallows and Amazons, not wanting to. I'd watched them with confusion rather than envy, puzzled by their curiously unstructured games.

'Hello!' My mother came striding into the kitchen, tall and confident, her long hair swinging freely, her arms full of dahlias and leaves she'd picked from the garden. Her fingers were stained with soil and her shoes were wet from the long grass, but there was an eager freshness about her. She was shining in sympathy with the dew on the dahlias. 'You must be Andrew.'

'Yeah,' said Andrew, getting up awkwardly. I grabbed his cup of coffee before it tipped on to the floor. 'Hi.'

'Hi,' she said. My mother worked very hard to make herself part of young people's culture. She was better at it than me. She got the language from the television and Harriet. 'Jess tells me you're a brilliant violinist.'

'Yes,' he said.

'I don't suppose you brought your violin with you? I would love to hear you play.'

'No you wouldn't,' I said. Why would she say that? My mother had never shown any interest in my playing, except when she moved the television out of the music room into a room of its own, so that the rest of the family could watch it in peace.

'Jess,' she said with reproach and gave me a strange, private look.

'I don't play unless I have to,' said Andrew.

'Really? Don't you enjoy it?'

'It's OK,' he said with a shrug.

I was annoyed. He was always so casual about his great talent. 'Take no notice of him,' I said. 'Of course he likes playing.'

'Of course,' he said, and grinned at my mother.

She smiled back. 'I imagine you get tired of playing all the time. How long do you practise for?'

'Three hours a day when I was living at home. Not so much now.' He hesitated. 'Only don't tell my mother that.'

'Do you fancy a game of tennis?' I said.

'Not especially.'

'Croquet then.'

'I don't play croquet.'

'I'll teach you,' I said.

'I'd rather go on the lake.'

'It's a bit cold for boating.'

'Find Andrew some jumpers and a waterproof jacket,' said my mother. 'There's no reason why you shouldn't take him on the lake if he wants to. Perhaps we could all play croquet after lunch if the ground isn't too wet. It's not difficult to learn, Andrew.'

'Great,' he said, and watched her as she left the

room.

We finished our coffee in silence. I found it difficult to know what to say to him now that we were away from the university and not rushing from lecture to seminar with work to do.

'She's all right, your mother, isn't she?' he said.

CHAPTER FOUR

'Jessica! Harriet! Come and see this!'

Connie waited for her two young daughters to appear, then led them by the hand up the wide marble staircase. She was trembling with anticipation, but wanted to present them with the spectacle in exactly the right way. She'd been waiting all day for this moment, looking out of the windows at the dying sun, willing the last light to leave the sky. At the first landing, where the stairs divided into two opposing sweeping curves, she stopped and turned Jessica and Harriet round to face the hall. 'OK,' she called out softly to Roland, who was standing by the front door.

The lights went out with a click.

'Look!' she whispered.

Jessica and Harriet stood on either side of her. Connie knelt down to their level and put an arm gently round Harriet's waist. Jessica stood slightly apart, her head lowered, but her eyes drawn upwards to the chandelier. Constructed from glass in a many-tiered half-sphere, it had mysteriously taken on a powerful life of its own. All fifty candles were alight, shifting, shivering, fluttering in the emptiness of the high-domed hall. Mirrors on opposite walls reflected the candlelight back on to itself, so the space had become a mass of twinkling stars. The tired, everyday dust had altered and become beautiful, a screen for the shifting nuances of colour and uncertain patterns of light.

'They called them lustres,' said Connie, 'rather than chandeliers.' Her voice, hushed in honour of the occasion, nevertheless rang out clear and knowledgeable. 'It's a good name, isn't it?'

'Oh,' said Jessica, letting her breath escape in a long hiss.

'Mummy, it's lovely,' said Harriet.

'Yes,' said Connie. 'It is.'

'Quite impressive, Connie.' Roland's voice floated up from the door in a tone of grudging admiration.

'Can we have them everywhere?' asked Harriet.

'Oh, yes, there'll be candles in every room, but not until tomorrow.'

Everything had been in place for several days now. Connie had spent many hours in each room, climbing up stepladders, finding places to put the candles out of reach, moving ornaments and pictures, clearing bookshelves and mantelpieces. She'd been collecting brass and ceramic candlesticks from jumble sales, secondhand shops and school fetes over the last few months. There were already several sconces fixed to the wall, backing on to mirrors, a whisper from the eighteenth century.

'You can't do this, Connie,' Roland had said. 'It's not safe.'

'Of course it is. Audlands couldn't burn down. The walls are too thick. Anyway, I'm putting them high up. Nobody will be able to knock them over.'

36

'It'll be difficult to see what we're eating.'

This was probably just as well, since Connie's cooking skills were not particularly sophisticated. She'd been planning this celebration—a midwinter party, she called it, to lift her spirits in the middle of February—for weeks, and much of the food had been prepared well in advance. There were piles of cocktail sausages in tins in the pantry, which was so cold they'd almost frozen; squares of cheese, shaped and ready to be put on sticks with pineapple chunks; cheese straws, no longer fresh, but still crumbly, lined up on baking sheets; a vat containing a chicken and mushroom concoction for the vol-au-vents; fluted cardboard dishes of trifle set out in rows, waiting for their final cream topping; dozens of cartons of Fontaine's Crunchy Chocolate Brownies standing in piles on the floor. Cases of sparkling wine towered over everything.

China and cutlery and glasses had been borrowed from anyone who was willing. 'But it can't be modern china,' Connie had stipulated. 'It must at least look antique, even if it isn't.'

Earlier in the day, Roland had set up tables in the entrance hall. They were draped in crisp white linen and covered with dozens of champagne glasses placed upside down and arranged in meticulously ordered rows. The flickering candlelight imprinted a thousand pinpoints of light on to the polished crystal.

'Make sure you put the candles out for now,' said Roland as he switched the lights back on. He walked off towards the drawing room with a pile of logs. 'I'm going to start setting the fires.'

The doorbell rang and Connie and Harriet raced down the stairs. Connie, in the lead, let the

37

pleats of her lime-green miniskirt billow up behind her as she jumped the last three steps in one go. 'Coming,' she called.

It was her sister-in-law, Cathy, with the cousins, Philip, Colin and Judy. 'Quick,' said Connie as she opened the door. 'We need to shut the door.' It was windy outside and bits of debris were swirling up the steps into the hall—leaves, twigs, a dusting of soil. A sudden gust slammed the door shut and the chandelier swayed dangerously in the draught. Half the candles went out.

'Oh no,' said Cathy. 'It won't be much good if you can't open the door.'

But nothing would dampen Connie's optimism. 'It's all right. The wind will have died down by tomorrow evening.'

'If Connie says it won't be windy,' said Roland, coming out of the drawing room, 'it won't be windy. All the weather experts check with her first.'

'Quite right,' said Cathy. She was wearing a white polo-neck jumper with a very short purple skirt, which revealed sagging in-turning knees and plump thighs. A three-inch belt with an elaborate buckle drew attention to her wide hips.

The cousins were off, the boys and Harriet racing from one room to another, counting up the candles, exclaiming at Connie's elaborate displays of laurel branches and red ribbons. 'Hey,' called Colin's voice in the distance. 'It's spooky.' They started to hoot and wail, wanting to find ghosts.

The desperate voice of four-year-old Judy followed them. 'Wait for me . . .'

'Careful,' called Connie after them. 'Don't disturb anything.'

She looked up at Jessica, who was still on the

38

staircase with her eyes on the chandelier. She had crouched down and was peering through the balustrades, still mesmerised by the candles, even though they had lost much of their magic against the background of electricity. Light danced and shimmered over her face, changing with every passing moment, illuminating her round eyes and creating shining highlights in her glossy plaits.

Connie watched her for a few seconds and sighed. 'Go and play with the others now, Jess,' she called. 'Cathy and I have too much to do, and we don't want you under our feet.'

But Jessica didn't move.

* * *

Connie spread the butter, mixed with margarine, on the bread while Cathy put fillings into the sandwiches and then cut each one into four neat little triangles. They'd started out with Connie filling and cutting, but she couldn't seem to get the edges sharp enough, so they'd swapped. Ten sliced white loaves were piled at her side, ready for her attention.

Cathy had been doubtful at first. 'Won't they be stale by tomorrow?'

'They'll keep all right in the pantry,' said Connie. 'Nothing ever goes off in there.'

Cathy was full of an unusual good humour. 'I don't know why you didn't think of having a party earlier,' she said. 'All this space crying out for people.'

'Oh, I know,' said Connie. 'I just needed to get Audlands into an acceptable state. Even now—'

'Nobody'll see the details. It'll be too dark.'

'And Roland took some persuading,' said Connie. 'But he agreed that a ten-year anniversary was a good idea.'

'He's so mean. I don't know how you get any money out of him at all.'

'Well, the business isn't doing as well as it used to—'

'Rubbish. It's thriving. He just doesn't want to admit it. He can't allow himself to be optimistic. It might make him generous.'

Cathy resented the fact that the business had been left to her brother, maintaining that her financial inheritance wasn't adequate. But Roland always said that she had the better deal: a generous sum of money and no worries about lemon meringue pie.

Connie smiled politely. 'He's been very generous about the party,' she said. 'Once he's persuaded something is worthwhile, he dedicates himself to it. This'll be the first of many parties, you'll see.'

Cathy snorted and pushed the bread knife down with a rapid twist, cutting through a sandwich with deadly accuracy.

Connie was getting ahead of Cathy, so she started piling some fairy cakes from the pantry on to trays covered in foil. Each one was topped with pink icing and a single cherry.

'They're nice,' said Cathy.

'Jessica made them this morning.'

'Really?' Cathy stopped filling the sandwiches for a second and looked up in surprise. 'Jessica?'

Connie flushed with irritation. 'She likes cooking.' Jessica had spent all day on them, mixing, measuring, pouring out the icing and plopping the cherry on top of each one. She'd seemed almost happy, accepting Connie's occasional direction without argument, persisting well into the afternoon.

Cathy continued filling the sandwiches. 'I just didn't expect her to stick at something like that, that's all.'

'If Jessica wants to do something, she'll do it.'

'And they're so neat.'

'Of course they are.' Connie chose not to mention the pile of rejects at the back of the pantry, which Jessica and Harriet had been dipping into at every available opportunity.

They continued in silence for a while. 'Connie?'

'Yes?'

'Have you ever thought about taking Jessica to the doctor's?'

Connie rammed her knife into the margarine container and whipped it round sharply, beating in the butter. 'Why would I need to do that?'

'Well—you know.'

'No.'

'Oh, come on, Connie. You must have noticed there's something wrong with her.'

'She's just shy, that's all.'

'No, it's more than that.' Cathy was clearly making an effort, softening her voice with a kindness unusual for her, adopting a tone of sisterly understanding. 'It's the way she won't look at you, and refuses to speak if you ask her anything. She never plays with other children, you know.'

'She plays with Harriet.'

'Does she? Or is she just telling Harriet what to do? Harriet's a very amenable child, she'd get on

41

with anyone.'

Connie sighed, weakened by the intimacy of their circumstances. They were working in harmony for once. The kitchen was warm, the kettle was starting to hiss gently in the background, and they were surrounded by food. 'She *is* very difficult,' she acknowledged.

Cathy's voice was still quiet and confidential. 'I don't know how you cope with her. Do you know, in all her eight years she's never once looked me in the eye.'

Connie started buttering again, spreading generously, making sure all the edges of the bread were covered. 'Actually, I did try to talk to the doctor once, when she was younger. I thought she might be autistic.'

'And?'

'He laughed at me. He said if I'd seen the kind of autistic children he had to treat, I wouldn't have suggested anything so ridiculous.'

'Was that the same doctor I met here when Harriet had measles?'

'Yes.'

'He should have retired years ago. He's far too old to be practising. Find a younger doctor who's more up to date.'

'He must know what he's talking about,' said Connie. 'He's a doctor.'

'Ask to see a specialist.'

The kettle boiled and Connie went over to lift it off the hot plate. 'She's not as bad as she used to be. She does talk to us now.'

'She may talk to you. Not to me.'

'No,' said Connie. 'You're more—more unfamiliar.'

'I'm her aunt. I've known her from birth.'

'Yes—but she manages at school. They just say she's quiet.'

'Hmm.' Cathy picked up her mug of tea. 'Well, I suppose that's something.'

Footsteps were clattering along the corridor outside and Harriet came bursting in with her cousins.

'Can we have a drink, Mummy?' asked Judy.

'Hey!' said Philip. 'Cakes.'

'You keep your greedy fingers off them,' said Cathy, pushing their hands out of the way. 'You'll spoil your supper.'

'Oh,' said Connie. 'I nearly forgot. The shepherd's pie needs to go in the oven.'

*   *   *

Connie and Roland invited everyone they knew to the party. Connie was proud of her renovation work, and she wanted as many people as possible to come and admire Audlands Hall. Roland was amenable, happy to reinforce his image as country squire. He invited work colleagues with their wives, and fellow managing directors he had met at the golf club. Connie invited mothers from school, old friends from university, acquaintances she had made in the village, the two single mothers who served in the Co-op, the butcher, the milkman. She liked the idea of extending the hand of friendship to people of different backgrounds. She wanted to be seen as generous, someone who was willing to share her good fortune with others. 'You can stay the night,' she told anyone who had to travel. 'There are plenty of spare rooms.'

43

She omitted to mention the lack of beds, the lack of heating and the faulty plumbing, but sent last-minute instructions to ensure that they knew what to expect when they arrived. So they came with sleeping bags and torches and flasks of hot water in case the electricity failed. 'It'll be fine,' she assured them. 'We have a good supply of candles.'

Connie was proved right about the weather. The wind had died down by early evening, and the draught from the open door wasn't strong enough to blow out the candles. The tiny flames swayed and leaned to one side in a show of mild rebellion, but they remained alight.

Ooohs of delight echoed long into the evening as each visitor was confronted by the spectacle of a living, breathing ball of fire.

The party was exactly as Connie had imagined it. When the first group of people walked up the drive, shrill with anticipation, their voices carried through the night air to the entrance. Cars started to congregate on the drive, engines revving up as they reversed into every available inch of space. Women stepped out of the cars in skirts so short they were little more than belts, their legs red and blotchy as the cold penetrated their tights. Or they came in long, full dresses that swept up mud as they approached the door, bringing in the debris that had been left by the wind. Men wore flowered shirts, or suits and ties.

Girls in lacy dresses and boys in smart trousers and shirts raced around like savages, darting from one room to another, picking Crunchy Chocolate Brownies off plates when no one was looking.

Roland had hired a group of his employees who had formed a piano quintet in their spare time.

The quintet consisted of a pianist, Jeff, who was an accountant, Dave, a sales rep, who played the viola, two violinists who were twins, known as Tweedledum and Tweedledee in honour of their size, both in middle management, and Gav, a cellist who worked in the icing department. Roland had asked them to come and play in his office, to ensure that they knew what they were doing. He knew nothing about music, but their rendering of a Schubert quintet minus the piano didn't sound too bad to him, so he'd booked them.

They arrived before the guests and unpacked their instruments in the music room, gazing up in awe at the freshly cleaned cherubs on the ceiling and the two magnificent chinoiserie panels of Delft tiles on either side of the fireplace.

'Well, well, well,' said Gav.

'The piano looks a bit ropey,' said Jeff.

'Oh dear,' said Connie. It hadn't occurred to her that pianos varied in quality. She blamed Roland for this. He should have checked.

Jeff sat down and played a few bars of the 'Moonlight Sonata', his long, slim fingers stroking the elderly keys with loving persuasion. 'OK,' he said, smiling at her. 'I'll manage.'

'Can't see too well, though,' said Tweedledum. He had half-moon glasses wedged on to his plump nose, and was squinting through them at the music.

'We could put the lights on,' said Connie, attempting to hide her dismay.

'No, no, no, no,' said Tweedledee, waving his hands at his brother. 'It would ruin the atmosphere. You can do it, you can do it.'

*   *   *

45

Jessica crept round the shadowy, magical house, staying close to the walls, not looking directly into anyone's face. She loved the candles. She kept holding out her hands in front of her, moving them slightly so that she could watch the pulsating light on her skin.

She went to the point where the stairs divided and looked down on the tops of people's heads. This was her favourite position, closest to the chandelier with its fifty candles. Everyone was squeezed so tightly together. How could they breathe with so little space round them? Different colours of hair blended into the half-light, so red became blond, and blond became brown, and brown became black. She liked the women's hair when it was long and tied up, some in exotic arrangements of perfectly shaped curls. Each curl was like a seashell, making her want to reach out and touch it. Other women had hair so short it was hardly worth having. She couldn't understand why they did this. Some of the men had long hair too, brushed into glossy helmets which looked as if they could be lifted off.

Most of all, she liked her mother's honey-coloured hair, warm and glowing, hanging loose to her waist. Jessica could see the way her hair swirled from the crown at the back, the white skin revealed by the parting, bare and exposed where the hair fell away.

The music started. There had been sporadic snatches of melody from the piano previously, and a strange whine as the notes of a violin changed slightly in pitch, two notes together, then another two. But now they were playing real tunes, an insistent beat, complex rhythms.

A prickling excitement crept through Jessica. A whole new harmony had just appeared, fully formed, sophisticated, thrilling. The wall of sound hit her like a tidal wave, flowing into the empty spaces in her mind. People stopped talking for a while. Or did they? Maybe she was just blocking out extraneous sounds in her anxiety to hear every note.

She stood up and went down the stairs, walking first, then trotting, then running towards the sound. It was moving music that forced its way in and blasted through locked doors. She couldn't stand still while it was going on.

'Jessica,' called her father as she pushed past him. 'Don't run. It's bad manners.'

But she had left him far behind. He was in a different universe. She entered the music room and finally stopped, breathless and trembling, letting the music flow through her. She watched the musicians, their movements, and began to mirror their actions. Her hands moved in front of her like the pianist, she bowed into the air like the cellist.

'Hey, look at Jess.'

Entranced, she hadn't heard her cousins, Philip and Colin, approach. She didn't realise they were there until Philip pushed her shoulder and knocked her off-balance. She turned around angrily and then relaxed as she recognised them.

Philip was the same age as her, tall and slim, with blond hair that used to be carefully parted and combed down, sweeping attractively over his right eye, but was now getting longer and more hippy in style. He had wide eyes that seemed to be interested in everything. And he laughed a lot, like her mother—

But the laughter that Jessica had allowed herself to admire had an unfamiliar, vicious edge today.

'Hello, Jess. Are you playing the piano? It doesn't work, you know. You can't hear it.' He mimicked her, exaggerating the action.

She dropped her hands to her side, deeply embarrassed, an unbearable warmth rushing into her cheeks.

Philip poked her in the side with his finger. She tried to step away, but he followed. Colin came up on the other side, so they had her hemmed in between them. 'Can we have a word, Jess?'

She shook her head, heavy with heat, incapable of clear thought.

They started to push her towards the door. She didn't have to go with them. She wouldn't go with them. She stood stolidly, refusing to move.

Philip pinched her arm very hard, holding on for a long time.

She bit her lip, determined not to respond, not wanting them to see her fear. Colin took her other arm and put his hands round her wrist—a Chinese burn.

She resisted the urge to cry out, concentrating on the pain. Tears were forming in her eyes and she hoped desperately that they wouldn't spill out.

Philip placed his foot on hers, his new, shiny lace-up dwarfing one of her light silver sandals that had been bought specially for the party. He pressed down hard.

'What's going on?'

It was her mother, standing over them, looking mildly perplexed. 'What are you doing? Philip,

48

Colin?'

'Hello, Auntie Connie,' they said almost together, stepping back.

Jessica stayed where she was, still staring ahead, not reacting to her mother.

'What were you doing to Jess?'

'It was just a game,' said Philip. 'Wasn't it, Jess?'

She didn't reply. She had stopped listening to him. The music was swirling around her, fast, passionate, overwhelming. She couldn't hear anything else.

Behind her there were muffled words, a short burst of laughter from Philip, and then her mother bent over. 'Are you all right, Jess?'

Jessica kept her eyes fixed on the musicians. She couldn't let anyone know that she had been upset. She swallowed everything down, nodded without looking at her mother and waited. It would all go away if she didn't move and a sense of space could open up around her.

*   *   *

'We must put the candles out before we go to bed,' said Roland, bringing Connie a glass of sparkling wine.

She lay back on the Chesterfield sofa and sipped thoughtfully, relieved that she no longer had to worry about her strapless dress. It was long, ruby-red, diaphanous, floating around her legs with a princess-like quality, but she had spent all evening being aware of its desire to succumb to gravity. She had had to keep disappearing into a corner to hoist it back up before it became too indecent. A cleavage was fine, but there were

49

limits. Now if it wanted to fall down, it no longer mattered. It could do whatever it wanted. 'It was a wonderful party,' she said. 'Wasn't it?'

He smiled and sat at the end of the sofa by her feet. He gently removed her sandals, three-inch wedges, undoing the buckles with meticulous precision, and started to massage her feet. She sighed with pleasure.

'Did you see the Telfords?' he said, bending over her feet and pressing his thumbs into her soles with deep, sensuous movements. 'I do believe they were impressed.' She could feel the warmth of his body, his breath over her arches, a tingle of pleasure running up the nerves in her legs. 'It takes a lot to make an impact on him.'

She put her drink down, leaned back, and reached her arms out over her head. The dress shifted, but held. She stretched luxuriously, right through her body, down to her feet, her toes, the gaps between them, pushing her heels into his palms. His fingers were reaching round her ankle bones. 'You were wonderful, darling.'

His hands started to move up her legs, barely touching her skin, brushing against her calves, lightly, lightly—

'Did everyone get off to bed?' murmured Roland in a slurred voice. 'You don't think anyone's going to come down?'

'Of course not,' whispered Connie, waiting for his hands to increase their pressure. The dangerous thought that someone might disturb them added to the tension. Her anticipation was desperate, urgent—

'Mummy—'

For a moment she thought she'd imagined it,

that Roland had changed his voice. Then she felt him sit up.

She looked over and saw Jessica standing there, small and round in a white flannelette nightie. Groaning, then suppressing her irritation, she sat up, her whole body aching with the effort, and grabbed the top of her dress just in time. 'Yes, darling?' she said.

Jessica didn't speak. With a pang of guilt, Connie remembered the scene in the music room. The boys had been bullying her. She had intended to speak to Roland about it and then Cathy, but she'd been distracted, and had forgotten.

She wondered if she should send Roland away, since this could be a rare opportunity to talk with her daughter, to find out what she was really thinking. She just wished the timing had been better. She forced a smile. 'Shall I come up to your bedroom with you?'

But Jessica shook her head. 'I want piano lessons,' she said.

CHAPTER FIVE

Leaving Joel with his spaghetti bolognese, I drive to Mary's house, which is large and semi-detached. It's in Harborne, at the end of a Victorian terrace, with windows on three sides, always full of light and sun. Weeds and cultivated plants flourish side by side in the front and back gardens, bursting with colour, not crowding each other out, but comfortably sharing the same space. Mary and her husband, Eamon, are dedicated to growing things,

51

but they don't give much priority to tedious details like weeding or cutting grass. Their fingers are not green, but olive, jade, emerald.

As I walk towards the front door, I can hear the boys' shrill voices through an open upstairs window.

'Yes!' It sounds like Angus.

'Aargh!' yells Tim.

Then they dissolve into hysterical laughter.

The Finnegans are always laughing. Mary's the same age as me—we were at university together—but her children are much younger, because she planned everything with common sense, waiting until she was older and settled before starting a family. As soon as she had her first child, I realised that being a mother was her mission in life. She didn't just fall into domesticity, she leapt in, her eyes wide and eager, cheering with delight. She had a built-in, unassuageable need to nurture. The boys remind me of my cousins, mad and violent, forever fighting, yelling, jumping on top of each other.

Sometimes the laughter energises me as I approach the front door, and I experience a strong desire to be part of it. At other times, like today, it makes me feel inadequate. Joel doesn't laugh like that, and Andrew didn't use to laugh at all. He threw his comments at people in a challenging way, his humour dark and cruel, but he had no time to wait for a response. Other people laughed for him, often from awkwardness when they didn't know how to react.

What do the Finnegans laugh about? I've been there with them when some small event becomes suddenly funny. I can join in with them, seeing the situation through their eyes, and it all feels perfectly natural, but I can't reproduce this sense of fun when I'm on my own.

Maybe this is a characteristic of happy people. An ability to be entertained by the world.

But what if one of them gets run over by a lorry? What if the house gets hit by lightning? Where would all that laughter go?

'Jess!' cries Mary, opening the door almost as soon as I put my finger on the doorbell. 'I thought you were never coming.'

We meet twice a week to practise, and average one concert a month. Yet she always greets me with an inexplicable pleasure, like a long-lost friend. Does she really hover by the door, longing for me to arrive? She gives that impression, but it can't be true. Sometimes it must be irritating to have visitors—if she has a headache, or she's having an argument with Eamon, or the boys are getting out of control and hurting each other. I wish I could catch her out occasionally and prove that the Finnegans are as flawed as everyone else.

'Am I late?'

'No, of course not. You're always on time. I was just looking forward to you coming. It's fish for supper. Will that be all right?' She looks worried, as if I'm going to tell her I'm allergic to fish, even though she knows I'm not.

'I think so,' I say, trying to give the impression that there's a decision to make.

Eamon turns round from the Aga as we go into the kitchen. 'Hello,' he says, waving a spatula. 'Salmon fish cakes tonight. I made them.'

Eamon is a barrister, so they're not dependent on Mary's meagre income from her musical activities. He's calm and sensible and one of those people who are interested in everything—art, music, literature, astronomy, science. The boys are clever too, constantly asking questions, pushing for more information. They have odd, grown-up conversations with their father, standing around with hands in their pockets, sighing in a tolerant, knowing way at the irrational behaviour of other people. Mary just laughs at all three of them.

Mary calls up to the boys. 'Come on, Angus and Tim. We'll be eating in a minute.'

'Beat you down,' shouts Angus, and I hear them tumbling over each other as they descend. There's a brief pause.

'Get off!' Tim's voice is muffled.

Eamon goes to sort them out. 'Stop it this minute.'

'It wasn't my fault,' says Angus. 'He stopped too suddenly.'

'Have you washed your hands?' says Mary.

'Hello, Jessica,' says Angus. 'Didn't you bring Joel?'

The boys are inexhaustible with their long, angular bodies and their straw-thin limbs. They fight with such energy and strength, play football with a speed that seems impossible for such spindly legs. They're a different species from Joel when he was their age.

'Sorry,' I say. 'He's too busy making plasticine cats.'

'What for?' asks Angus.

I smile. 'I have no idea.'

'How is he?' says Tim, who is ten.

'Great.'

Angus and Tim love Joel. They spend hours

54

watching cartoons with him, discussing ideas for computer games, making paper models, improvising storylines. He says he'll employ them when they're old enough.

'I wish he'd get a hobby,' I say to Mary, once we've settled down to eat. 'I don't think he lives in the real world.'

'He never did,' says Mary. 'Don't you remember how we had to drag him to the cinema to see *Star Wars* because he was too busy writing a science fiction story?'

'How could I forget?' I say. 'His main character was a purple mist.'

'It's difficult to believe he nearly missed *Star Wars*.'

'You mean our technical discussions about the fighting techniques of a Jedi knight might have been lost for ever?' I say. 'What a tragedy.'

'He'd have found something else,' says Mary.

'Has he got a girlfriend yet?' asks Eamon.

'No.' I don't want to tell them how much this worries me.

'He's probably gay,' says Angus.

'I don't think so.' Although I'm not at all sure how you can tell. 'It's just that he never goes out. He doesn't have a social life.'

'Does he want one?' asks Mary.

I shrug. 'I have no idea.'

'He will when he wants to,' she says. 'They always do.'

She may not be right. She likes to believe in people. She accepts them by their own standards and always assumes good motives, even if their behaviour doesn't correspond with her own. The strange thing is that everybody tries harder when

55

Mary is around. As if they pick up some of her goodness and want to reflect it, without even knowing they're doing it. Mary's view of the world is through rose-coloured spectacles, because that's how the world behaves with her. It's more rosy in her presence.

'Can I get down, Mummy?' asks Tim.

'No,' says Eamon. 'Finish your broccoli.'

'But I don't like broccoli.'

'Irrelevant,' says Angus. 'It's good for you, therefore you must learn to like it.'

He sounds exactly like his father. 'He's right, I'm afraid,' says Eamon. 'Although it's not for him to say so.'

'It's home-made strawberry ice-cream for pudding,' says Mary. 'But only for those who eat their broccoli.'

'Oh,' says Tim and eats the broccoli, messily, with his mouth open, swallowing it as if he's being force-fed.

'Stop that,' says Mary. 'Or you still won't get the pudding.'

He shuts his mouth, but gulps it down with grim resentment.

My battles with Joel never went like this. I used to give in, if Andrew wasn't around. There was no other way. Otherwise we'd still be sitting there now. I would go out of the room for a while, and come back later to find the plate half-empty. I'd let him leave the rest. Years afterwards, when workmen came to remove the old gas fire, they found piles of tiny, shrivelled pieces of meat that Joel had pushed through a hole in the side.

Mary and Eamon wouldn't understand any of this. But then, they'd never have had a child like

Joel because they're nice, amiable, easy-going people and their children are genetically programmed to be nice too.

After supper, Mary leaves Eamon to deal with the boys' homework and get them ready for bed, while we head for the Steinway in the living room.

We like to warm up with scales for about fifteen minutes, right hands together, then left, as if we're two halves of the same person. C sharp melodic minor, E flat harmonic. Fingers synchronised, joints lubricated by the movement, our minds cleared of all the day's distractions. I love the scales, the clean, satisfying patterns of keys. I'm not sure that Mary is quite as enthusiastic but, as always, she humours me.

Then we start on the pieces. We've been playing together for about twenty years, but only doing well for the last five. Our bookings are picking up, and we've been invited to do a tour of Cornwall next year, performing in six different secondary schools. We're not making much money, but even a small amount is a welcome addition to my income, now that I've abandoned teaching.

I hadn't been a great success as a teacher. I'd had to battle with the neighbours when I first started. They would bang on the wall while I shrivelled with embarrassment in front of six-year-old children and their parents. I pretended it was nothing, just people doing their housework, but nobody was fooled.

'I think the lady next door doesn't like my playing,' said Katy.

'How could anyone not like your playing?'

She looked at me with scorn on her face. 'Well, I'm only a learner, aren't I?'

57

'Maybe you should practise more, then they'd like it.'

Sometimes the children did practise, at least well enough to impress non-players who lived next door, but it didn't make any difference. They still complained. I made promises. No playing after eight o'clock. I moved the piano against an internal wall. They learned to accept it.

But I didn't enjoy the teaching. I found it frustrating, rather than fulfilling. 'No! You lean on the *first* beat of the bar.'

'I am.' This was Richard, who never accepted he could be wrong. Fifteen and arrogant before he'd even started real life.

'No, you're not.'

So then he'd sulk, because he'd been told by his parents it was rude to argue. 'Come on,' I said. 'Let's have another go.'

He would either play mechanically, with no feeling, or furiously, thumping out the beats so that they were equally violent, with no sense of style.

In the end I just sat back, looked out of the window and let him get on with it. 'OK,' I'd say when he'd finished. 'Let's try another piece.' He didn't like it. He wanted me to be aggressive and get angry, but I refused. It didn't seem worth the effort. He would find out when he failed Grade 7.

Then there were all the children who never practised, whose parents would write little notes of excuse in the book, as if it would be all right because they had told me. The lessons became tedious and repetitive. 'Play it again,' I'd say to Petra. 'And again.' She would sigh and shuffle on the stool, scowling at the music, never improving because she hated the repetition.

Most of my successful pupils were under eleven. They would get merits or distinctions in exams, responding to encouragement and guidance. But once they entered puberty, they followed the same line of rebellion as everyone else.

'Your fingernails are too long.'

'No they're not.'

'Can't you hear them click?'

'No.'

'Have you had a good week?' This was my attempt at small talk to relax them, to make friends, so they wouldn't resent me telling them what to do.

'It was all right.'

'Did you do anything exciting?'

'No.'

I have concluded that I'm not good with children. Mary's pupils are different. They like going to lessons and progress steadily to Grade 8, staying in touch with her when they leave for university. They send her postcards as they go on their gap years, hug her when they meet her in the street. Although she probably hugs them first.

Mary knows how to make people like her. I don't. I'm happy to have stopped the teaching.

Maybe this is why I never had much success with Joel. Or maybe I didn't have much success with children because they all reminded me of Joel and I knew before I started that I wouldn't be able to connect with them.

Mary and I begin with Mozart because it's clean and satisfying, with scale passages and comfortable chords that we have to play perfectly together. We're good on fingerwork, although Mary is better than me. She has perfect pitch and everything she does is tidy and precise. I make mistakes, rush at things, want to play huge romantic pieces with passion, while Mary wants neat music—Mozart and Haydn. But we learn from each other, and we're both better than we used to be.

We sway with the music, building up the crescendos, and there's a wonderful sense of working together that I don't experience anywhere else in my life. We are one, instinctively knowing each other's responses without discussion. There's nothing in the world more satisfying for me than playing duets with Mary. We understand what is never spoken, what couldn't be spoken because there is nothing to say.

*   *   *

I arrive home just before ten-thirty, contented with the duet playing, the food, the good company. Eamon is such an easy man. He washes up, puts the children to bed when he needs to, and talks to me as if I'm his sister.

I live on a council estate. The houses are crammed together in a long terrace, each one squeezing the edges of its neighbour, struggling to breathe and assert its individuality. Inside, husbands who like DIY have built fitted kitchens, put in wooden floors, installed fireplaces that make the living rooms cosy even though they have central heating. It's harder to make a mark on the outside. Several of the houses have been bought under the right-to-buy scheme and the owners have built porches, which break up the monotonous lines. But they don't make enough impact. They look tiny, shrunken, overpowered by

60

the conformity of the row. The Council have fitted double glazing, but after the initial excitement, the houses have all started to look drab again.

I don't have a husband to improve my house. I've got Joel.

He's watching the news when I come in.

'Hello,' I say.

'Hi.' You can't talk to Joel when he's watching television.

I go into the kitchen and find the remains of his meal lying on the side on a tray, not washed up, not tidied away. 'Joel!' I call, determined to be annoyed.

He doesn't reply. I go into the living room and stand in front of the television.

'Mum—' He sounds as if he's still sixteen.

'How old are you, Joel?'

He doesn't understand the question.

'When are you going to start behaving like an adult?'

He sits up from his prone position on the sofa. 'I am an adult. I go out and earn money, don't I?'

'Then perhaps you should use some of it to pay for a cleaning lady?'

'Why would I need—' He stops as he realises the implication of what he's about to say.

'Yes? Why do you think?'

His face clears. 'Oh, my tray. I get it. Don't worry, Mum. I'll put it all away. I was just waiting until the end of the news.'

'But it offends me.'

'In a bit, Mum. Trust me. Can I just watch the end?'

Reluctantly, I move aside.

I feel cramped, squeezed by the smallness of the

61

rooms. The walls seem to advance inwards and the enclosed area shrinks a few more millimetres every day, forcing out surplus air, making breathing more and more exhausting. At Audlands, I could go wherever I wanted and more or less guarantee that I wouldn't meet anyone all day. Here, it's so crowded. Other people's children leave home, get girlfriends, find a flat, go to university, apply for jobs in London, learn to be independent.

I return to the kitchen, trying to ignore the tray with the dried-up remnants of spaghetti bolognese. I would like to come in and find an immaculate kitchen with no trace of cooking or eating or living. A kitchen with clean, clear lines, bare and open. It will never happen with Joel in the house.

'Mum! Come here, quick!'

I go back into the living room, alarmed. Joel is sitting up on the sofa and leaning forward with his elbows on his knees.

'What's the matter? Are you ill?'

'No, look.'

He's pointing at the television. It's the local news—they're showing the outside of Waterstone's in New Street. The commentator is directing attention to a small figure standing at the top of the building, on a small ledge just under the roof. He has both hands in the air, waving as if he knows he's on television.

'It must be for charity,' I say.

'No,' says Joel. 'It's not for charity. Look at him.'

I study the figure and there's something familiar about him. His long, gaunt droopiness—

The picture reverts to the studio, and another story appears.

'It was Dad,' says Joel.

'It can't be.'

'Why not?'

'Your father doesn't do crazy things like that.'

'How do you know?'

'Well—I just do.'

'No you don't,' says Joel. 'You just think you do. He does lots of childish things. Why not climb buildings as well?'

'Do you think he intended to jump off?'

'No, of course not. You don't wave at people if you want to commit suicide.'

'So what was he doing?'

'If you want an analysis of the ridiculous way my father behaves, ask him, not me.'

He gets up and leaves the room. I remain glued to the screen, hoping they will show the item again, but of course they don't. It was a small incident, trivial amongst major disasters, just a way of ending the news with a light-hearted item.

But it was Andrew. The whole way he stood, that defiant position at the top of the building, broadcasting his conviction that he is the only important person in the world. I would recognise it anywhere.

CHAPTER SIX

'You won't like my mother,' said Andrew, on the day when I was going to meet his parents for the first time. 'She's the stepmother from Cinderella, the Queen in Snow White, a female Pol Pot.'

I couldn't work out if he was joking. 'Did she beat you?'

'It was a beating of the mind, the spirit.' He paused. 'If you take away a child's autonomy, you beat him into submission. I think that just about sums her up.'

'Don't exaggerate, Andrew,' said Mary. 'She can't be as bad as all that.'

Mary was my first real friend. Until I met her, I thought I'd had lots of friends at school, but she taught me that they weren't friends at all, only acquaintances.

In our early days at university we recognised something in each other, an inadequacy, a belief that we were there under false pretences. So at the beginning it was a friendship of convenience, a mutual desire for someone to cling to. Everyone else seemed to know everything. We hadn't even worked out that the Student Union was a building and not just a militant political organisation until Andrew explained it to us. Mary and I groped our way to lectures together, terrified that we would be found out, that someone would suddenly realise we weren't good enough to be there and we'd been offered places by mistake.

Against all my expectations, we remained friends. I was no longer the odd one out, the outsider. There was someone to sit next to in lectures.

'Jess!' Mary would call if I arrived after her. 'Over here.'

How important it felt, climbing over other people's legs, making my way to a saved seat.

When I worked in the music library, or met Andrew for lunch in the refectory, Mary would be there too, an equal partner in our conversations. She and I discussed our seminar work—Mahler's symphonies, Byrd's madrigals—while Andrew threw in enlightening, cynical observations. We went to *Aïda* together when the Welsh National Opera came to Birmingham, bought books and orchestral scores from the university bookshop, stretched out on the grass in the late autumn sun and analysed life and other people's liaisons.

Me and Andrew and Mary. I had a boyfriend and a girlfriend. I was just like everyone else.

Mary was small and neat, with dark hair that bounced into natural waves round her pale freckled face. She was quiet, not someone who contributed anything to seminars unless she was asked, but she had an unexpectedly clear knowledge of Haydn, who pleased her more than any other composer. She soon learnt how to fit in and adapt, although she had occasional bouts of longing for her family and often returned home at weekends.

I was baffled by this. I thought I might be homesick for Audlands if I left, but couldn't imagine missing people.

Mary was most comfortable as a supporter, a strong stable friend who enjoyed being in the background. She accepted Andrew in the same way that she accepted me. Without question, somehow identifying a need in both of us.

'My mother is Lucrezia Borgia,' said Andrew. He looked past us, at the silver birches across the road. Dappled patches of light shivered and shifted on the lino. 'Mrs Ceausçescu, Imelda Marcos without the shoes.'

'Doesn't your mother wear shoes?' I asked in surprise.

He rolled his eyes.

Mary smiled. 'She brought you up. She must have done something right.'

'You haven't met her,' he said.

We were squashed into Mary's room in hall, because Andrew had arranged to meet his parents by the porters' desk, just inside the entrance.

'Why are you meeting them here?' asked Mary. He was sharing a house in Selly Oak with four other students, and it would have been easier for his parents to go there.

'They think I live here,' he said.

We stared at him.

His eyes, dark and agitated, were now flickering restlessly around, refusing to meet mine, not focusing on anything. 'I just like the idea of them not knowing where I am.'

'What happens if they want to write to you?' asked Mary.

'No problem. I lived here last year, so I have a relationship with one of the porters.'

'What kind of a relationship?'

He sighed. 'Whatever kind of relationship you would like it to be.'

I was bewildered. It seemed so unnecessarily complicated.

'Anyway,' he said, 'they don't write letters. I telephone them.'

I was surprised that he had never mentioned this before. 'How often do you phone?'

'Never,' he said.

'So how did you arrange where to meet them today?'

'Well—I phone if I need to.'

It was five minutes before we were due to meet them, but Andrew suddenly grabbed me by the shoulders and studied my face. 'You'll have to wear lipstick,' he said.

'I don't have any lipstick.' He had known me for nine months. Hadn't he realised that I didn't use make-up?

Apparently not. 'You must have. All women wear lipstick.'

'There wouldn't be much point, though, would there, bearing in mind that you've never noticed that I don't?'

'Mary,' he said, turning to her. 'Can we borrow some of yours?'

'There isn't time,' I said. Punctuality was very important to me. I couldn't think clearly if I could hear time ticking towards a deadline and I wasn't ready and waiting, fully polished, five minutes early. And I didn't like make-up.

'No rush,' he said. 'They can wait for us.' But his eyes kept seeking out the clock, and he was rubbing his fingernails up and down against each other, the noise insistent and irritating.

Mary rummaged in a drawer and produced an assortment of lipsticks, which she held up against my face. 'Yes,' she said. 'Either of these should do. Let's go for Cupcake. Hold still.'

She applied it to my mouth, and we examined the effect in the mirror. I held my lips apart, conscious of the artificiality of my pose and the sticky, slithery texture of the lipstick. 'It's horrible,' I said.

'No,' said Mary. 'You look lovely.'

But I didn't. I couldn't bear the feel of it on my lips, the way it made me feel like an imposter. I resisted the urge to wipe it off, knowing how anxious Andrew was to impress his difficult

67

mother. 'Cupcake!' I said.

'Let's have a look at you,' said Mary.

I was wearing a brown tweed skirt and a white shirt with a V-neck beige jumper. They were the smartest clothes I possessed. The jumper, which I'd bought from Marks & Spencer about six months ago in an unusually extravagant moment, was made of Shetland wool.

'The lipstick's better,' said Andrew. 'But you don't look glamorous enough.'

'Forget it,' I said. 'I'm not glamorous.'

'Wait a minute,' said Mary, and opened another drawer, searching through piles of tights and bras while Andrew and I watched her. There was a fear hanging over us. Fear of the unknown for me. Fear of something indefinable for Andrew. Was his mother really this terrifying? I glanced down at my watch, pretending to be nonchalant. There were two minutes to go.

'Here it is.' Mary pulled out a small gold necklace. 'This is what you need,' she said, and put it round my neck. She had trouble with the clasp, but her breath was warm and calm underneath my hair as she struggled to fasten it.

'There!' she said. 'Lovely.'

'Yes,' said Andrew. 'That's good.'

'They'll be there before us,' I said.

'Off you go,' said Mary and kissed my cheek. 'Hope it goes well.'

'It won't,' said Andrew. We left the room and ran down the stairs.

As we reached the bottom, his mother was coming through the door, but I didn't know it was her until Andrew stepped forward to greet her. She was much taller than I'd expected, and thin, but large-boned. There was an impression of internal conflict in her appearance, her skeleton swelling inside the inadequate skin, pushing outwards, refusing to be restricted. Her angular face was dominated by large brown eyes, with eyelids which never fully opened. They hovered, almost half-shut, over her protruding eyes, giving her the look of a Renaissance painting. A Michelangelo madonna without the necessary plumpness for genuine beauty. Her greying hair was cut short, close to the head, and she wore pearl earrings, her only concession to femininity. I couldn't see why Andrew had worried about me not being glamorous enough.

'Andrew!' she said, and her face lit up, as if a shaft of sunlight had squeezed its way through the glass doors and sneaked round the potted plants to illuminate our awkward little group. The Renaissance beauty was there after all, waiting to be activated by maternal love. I was relieved. She wasn't the monster I had been led to believe.

Andrew looked gloomy and didn't reply. She turned to me. 'You must be Jessica. I'm Miranda, Andrew's mother.'

'Yes,' I said, smiling.

'Hello, I'm Donald.' Andrew's father had crept up in the shadow of his wife. He stepped out from behind her with an outstretched hand, a worn-down version of Andrew, round-shouldered, his hair receding over a domed forehead. He wore thick glasses, and had to tilt his head upwards so that he could peer through the lower half of his lenses.

'Hello,' I said, shaking his hand reluctantly. I was inexperienced at this kind of formality.

I began to understand the need for the lipstick and the gold chain. They had the effect of watering down Miranda's intense gaze, creating a shield to deflect the full heat of her alarming inspection.

'How much practice have you done today, Andrew?' she said, turning to him.

He answered without a pause. 'Three hours. I got up at six o'clock and got it in before breakfast.'

I looked at him in astonishment. He boasted about his ability to roll out of bed at half past nine, dress, have breakfast and still be only five minutes late for the ten o'clock lecture. I couldn't swear he hadn't practised this morning, but it would have been unprecedented if he had. Did he behave differently when threatened by the appearance of his mother? Or was he lying? He only seemed to practise when there was nothing else to do. I'd tried to encourage him once or twice, but he quickly became annoyed. 'Leave it, Jess. I know what I'm doing, all right?'

His mother accepted his response, which seemed to fulfil her expectations. 'Good. I'm looking forward to the concert tonight.'

Andrew would be playing the first movement of the Sibelius concerto, a significant privilege which was usually given to a third-year student. Tickets had sold out almost immediately, and I'd only managed to get two for my family, so Harriet wouldn't be coming. We were also playing *The Swan of Tuonela* and Schubert's Unfinished Symphony, so it should be a good concert.

*   *   *

We went out for lunch at a Chinese restaurant.

70

'Andrew has told me all about Audlands,' said Miranda, starting to pour some wine.

'I don't drink,' I said, covering my glass with a hand.

'Oh.' Miranda paused with the bottle tilted in the air, her eyes large with amazement. 'Is there any particular reason for that?'

'No. I just don't like the taste, and it's cheaper to drink water, so I can't see the point.'

Donald was appalled. 'But it's one of the great pleasures of life, my dear.'

'Sorry.'

'You must try, although it takes a little time to develop a good palate. You'll have to go to the university wine-tasting club with Andrew. A bit of training and experience would make a lot of difference.'

'I didn't know there was a wine-tasting club,' I said. 'When do you go, Andrew?'

'Thursday evenings,' he said. 'After choir practice.'

What was this all about? We went to the pub after choir practice. Every Thursday.

'I gather Audlands Hall is not an old family home,' said Miranda.

'Well, it's our family home and it's over two hundred years old.'

Miranda smiled, and her face softened into natural lines that must have been there all the time, waiting to be used. 'But it's not a family seat.'

'She means your family didn't inherit it. It hasn't been in your family for generations,' Andrew said.

'Oh no. My parents bought it just after they got married.'

'We've admired it from the road,' said Donald.

71

'You can't see it properly,' I said, 'unless you go up the drive.'

Miranda leaned forward as if she was going to say something important. 'We went up the drive—just a little way—to have a peep. It's beautiful, isn't it?'

They had trespassed on our property. I thought of them driving in, going halfway up the drive as if they lived there. How would they like it if my family drove into their garden and peered through the windows? 'It's a private drive,' I said with indignation.

She sat back, surprise making her eyelids open wider.

I glanced across at Andrew, who was grinning at me. 'I think it's Georgian,' I added, aware that I'd said something wrong and anxious to change the subject.

'Mid-Georgian, I thought,' said Miranda.

'Yes, maybe.' I knew nothing about history or architecture. I just lived there.

'I hope we'll be able to come and see it properly some time,' said Miranda.

I didn't think it would be a good idea for them to visit Audlands, with its battered pillars, the dusty entrance hall and my mother's amateur attempts at restoration. Unless they came to a candle-lit evening party where everything was camouflaged.

'I'm sure you'll get the chance one day,' said Andrew, and I realised that his mother had been waiting for me to answer.

'Yes,' I said. 'I'm sure you will.'

Miranda had short, very clean fingernails. She leaned forward and touched my necklace with a finger. 'What a lovely chain. Is it a family heirloom?'

I was alarmed. Was it worth a lot of money? People shouldn't lend me valuable things. I tended to break them, lose them, damage them.

'It was given to Jess by her grandmother,' said Andrew. 'She escaped from Russia during the revolution—she was a White Russian, from an old aristocratic family.'

'Really?' Miranda asked, raising her eyebrows.

I looked at him, confused, and he returned my gaze, his eyes steady and unblinking. 'Jess has told me all about her,' he said. 'Her grandmother couldn't speak a word of English, but fell in love with a penniless English nobleman—Jess's grandfather. All she brought with her was the gold necklace.'

'It sounds like a romantic novel,' said Miranda, her voice sharp with scepticism. She looked across at me, and I smiled earnestly, stretching the corners of my mouth, forcing my face to convey agreement. For some reason this seemed to satisfy her, and she gave a brisk nod of acknowledgement. 'Well, well,' she said. 'Life never ceases to amaze.'

I tried to work out dates. Should it be grandparents or great-grandparents?

'And there was a pair of sealskin gloves,' said Andrew. 'Jess keeps those safe at home.'

My thoughts were fluttering round my head, trapped and bewildered, not knowing how to find the exit. I knew what he was saying wasn't true, but he sounded so convincing. Had my mother told him something I didn't know about? Was he lying or just making up stories?

'She's dead now, of course,' said Andrew. 'But

Jessica remembers her as a tiny old woman, always dressed in black, with a very strong accent.'

'How interesting,' said Miranda. 'You must tell me more about her.'

Heat from the kitchen was rolling out towards us, sweltering, full of unfamiliar smells. Miranda was too interested. You shouldn't lead anyone as far as this down a garden path. They might like it too much and want to return for another visit, hungry for non-existent details. I thought Andrew might also feel he'd overdone it, but he just looked pleased with himself. He was gazing thoughtfully at a Chinese waiter, who was ushering a group of elderly Indians to the next table. I suspected he was plotting the next instalment, preparing to invent a whole army of relatives with lockets inscribed by the Tsar and eye-witness accounts of Anastasia.

'I'm leading the Seconds tonight,' I said.

The atmosphere shifted back to the present. 'Goodness,' said Donald. 'What a privilege.'

'I was moved up at the beginning of term. The last leader wanted to play in the Firsts.'

'It's going to be a great concert,' said Andrew.

There was something unconvincing about the way he said it, as if he was acting out a script prepared for his parents. He didn't like talking about the music he was going to perform. I assumed familiarity had made him off-hand and he preferred to play rather than analyse. He'd done so many concerts before he came to university, and this was by no means his first concerto.

After the meal, Donald drove us back in his BMW. Leather seats, air conditioning. I wasn't accustomed to such luxury. We strolled around the

74

grounds of the halls of residence for a while. Huddles of students clustered on the grassy slopes leading down to the lake, their voices subdued in the hazy summer heat. Most were stretched out horizontally, half-naked, getting in some serious post-exam sunbathing. The lake was still and luminous in the afternoon sunshine. A group of Canada geese glided effortlessly around, sending a ripple of gentle waves towards the edges. The sound from the casual splashing of their beaks as they lifted their heads in and out of the water was cool and refreshing.

'What a glorious setting,' said Miranda. 'How lucky you are, Andrew. I wish I could wake up to this view every morning.'

I thought that Andrew probably wished he could wake up to this view every morning.

'You know,' said Donald. 'Those geese are the only animals I would ever consider shooting and having for dinner.'

'Donald!' said Miranda.

But I warmed to him. They were frightening birds. They hissed and snapped if you tried to walk through them when they crowded the paths. Their droppings littered the ground and stuck to your shoes, however hard you worked at avoiding them. Underneath their charming exterior, they were unpleasant and aggressive.

'We have to go soon,' said Andrew. 'We need time to get ready.'

'I expect you'll be wanting to do some practice,' said Miranda.

Andrew turned his head away from her and stared into the distance. I followed the line of his gaze, but there was nothing there. The road, a few passing cars, the trees beyond.

'Of course,' he replied, with a noticeable tension.

Miranda acted as if she hadn't noticed. 'Good,' she said.

He started walking back up the hill ahead of us, his mood strangely altered. A cloud had descended over him, bleak and damp, an oppressive presence that seemed to crush and reduce him.

I ran to catch up with him, but he ignored me. At the entrance, I turned to say goodbye to his parents. 'Sorry,' I said, embarrassed by Andrew's rudeness as he disappeared without another word.

Miranda smiled, her face over-bright. 'Oh, you mustn't worry about Andrew. Don't forget we've known him for twenty years.'

I went upstairs to Mary's room, where I found him sitting on the side of her bed. He stopped talking as I came in.

'You really should have said goodbye,' I told him.

He shrugged. 'I'll be seeing them later.'

I squeezed next to him. 'Shove up,' I said. I took some salt and vinegar crisps from a packet on the floor. 'Your mother didn't seem that bad.'

'Don't be fooled. You just got her caring-mother performance.'

'Andrew!' said Mary. 'You mustn't be so cynical.'

'They liked Jess,' said Andrew.

I was surprised but pleased. 'How do you know?'

He stretched his legs out in front of him and yawned. 'I can read my parents like a book. It's like looking into someone's room at night when they've forgotten to draw the curtains.'

But did he have the right room?

'Why did you say all that stuff about my grandmother?' I asked.

'Why not? They loved it. Just the kind of thing they enjoy. It confirms their belief in society, in prejudice, in social divisions. It meant they liked you.'

'Oh.' They liked me for my grandmother who didn't exist. 'But she's not real.'

'They don't know that, though, do they?'

'But now they've got the wrong impression.'

'Don't lecture me, Jess. It was just a bit of fun. They didn't really believe it.'

How could he be so sure?

'They did think you were a bit odd,' he said.

'When did they say that?' I said.

'They didn't need to. I could tell.'

'I thought you said your mother liked me.'

'She did, but she also thought you were odd.'

I was puzzled. 'In what way?'

'Well—the way you didn't invite them to Audlands, your clothes, that sort of thing. You know . . .'

I didn't know. It seemed unreasonable. I couldn't have invited them to Audlands—my parents would have to do that. I was wearing my best clothes. What more did they want from me?

What did Andrew want from me? Why did he pass on their disapproval? He should have told me the good things, tried to build up my relationship with his parents. Did he secretly agree with them and want their observations to do his criticism for him?

'Hadn't you better go and do some practice?' I said.

For a moment, the blankness descended again.

77

Then he got up. 'I know the music. I've performed the concerto before, lots of times. But if you want me to practise, Jess, I'll practise.'

He kissed my cheek and left.

'He really doesn't like his mother, does he?' said Mary.

'Was that what you were talking about when I came in?'

'She kept going on about his practice, apparently. He was furious with her.'

'Yes,' I said. 'I picked that up.' I didn't know he discussed things with Mary. I had a brief, desolate picture of myself outside, peering in at everyone as they leaned towards each other, communicating, lit by soft, intimate lamplight. How did Mary manage these cosy chats? Nobody ever told me anything.

'Actually,' she said, 'he seemed rather low.'

*   *   *

Mary and I had supper in hall and then we changed in her room. We had to wear black, so I put on a long skirt and a black blouse, my normal concert dress. I returned Mary's gold necklace, relieved to take it off. It had become too restrictive round my neck.

'Andrew's mother admired it,' I said.

'It was my grandmother's.'

'Don't tell me. She came over after the Russian revolution.'

She looked confused. 'Wherever did you get that idea? She was Irish.'

'Is the necklace valuable?'

'Oh yes, it's eighteen carat gold.'

So Andrew's mother was more discerning than

78

I'd realised. 'You shouldn't have lent it to me.'

'Why not? It suited you.'

'But I might have lost it or stolen it.'

'No, you wouldn't, Jess. You're my friend. I trust you.'

I wasn't sure if this was wise. Why should anyone trust me? Mary had no idea what was going on in my mind. I'd always assumed that you could believe what people said and did, but I'd just seen Andrew with his parents and nothing was as clear as I'd thought. There were no clues to help make sense of the situation, no indications, nothing.

Lying undermined everything. Once a big lie had been put in place, there had to be other smaller lies, to back up the big one. And then the whole fabric that made up what you saw was called into question. What was real and what was false? Was Andrew's lie about the wine club the big lie, or a small one to cover up something bigger? If you lived with lies you lived in a floating world where the horizons weren't steady. You couldn't be certain that the ground would be there when you put your foot down.

*   *   *

The Great Hall overflowed, with people standing at the back and along the aisles. The orchestra was seated, waiting for the conductor. I enjoyed concerts. I loved to see the men become civilised, hair shiny and brushed, or tied back into neat pony tails, faces transformed and matured by white shirts and ties. Most of all I liked to see them from behind, to admire the broad sweep of their shoulders in black jackets, the back of a neck rising with sophistication from a crisp shirt collar. They hated dressing up, but they looked stunning.

Many of the women appeared in tight dresses and sparkling earrings. They normally wore the same uniform as the men—jeans and trainers—but now several of them turned out to be beautiful. I was fascinated by the way people changed when they dressed up, became someone different. They shimmered and glittered and it was like placing them in front of a mirror, turning them through 360 degrees, and finding them altered when they came back. The same people, the same features, but subtly different. The nose that had seemed too big became elegant, the lips that protruded too much became full and individual. Skinny people became slim, fat people warm and shapely. I began to see what attracted people to each other. A glistening aura that was not normally on show. But then again, maybe they were able to appreciate the potential without all the dressing-up. Maybe I was the only one who couldn't see it.

Every time I looked at Andrew, I experienced a stab of pleasure at his appearance. My first and only boyfriend, looking more substantial than usual in a jacket, blond curls resting neatly on his black-suited shoulders. He was leading the orchestra until his concerto, so there was applause as he came on and sat down. He made himself comfortable, adjusted his trousers, bent those long ungainly legs under the chair.

I couldn't see my parents in the audience and I didn't want to spend much time searching for them. It wasn't professional. Too much like the child in the back row of the school play, waving at Mum and Dad.

The conductor entered to more applause. I caught Mary's eye in the oboe section and then looked back to the conductor. There was electricity in the air. I could feel the keen edge of anticipation rippling through the seated musicians, the violins nervous about that exposed high passage in seventh position, the first clarinet worrying about the clarity of a section with awkward fingering, the second trumpet silently playing his brief solo.

Robin, who sat next to me, leaned over. 'How do you get two elephants into a Mini?'

'I don't know.'

'One in the front and one in the back.'

The conductor raised his baton. We put our violins under our chins, watched the baton, placed the points of our bows on the strings, and started the tremolos, the sound shimmering and trembling as we waited for the cor anglais to come in. *The Swan of Tuonela*—calm, unhurried, gliding gracefully across a still, idyllic lake on a summer afternoon.

*   *   *

Before the concerto, Andrew went out and the platform was rearranged. The First Violins shuffled around, making space for him to stand. Janet, who usually sat next to him, took over as leader.

Silence fell. We were ready.

'How do you get two whales in a car?' whispered Robin, who refused to be over-awed.

'Shh.'

'Take the M50 and keep going.'

81

I frowned.

'Wales, idiot. The place. How do you get to Wales?'

'Oh.'

The audience started clapping. I could see Andrew's parents sitting in the front row, pretending to be nonchalant, but sitting up straighter. I could feel their tension, their expectation.

Andrew made his way through the desks of the Firsts with his violin in his hand, brushing against people's shoulders. There was something odd about him that I couldn't quite place. He didn't seem his usual self. Was he nervous? I'd seen him perform several times and he was usually a little tense, enough to give an edge to his performance. But today was different. He seemed more jittery. He stood for a moment, with his back to the audience, sweeping his eyes round the orchestra, and when he came to the Second Violins he rested his eyes on mine for a moment. I tried a smile, but he didn't respond.

He looked up at the conductor, who nodded, and we started. The violin comes in right at the beginning, in the fourth bar, with an expressive melody made bleak by a series of falling fifths. We concentrated on the repeated semiquavers, counting furiously—there were twenty identical bars and it was easy to lose your place. Everything was going well. The bassoons entered in the right place without squeaking, the brass rang out, without dominating.

The sound died down, until the cellos and basses were holding their long dark B flats, ready for Andrew's display of technical brilliance. We'd heard it before. We knew he would make it sound effortless. We played one more explosive chord and put our instruments down while Andrew's resonant A took over, soared up an octave—and stopped.

The space where there should have been music was filled with silence.

The conductor turned towards him.

Andrew put his violin down.

The conductor leaned over to speak to him. 'Is everything all right?'

Andrew didn't react.

'Shall we omit the solo? Pick it up at the tutti?' He raised his baton in expectation.

'No,' said Andrew loudly.

Nobody knew what to do.

Andrew glanced at his parents in the front row. His mother was staring at him, an expression of disbelief frozen on to her face, her eyes dark and fierce.

'I don't think I want to do this,' said Andrew, and turned to walk off the platform.

His mother rose from her seat. 'Andrew!' she called.

He ignored her and started moving away, knocking music off the desks in his wake.

'Andrew! Come back immediately!' Her voice was steely. She did not expect to be disobeyed.

Andrew flinched, but didn't stop.

She leapt up on the platform and ran towards him, pulling on his arm, oblivious to her lack of dignity. 'Don't do this to me. Play the concerto. Do you hear me?'

He pushed her out of his way and left the stage.

She faltered, stepped back, lost her balance, and

fell into the fifth desk of the Firsts.

CHAPTER SEVEN

Miranda was helped to her feet by Willard, an American French horn player with a tangled beard and hair that bushed out wildly, adding about four inches to the circumference of his head. He leapt up with an easy athleticism, long before anyone else could react, and was at her side immediately, lifting her up with one arm round her back and the other under her right elbow.

She stood dazed for a second, and then straightened her jacket. Dignity returned rapidly. 'Thank you,' she said with perfect clarity and followed Andrew off the stage.

'No problem, ma'am,' he said and returned to his horn, checking that his tie was still straight.

I wondered if I should offer to get up and go after Andrew, but I was crowded in by violas and Second Violins, and Miranda had gone before there was time to negotiate an exit.

The conductor turned to the audience and raised his arms, baton in hand. The talking died down. 'Ladies and gentlemen, I must apologise for the break in the proceedings, but I'm sure you will appreciate that in any gathering of musicians, who also happen to be students, there'll always be a certain element of unpredictability. May I suggest we have the interval early and resume in about forty-five minutes? Coffee will be served outside on the lawn.'

The audience murmured appreciatively and

applauded as he left. Members of the orchestra started shuffling to the exit and I pushed my way through them, holding my violin up in the air to keep it safe.

I could hear people muttering.

'Typical Andrew Courtenay. Never does anything without a fanfare.'

'Still, you've got to admire his nerve.'

'He did it on purpose. You could tell. There was a smirk on his face.'

I'd seen that look too, just as he'd turned away from the audience, before he said he didn't want to do it, but I'd interpreted it differently. I'd seen despair, an urgent need to escape. Had he been planning the whole thing, intending to disobey his mother and create mayhem at the same time? I had completely misread his relationship with his mother, thinking he just found her irritating. I should have been warned by the lying, which now appeared to be a manifestation of something more alarming.

'I always said they shouldn't have given him the solo. He's too unstable. Everyone knows that.'

Everyone except me, it seemed.

I couldn't find Andrew in the room behind the stage where we'd left our instrument cases. I ran along the labyrinth of corridors, not sure where to go, and bumped into someone. 'Sorry,' I said, impatient and irritated that people should get in my way.

'Jess, it's me, Mary.'

I stopped and focused on her face. 'Where is he?' I asked, confused by the sight of members of the orchestra walking down the corridor. It had been deserted a minute ago.

85

'I think he's in this room,' she said, and guided me back along a corridor I'd just left. 'I heard voices.'

The only voice we could hear as we approached was Andrew's mother's. She was talking loudly, but not shouting. It was a long, rational monologue, her voice crisp with authority, and the tone reminded me of my old headmistress. '—get back on that stage—finish what you started,' she was saying. '—regret this for the rest of your life.'

There was no reply from Andrew.

We paused at the door. 'I can't come in with you,' said Mary. 'It's not really my business.'

I took a deep breath, turned the door handle, and went in.

Andrew was sitting on a chair facing his mother, and his father was standing in a corner, some distance from them both. I was surprised that Donald had found the room before I had. He must have left the hall immediately after his wife and followed her.

Miranda was still talking, but she stopped in mid-sentence as I entered. She looked outraged that someone had intruded on their family row, someone who had nothing to do with them. 'Sorry,' I said, and stepped back to the door.

'No,' said Andrew. 'Jess has as much right to be here as you have. More, actually.'

His words sent a surge of pride through me. I belonged to him, and he wanted his mother to know that.

He was leaning forward, running his hands through his hair, his awkward legs folded and cramped under the chair. There was an air of desolation about him. I walked over and perched

86

on the edge of an adjacent chair, feeling guilty that I'd listened to the other students and doubted him. I had a strong desire to put my arms round him, but it didn't seem appropriate in his parents' presence.

'Are you all right?'

He nodded.

'Was it panic?' I wanted to give him a way out. I could discuss it with him properly when his mother had gone.

'Well,' he began, then stopped.

'Panic!' said Miranda. 'When did you ever suffer from nerves?'

'What would you know?' he said, his voice thick with contempt.

She softened her voice. 'Well, of course I know you can get a little wound up before a performance, but you've never allowed nerves to get the better of you before.'

'Did you give me a choice?'

'Don't be dramatic. I wouldn't have asked you to do something if I didn't think you enjoyed it.' She was starting to sound defensive, but recovered herself. 'You've always enjoyed performing.'

'How do you know?'

For a moment she was silent, looking at me, presumably weighing up how all this would appear to an outsider. Donald was almost invisible. He was standing with his feet apart, rocking slightly, with a neutral expression on his face. As if he wasn't part of all this, not even interested in what was going on. I couldn't contribute to Andrew and Miranda's private duel either, and wondered if I should go and stand beside Donald, taking a position as another impartial observer.

Andrew stood up. He was taller than all of us, and, taken by surprise at his sudden proximity, his mother stepped back.

'You've told me what to do all my life,' he said quietly. He turned to me. 'I had to get up at six o'clock every morning to practise, even in the holidays. Imagine that, Jess.' I blushed at the way his parents followed his direction and stared at me. I wanted to say, 'It's not my fault.'

'How long do you reckon most children practise when they're very young?' he asked me.

I didn't know what he wanted me to suggest. Fifteen minutes? Twenty? I stared at him helplessly.

He answered his own question. 'Most children practise for five minutes when they start.'

I nodded encouragingly. That was the answer. Five minutes.

'We did half an hour. I was three years old. What kind of mother does that to her only son?'

I wondered if it would have been more reasonable if she'd had more sons.

'I think you're exaggerating,' said Miranda, her voice steady and controlled.

'She was obsessed,' said Andrew. 'Every workshop, music festival, county youth orchestra, National Youth Orchestra, I was there, doing it all, winning every scholarship available.'

'And you loved it.'

He stared at her, moving closer to her, but she didn't flinch. 'How do you know? How can you assume I loved it?'

'I could see it. Your involvement with the music, the pleasure on your face when you won.'

'Everyone looks pleased if they win.'

88

'There you are, then.'

'Where? Where am I? Doing as I'm told, playing your tunes, acting out your ambitions.'

'It wasn't like that, Andrew. I did it for you, even though you argued with everything I did. If I hadn't helped you, you wouldn't have achieved anything.'

He started to laugh, gulping deep breaths in between bursts of laughter, while we stood and watched him. I'd never heard him laugh before.

'Stop it, Andrew,' said his mother sharply. 'You're being hysterical.'

He wasn't being hysterical, because he gave one last laugh, then shut his mouth and straightened his face. 'Then you admit you had to force me to practise?' he said.

She thought before answering. '"Force" is the wrong word. You can't just let children do what they want. They have no concept of personal discipline and become frustrated by their lack of success.'

'You've ruined my life.' His voice was calm now, like a very sharp cooking knife, deceptively innocent, capable of slicing through thick cuts of meat with innocuous ease.

Miranda stared at him for some time without saying anything, her large eyes still and thoughtful.

Donald cleared his throat. 'Well,' he said. 'We will have to go and apologise to someone. Who do you suggest?' He turned to me.

'I don't know,' I said. 'Gregory Ridings, the conductor, I suppose, or the professor.'

'Let's find the professor, shall we? Might as well go for the top.' He didn't seem to be as disturbed by the situation as Miranda, almost as if he'd expected it, or as if this kind of argument went on all the time. Was the apparent crisis of a lifetime just an everyday occurrence?

I'd observed my cousins and girls at school with their families. They seemed to argue all the time, digging away at each other, undermining, attacking with huge emotional outbursts, then going back to normal the next day. I'd never really understood this blatant display of personal feelings. It made me uncomfortable. I preferred to walk past people. Certain things were better left unsaid, allowed to gather dust in another room.

The door opened and Gregory Ridings entered. 'Ah,' he said. 'There you all are.'

Miranda instantly resumed her polished, controlled manner, stepping forward to offer her hand. 'I'm Miranda Courtenay, Andrew's mother. I must apologise for this evening's disaster. He seems to have suffered from an entirely unexpected attack of nerves.'

Gregory took her hand and kept holding it, gazing round at all of us, his amiable expression implying that he wanted to believe good of the situation. 'I didn't know you suffered from nerves, Andrew.'

'I don't,' he said.

Gregory looked back to Miranda politely.

'It's most unusual,' she said. I think it must be the result of a stressful term. I'm so sorry it's had to end like this.'

'Don't worry, Mrs Courtenay. Everyone was delighted to have the chance to get out of the overheated Great Hall. They're all strolling around happily outside, taking the air, discussing other high-profile musicians struck down by disaster. Jacqueline du Pré, John Ogdon, that sort of thing. It adds drama to their lives—gives them anecdotes for years to come. People are remarkably tolerant and forgiving, I always find.'

'I think I'll go home now,' announced Andrew. 'Are you coming, Jess?'

I didn't know what to do. 'What about the rest of the concert?'

He shrugged. 'OK, then,' he said, and walked out of the room.

I wanted to rush after him. I'd seen the look of hurt in his eyes when I didn't go with him. But I was leading the Seconds. He should have been leading the orchestra. We couldn't all just disappear.

Donald took charge. 'Leave him to calm down,' he said to his wife. 'He'll see it differently tomorrow.'

'Do you think he believes what he said?' she asked as they edged towards the door. 'Am I the monster he thinks I am?'

'No, of course not,' he murmured, ushering her though the door. 'You know how he likes to make everything so dramatic.'

Gregory and I looked at each other. He raised his eyebrows. 'Musicians,' he said. 'What can you expect?'

I smiled and tried to swallow the guilt that was growing in me, the realisation that I should have gone with Andrew.

*   *   *

Our performance of the Unfinished Symphony was inspired, as if the earlier drama had heightened

91

our emotions, touched something familiar inside us all. An inherent vulnerability, the tightrope between musical brilliance and failure. I could feel it in myself and all round me, the desire to commit every ounce of energy, an unwillingness to hold back in any way.

Schubert's melodies, each one effortlessly simple, tangled and overlapped, gaining strength as they came together. Woodwind and brass blended with the strings. We'd arrived as individuals, but learnt how to cooperate by listening to each other. Discords developed and then melted away into calm resolution. The crescendo of commitment, the power of harmony. An unfinished symphony which created its own completeness. Already the concerto was taking its place in history, as Gregory Ridings had predicted. It was a wonderful scandal, a highlight of embarrassment. They could go on discussing it for ever, marking it down in the diaries of their life events. 'I wonder what happened to Andrew Courtenay,' they would say.

I told my parents I was going to stay the night with Mary.

'Wonderful,' said my mother as she climbed into the car. 'Lovely evening.'

'Yes,' said my father. 'Great music.' He didn't appreciate classical music or music of any kind.

'We spoke to Andrew's mother at the beginning,' said my mother. 'I must say she seemed a bit strange. Kept talking about Russian grandmothers.'

I closed my eyes. Everything was so complicated.

'Shame about the concerto,' she said. 'Nerves, I

suppose. Give Andrew my love. I'm sure he'll be fine next time.'

She would think that. She'd only seen the charming side of Andrew, so she wouldn't know about his distress. She couldn't even visualise it, because darker things were alien to her nature.

She laughed. 'What a way to do it. Such style. He knows about dramatic climaxes, doesn't he?'

I waved as they drove off, then headed for Andrew's house in Selly Oak. It was after ten, not late for his housemates. They were probably still at the Gun Barrels, contemplating their usual gallons of beer, competing for best drinker of the evening.

I rang the doorbell, but nobody answered. I stood outside the front door, uncertain what to do. Should I use my key to go in and wait, or should I wander round the streets trying to find him? Was this a major crisis in his life, or just a blip? Did he need to be alone, or did he need me? How did you ever know these things? I thought of all the books I'd read, the films I'd seen, the conversations I'd overheard, and realised that I knew nothing. I couldn't interpret events. I didn't know how people would react, or why they said what they did. I didn't even know how my own boyfriend would be expected to behave.

Johnny, one of the students who shared the house with Andrew, came round the corner in his rust-ridden Ford Anglia, and parked it in the tiny space outside the house. I watched him manoeuvre, swinging the steering wheel with masculine assurance, confident of his own ability.

'Hi, Jess,' he said as he climbed out and slammed the car door behind him. 'Are you looking for Andrew?'

93

I nodded.

'Sam said he'd just seen him. Now where was it?' I could smell the alcohol on his breath. 'Oh, I know. He's at the station. Gazing into space. Looking serious.'

He raised his eyebrows at me on the word 'serious'. As if it was hilarious when people stopped laughing occasionally.

I started to run down the road. 'Thanks, Johnny,' I called back.

I found Andrew on a bench at the far end of the platform, as if he was waiting for a train. The station lights illuminated his yellow hair so that it seemed to generate its own electricity. From a distance, he looked like Rodin's Thinker, leaning forward, his chin on his knuckles, profoundly removed from the world around him. But he also reflected the desolation I had seen earlier, an untouchable bleakness. I stood and watched him for some time, wanting him to see me first, waiting for him to sense that I was near and to respond to me.

But he didn't. After a while I walked over and sat down next to him. He made no acknowledgement of my presence.

'Hi,' I said.

He still didn't reply.

'Are you all right?'

He looked away, and I thought he was ignoring me. Then I realised that his eyes weren't focused on anything, that they were full of water, that he was crying.

'Oh, Andrew,' I said. I put my arm round his shoulders, and he buried his face in his hands. Love rose up within me, so powerful that it overwhelmed every familiar function of my body, so potent that I thought I would suffocate.

*   *   *

The following morning, Andrew's parents came to the hall of residence. I watched them through the window as they arrived. After about ten minutes, they left again. They must have spoken to the porter and discovered that Andrew didn't live there at all. I imagined their disbelief, their refusal to accept the porter's word and finally their defeat. His mother looked pale as she descended the steps, but she was smartly dressed and her manner upright and controlled. I admired her ability to maintain her dignity.

I went over to Andrew's a bit later, and told him I'd seen them go.

'Good,' he said.

'You're so cruel.'

'They deserve it.'

Did they? It seemed very unkind to treat them like this.

'Why did you stop playing?' I asked.

He shrugged. 'I don't know.'

'But did you plan it beforehand?' I needed to know. Was it a cynical act of rebellion, or a snapping of something, a moment of insanity? Or had he simply forgotten the music?

He couldn't answer. 'I don't know,' he said again.

And that must have been the truth. It just happened, unexpectedly, unplanned. Not cynical, not deliberate. A flash of clarity in his uncertain world, a lucid conviction that he might never

95

encounter again.

He didn't play another note after that concert, refusing even to pick up his violin. He left the music department, despite everyone's assurances that the concert didn't matter, and didn't finish his degree. His mother found out where he was living and came to take the violin away. It was too valuable to be left in the care of a drop-out. He found a job as a trainee electrician.

Two weeks later, we went out for a curry to celebrate his new job. 'I'm going to be doing proper work now,' he said.

I studied his long, pale hands. I just couldn't imagine them connecting wires, manipulating hammers and pliers. 'Are you sure you can do it?'

He looked amazed. 'I can do anything. I learnt the violin, didn't I? Hardest instrument in the world.'

It's not the same, I thought. Not the same at all.

'Marry me, Jess.'

I stopped eating and stared at him. Had I heard him correctly? 'Sorry?'

'I want you to marry me.'

'Oh.'

'Is that all you have to say?'

I needed time. 'Can I think about it? You've taken me by surprise.'

'Of course,' he said cheerfully.

But I didn't need to think about it. I loved him, of course. I always had. Every time I saw him I wanted to be near him, even though that proximity was often exhausting. Now that I'd seen into his deepest thoughts, I was tied to him for the rest of my life. I could see his flaws. I knew he was unreliable and insecure. But I had never loved anyone before. Every time I had doubts, I thought back to that night on the station, the way he had cried, and I was hit again by those extraordinary emotions. Irresistible, unstoppable.

'OK,' I said softly.

His face lit up. 'Great,' he said.

CHAPTER EIGHT

Thelma Gulliver had been teaching the piano since the end of the Second World War, and over the years she'd constructed a method for maintaining her sanity. She refused to teach children who wouldn't practise and children with no talent. She gave everyone a trial year, then selected the ones who interested her.

She quite liked children, but she liked Chopin more.

She was tall, but sat at the piano with a rounded back. In the last fifteen years a hump had started to form and it interfered with the alignment of her whole body, so that she could no longer sit up straight. Her hair was coarse and crinkled, fizzing out from her head, as if she had a finger permanently in an electric socket. She knew she looked like a witch but didn't mind, since it meant that the children would feel sufficiently insecure to be obedient. She'd cultivated a kind, gentle voice as a conciliatory gesture.

One Saturday morning she opened the door to Connie and Jessica. 'Mrs Fontaine?'

'Yes,' said Connie, smiling, but betraying her anxiety with restless, darting eyes. 'And this is

97

Jessica. She's eight.'

Connie's hair was pinned into a weak bun which was gradually unravelling, ethereal veils of wisps dripping down each side of her face. She was wearing a navy linen suit, crumpled and close-fitting, with a skirt that ended several inches above the knee. She's a flower-child, pretending not to be, but failing, thought Mrs Gulliver.

Jessica stared past Mrs Gulliver with unresponsive brown eyes, while a deep flush radiated from her cheeks. She looked far too tall for an eight-year-old. This is not a normal child, thought Mrs Gulliver, sighing to herself. How in the world am I supposed to teach someone who doesn't acknowledge my existence?

'I'm glad you could manage the early time-slot,' she said. 'Do come in.'

She led them into her music room, originally intended as the dining room, at the back of the house. The piano was on the wall opposite the window, and a little lamp stood on top, small tassels dangling down from the yellowed, slightly distorted, parchment shade. A duet stool with a seat of well-worn leather stood in front of the piano. Mrs Gulliver kept her music from the Classical period in this stool: Haydn, Mozart, Beethoven. On the wall to the right of the piano there was a table, covered in a red velvet cloth, where piles of music were neatly sorted into categories. Most of it had been inherited from her uncle, who had died in the First World War. The covers were an ancient, brittle brown, crumbling at the edges. There was a section for Baroque music and another for the Romantic composers, with the largest pile devoted entirely to Chopin. A very small pile in a corner represented the twentieth century. Mrs Gulliver was not keen on modern music. She liked passion.

'If you want to,' she said to Connie, 'you can stay and listen for the first lesson.'

'Oh,' said Connie, looking shocked and then embarrassed. 'I didn't realise . . . I have such a lot of shopping . . .' She edged her way to the door, smiling more than she needed to. 'You'll be all right, won't you, Jessica?'

A moment of panic swept across Jessica's face, replaced quickly by a blank, impassive expression. She nodded once, a short, sharp nod, but kept her eyes fixed on Mrs Gulliver's brown speckled carpet.

'She'll be all right,' whispered Connie.

'Of course she will.' She's with me, thought Mrs Gulliver. How could she not be all right?

'She's just a bit shy.'

'I understand,' said Mrs Gulliver.

And then Connie was gone, springing down the steps lightly as if she were the child, let out to play early, absolved from responsibility. 'I'll be back in half an hour,' she called.

Flighty, thought Thelma Gulliver.

She returned to the music room where Jessica was still standing in the same position. 'Come and sit here,' she said, gesturing at the music stool. Jessica didn't move. They stood facing each other.

I'm too old for this sort of thing, thought Mrs Gulliver. She moved over to take Jessica's hand and tried pulling her towards the piano, but she resisted. 'Well,' she said, 'this is going to be a bit tricky, isn't it?'

Jessica shifted slightly, so that she was leaning

99

on her left leg instead of her right.

'Do you like music?'

There might have been an imperceptible nod, but it was difficult to be certain in the half-light.

'Was it your mother's idea for you to have lessons?'

A very slight shake of the head. Good news. The child wanted to come. She hadn't been forced. Now all they needed was a way to get her to the piano.

Mrs Gulliver had an idea. She leafed through her Chopin collection and found a volume of the Preludes. She took it over to the piano and sat down, reaching up to turn on the lamp before starting. A pool of light flooded out and illuminated the music. She lifted her hands, wrists up, elbows down, fingers loose and relaxed, and placed them elegantly on the keys.

Her left hand started to stroke the repeated A flats with a gentle insistence, establishing a constant presence, but taking a passive role, hardly there at all. The right hand sang out, *cantabile*, easing its way through the simplicity of the melody. *Rubato*, indulgent, taking its time. Each phrase rose and fell, shaped and polished with love. This was how you played Chopin. It was music for the nineteenth-century salon, a piece to impress George Sand and the cultured circles of Paris, who, like Thelma Gulliver, were all slightly in love with the consumptive, temperamental composer from Poland.

A slight movement from behind reminded her why she was playing and she glanced sideways. Jessica had approached the piano and stood beside her, her face lifted slightly as she swayed with the music.

Aha, thought Mrs Gulliver. The dreadful mother might have been right after all about her daughter's desire to play the piano.

She continued to play. The A flat sank enharmonically into G sharp. Chords developed and built up to a crashing, resonant climax before dying away and starting all over again. There were a few wrong notes, where her arthritic fingers slipped a little, but they didn't matter too much. The shape was there, the drama, the emotion. The music started to wind down, losing the chords, falling back to a single repeated note and the final chord.

There was a long silence. Mrs Gulliver lifted her hands with the fluid, ballet-like movement she had once seen Rachmaninov make at a concert when she was a child, and placed them in her lap. She knew she had won. Jessica's response to the music was satisfying. She was close to the piano, breathing deeply, her hands reaching out and touching the keys.

Mrs Gulliver moved to her teaching chair and gestured at the piano stool. Jessica sat down.

I'm good, thought Mrs Gulliver.

'Well,' she said finally. 'It'll take a bit of time before you're ready to play that. It's by a man called Chopin, the greatest composer of piano music who ever lived. He was Polish.' She pointed to a picture on the side wall. Chopin looked past them, his hands folded, a strangely solid man with hollow cheeks. There was confidence in his expression, a belief in his own genius. 'That's our Frederic,' she said.

Jessica studied the picture for a few seconds.

But her eyes slid back to the piano, greedy for the music.

'We'll have to start with something a little more straightforward,' said Mrs Gulliver. 'Let me tell you about middle C.'

*   *   *

Connie watched Jessica and Harriet at the dance show, and placed a smile on her lips. She ensured that her eyes shone with pleasure, mirroring the other mothers, all of whom were clearly delighted by the performance. In reality, her mind was on the drawing room at Audlands Hall. She was distracted by thoughts of the eighteenth-century gilt-framed mirror over the Adam fireplace. A complex pattern of gold lilies and reeds weaved and twisted round each other in elaborate spirals, reaching a good three feet above the mirror itself. She'd looked up the design in her abundant supplies of books, and was fairly certain it originated from China. Connie was very excited by this mirror.

A ripple of applause broke out around her. People were chuckling and whispering to each other.

'They're very good, aren't they?'

'Debs never practises—you wouldn't believe she could do all that, would you?'

'The Wilden girls' costumes are home-made, aren't they? They don't have quite the same polish.'

My girls' costumes are home-made, thought Connie in a panic. Can you tell?

She forced herself to concentrate on the finale, where all the classes were performing together.

Harriet was at the front, putting energy and dedication into her dancing as always, a natural performer, even though she was one of the younger ones. Her willowy body bent and stretched and her supple arms fell naturally into graceful shapes.

Then there was Jessica at the back, behind the older girls, so no one could see her. Solid and awkward, black plaits tied up round her head, German-style, never quite in step with everyone else. She didn't want to be there. That was obvious from her manner whenever Connie caught a glimpse of her. Her face was red and sweaty and her movements heavy with embarrassment. Unlike Harriet, she made no attempt to lose herself in the spirit of the music.

Connie sighed. She'd been so impressed by Jessica's response to the piano lessons that she'd decided to offer ballet as well, but Jessica had initially refused. 'You'd love it,' said Connie, her voice rising with her own enthusiasm. 'They play music and you learn to move better. It'll make everything easier. When they play games at school, you'll know what to do. It'll stop you being—' She stopped. She'd been intending to say 'clumsy', but realised that this would not be tactful. 'You won't fall over so often, because you'll be even more graceful than you are now.'

Jessica looked at the ground while she contemplated this information. 'I'm not graceful,' she said after a long pause.

'No, Jessica, but you could learn to be.'

'All right,' said Jessica.

So she went to ballet lessons. The teacher talked to her at the beginning of the first lesson, with an extravagant smile and elaborate hand gestures. 'Just copy the others. You'll soon get the idea.'

For a whole term, Jessica stood against a wall and refused to join in.

Connie made Jessica a little white tunic with a red belt and bought her some satin ballet shoes, which Jessica obediently put on every week. She then continued to stand in a corner with a flushed, agonised face. She leaned backwards on one leg, the other leg bent in front of her, her tummy sticking out.

'Come on, Jess, I'll do it with you.' Connie slipped her shoes off one day and led Jessica by the hand to the middle of the room. They stood side by side, both of them towering over the line of eight-year-olds.

'First position,' called the ballet teacher. 'Point to the side, second position, demi-plié, bend the knees, hold it—and up.'

Connie did all of this, much to the amusement of the other children, while Jessica stood motionless at her side. She started to enjoy it herself. Each week, she put on a close-fitting T-shirt and her shortest skirt, which barely covered her bottom, and tied her hair up in a bun, waiting for the moment in the lesson when she could give the impression that Jessica needed her help. She began to practise in the drawing room every morning when the girls were at school.

Then one day, after about three months, Connie was painting the walls in the study—green, calm and sophisticated—when she heard voices from Jessica's bedroom above her.

'First position, point to the side, second position, rise on the toes, hold it, a little longer, raise the arms above your head. No, no, no, your arms go like this. Pas de chat. Pas de chat.'

She put down the paintbrush, crept up the stairs and peeped through the doorway to see Jessica giving Harriet ballet lessons: Jessica in her tunic and red shoes and Harriet in shorts and pumps. They had clearly been doing this for some time, because Harriet understood all the directions and she even knew the French words. But Jessica was doing it too, stretching with long clean lines, her turned-out legs under perfect control, as if she had been dancing for years. Connie felt a twinge of jealousy at her loose limbs and her unexpected lightness.

Well, thought Connie. She takes in more than you think. She fought down a twinge of irritation. She'd worked so hard to do the right thing. Why couldn't Jessica at least have let her know she was interested?

At that moment, Jessica saw her peering round the door and stopped. She stood rooted to the spot, instantly heavy again, her face reddening. She stared at her feet.

'Hello, Mummy,' called Harriet. 'Look at me. I'm learning to do ballet. Jessica's the teacher.'

'So I see,' said Connie loudly, walking into the room and pretending she hadn't been secretly observing them. 'You'll have to go to lessons with Jessica.'

In the end, that was the solution. Both girls joined the class after half-term, and together they took part as if they had been doing it for years. The teacher was amazed.

'What talented girls you have,' she said to Connie.

But Jessica was only any good if she could dance at the back of the class where she thought she would be unobserved. If anyone's attention was focused on her, she became clumsy and self-conscious. Out in the rose garden, surrounded by four walls, she made up ballet stories with Harriet, free and easy in a way she would never be in public. Connie could hear them when she was hanging up the washing. She longed to go and see, but knew it would all stop if she appeared.

*　　　*　　　*

After the show Connie went round the back to help them dress, but they'd already changed. 'That was quick,' she said. 'Aren't you clever?'

'It's not clever to get dressed,' said Jessica. 'We do it every morning.' She still had make-up on her face, bright red lipstick and painted eyes. She must have forgotten, because when she caught a glimpse of herself in a mirror on the way out she stopped with a shocked expression. 'I need a handkerchief,' she said.

Connie found a grubby handkerchief in the bottom of her bag and handed it to her. Jessica began dragging it across her face, scraping at the make-up with a desperate urgency.

'You don't need to do that,' said Connie. 'It looks very pretty.'

'It's horrible,' said Jessica.

'But Harriet still has hers on.'

Jessica wouldn't look at Harriet. 'It's not real,' she said, her voice low and angry. 'I hate it.'

*　　　*　　　*

106

In the evening when the girls had gone to bed, Connie tried to talk to Roland about Jessica. They sat in the dining room at one end of the long table, but with plenty of space between them. 'Most girls love the idea of wearing make-up,' she said.

'Jessica isn't like most girls,' he said. He sounded pleased.

'She's so difficult to deal with. I never know how to respond to her.'

He sipped from his glass of wine. 'You mustn't assume that everyone is going to behave in the same way that you do.'

'Well, of course I don't.'

'She's highly intelligent. Picks things up very quickly if she wants to.'

'Yes, if she wants to. So will you come to her parents' night with me?' She usually went on her own, but Jessica's present teacher, Mr Kelvin was alarming. He was not the kind of man who would take her seriously.

Roland frowned. 'I was like her when I was a boy. Wanted to follow my own interests. Wouldn't be told by anyone. It hasn't done me any harm.'

Connie felt this might be a good time to talk to him about his unapproachability, his transformation from energetic and eager-to-please young man to boring businessman, whose mind was constantly on work, particularly now. Fontaine's Crunchy Chocolate Brownies were starting to lose sales. Mr Kipling was in the ascendancy. But she knew she wouldn't be able to penetrate. 'Do you think we could afford a carpenter? There are so many little jobs that need doing. Some of the window frames are sticking.'

He finished his meal and lined up the knife and fork at an exact right-angle to the edge of the table. 'You don't need to worry about window frames. If one sticks, open another. There are plenty to go round.'

She pretended to smile. 'But if they stick open, the rain comes in.'

He nodded. 'Yes, I see. I'll think about it. Depends how the new campaign goes. We're putting everything into Bakewell tarts.'

*   *   *

'Your daughter is very bright,' said Mr Kelvin. He had overabundant black eyebrows that descended dramatically when he wanted to emphasise a point.

Connie stared at him, not sure whether he was serious. 'Are we talking about Jessica?' she said. 'Or Harriet?'

'I only teach Jessica,' he said and sat back in his chair, observing her through his thick-lensed glasses, the tangled eyebrows visible above the metal frames. 'She's quite exceptional.'

Connie didn't know what to say.

'Of course she is,' said Roland. 'She picks things up very quickly when she wants to.'

'Her reading skills are years above her age,' said Mr Kelvin.

'But does she understand what she's reading?' said Connie.

He frowned. She thought he could read her disbelief and was dismissing her opinions without considering them properly. She felt herself flush. 'Of course she does,' he said. 'If she can read the words, she can understand them. Words are the

108

tools to comprehension.'

'What about arithmetic?' asked Roland.

'Excellent, excellent.'

'But . . .' Connie began, unsure how to express what she wanted to say. 'Does she play with other children?'

Mr Kelvin's gaze moved into the distance, a bored expression creeping into his eyes. 'I have no idea, Mrs Fontaine. I think you should concentrate on her intellectual abilities and not worry about how well she can play games.'

'We've arranged for piano lessons,' said Connie, wanting to show that they'd already put an effort into expanding her abilities.

He was not impressed. 'Waste of time. All these extra-mural activities are just a modern fad. I didn't allow my children to do music or sport. "Plenty of time for that sort of thing later", I said. It paid off. One's a doctor, the other's a lawyer.' He sat back and beamed. 'That's where Jessica's heading, you know.'

'I don't think music is that modern,' said Connie. 'Mozart was around . . .' she took a guess, 'two hundred years ago. And what about Beethoven, or Tchaikovsky?' She couldn't think of any more composers and gave up.

'I always knew she was clever,' said Roland.

'Supposing she doesn't want to be a doctor or a lawyer?' said Connie.

'She will. She's Oxbridge material.' He rose to his feet. 'Thank you so much for coming. The school report will give you more details.'

'See,' said Roland, as they walked to the car. 'I told you there was nothing to worry about.'

'But he didn't seem to understand her very well,

did he?' She paused. 'I didn't like him.'

'I thought he was a good sort,' said Roland. They climbed into the car and he started the engine. 'If she's that intelligent,' he said, 'she could come into the firm and take over when I retire.'

Connie snorted. 'She won't want to do that.'

'Give her time. She's only nine.'

'So why doesn't she give us any indication that she's clever?'

He smiled. 'Well, you might not see it, but I do.'

Connie looked across at him. Where did this optimism come from? He spent most of his time telling her that Fontaine's were about to collapse and he couldn't possibly afford a plumber, a plasterer or a carpenter, and yet here he was planning for the future, with Jessica as the managing director. It didn't make sense.

Roland had seemed so deliciously mature when she married him, so wise, so dependable. Now, only eleven years later, his hair was receding, furrows had appeared in his forehead and there was a stoop in his shoulders.

'You don't always have to wear a suit and tie,' she said. 'There are alternatives.'

He reached out his left hand and patted her knee. 'Stop worrying,' he said. 'Jessica's clever. Clever children always survive.'

But Connie knew that they also played with other children, and discussed things and generally made an impression on people. They didn't look into space and ignore you.

*   *   *

'Mr Kelvin told us you were doing really well,' said

110

Connie when she went up to see Jessica in bed.

Jessica lowered her eyes and smiled to herself. 'What else did he say?'

Connie couldn't remember any of Mr Kelvin's comments clearly. 'Well . . . not much . . .' The conversation was already faltering. 'Do you want me to read something?'

Jessica shook her head. 'No, thank you.'

Connie sat on the end of her bed for a bit longer because she thought she ought to, without knowing what else to talk about. It was always like this when she was with Jessica—a struggle between her conscience and an urgent desire to escape. She knew she should keep trying, but it was such hard work, so unrewarding. She was looking forward to reading to Harriet. 'Your arithmetic book was a bit untidy.'

Jessica flushed. 'I didn't think it was.'

'No, but I did.'

'Mrs Gulliver says I'll be able to play Chopin one day.'

'Good,' said Connie and stood up. Harriet would be waiting for her. She could tease her and they would giggle together and then she could read some of *The Magic Faraway Tree*. Harriet loved the goblins and the pixies and the fairies. She wasn't contemptuous about them and didn't demand proof of their existence. It was fun reading to Harriet.

'Night night, sleep tight, mind the bugs don't bite,' she said to Jessica.

Jessica started to scrabble through her bed. 'Where?'

'Stop untucking the blankets,' said Connie. 'You're making it all messy.'

111

'Where are the bugs?' said Jessica, her voice rising in panic.

'It's just a joke. It's not real.'

Jessica lay back and turned away from her, breathing heavily. 'Well, it's not funny.'

'Night night,' said Connie again.

But Jessica wasn't listening. Her eyes were fixed on a corner of the ceiling, her mind already removed from their conversation. She doesn't need me, thought Connie, with a mixture of relief and guilt. She's happier on her own, thinking her private, unknown thoughts.

Connie turned off the light and headed for Harriet's room. She was a good mother. She knew she was a good mother.

CHAPTER NINE

'Andrew?'

'What?' His voice is muffled and irritable. 'Go away. I have to get up at five o'clock.' He puts the phone down.

I start to doubt what I've seen on the television. If it had been him standing on top of Waterstone's, surely he would have known he was being filmed, and therefore he'd have been watching every edition of the news, hoping to catch a glimpse of himself. Maybe I've been influenced by Joel's certainty, unable to see properly for myself. I often make mistakes with identification. After all, there isn't a lot to go on. Two arms and two legs, two eyes, a nose and a mouth—

The phone rings and I snatch it up. He must

112

have recognised my voice after all.

'Jess?' It's Mary.

'Aren't you in bed yet?'

'We've just been watching the news. And at the end—'

'You saw Andrew.'

'You saw him too, then?'

'Well, I thought I did, but now I'm not quite sure.'

'Oh, it was definitely him. Both Eamon and I recognised him immediately, without any discussion. Extraordinary, after all this time. Whatever is he up to?'

'I don't know.' I feel stupid, as if I should know what my ex-husband is doing, as if our long separation doesn't count. I can't admit to Mary that I've been in contact with him and that he made no mention of climbing buildings. She would be so shocked.

She's as practical as ever. 'You ought to ring him. Do you have a telephone number?'

'Joel must have it.'

'We ought to check he's all right.'

'Of course he is. Have you ever known a time when he wasn't?'

She pauses. 'You sound annoyed.'

'Yes. I probably am.' Being annoyed means I don't have to worry.

'Jess—you don't think he was trying to throw himself off the top of Waterstone's, do you?'

'No, of course not.' I'm starting to feel guilty. He's not used to rejection. If he wanted to make a point he would never go for the easiest option, and the melodrama of an attempted suicide would appeal to him. 'There's a group, isn't there, who

113

climb up buildings, dressed as Batman or Spiderman?' I say. 'Rights for absent fathers, or something. He's probably got the idea from them. Let's hope he hasn't joined them under false pretences.'

'Oh, Jess. How sad. Do you think he misses Joel that much?'

'He doesn't need to miss him,' I say. 'He could make an effort, go round and see him at work, attempt to communicate. Joel isn't a child. They could talk to each other as adults.' I pause. 'Well— maybe not. But they could pretend.'

Mary is taking it very seriously. 'Just phone him, Jess. For my sake.'

'He's not our problem, Mary.'

'What if there's no one else who cares? You hear about lonely people who die in their flats and it's six months before anyone finds them.'

'That wouldn't happen to Andrew. He's more interested in making a splash. If he did anything, we'd know about it.'

'That may be exactly what he was doing at the top of Waterstone's. Please ring him. Otherwise I won't get any sleep tonight.'

I smile, despite myself. 'Go to bed. I'll do it.'

'Thank you, Jess. I'll ring you tomorrow.'

I put the phone down, wondering how she can be so sure that I'll do as she asks. Years ago, there would have been no doubt. I always kept my word, however difficult it might be, because it never occurred to me to do otherwise. But I've begun to realise that the world doesn't always operate as I'd imagined. People half do things, drift to the side, refuse to be moulded by other people's expectations. I'm interested in this. I've been trying to cultivate the art of unpredictability.

I dial Andrew's number, and he answers with the same lack of curiosity. 'I'm asleep. Call back tomorrow.'

'Andrew? It's Jessica. I need to speak to you.'

His voice wakes up. 'Jess! You've changed your mind?'

I'm confused. 'What about?'

'A reconciliation, a new start.'

'No!' I nearly put the phone down. Once again, it feels as if the only way I can resist him is to go physically in the opposite direction.

'So why did you phone?'

'Was it you on the top of Waterstone's this afternoon?'

'Ha!' He sounds pleased. 'How did you know about that?'

'The whole of West Midlands knows about it.'

'Really? You mean I've been on television?'

'Local television. *Midlands Today*. What were you doing there?'

He whoops with delight. 'Do you think my mother saw me?'

'I've no idea. Ask her.'

'No way. She'd want to know why I hadn't taken the violin with me. Hey, there's an idea—playing Shostakovich at the top of Waterstone's—I never thought of that—'

'Andrew! What's it all about?'

'Do you think they'll recognise me in Northfield tomorrow?'

'Not if you start work at six o'clock. Nobody will be awake.'

'I'll go in later, pretend I've overslept, give people a chance to meet me in person.'

It's only about nine hours since I last saw him. During our short meeting I watched him argue with the lady in the BHS restaurant and take on the world of pedestrians, yet it's still a shock to discover how little he's grown up. Even if he picks up the violin that his mother has delivered to him and starts again, he'll only ever be an infant prodigy, stuck at the age of twelve.

I remember myself at eighteen, listening to him playing Brahms. He was able to construct an exquisite world around us, an edifice of glass that reflected and refracted the light, where every note shimmered, became a prism, broke up into rich fragments of flickering colour. I thought his violin was speaking of things he couldn't say. Now I wonder if he really wanted to say anything at all. He was just a spoilt young man with an expensive instrument.

Other people recognised this, but I thought they were jealous: 'He's just a showman' they'd say. 'You can tell from the music he chooses.' Or: 'He's all technique. There's no soul.'

Why did I never see beyond the music? Even when we were married I only saw the conductor, only heard the sounds of instruments close to me. My perceptions were so limited, as if being confined in a small world controlled by someone else had stunted my growth. It never occurred to me to stand back from it all, hear the symphony as a whole and recognise that the French horns were also there, taking part, liaising with the bassoons, the double basses, the timpani. There were elaborate strands of melody going on around me, contributing to a harmonious whole that I knew nothing about, because all I could hear was

116

Andrew's solo.

So why had I allowed this pre-teenager, this wayward boy, to invade my life again?

'Andrew! What's going on?'

'It was superb. I was so high, looking down on everyone else. Mark my words, Jess, this is only the beginning.'

'The beginning of what? What are you talking about?'

'My future career.'

'I thought your future was on the streets of Northfield. A man of the people, you said.'

'Very funny. It may be the streets of Northfield today, but it'll be the streets of New York tomorrow. Paved with gold. Only it won't be the streets, it'll be the buildings, the Statue of Liberty—'

'It's a wonder you didn't get yourself arrested.'

'I nearly did—I could hear the sirens, but I abseiled down and made a quick getaway.'

'Didn't you see the television camera?'

'There wasn't time to look. As it was, I had to leave my rope.'

I sigh with exhaustion. 'It's very late. I'm going to bed.'

'Great. I might ring you before I go to work.'

'Don't even think about it.'

'Why not? You woke me.'

'Did I? I'm not entirely convinced.'

'Jess, you cynic! You must learn to believe what people tell you.'

I used to, and look where it got me.

'All right,' I say and put the phone down.

Joel surprises me by coming in with a cup of hot chocolate. 'Thank you,' I start to say, until I realise it's for him, not me. 'Where's mine?' I ask.

He has the decency to look embarrassed. 'Sorry, Mum. I didn't realise you would want some too.'

'Did you ask?'

'Well—you were on the phone and I thought I was being helpful, making my own.'

The idea that he might look after me occasionally has never occurred to Joel. Why should I expect anything else? Andrew didn't set a good example. What could Joel have learnt from him? All he'd have picked up from his father would have been selfishness, how to be waited on, how to dominate. I tried to teach him, seeing myself as authoritative, consistent and decisive, but I'm not convinced I've made any impression. Joel was eight when Andrew left, already shaped and influenced.

I lean back on the sofa and kick off my shoes. 'I didn't really want a drink anyway.'

He sits down opposite me. 'No, I thought you wouldn't. They always feed you well at Mary's.'

He smiles at me, his face open and good-natured, and I find myself smiling back.

'It was him, wasn't it?' says Joel.

'Yes—he's rather pleased with himself. He's keen on the idea of being famous, so even if it was only a whim he's just realised he's on to a good thing.'

'Typical Dad. Anything to draw attention to himself.'

'Yes. Have you washed up yet?'

'Wait until tomorrow. Then you'll find out.' He starts fiddling with some plasticine models of cats that he's placed on the coffee table. He twists their tails round thoughtfully, manoeuvring them into

118

aggressive postures. 'Rossini,' he says, pointing to one. 'And Gershwin.' The cats all look the same to me. They stare into each other's eyes.

I would like to play the piano but the neighbours would complain, so I go back to the kitchen and run hot water into the washing-up bowl, adding Fairy liquid. I know I shouldn't do it, but I hate coming down to a messy kitchen in the morning.

*   *   *

The next day, I leave at 8.15 for my part-time job in the local library. I enjoy the work—the soothing quietness, the dusty, calming presence of books. Things have altered in the last few years, with the advent of computers and virtual knowledge, but my interest still lies with books. I'm good at recommendations because I read newspaper reviews. I get the story from the back cover, read the first page for the style and the last four pages to find out what happens and I've got them sorted.

Isolde, the other librarian, reads everything from cover to cover. Whenever she sits down, five minutes before we open, during a coffee break, while she has a quick sandwich in the back for lunch, there's a book open on her lap. She can break off and pick it up again without confusion. She averages a book a day, taking it home to finish, because there's always a new one on her lap the next day. She lives alone, and I think of her with envy, reading as she eats her supper, going to bed early, racing through the last exciting pages. She devours everything—literary novels, romances, thrillers, non-fiction. She's acquired more knowledge from books than anyone else I've met.

119

Neither of us is very interested in the computers. Most people know how to do it these days, and if they come and ask we can get them going. Otherwise, we bluff it. There's nearly always someone else there who knows what to do if we don't.

We often ask Joshua. He's either homeless or lives in a hostel, we've decided, and he's ancient—a human version of a hundred-year-old oak tree. The way it turns in on itself, the branches bent and gnarled, untidy, but with an inner strength that's all set to tackle its next century. Joshua comes in every day for several hours, clicking through the on-line property pages, jotting down the prices of houses that interest him. Never fewer than five bedrooms, or under £300,000. He knows everything about computers there is to be known. He sits, bowed over the keyboard, his huge black head covered with a dense mass of tight white curls. He doesn't say a word unless asked a question, at which point he'll come to life, animation and interest lighting up his face as he explains everything in his deep, melodious voice.

Otherwise, Luke will help out. We think he should be in school—he looks younger than sixteen—but we've given up asking about his age, since he never answers. He's pierced by little rings which pop out from every available area, in neat lines down his ears, across his eyebrows, in clusters on his nose. His interest is in figures. Huge, long, complex calculations. He and Joshua sit side by side, never communicating, but willing to explain anything if asked.

Isolde is already there when I arrive at the library, half an hour before opening time. She's about fifty, and always well dressed. Her ginger-blonde hair bounces out from her head in random waves that alter from day to day, in endlessly fascinating ways. I've wasted many hours trying to work out the patterns—where the parting is, which bit sticks up where, whether it's symmetrical—but there's no inner logic.

'Did you see that man who climbed to the top of Waterstone's last night?' she says. 'Such a good idea, standing above all those books. Man conquers knowledge. I wish I'd thought of it. I'd have had a banner. Don't buy your books—use the library.'

The power of local television. How many people have seen Andrew? 'Actually,' I say, 'it was my ex-husband.'

Her eyes widen with disbelief. 'No!'

'Yes.'

'The one you met recently?'

'How many ex-husbands do you think I have?'

'So what was he up to?'

'I have absolutely no idea.'

Isolde smiles, convinced I know more than I'm letting on. She'll wear me down through the morning, as usual. You can't keep secrets from her. I end up telling her all sorts of things I don't mean to. I tell her plenty of other things too, exaggerated anecdotes, in order to satisfy her insatiable appetite for information. I can do this these days. I'm developing an imagination.

'Was it charity?'

'Yes,' I say, smiling at the thought. Andrew would no more support a charity than he would go back to university. Although you can never be absolutely certain.

'Which charity?'

'I don't know.' I go behind the desk and sort through deliveries from local libraries, checking them against the list of ordered books. 'He doesn't tell me much.' He doesn't tell me anything, but I'm not prepared to say so.

Isolde picks up her book for the day. It's science fiction, so we can expect some practice with imaginary phaser-guns this morning, and odd eye signals as she examines customers for evidence that they are aliens in disguise. I study the back of the latest Ian McEwan. I think I've got the general idea.

*   *   *

I finish work at one o'clock on Saturday. I intend to go home for lunch, so I leave by the side entrance and head towards the small staff car park at the back.

'Jessica!'

I ignore him at first, half-hearing, wishing that I haven't, pretending that the voice is someone else's.

'Jess!' Andrew comes bounding round and plants himself in front of me so that I have to stop. 'It's me.'

'Yes, I rather thought it might be.'

He's fresh, bouncy, expecting me to be delighted to see him. 'Somebody stopped me this morning, on his way to work, and said he'd recognised me on television. Wanted to shake me by the hand, thought I was doing a good job for absent fathers, and why wasn't I wearing a Batman outfit?'

'What did you say?'

122

'I said thank you very much and I was doing the best I could for justice.'

'Andrew, you shouldn't have said that. It wasn't true.'

'Why not? It wasn't not true. I'm in favour of justice. Nobody else said anything. I thought there would be lots of people. Strangers.'

'Nobody remembers faces that they glimpse for a second on the television. That man probably recognised you because he's seen you cleaning in Northfield and he had something to relate to.'

'He always says good morning.'

'There you are, then.'

We're standing in the middle of the pavement. Someone wheels a shopping trolley over Andrew's foot, and he swings round in a fury.

'Hey!' he shouts.

If only it had gone over my foot instead of his. 'Did it really hurt that much?' I ask, longing for him to disown the pain, to act as if it was a small inconvenience, not a major disaster.

The woman who turns to confront him is short but solid, with furious eyes. She glares at Andrew. 'Don't you hey me, sunshine,' she says, a sense of menace permeating every tight word. She doesn't have any front teeth.

It's immediately obvious that he's chosen the wrong person to argue with, but he doesn't seem to have discerned this. 'You've just driven your vehicle over my foot,' he says.

She pushes a strand of iron-grey hair behind her ear. 'You shouldn't have such big feet,' she says.

'Big feet? You think I chose my feet? You think I explained to my mother in the womb, I want big feet, so I can annoy all the ex-women Gestapo

123

officers that I meet in the street? So it's my fault?'

'Yes,' she says and turns away, pulling her trolley behind her.

'Leave it, Andrew,' I say. I can't cope with the embarrassment. Everyone has stopped to watch. I gave up this way of life a long time ago. I don't have to deal with it.

'No way,' he says. 'She can't get away with talking to me like that. Who does she think she is?'

'Fine,' I say and turn my back on him. He can choose. Either he wants to talk to me or he wants to have a row with a stranger. He can't do both. I walk towards the car park, and for a brief second think I've got away with it, but then I hear footsteps behind me. This time I keep going, but he appears at my side, panting. I have visions of the woman lying in the street in a pool of blood, or slumped against a wall, battered by his words, but there were no screams or shouts, so I assume one of them gave in. Does he think I'm more important than a big bust-up? I try not to think about it—it's too depressing.

'Shall we have lunch?' he says.

'Again?'

'Why not? It was fun yesterday, wasn't it?'

'Can't we talk here?' I say.

'How can we possibly have a decent conversation while the whole world assaults us? It's not civilised. Most people sit down to talk, ease their words with the lubricating power of coffee, the occasional mouthful of food—'

'I'm really busy—'

'That's OK. We could go back to your place and you can get on with things while we chat.'

This is becoming alarming. It's the same house

124

we moved into together when Joel was born, but I've bought it, decorated it, made it my private domain. I've replaced everything from the early days. I don't want to allow him into the context of my life and possessions.

He's fidgeting in front of me, his eyes darting from side to side, his feet agile and active as he tries to avoid being jostled by passers-by. I wish he wouldn't do this. I don't want to feel sorry for him. 'We could go to Costa up the road,' I say.

We walk back the way we came. There's no sign of the woman with the trolley. In Costa we buy coffee and sandwiches.

'Thanks Jess,' he says, as I edge him towards a corner table where he can't bother anyone. He sits down and bites into the sandwich, taking an enormous first mouthful. 'I'm starving.'

I watch him for a few seconds. How could he allow himself to end up here? The man who could play the Sibelius violin concerto, the Beethoven, the Tchaikovsky?

'So what's going on, Andrew?'

He swallows his mouthful and pauses before biting into the sandwich again, studiously innocent. 'What do you mean?'

'You know very well what I mean. Waterstone's. What were you doing there?'

'It was the most mind-blowing thing I've ever done.'

'But why?'

'Waterstone's, you mean? You should appreciate the value of bookshops, Jess. You're a librarian.'

I take a sip of coffee to give myself time to hide my irritation. 'That wasn't what I meant. What were you doing there? You don't climb up buildings if you want to buy books.'

He grins. 'Some people might have to.'

'But you don't.' I give up and wait. He's dying to tell me, but he won't be pushed.

'I've taken up climbing. I've got all the kit. Bought it from the man in the flat below me. He broke his knee climbing in the Lake District and the doctors told him he could never climb again, so I bought the whole lot for a couple of hundred pounds. Bargain.'

'It's odd that you didn't mention this yesterday.'

He frowns. 'It must have slipped my mind.'

'But if you take up climbing you're supposed to go and find mountains, or at least hills—not buildings.'

'You can climb anywhere. It's all good stuff. Climbing walls is good training. It's what the SAS do.'

'You are not the SAS.'

'Well, I'm glad you pointed that out, Jess. I might not have realised without your help.'

Unexpectedly, he gets out of his chair and walks towards the door where a young woman with a pushchair is having difficulty negotiating her way through the tables. She's very young, little more than a girl. She has a thin pony tail with pink streaks in it and long false eyelashes. The baby is asleep, a rim of dried ice-cream plastered to its cheeks.

Andrew goes over and starts moving chairs out of the way so that she can reach the counter. She doesn't know how to deal with his efficiency, and won't look him in the eye. 'Thanks,' she mutters eventually, and he waves his hand in a carefree,

126

amiable manner. He comes back to the table.

'Do you know her?' I ask, confused by all this.

'No.'

'So what was that all about?'

'I just felt sorry for her, OK?'

However hard I try to control the situation he has a way of taking over, and I can't win. I don't understand why I give in to him, why I've allowed him to reappear in my life. I thought I was winning, beating the current, striking out for land—and here he is again, in front of me, mocking, making me believe I can't do it.

'Mary phoned last night, after the news.'

He looks pleased. 'She saw me then?'

'Yes, she was worried. And Eamon.'

'Good chap, Eamon. How are they both?'

Why would he think of Eamon fondly? The last time he saw him was fifteen years ago when he put him in hospital. Does he really not remember?

'Eamon's fine. And Mary. But they want to know, as I want to know, why you climbed to the top of Waterstone's.'

His expression becomes serious. He abandons his performance, the nonsense, the light-heartedness and leans towards me, his voice low. 'All my concentration was on that wall. Nothing else. No orchestra behind me, no mother, no wife, no child. Just me and the wall. All I could see were the bricks in front of me. And when I got to the top, it was like I'd climbed Everest. I don't need to go to the Lake District or Scotland, or Nepal. It's all here, the whole of Birmingham, then London, then wherever I want to go. I could see for miles, as far as Spaghetti Junction, beyond the motorway.'

'You can't possibly have seen that far,' I say. 'Waterstone's isn't high enough.'

He ignores me. 'It was completely different from any other view because I'd got there on my own. Nobody had made me, nobody had persuaded me, and nobody had even suggested it. It was me, and me alone. Jess, it was the best feeling I've had all my life.'

His face is solemn and still, his eyes alight with his achievement, and I can't organise my thoughts. I just know that this is not good news.

CHAPTER TEN

We were going to have to wait until the end of my second year at university before getting married. There was a problem with money—we didn't have any. Andrew's parents offered to pay for the wedding, but Andrew refused. My father was prepared to let us have the reception at Audlands as long as it didn't involve too much expense. 'Profits are low at the moment,' he said.

'Nonsense,' said my mother. 'The macaroons and iced fancies have been doing really well.'

'Your mother imagines she knows everything about the business world, Jessica,' he said. 'She's wrong, but I'll do my best. Just don't expect unalloyed extravangance. Unless Andrew wants to contribute, of course.'

'I don't think he'll be able to,' I said.

'No,' he said. 'I didn't think he would.'

Andrew wasn't interested in details. 'We could get married tomorrow, Jess, if we wanted to. Or in fifteen days' time, anyway, if we go down to the register office tomorrow.'

I didn't want to sneak off as if we had something to hide. I wanted to show everyone that it was a sensible decision to get married while I was still a student, that it was a proper event, worthy of serious attention. 'If we wait till next summer and let my mother save a bit, we could have the reception at Audlands.'

'Brilliant.' I knew he would agree. He loved Audlands. But then he had another thought. 'Ask your mum and dad if we could have a few spare rooms for a flat. It would save us a fortune.'

We didn't have a fortune to save. 'I don't think it would be very practical,' I said. 'There'd be too much work.'

'Your mum knows how to restore everything.'

'She's spent a lot of money on it.' Besides, not many of her renovations would stand up to a detailed inspection.

I couldn't think of anything more alarming than living at Audlands. I didn't want to look out of my bedroom window every morning and see my mother on an early morning jog in scarlet shorts and headband, hair tied up into a pony tail, sweat pouring down her face and dampening her vest. Or hear hysterical laughter from Harriet and her friends as they messed around in boats on the lake, played croquet, thumped tennis balls at each other in the distance. Or come out of my door and collide with my father as he shuffled off to the library with a tray of breakfast and *The Times* tucked under his elbow.

'We need to find somewhere else,' I said. 'Mary says we could get a rent rebate.'

129

Andrew refused to abandon the idea. I found him one evening, crouched over the kitchen table with my mother, examining a diagram of the first floor.

'You could have this room as a living room,' she was saying. 'And you could use a back staircase up to the next floor for your bedroom. Use the maids' rooms. Nobody ever goes up there.'

'What about a kitchen?' I asked.

My mother ignored me. I didn't feature in this little conversation they were having together about their plans for my future. 'Of course, you'd need to do a lot of work.' I could see her eyes running up and down his body, assessing his strength, measuring his muscles. I guessed what she was thinking. It would be useful to have a young man on the premises. She could send him up on the roof, into the attic, get him to move heavy furniture around, paint ceilings. He would be an improvement on my father, who never did anything. But I knew that my mother had the wrong man. Andrew was no good at fixing things. She would only be disappointed in the end.

'No problem,' said Andrew. 'I can do anything.'

Except finish his degree, or do something he could do, like play the violin.

'What about heating?' I said. 'It's freezing up there.'

'Why don't we go upstairs and have a look?' suggested my mother.

'Great,' said Andrew, springing lightly to his feet. In my mother's presence he acquired energy and agility, became physical in a way that was not normal for him.

I sat down at the kitchen table and let them go

off without me. There was a heaviness inside my head, an ache behind my eyes, and every action seemed to require enormous effort. Recently I had been waking too early in the morning. I'd be fresh and clear for a few seconds, then a desolate, sinking sensation would creep into my mind, spreading like melting ice, steadily numbing all the earlier optimism. I would lie there for some time, struggling to give the feeling a shape, or at least bring back the dream that must have set it off, but I was never able to reach the centre of the problem.

I could see the lake through the window. An autumn gale was sweeping rain through the willows on the central island, whipping them backwards and forwards with a malicious glee. Sometimes the branches were bent double, then they were released and sprang back up, ready for the next gust to blow them over again.

I wasn't sure how I felt about growing up or getting married and leaving. I had always seemed to be wandering without a map through a confusing and unexplained world. How did I know if I was doing the right thing?

It'll be fine, I kept saying to myself. We'll grow up together, mould each other. You can manufacture your own future.

Harriet came into the kitchen. 'Hi. What are you doing here on your own?'

'Andrew's gone with Mum to look round upstairs. He wants to live here when we're married.'

Harriet stopped in front of me, her face serious. 'That's a really bad idea, Jess.'

'I know.'

She went over to the Aga and opened one of the lower ovens that was used for slow cooking. 'I've got such cold feet.' Sitting down on the small rocking chair next to the cooker, she put her feet inside and sighed. 'That's better.'

'Don't let Mum catch you doing that,' I said. 'You'll get chilblains.'

'She does it herself all the time.'

'Only when there's no one around.'

She grinned. 'Mum's very immature sometimes, isn't she?'

Harriet was two years younger than me, and in the Lower Sixth, but she was frighteningly like a middle-aged woman. Where did she get all that common sense, her ability to judge situations and assess people so accurately?

'You don't have to marry him, you know,' she said.

I sprang into an instant position of defence, mentally crouched down and wary, resentful of the implied criticism. 'I want to,' I said.

Harriet got up to lift the hood on the cooker and place the kettle on the hot plate. She had her back to me. 'Do you?' she said. 'He's not very— considerate.'

What did Harriet know? Seventeen years old, the world's greatest oracle, in training for the post of guru to anyone who would listen.

'He's fine,' I said. 'You don't always see the best side of him.'

'But has he got a best side?'

I got up from the table. 'I'll go and see how they're getting on,' I said, and left the room.

I could hear my mother and Andrew laughing as I climbed the stairs. My mother was the real teenager at Audlands, giggling too much at things that weren't funny, full of an unnatural excess of energy. She was always ready to leap up and race around, as if she had a desperate need to wear herself out. Like a gas fire that has to burn on full for a while until it stabilises and you can turn it down. She was in her forties. She should have been calm and motherly, but her growing-up mechanism had somehow failed.

'The view,' she was saying as I came through the doorway. 'Have you admired the view yet?'

I tested each floorboard before putting my full weight on to it. They all creaked alarmingly. There was a large hole in the ceiling where plaster was hanging down, held together by a mass of cobwebs.

'I love the view,' said Andrew. Laughing didn't suit him. Lines appeared in all the wrong places, and his skin seemed to stretch unnaturally, stiff from years of neglect.

The window where they stood together was letting in the rain, its swollen, rotten wood jamming it perpetually open. I decided to go and look for a flat on my own.

*   *   *

I stood in the centre of the bedsit and tried to work out how big the space was.

'You'll have to share the bathroom, of course,' said Miss Stacey. She was very wide—I'd already wasted precious time trying to calculate her hip measurement, but given up as the numbers became too unrealistic to contemplate—and tightly contained in a tweed suit. Her face was smooth with foundation, a large, empty expanse with a

133

careful blush where the cheekbones should be. 'But there's an extra loo just along the corridor.'

There was a brown velour sofa and a low sideboard in light oak. The bed fitted into an alcove on one side of the fireplace, up against a wall, with a small bedside table next to it. The other alcove was filled by a built-in wardrobe. A tiny kitchenette was separated from the rest of the room by a beaded curtain. It contained a wall cupboard, a cabinet, a cooker and a sink. A square table just fitted into the corner, with two stools tucked underneath. I imagined sitting there with Andrew, eating toast and marmalade.

Despite its lack of space, I was pleased by the bare, unlived-in emptiness of the room. Audlands had begun to feel crowded recently, with too many people around, talking, planning. I wanted to be alone with Andrew, not share him with my mother.

'How many other flats are there in the building?' I asked Miss Stacey.

She was surprised by the question. 'Oh—let me think—at least four, I should think—no, five. There's one in the attic.' She seemed to be proud of this. The more the merrier. 'Of course they're all out during the day. Medical students, most of them.'

I saw myself lying in the bed under the window, hearing the future doctors moving in their flats, their footsteps squeezing through the walls, their low voices echoing under the ceilings, breathing into every available space, exhausting the oxygen—

It wouldn't be like that. They would be separate from us.

'Can I check with my—boyfriend?' I couldn't quite bring myself to say fiancé. It sounded so pretentious.

'Of course,' said Miss Stacey. 'But you'll need to let me know quickly. There's a very high demand for flats near the university.'

*   *   *

'It's great,' said Andrew. 'Just what we need.' He seemed to have abandoned his plans for Audlands—maybe he appreciated the built-in kitchen, knowing he wouldn't be required to do anything practical.

'You don't think it's a bit small?'

He put his hands round my waist and whizzed us both round, just missing the coffee table, forcing Miss Stacey to step back into the kitchen area with a cry of alarm. 'See,' he said as we came to a halt. 'There's even room to swing a cat. This is it. Our first home.'

He was impressed by how low the rent was, although he didn't give Miss Stacey any indication of that. 'We'll take it,' he said.

It was an ideal first home. We couldn't expect much more. If the other tenants were students, there would be long holiday periods when they weren't there. There was a good view across the city. The space was in the sky, around us. I could lean out of the window to breathe.

'Can we afford the deposit?' I asked.

'No problem,' he said.

'No unmarried couples,' said Miss Stacey.

'We're going to be married,' I told her. 'Soon.'

'Good,' she said. 'Meanwhile, you can't share the flat.'

'Wow,' said Andrew. 'You really stick to your

principles.'

'She still gets the rent,' I said. 'She doesn't lose out.'

So Andrew moved in, and I stayed at Audlands until the wedding.

*   *   *

Andrew's mother arranged to meet me outside the Barber Institute one lunchtime a few weeks before the wedding and offered to buy me lunch. I hadn't been able to find a way to avoid it, so I took her to the Students' Union. We carried our trays of steak and kidney pudding, peas and mashed potatoes to a table near a window. We were surrounded by groups of smoking students devouring platefuls of egg and chips and arguing about effective protests against the Falklands War.

'They all look like Andrew,' said Miranda, leaning towards me and attempting to smile.

'That's because he was born to be a student,' I said.

'Except that he isn't one any more.'

'No.' Every time we met, Miranda told me how much she wanted him to go back to university and finish his degree. She seemed to imply it was my fault. 'He didn't really like doing the work,' I said.

Miranda tackled the steak and kidney pudding with unexpected enthusiasm. 'Well,' she said after a few mouthfuls, 'this is fun.'

Did she mean the atmosphere and the intense debates going on round us, or was she enjoying the meal, appreciating its nostalgic school-dinner flavour? I didn't believe her. She would be much more at home with waiters, a respectful hush and a

136

huge bill.

'And what job is Andrew doing now?'

He wasn't communicating with his parents. I was the one who told them about the engagement, rang them occasionally to let them know what was happening, turned down their offer to pay for the wedding. I did this because Mary told me to. 'You shouldn't disown parents,' she said. 'It can lead to terrible unhappiness. I know families who haven't talked to each other for ten years, and nobody can remember what it was all about in the first place. It's not worth it.'

How did Mary know people like that? She was a peacemaker, someone who saw the good in everyone. How did she cope with a situation that involved taking sides?

But I took her advice and maintained the contact. 'You know that his idea of becoming an electrician didn't work out? He couldn't get on with the man who was training him.'

'Of course not,' she said.

'It wasn't his fault. The man hit him, you know.'

'Why ever did he do that? Andrew must have antagonised him.'

'Well—it was something to do with Andrew refusing to climb on to the roof when he was asked to, because it was too dangerous, and being told that he was the apprentice, and that's what apprentices did. Then Andrew told them that things had moved on since "The Little Chimney Sweep" and that Dickensian Britain had passed away with the nineteenth century.'

'That sounds like my son.'

Her voice was hard and cynical, so unlike her manner a year ago on the day of the concert, when she had sat in the front row of the audience radiating pride and belief, anxious to be identified as his mother. I took a sip of water and felt it wash through me, tainted by a guilty wave of sadness. Maybe she was a bit arrogant, but it wasn't pleasant to see her lose her dreams for her son in such a brutal way. I felt as if I had contributed to the end of her hopes. 'He'll be all right,' I said. 'He was thinking of trying bank work.'

'Could you really see him in a bank?'

I couldn't see him anywhere except with a violin under his chin, and Miranda was obviously thinking the same thing.

'I expect he's told you all sorts of terrible stories about how I pushed him, forced him to practise against his will?'

I hesitated, then nodded. I had been given a very clear picture of a monster mother. Miranda went to every violin lesson until Andrew left home. She took notes and even taped the lessons so that they could go through the whole thing again, daily.

'He was a gifted child. He could sing in tune at the age of two, pick out melodies on the piano, even before he talked. He was always meant to be a musician.'

Andrew's perspective didn't allow for talent. How easy it was to take a set of facts, rotate them slightly and find that there were two opposing versions of the same story, equally convincing. How did you know which to believe? Each side was true.

'But children need to be happy,' I said.

Miranda smiled, the skin drawing so far back from her mouth that she revealed the gums over her upper teeth. 'He was happy. He's just forgotten.'

How could she be so certain? 'He says he never enjoyed it,' I said.

'Then he's not telling you the truth. It gave him pleasure and a sense of pride that he doesn't have any more. You've heard him. Nobody could play like that without wanting to. Don't you think he enjoyed it?'

'Maybe he didn't have the chance to try anything else. He thinks he was deprived of a normal childhood.' This was a bit bold, but it seemed better to talk about it openly rather than whisper in secret with Andrew.

Miranda's eyes stared out from beneath her drooping eyelids, and I could feel my cheeks start to burn. 'He didn't miss out on anything,' she said, 'until he was a teenager, when he couldn't be bothered to move a muscle more than necessary.'

'He's older now,' I said. 'Let's wait and see. Once we settle down, he'll sort something out.'

'Of course.' It was clear from her tone that Miranda didn't believe this. 'I'm sorry I had to take the violin away,' she said. 'But I couldn't risk him selling it.'

'Andrew wouldn't do that.'

She laughed. 'Oh, dear. You don't know him very well, do you?'

I know him better than you do, I thought.

'We made huge sacrifices for that violin. We're still paying for it.'

I was shocked. I'd assumed it had been easy for them to afford. 'So you'll sell it, then?'

'Oh, no, we'll hang on to it for the time being.' Just in case, she meant, although she didn't say so.

'There's no point,' I said. 'If he ever decides to

139

play again, we could buy something cheaper, one that doesn't matter so much.'

'But it would matter, wouldn't it? He'd know the difference.'

She was right, of course. Once you'd played on an instrument of such quality, nothing else would do. I had fallen in love with Andrew through the sound of that violin. What was he without it? 'How will you know if he wants to play it again?' I asked.

'He'll tell me,' said Miranda with complete conviction.

I was ninety-nine per cent certain that she was wrong, and it made me feel better.

When we got up to leave, Miranda grasped my arm briefly. 'You will let me know what's going on, won't you? I want to help you both.'

'Of course.' I was surprised by the small intimacy of her touch. She was trying to express affection in a way that was unfamiliar to both of us, and I felt the need to reciprocate, but didn't know how.

'Have you found somewhere to live?'

'Andrew wanted to use some rooms in Audlands, but even he had to agree it wasn't practical. Plastering ceilings and putting down floorboards isn't quite his scene. So we've found a flat—well, a bedsit really. It's not brilliant, but it's cheap, and we've put our names down for a council house.'

Miranda's smile was bright but unconvincing. A council house would not be what she'd had in mind for her son. 'Jessica . . .'

'Yes?'

She hesitated, her manner less confident. 'You know, you don't have to—'

I was confused by her uncertainty. 'What?'

'You don't have to go through with it—the wedding—if you don't want to. Nobody would think any less of you for changing your mind.'

I couldn't acknowledge my doubts. They did exist, but they were deep inside, in a safe with a timed lock, reinforced in concrete. Because Miranda and Harriet had both challenged me, the steel bars descended even more rapidly, alarm bells rang and security forces came charging in.

'I don't want to change my mind,' I said. 'I want to marry Andrew.'

We said goodbye outside the Barber Institute, and I watched her walk away. Had Andrew painted a fair portrait of her? Who wielded the more honest brush, him or her? I longed to see clearly through the accumulation of paint, the technique, the brushstrokes, to the canvas beneath. Why wasn't it easier to go straight to the truth without having to scrape through layers and layers of camouflage?

*   *   *

My dress was borrowed from Mary's cousin. It was made of white polyester satin, tailored above the waist with yards of material sweeping out generously below. I put it on every night in my bedroom, wondering at its ability to transform me from my familiar clumsy self into someone elegant and unrecognisable.

My mother had been racing round Audlands for weeks in preparation for the reception, applying fresh coats of emulsion, supervising a group of cleaning ladies from the village as they scrubbed and polished and hid clutter behind cupboard

141

doors. The marble busts in the Long Gallery shone as white as they could, mirrors gleamed, the wooden floorboards basked with pleasure after their first contact with polish in years. Nobody dusted the chandeliers—they were too high to matter—but the cobwebs were swept away. And somebody removed the advertisements for Fontaine's Crunchy Chocolate Brownies in the entrance hall.

Harriet had made buttonholes for everyone from the roses that were still flourishing in the neglected rose garden. They were held together by silver foil and a safety pin, but they didn't stay in place very well. The flowers kept bending round in the wrong direction, so you could only see the stems. I had a bouquet of white carnations and violet asters, round and pretty with a lace doily behind them, keeping them in shape.

'You must wear make-up,' said Harriet. 'Even if you never wear it again in your entire life, you should put some on for your own wedding.'

Nail varnish, lipstick, mascara. I sat motionless while she applied them, prepared for once to accept her advice. I was no longer myself. I was capable of doing anything.

Then she pinned a veil on my head with a headdress of daisy chains. We'd sat in the middle of the croquet lawn the night before, weaving the daisies together. We tried floating them in water overnight to keep them fresh, but they shrivelled and lost their dewy whiteness. So we started all over again early in the morning, cutting slits in the plump stalks with our varnished fingernails, trying not to damage them in our haste.

When I was ready, I stood in front of my

142

bedroom mirror and stared with astonishment. Was it really me?

'Yes,' said Harriet, pleased with herself. 'You'll do.'

Mary had given me the gold necklace that I'd worn on the day of the concert. 'I can't take that,' I said. 'It was your grandmother's.'

'I want to give you something special, something that requires a sacrifice from me,' she said, 'and this is ideal.'

I couldn't think of a single occasion when I'd sacrificed something of real value for anyone else. 'I don't deserve you, Mary.'

'It's not a question of deserving. If we're friends, we're friends.'

Harriet left me alone for the last half-hour before we were due to leave. I sat quietly on the side of my bed, trying to make sense of it all, wanting to appreciate the enormity of the step I was taking but not able to think clearly enough. The whole thing had become an unstoppable machine, lumbering heavily forward, crushing everything in its path. There was no brake, no one with the expertise to disconnect the right wires and bring it to a halt. It was better to let it go rolling on until it ran out of petrol and regulated itself naturally.

Andrew came in through the door. He was wearing a pale blue suit with a waistcoat and a white tie. He hadn't managed to harness his hair, which looked as abandoned as always, but otherwise everything was perfect. It was the first time I'd seen him in a suit for a year, and I was instantly captivated, thrilled that he'd made an effort, despite his performance of casual

143

nonchalance.

But I couldn't believe he had come. 'What are you doing here? Shouldn't you be at the register office?'

'Not likely. My parents are there. I don't want to talk to them.' He shut the door behind him. 'You look very nice, Jess.'

'Is that all? Nice?'

'What do you want from me? Amazing, beautiful, astonishing, chic, elegant, gorgeous—'

'Any of those would do.'

He nodded. 'OK. Take your pick.'

A sense of disappointment was creeping through me. The same indefinable heaviness that appeared every morning when I woke up.

'I just wanted to let you know we're leaving straight after the wedding,' he said.

'I thought we were going back to the flat after the reception.'

'Everything's changed. My ex-housemates have paid for a honeymoon as their wedding present. A last-minute offer. I booked it yesterday.'

This was unexpected—Andrew's dealings with his housemates had not been harmonious. Maybe they were worried he would change his mind, abandon the wedding and return to live with them. They must have felt that a generous gift would help him on his way.

'Where to?'

'Let's just say we're flying there.'

'But what about passports?'

'You've got one and I've got one. Where's the problem?' He tapped his pocket. 'I've got the tickets. It's a surprise. We have to leave immediately.'

144

'After the reception?'

'No, straight after the wedding.'

I stared at him. 'We can't do that. Everything's arranged. Audlands is all ready for the reception.'

'That's the surprise. We'll be gone.'

'But we have to have photographs.'

'Oh, there'll be time for a few and we'll need to come back here anyway, to change. Then we go.'

'What about cutting the cake?'

'Absurd ritual. I don't want to stand there, one arm round your waist, the other brandishing a knife, poised over a nonsensical edifice of white icing, pretending to smile.' He demonstrated, one arm bent round a space beside him, the other holding an invisible knife like a dagger, bringing it down dramatically to carve up the air.

But I wanted to do all the traditional stuff. 'Our families, our friends, they'll all be expecting—'

'They can enjoy themselves without us. There's plenty of food, they can dance. Whether we're there or not is irrelevant.'

There was some logic to his argument, but it upset me to think of them doing all this without us. 'It's our wedding,' I said. 'We should be there.'

'Rubbish. They won't care. Why should we?'

'They will care. Your parents—'

His lip curled and I regretted mentioning them. 'We don't need to worry about them.'

'What about my family then, and Mary?'

He smiled, and the two creases appeared in his cheeks, familiar and intimate, illuminating his face. 'Wait until you find out where we're going, Jess. Then you'll see that none of the rest of it matters.'

'It matters to me.' I tried to hang on to the argument, desperate to assert myself. I could imagine everyone's surprise and disbelief when we disappeared. I didn't know how to explain it without embarrassment. Tears were forming in my eyes, and I blinked rapidly. I was wearing mascara for the first time in my life and didn't want it to run.

He was watching me, so I tilted my head back slightly to hide the tears. 'I hope you're not going to be difficult,' he said with a hard edge to his voice.

'No, of course not, only couldn't we delay it all by an hour or two?'

'Oh come on, Jess. What do you expect me to do? Phone the airport? Frightfully sorry, could you just delay the flight for two hours? It'll affect your other flight patterns? Surely you could be more flexible. It is our honeymoon, you know. Everyone else can wait.'

'Since when have you cared about other people?' I shouldn't have said it. I knew I was being unreasonable. If the tickets were for a certain flight, there was no choice.

He stared at me, his smile fading. 'Oh, I see. I never think of you, of course. I wouldn't dress up in a ridiculous outfit for the wedding or book tickets for a honeymoon to please you. I do all that for myself, I suppose, because I like making a fool of myself.'

'I'm sorry,' I said, and the tears were spilling out now. I tried not to think about the mascara.

'I didn't realise it was so important to you, being in the limelight, dressing up, prancing around for the sake of ancient rituals.'

What could I say? To defend it all seemed petty and hypocritical. But I loved the new person I had

146

become in my wedding dress. I'd thought that I would be able to forget myself for a while and act out a new role, transform myself into a traditional bride for a day. I would slip back into my normal self tomorrow, but it seemed that tomorrow was going to come sooner than I expected. 'I thought it would be fun for a while,' I said eventually.

'Fun? Fun?' He placed his face directly in front of mine. 'Who are you, Jess? I was under the impression we saw things the same way.'

I wanted to look away, but he was too close. 'We do,' I whispered. He was unravelling before me, redesigning himself into my cousin Philip, tall and blond, a hard cruel mask instead of a face. Why had I never seen the resemblance before?

All I could see was his eyes, right in front of mine, still and expressionless. Green, surrounded by a clear, innocent white, his eyelids pale pink and edged with long pale eyelashes. How did people read expression in eyes? They were just physical objects. There was nothing there that could speak. They were not even attractive.

I tried to move, but he put his hand behind my head to hold it there. 'Let's start as we mean to go on,' he said in a tight, clipped voice which I hardly recognised. I started to shake, my legs juddering uncontrollably.

'Jess!' It was Harriet calling from downstairs.

I made myself stare back at him. I didn't want him to know that I was afraid.

'Jess!'

He released the pressure suddenly, so that I nearly fell over, and smiled, charming again. 'It's all right,' he said gently. 'Don't cry.'

He held his arms out and I stepped into them,

147

my cheeks hot against the rough fabric of his jacket. 'We need each other, Jess. We're not like other people. No one else would have us.'

'I'm sorry,' I whispered.

'I know,' he said. 'It's just nerves.' He reached over, took a paper tissue from the box on the dressing table and wiped my cheeks.

He examined my face. 'Perfect,' he said. 'Beautiful, angelic, divine. See you at the register office.'

And he was gone.

'Jess, it's time to go!'

'Coming!' I called, testing my voice to make it sound normal. 'Won't be a second.' I glanced quickly into the mirror and discovered that waterproof mascara really worked.

*   *   *

My father had asked his accountant to drive us to the registry office in his Rover 2000. He had tied white ribbon on the front of the car and scattered orange blossom along the shelf in the back window, although it was already starting to wilt in the heat.

I sat in the back with my father, the spare seat between us, and we looked out of opposite windows. I was trying not to think of what had happened in the bedroom with Andrew, worrying about how to explain that we wouldn't be at the reception. I could say it was very last-minute, that all the later times were booked. Andrew's friends had bought the tickets, and we could hardly refuse them. It was sounding reasonable. I began to feel better.

148

My father cleared his throat. 'Jessica . . .'

'Yes?'

'You know, you don't have to do this if you don't want to. We can cancel it, even now.'

Had he been talking to Harriet? Had he heard my conversation with Andrew?

'Don't worry about all the arrangements. It's better to be happy than to do things because you feel you have to.'

What could I say? All those people. All those presents. All the food waiting at Audlands.

I thought of Andrew playing the violin. The way he had reached inside me and touched a part previously unknown to me. I remembered how his tears outside the station had moved me, and the thundering sense of pride as I realised that he needed me.

I could handle him, help him to mature and mellow.

'It's all right,' I said. 'I want to do it.'

We arrived at the register office and my father climbed out first, then put out his hand to help me. Nobody had ever helped me out of a car before. I stepped on my train, caught a sleeve on the door handle, nearly lost my balance and grabbed my father for support. He remained solid and still.

There were people with cameras waiting for us, and I stood bewildered for a few seconds, trying to work out who they were. Eventually I recognised Harriet, Mary and other friends. My father stood by my side for a while as we beamed into the cameras. Then he put his arm out, horizontal to the ground, elbow bent. It looked odd and unnatural.

'Put your hand on my arm,' he whispered.

149

I met his eyes. We smiled at each other and walked towards the entrance.

I like my father, I thought. He's a kind, supportive man. Why had I never noticed this before?

CHAPTER ELEVEN

I sat on the plane next to Andrew, my stomach churning as we started to taxi. I had never flown before. I had been to France every summer with my family, but only on the ferry. My father had never been persuaded that air travel was worth it, despite my mother's desire to be more adventurous.

'Far too expensive,' he always said. 'And you can't take the car.'

'Relax,' said Andrew, taking my hand in his. I could feel the warmth of his skin, but it wouldn't penetrate. There was a wafer-thin barrier between us, like a film of hand cream, that meant our contact was only superficial. My mind was still on the wedding.

'What do you mean you're not staying?' said Harriet, a plastic cup of champagne hovering just below her mouth. Her bridesmaid's dress, a pale, watery pink, draped elegantly. She'd chosen the pattern and made it herself.

'The flight is earlier than we expected . . .' My voice wasn't secure enough to be convincing.

Harriet turned to Andrew. 'You're not serious?'

'Can't be helped,' he said. 'It was a cancellation—the only one we could afford.'

'So what about all this?' She waved her hand in a grand gesture, indicating the people, the food, the freshly cleaned drawing room, the French windows opening out into the garden to let in the warm summer air.

'What about it?'

'What's it all for?'

He leaned towards her and spoke softly into her ear. 'It's for our wedding. It's called a reception.'

She flushed with irritation. 'What's the point in having a reception when the bride and groom aren't present?'

'We are present,' he said, his face slipping into the boyish, amiable look that I couldn't resist and Harriet could.

'But you're going in a minute,' she said.

'Yes,' he said.

The photographer came over, a well-built, well-padded man. 'We need to cut the cake,' he said. He worked for my father as a quality controller. I imagined him spending every day eating cakes and biscuits, rolling them round in his mouth while his eyes drifted up to the ceiling in appreciation. 'Yes,' he would say. 'A delicate marzipan with a subtle aroma of Mediterranean breeze.' Or, 'No. A touch more sugar would do it, I think, to chase away that aftertaste of swamp gas. Mustn't let our customers believe we're skimping on quality.' Did he spit the samples out again, like a wine-taster?

'I don't think we're doing the cake,' I said.

The photographer raised his eyebrows. 'Everybody cuts the cake. It's part of the tradition.'

Andrew took my hand. 'Come on, Jess. There's no need to be melodramatic. We can do it quickly and still be in time for the flight.'

151

He put his arm round me, exactly as he had demonstrated earlier. We held the knife together and thrust it into the cake with an exaggerated, artificial movement. He's enjoying this, I thought. Who does he imagine is on the receiving end of the knife? His mother?

'You'll be so pleased you have that photograph,' said the photographer to me. 'Now, we just need a few more portraits. On the steps by the entrance, perhaps.'

'No,' said Andrew. 'There won't be time for that. We have to get away.'

'Jessica,' said my mother, coming up behind us. 'What's Harriet talking about? You're not leaving already?'

'We have to,' I said. 'It was the only flight available.'

She stared at me. 'But this is your wedding. We've done all this for you.'

Andrew beamed at her. I couldn't get used to this smile, which had been hovering all day, brought out with a flourish, fully polished, whenever anyone expected it. It didn't suit him. 'We really appreciate it. You've done a wonderful job.'

'But what about the dancing?'

Even I could see that this was a thin argument. We all knew the dancing was for my mother, not for me or Andrew. 'You're the world expert, Connie,' said Andrew. 'You don't need us.'

'Yes, well . . .' she said. 'I'd expected you to join in.'

He put an arm round her waist and grabbed her other hand, swinging her towards him dramatically. They danced away, through the hall and towards the drawing room, where the heady scent of freshly picked roses wafted through the crowd of guests. Andrew was talking as they bounced inexpertly together and I could hear my mother's rich, open laughter echoing in their wake.

I turned to the photographer and shrugged an apology. He moved away, pointing his camera at groups of guests, calling them to look up just before he snapped.

Harriet came up again and I tried to smile. 'You shouldn't have let him talk you into it,' she said. 'It's not right.'

'It wasn't a matter of letting him,' I said. 'We had no choice.'

She studied me for a while, and I started to feel threatened by her intensity. She opened her mouth to speak.

'Yes?' I asked, knowing that I didn't want to hear what she was about to say.

'Nothing,' she replied.

Andrew came back without my mother. 'Time to get changed,' he said. 'Tim's coming for us in fifteen minutes.'

I went upstairs to my bedroom. This won't be my room any more, I thought. I gazed round, gripped by a sudden sense of loss that bordered on panic. Would I ever be able to sit on my own and study the fir tree outside my window again? I caught sight of myself in the mirror, and examined the unfamiliar image. Not bad, I thought. Quite nice, even. I would probably never look this good again.

I became aware of the time and unzipped the dress. It fell rustling to the floor, too eager to leave me. As I stepped out, it settled into a round,

153

puffed hollow with a life of its own, barely affected by my absence.

Andrew called through the door. 'Are you ready, Jess?'

'Coming,' I said, throwing on my jeans and T-shirt.

As we came downstairs, we could hear Andrew's housemate Tim hooting outside. Music had started in the drawing room, and the volume was increasing, becoming more earnest. Everybody was in there—I could hear the DJ talking through a microphone, the pounding beat, the thumps of mass movement. Plates of half-eaten food and discarded plastic cups lay on the sides of the stairs. There was no one in the hall.

'Come on,' whispered Andrew. 'Let's go before they see us.'

I hesitated. It seemed so ungrateful. 'Surely we should say goodbye.'

'No,' he said. 'They'll know we've gone. It's traditional to creep off unnoticed.'

I didn't know that.

He held out his hand. 'Are you coming with me, Mrs Courtenay?'

I smiled and stepped towards him.

*   *   *

The aeroplane gathered speed. I was overwhelmed by the scream of the engines, the power beneath my feet, the thrust as we surged forward. I gripped my armrests and looked out of the window. We had already left the ground. The airport buildings were below us, getting smaller, dwindling in the distance as we tilted upwards and climbed into the sky.

It's all right, I thought. I can do this.

*   *   *

Our hotel was on the east side of Majorca, away from the popular beaches near Palma. It had character, but not much luxury. Not as good a bargain as Andrew had thought. In our bedroom the light bulb was so dingy you couldn't read by it. When I switched on the bedside lamp in the morning, sparks flew out from a kink in the wire. I turned it off immediately and opened the curtains instead.

'We'll complain,' said Andrew, stretched out in bed, watching me.

'No, it's all right. I don't mind. We won't use it.' I didn't want any rows or unpleasantness. This was our honeymoon.

'No point in paying good money for rubbish.'

'You didn't pay. Your housemates did.'

'Hmm.'

'Shall we go for breakfast?'

'Come back to bed. We've only had five hours' sleep.'

'I'm hungry.' We'd not had time for food at the reception, and there hadn't been much opportunity to eat on the journey.

He turned his back on me. 'Please yourself. I need at least two more hours.'

I went down by the stairs. We'd come up in the lift the night before and I wasn't willing to repeat the experience. Two of us and our luggage seemed to have placed a great strain on its ability to function and we'd juddered upwards for several nerve-racking minutes, not at all certain that we'd make it. The stairs creaked with every step, but at least I felt in control.

In the dining room I sat at a table on my own, eating with my eyes down, in case anyone tried to talk to me.

When I went back up Andrew was asleep, stretched out diagonally across the bed. I didn't know what to do. A thin shaft of sun was creeping past the buildings on the other side of the road and into our room, a dazzling slice of light piercing the dust and gloom. I wanted to go outside and explore but I didn't like to wake him. I went to the window and looked out. Most of the windows opposite were hidden behind shutters, as if everyone's purpose in life was to avoid the sun. There weren't many people in the street below, mainly women and old men with bags of shopping. I imagined them all hurrying home before the town was flooded by midday sun.

I didn't feel normal, standing here alone in a foreign country. I'd never before spent a whole night in the same room as someone else, let alone in the same bed. I had the sense that I'd given up something precious. I was now Jessica Courtenay, wife of Andrew, grown-up, a married woman for the rest of my life. But I felt like a small child, sent off to boarding school and forced to sleep in a dormitory. The space around me had shrivelled and compressed, as if I was breathing with a plastic bag over my face.

'Andrew,' I whispered.

He didn't respond.

'Andrew,' I said a little louder. 'I'm going out. I'll be back in an hour.'

He was burrowed into the pillow, his skin slightly damp from the heat of sleep, the side of his face squashed and creased. He didn't look like the Andrew I knew, but a stranger, someone who had no connection with me.

I wrote a note on a piece of paper and put it on his bedside table—'Gone for a walk'—then left the room quietly.

The light outside had a brightness and intensity that took me by surprise, and I had to shade my eyes with my hand until I grew accustomed to it. I climbed the steps down to the beach and slipped my sandals off.

I'm abroad, I thought. I'm doing what everyone else does. My family had never reached the Mediterranean on our French holidays, preferring Brittany and the Dordogne. Small waves lapped at the edge of the beach and I walked towards them, expecting warm water.

'I only swim in the Mediterranean,' a girl had once told me at school. 'The water's far too cold anywhere else.'

'No it isn't,' I'd said. 'It's fine.' But I knew she was right. She was rich and experienced and I was just an ignorant peasant who only knew about shivering in the Atlantic when we went on holiday, swimming as fast as possible so that we wouldn't freeze.

I stepped into the water and back out again with shock. The water wasn't warm at all. It must be too early in the morning. Two girls ran past me in skimpy polka-dot bikinis, their pony tails wet and stringy, their teeth chattering. I recognised them from the plane the night before and looked over to where their mothers sat on a blanket farther back.

They were wearing shorts and strappy tops, which revealed vast expanses of white, unprotected skin.

I sat down in the soft sand and examined my surroundings. The bay had rocky cliffs on either side. Our hotel was behind me, small and picturesque. White plastic tables and chairs were scattered around on the veranda, facing the sea. It was too far away to see the peeling green paint and the cracks in the tiled floor. A new hotel was being built on the edge of the bay, about twenty-five storeys high, already superior in design and ambition. I could see men in hard hats, busy behind glassless windows while the sound of their labour echoed out into the morning air.

There weren't many people on the beach yet. A boat drifted lazily across the sea, its little motor chugging, missing a beat every now and again, gasping for a last breath but then recovering just as you thought it had died. It parted the still, glassy water, leaving an ever-expanding arrow behind it.

I sifted the sand with my fingers and examined the tiny, multi-coloured grains. It was warm on the surface, but cold lower down. I dug into it with a piece of driftwood, expecting to find a damp layer, but it remained dry and loose. I could feel the sun on my back, warm and friendly, soaking into my bones.

I knew I should return to Andrew, but I didn't want to move. It was pleasant sitting here alone, no one to speak to, no one to know me. A curious lethargy crept through me, an inability to move. I wanted to stay here for ever. Would anyone ever notice? They would in the evening when the beach cleared. They probably had lifeguards who would ask me what I was doing there.

Waiting, I would say.

Who for?

Nobody.

You can't stay here.

Maybe I'm not waiting. Maybe I'm escaping.

A family walked across the almost empty beach and put their things down about five yards from where I was sitting.

'Can we swim?' asked the little boy. He was pulling his T-shirt over his head.

'No,' said his mother. 'You've got to wait an hour after eating.'

'Old wives' tales,' said his father, who was setting out chairs and blankets and bags. It was a military operation. They were camping down for the day. He started to put up a screen, knocking the posts deep into the sand.

It won't stand up, I thought. The sand's too soft.

'It's not an old wives' tale,' said the mother, who was pale-skinned and freckled. She was pouring suntan lotion into her hand and smothering both children while they hopped up and down. 'Stand still, James.'

'I want to go in the water,' he wailed, his voice rising on a wave of resentment.

'No. When you eat, the blood collects in your stomach and you can get cramp.'

'I really wanted to know that,' said her husband. 'About the blood.' He went back to the first post he'd knocked in, which was already tilting at a dangerous angle.

Actually, she was wrong. It's a myth. Our biology teacher explained it to us in the upper fifth.

I got up. I didn't want to, but I couldn't stay and listen to this family.

I knew as soon as I opened the door that Andrew was angry. He was standing by the window and the light behind him made him tall and dark, his face unreadable.

'Where have you been?' he said in a low voice.

'I went for a walk. I told you.'

'No,' he said. 'You told me you were going for breakfast.'

'Well, I did. And then I came back up, but you were asleep, so I went for a walk. I left a note.'

'You didn't think I might worry?'

I'd thought he might be annoyed. I hadn't considered worry. 'I just wanted to explore a little.'

'Oh, I see. I was expecting us to explore together, but you thought you'd do it alone.'

'I can go again. I don't mind.'

'It won't be the same, though, will it? Now that you've been first?'

When I was in the sixth form, we'd had a discussion forum once a week and I remembered the time we'd discussed the traditional roles of men and women.

'Some men like to dominate,' said Mrs Taylor. 'They want you to be a victim.'

None of us could understand battered wives. 'Why don't they just leave?' asked Helen.

'It must be partly the women's fault—they must enjoy it.'

'You have to stand up to bullies and then they'll give in.'

I knew it was more complicated than that. Philip was never far from my mind.

160

'I'd kill him,' said Jane. 'When he was asleep.'

'But then you'd go to prison. It's easier to leave.'

That's right, I thought.

'If you want respect,' said Mrs Taylor, 'you have to make it clear that you won't accept the situation.'

'That's silly,' I said to Andrew, turning away with a smile. 'Do you want to go into the bathroom first? You'll miss breakfast if you don't go down soon.'

He grabbed me by my arm and dragged me back.

'What?' I said.

'Did you just call me silly?'

'I didn't mean you personally,' I said. 'Just the idea that we can't explore together.' My voice was light and I could still breathe.

'You know very well what I mean.' The Andrew that I'd encountered just before the wedding had returned, all fired up and ready for action.

'You have to make it clear that you won't accept the situation.'

'Let go,' I said. 'You're hurting.' I tried to pull away, but his hand was clamped round my arm like a steel bracket. My powerlessness against his strength was frightening.

'Let's get one thing straight,' he said. 'You're married now. You can't do whatever you want any more.'

'They want you to be a victim.'

'I'm still a person,' I said, refusing to allow my voice to tremble, refusing to cry. 'I can make my own decisions.' I would not let him take over Philip's role.

'I'm your husband. We made vows. Remember

161

the words yesterday?'

I struggled to remember anything from yesterday. Somewhere in the distant past there was a crowd of people laughing, eating, dancing. Audlands was watching over them all. There was space around them, everywhere, in the rooms, in the garden, down by the lake, high above them, in the arched ceilings and the dome of the hall.

But Andrew and I weren't there. There was a vacuum where we should have been, and nobody seemed to have noticed our absence.

I'd lost my silence, my spaces, without even realising that I'd done it.

Reality was here, in this dingy hotel room where light struggled to penetrate, where the people above us were stamping around as if they were trying to defeat a plague of ants, where there was a choice between rickety stairs and a lethal lift if we wanted to escape. There wouldn't be any fail-safe emergency mechanisms here. It was too old. Reality was the Andrew in front of me.

'You have to stand up to bullies.'

'What about you?' I said. 'You promised to love me too. Does that involve twisting my arm and threatening me?'

He blinked for a few seconds and laughed. 'OK,' he said softly, letting go of my arm.

I thought it would be all right again. A brief slip into irrationality and then out again. An uncomfortable stumble before he recovered his balance. 'Do you want to go into the bathroom first?' I said.

'Why would I want to go into the bathroom?'

'For a wash, a shave?' This was such hard work.

'Why would I want to shave on holiday?'

162

'Please yourself,' I said, opening the bathroom door. 'I thought you might like to keep up some appearances.'

I shouldn't have said it. He grabbed me by the shoulder this time and swung me round. 'What are you playing at?' he said.

'I'm not playing at anything.' I tried to keep my voice innocent, convincing myself that I wasn't criticising him, just making an observation. All the anger that had dissipated a few moments earlier was back, a sheet of flame shooting up from dying embers, aimed directly at me. As if he spent most of his life hiding it, while all the time he was secretly feeding it, offering it little scraps of wood, holding it back until it was ready to flare up and prove its worth.

He pushed me against the wall and held me there with his arm. 'Cut the games, Jess,' he said. 'You are now Mrs Courtenay, and the sooner you recognise it the better.'

'I'm not denying it,' I said, resenting the tremble in my voice. 'But I still don't see that it gives you the right to order me around.'

He raised his hand and I watched him form it into a fist, tensing his muscles, closing the fingers deliberately, summoning the strength.

I put my hands up to pull away his other arm, but it was like trying to shatter concrete or pull iron railings out of the pavement. His eyes were distant, looking inwards, not really seeing me.

I gave in to my fear. 'Go on, then,' I screamed. 'Hit me! That's what you want to do, isn't it?'

He still didn't move.

I can't do this, I thought. I can't stand up to him. I dropped my eyes and let myself go weak.

163

'Andrew,' I said gently. 'Stop it.'

He stood motionless for what felt like hours until the tension slowly seeped out of his fist. Both arms dropped to his side.

'Come on,' I said. 'Let's start again. We don't have to be like this.' I even tried a laugh. 'What a way to start married life!'

His face started to crumple. 'Why do you do this to me?' he whispered. 'You know I love you.'

He hardly ever said that. I let my head flop on to his chest. 'It's all right,' I said.

I could hear his breathing, ragged and distressed, as his body folded in on itself and he put his arms round me, burying his face in my hair. 'I'm sorry,' he said in a muffled voice. 'I don't know what came over me.'

I didn't know what had come over him either, but I knew I couldn't go through that again. My sixth-form discussion group was wrong. Mrs Taylor was wrong. Sometimes you just can't stand up to people. They don't back down. They don't know how to.

I had to learn how to manage him, not let him fall into this state again. I patted his back rhythmically, complicated messages of love making me maternal.

'Let's go and find you some breakfast,' I said.

CHAPTER TWELVE

The dark green front door of Audlands stood half-open, its six Palladian panels glinting in the morning sun. The delicate, Adam-style tracery of

164

the fanlight above the door allowed shards of sunlight to scatter like mosaics on to the hall floor behind Connie, who stood waiting, her hand resting impatiently on the door knob. Just above her head, a life-sized brass lion's head glared down, its teeth bared, with the two sides of a knocker protruding from its nostrils like eighteenth-century nose studs.

Connie was watching a truck amble its way up the drive. Every time it hit a pothole, it lurched to one side as if it would never recover and caught the low-hanging branches of the horse chestnuts. She could hear them scraping over the top of the driver's cab, breaking off and falling into the open back of the truck.

In the distance, twelve-year-old Jessica was playing scales. Up and down, up and down, automatic and energetic, quite inappropriate on this languid summer day. This wasn't what Connie had expected when she'd agreed to piano lessons. Even when Jessica practised real music, with tunes that you could grasp hold of, she approached them obsessively, repeating sections so often that they ceased to have any meaning. The scales dominated, as if they had found a little niche in Jessica's brain that had been waiting for their arrival, a mathematical corner that was thirsty for patterns and shapes.

Connie had tried to discuss the matter with Mrs Gulliver. 'Is it necessary to play scales so much?' she asked.

Mrs Gulliver had reacted with appalled indignation. 'Mrs Fontaine, I spend my entire life arguing with my pupils about the need for scales. Jessica is a gift, a natural. I love her scales.'

She stood and glared at Connie, taller than her by several inches, tilting forward, her eyes steely. She did not look like someone who loved anything.

Connie could now see the driver and his companion inside the cab. Their heads were bouncing up and down with each bump, rolling loosely in rhythm with the truck.

Once they had passed the tenth tree from the house, she decided that she could allow her enthusiasm to show. 'It's here!' she called, in a brief moment between scales, expecting everyone to come running.

Nothing happened.

'Harriet!' she called. 'Jessica! It's arrived.'

The scales started up again. A door banged somewhere in the distance and Harriet came down the stairs, crossing the hall to join her mother in the doorway. 'Where is it?'

'There, in front of you.'

'Not the truck, the statue.' Harriet's voice was calm and matter-of-fact, as if she was explaining something to a younger child.

'The statue is in the truck, Harriet.'

At ten years old, Harriet troubled Connie. She was charming, friendly and helpful, with dozens of friends who regularly turned up at Audlands in groups. They participated in treasure hunts, played hide and seek inside on rainy days, or tumbled around rowdily on the tennis court. There were three-legged races, sack races, dressing-up races— all organised by Connie, who invariably joined in. This was what Connie expected of children; it was the right way to behave. Harriet was pleasant with everyone, about everything. Yet there was something unnerving about her common sense, her

166

ability to look at you as if she knew exactly what you were thinking. Connie sometimes had the feeling that Harriet was the mother and she was the daughter.

The truck drove up in front of the steps, reversed, levelled up and came to a halt. The driver turned off the engine and he and his helper, a young lad, jumped down, hot and sweating in their jeans and T-shirts. They looked up at Connie, who was standing midway between the two central pillars. 'Mrs Fontaine?' called the driver.

She ran down towards them and stopped a few steps from the bottom. 'Hello,' she said. 'You found us all right, then.'

The driver ran his eyes across the façade of the building. 'It's not easy to miss,' he said. He glanced at his delivery sheet. 'We've got a statue for you.'

Connie struggled to contain her excitement. 'Yes, Artemis. But I can't actually see her in the truck.'

'Lying down,' said the driver. 'We can't drive along country lanes with a dirty great female peering over the top of everyone's hedges, now, can we? How's the access?'

'Oh, you can drive round easily.' Connie smiled at him, positioning herself so that the sun was behind her head. She knew that the little wisps of hair which surrounded her face would be lit up like a halo, light and pretty.

She led them round the side of the house where the plinth was waiting for the statue on the edge of the lawn with the fountain, between the crimson rhododendron and the white lilac. If you took the gravel path to the lake, Artemis would gaze down on you, tall and elegant, her Greek robes draping into fluid stone folds.

'We might need to go on the grass,' said the driver.

'Oh, that's fine,' said Connie. 'Absolutely fine.'

As they returned to the front of the house, a white Vauxhall Victor appeared on the drive, negotiating the potholes with an enviable familiarity. It came to a halt beside the truck. Cathy got out, followed by Philip, Colin and Judy.

'Connie!' called Cathy. She was wearing strings of ethnic beads that bounced on her ample bosom, clicking and clattering as she moved. 'What's going on?'

'Cathy, how lovely to see you! And the children. Was I expecting you?'

'You invited us for lunch.'

Connie slapped a hand to her mouth. 'Oh no, did I really?'

'It's all right,' Harriet said to Cathy. 'The food's ready in the fridge. She just forgot the day.'

'Oh, yes, that's right.' Thank goodness for Harriet. There was cold salmon and salad. No cooking, but she would have to go and prepare it shortly.

The two men climbed into the truck and slammed the doors. The engine roared into life and revved up violently while they manoeuvred along the front of Audlands. The sound of their awkward progress persisted after they had turned the corner and disappeared from sight.

'I've bought a statue,' said Connie. 'Come and see.'

By the time they arrived, the crane had already started to lift the statue into the air. The head was emerging gradually, like someone rising from bed.

168

Her face was serene, her eyes bland and unpainted, hinting at a private, ancient knowledge. Slowly, slowly, she moved into an upright position and it was possible to see her ringleted hair, the little hunting horn that she held almost concealed in the folds of her dress. The crane inched her upwards until her feet left the floor and she hung above the lorry, monstrous but graceful, vibrating slightly above them all.

'Good gracious!' said Cathy.

Connie found it difficult to conceal her pleasure at her sister-in-law's reaction.

Philip and Colin had climbed up the side of the lorry and were leaning over, studying the mechanics of the crane. Judy was scrabbling at the wheels, trying to follow them.

'Philip!' cried Cathy. 'Get down from there. It's far too dangerous.'

An ominous voice came from inside the top of the lorry. 'Get them out of my way, lady. Or they'll be dead meat.'

'Harriet,' said Connie. 'Get the rackets and take your cousins over to the tennis court. You can have a game before lunch.'

'But Caroline and Hester are due in a minute. I'm waiting for them.'

'Are they coming today as well?'

'For lunch. You said I could invite them.' Harriet's thin, delicately moulded face was setting itself into an expression of stubborn resentment.

'That's fine,' said Connie. 'I'm sure we'll manage. Could you go and fetch Jessica for me, please?'

Harriet left, with Judy trailing behind her. 'Harriet, wait for me!'

After a couple of minutes they reappeared with Jessica through the French windows of the music room, and came over.

Jessica stood with her mouth open, watching the statue hover weightlessly in the air above the lorry. It looked as if it was ascending to heaven, blocking out the sun, casting a gigantic shadow over the lawn. It began to float sideways, gliding effortlessly, more an angel than a Greek goddess, movement bringing the stone to life.

'Jessica, darling,' said Connie, 'could you take the boys and Judy to play tennis? It's all a bit risky here, and I think Auntie Cathy would prefer it if they could be distracted for the time being.'

'No,' said Jessica, without taking her eyes off the statue. 'I don't want to.'

'I didn't ask if you wanted to, dear. I asked you to do it.'

The boys had now climbed down. 'Jessica will take you to play tennis,' announced Connie.

'Do we have to?' said Philip. 'I want to stay here.'

'Well, you can't,' said Cathy.

'We always play tennis,' said Colin.

'That's not true,' said Harriet. 'We do lots of interesting things.'

'Is there going to be a treasure hunt?' asked Philip, looking hopefully at Connie.

'Not today,' said Connie. 'I'm afraid I've been a bit distracted by Artemis.'

'Who?'

'Never mind,' said Cathy. 'Off you go with Jessica.'

The three of them walked back to the house to fetch the rackets, stopping regularly to check the

170

progress of the statue. 'The crane's going to break,' said Philip with some satisfaction. 'It'll crush them all.'

Judy ran after them. 'I want to play too.'

The boys groaned.

A car horn sounded from the front of the house.

'Mummy,' shouted Harriet. 'Caroline and Hester have arrived.'

*   *   *

Philip and Colin were not as tall as Jessica, who had always been big for her age, but they were better constructed, more streamlined. Philip ran backwards and forwards to the net, his tanned legs strong and athletic, full of latent energy and grace even when he remained in one place. His shoulders had already filled out from his sporting activities, and they were broad and mature. He was in all the first teams at school—rugby in the winter, tennis and cricket in the summer. He was successful in everything he did. His hair was allowed to grow past his ears, thick and luxuriant, but there was no danger that anyone would mistake him for a girl from behind. He walked with so much ease, swung his arms with such assurance.

Jessica swung her racket and sent the ball into the net.

'Idiot!' shouted Colin. 'Anybody could have got that one.'

She blushed with embarrassment, knowing that she hadn't been concentrating. The image of Philip racing around opposite her, alive with an inexhaustible source of energy, was mesmerising and she found it difficult to think of anything else.

Judy darted along the side of the net and retrieved the ball. Initially she had attempted to join in, but she soon gave up and decided to be a ball girl.

'Forty-fifteen,' called Philip as he prepared to serve again.

Jessica tried to keep her mind on the tennis. Philip, at twelve, represented something that she never encountered in her all-girls' school. She wanted him to like her, but everything she did inexplicably enraged him. She watched him run, his hair flying up behind him, fanning into a cascade of gold, a moving work of art.

'I'll get it,' yelled Colin, moving in front of her and hitting the ball with a satisfying thwack. It swept over the net, and Philip had to run backwards to reach it. He skidded round and returned the ball. It skimmed the top of the net and landed close to Jessica. She was prepared, her racket swinging back, but the bounce was false. This frequently happened on their court, since her father only used the roller once a year at the beginning of the season. The ball headed off at the wrong angle and she sliced through empty space.

She turned and watched the ball fall away behind her. 'Sorry,' she said.

Colin was furious. 'What's the point of playing? You never hit anything.'

'I couldn't help it,' she said. 'The bounce was funny.'

Colin's next serve was aggressively fast, only just clearing the net. Philip attempted to return it, but the ball bounced off the wood on the edge of his racket, up in the air and over the wire netting into the bushes beyond.

'Oh, no,' he groaned.

'I'll get it,' called Judy, running to the entrance of the court.

'We'd all better go,' said Philip.

Jessica didn't mind. She was happy to rummage through the undergrowth searching for balls. It was preferable to being humiliated by her clumsy tennis.

The land round the tennis court was a neglected wilderness, overgrown with trees, unpruned shrubs, ivy, brambles and nettles. Most of it was impenetrable, although the ongoing search for balls near the court had resulted in some more accessible patches. It was nevertheless a hopeless task. Somehow the balls seemed to know how to find secret places—wedged in the branches of a tree, caught in the holes left by moles or rabbits, or simply blending into their surroundings. Usually, looking for balls was more time-consuming than playing the game, but everybody did it, because they knew that Jessica's father would be infuriated by every missing ball. He was a mild-mannered man, but this one issue had the effect of stirring him up. 'Do you know how much these balls cost?' he would shout.

They all knew how much the balls cost. It was engraved upon their hearts. The price was nothing compared to the electricity bills at Audlands, the rates, the lawn mower repairs, the telephone bills, but they understood that the tennis balls mattered more. They were a symbol of extravagance and luxurious living. They epitomised waste.

'Ouch!' said Colin, scratching his arm. 'Nettles.'

Jessica handed him some dock leaves and he sat for a while, rubbing a leaf up and down, watching a

173

green stain spread through the hairs on his arm.

Philip was swinging his racket backwards and forwards like a scythe, sweeping rapidly through swathes of long grass. Jessica was more careful, pushing back dandelion leaves and brambles, peering through the branches of overgrown bushes, checking every small space.

A piercing scream broke into their concentration and their heads shot up.

It was Judy. Philip ran over to her. 'What's the matter?'

She had walked into a jutting broken branch and had fallen to the ground, clutching her leg and whimpering. 'It hurts, it hurts.'

Philip sat down beside her, his legs brown and muscular against the green of the undergrowth. 'Let me see.'

She moved her hand, and he studied the injury. 'There's no blood,' he said.

She stopped crying and looked. 'But it hurts.'

He rubbed it gently. Judy began to calm down.

'There, it's better now.' He looked up and saw Jessica watching him. 'What do you think you're staring at?' he said.

She turned away quickly, her cheeks aflame, a hot breathless sensation in her chest. She had been moved by his tenderness with his sister, the way his manner became soft and compassionate. She hadn't realised he could do that. But she didn't want him to know that she'd noticed his transformation.

'Found it!' yelled Colin triumphantly and held up the ball, smeared with dirt but intact.

'That can't be the right one,' said Philip, grabbing it. 'It's the wrong colour.'

174

'Doesn't matter,' said Colin. 'It must be an old one that nobody found. As long as we bring back the same number that we started with.'

They played for half an hour more. Judy continued to be a ball girl for a while, but soon became bored and settled down in a corner of the court, picking daisies, constructing her own private game.

Jessica concentrated fiercely and she and Colin began to take the lead. Philip wouldn't accept this, his temper deteriorating with each lost point.

'Out!' he shouted when Colin sent a good backhand down the line.

'No it wasn't,' said Colin, putting his hands on his hips.

'Of course it was. Anyone could see it was out. Judy, did you see it?'

'No,' she said. 'I wasn't looking.'

'Jess?'

It wasn't out, she was sure. 'I thought it was in,' she said apologetically.

'You can't have seen it properly.'

'I don't know. Maybe it was out.'

'See?' said Philip. 'It was out. Jessica saw it too.'

Colin came over and pulled her arm. 'What do you mean it was out? You saw it as plain as I did.'

'Yes,' she said, trembling with her desire to say the right thing.

'Jess says it was in,' called Colin.

Philip glared at her. 'What does that mean exactly? You say it's out, then you say it's in. Can't you make your mind up? What's the matter with you? It can't be both.'

She shook her head. 'I don't know. I can't remember.'

'You must remember.' His voice was getting louder, more aggressive. 'Tell the truth, Jess, that's all you have to do.'

'Let's play the point again,' she said, in a hopeless attempt to distract them.

'No,' said Philip. 'That ball was out. The point was mine. I'm not going to play it again.'

'I think we should,' said Colin.

'No!' shouted Philip. 'If you can't be fair, I'm not playing.' He picked up one of the balls lying at his feet, threw it into the air, swung his racket, and pounded it over the net, directly at Jess. He picked up another ball, then another. The first hit her shoulder as she tried to turn and avoid it. The next one hit her hip. She couldn't move. Her feet were planted firmly into the grass, invisible roots holding her in place. She knew that she made an easy target, so she hunched in on herself, desperate to shrink and fade away.

When he'd run out of balls, they stood there facing each other, Philip panting slightly, Jessica seeing everything through a distorted, misted window.

'Why didn't you run away?' asked Judy with a puzzled frown.

But Jessica couldn't speak. She could feel the places where the balls had hit her, each one throbbing with pain.

'Philip! Colin! Jess! Lunch is ready.' Harriet was calling from the house.

The boys threw their rackets down on the grass and sprinted for the house. Judy dropped her bunch of daisies and ran after them, her short legs unable to match their running skills. 'Wait!' she cried.

Jessica stood motionless for a long time. After a while, she felt as if she might cry, and she didn't want to, so she swallowed hard. She forced everything down her throat, packed it away in a secret compartment and shut the drawer. It was gone. She didn't need to think about the tennis, or Philip, or his legs flashing as he ran back to the house, his feet flying up in the air behind him.

The air was hot and heavy, and bees were buzzing in the hedge at the end of the tennis court. The scent of the lilac was strong, but she didn't identify it exactly as a smell. It was there, round her, in her head, part of the landscape. She bent down to pick up the rackets and collected the balls together.

As she walked back to the house, she was humming. It was a Mozart sonata that she had just started to play. One of her father's colleagues had cleared out his mother's house recently and found a pile of old music, which he'd passed on to Jessica. She was working her way through it all, trying everything, experimenting, playing the ones she liked over and over again. She could hear the music in her head, feel the shifting chords below the tune. Her fingers were moving, even as they held the rackets, sensing the vibration of the keys under her hands.

She thought she might miss lunch. She wanted to go and play the piano.

*   *   *

The statue was perfect. Connie brought everyone out to admire it again after lunch. 'It's just the beginning,' she told Cathy. 'I intend to fill the garden with statues.'

'Let's hope Roland keeps selling the cakes, then,' said Cathy.

'She's beautiful,' said Connie, wishing that she could drift around like a goddess, her arms hanging bare and loose at her sides, round and shapely.

'Where's Jess?' asked Harriet.

She looked around in surprise. 'I don't know. She was at lunch, wasn't she?'

'No,' said Harriet.

Connie looked at her suspiciously. 'Of course she was.'

'No,' said Cathy. 'I don't think she was.'

Connie experienced a familiar sensation, a feeling that events were fluttering past her, out of control, like dust motes in the sunshine that you couldn't grasp before they floated off. There were too many people at lunch, too many children. How could she be expected to count them all? 'Well,' she said. 'How strange. I thought I asked her to play tennis with the boys.'

'You did,' said Cathy.

'So did she play tennis with you?' she asked Colin, who was standing next to her.

'Oh yes.' He nodded enthusiastically. 'We won.'

'No, you didn't,' said Philip. 'You cheated.'

'Boys, boys!' said Cathy, with an indulgent look. 'You're so lucky, Connie, only having girls.'

'I know where Jess is,' said Harriet. 'Listen.'

Scales were cascading out of the house. Minor scales. Up and down, up and down, five times each, then up a semitone and the next one started.

'I do wish she would play something else,' said Connie.

CHAPTER THIRTEEN

The semiquavers are machine-like, clean and precise. They grow with controlled impatience, working through a long crescendo, *poco a poco*, until they burst out with delighted exuberance. The Queen of Sheba has arrived. Then it all swallows back into itself, drops to a whisper and starts again. Mary and I are side by side at the piano, our minds and movements in absolute harmony. We crouch down for the *pianissimo*s, small with the music, then straighten up as it gets louder, our movements wider and more expansive as we approach the tumultuous climaxes. This is what I love about duet-playing—the sensation of sharing, of being two halves of the same entity. Separately Mary and I are insignificant. Together, we are masters—mistresses—of the universe. Nothing compares with this. Nothing.

'The Arrival of the Queen of Sheba' makes an ideal encore, full of life and vigour. At the final triumphant chord, Mary and I leap to our feet and run in opposite semicircles to face the audience. Our evening dresses rustle with a counterfeit glamour, the sequins reflecting points of lights from the auditorium, everything absurdly sophisticated. We clasp hands and bow deeply from the waist. The applause is warm and enthusiastic, satisfying an internal hunger in me. It represents approval, acknowledgement that I'm doing something worthwhile with my life at last.

We now have an agent, Stuart, who organises everything, and he has increased the number of engagements dramatically, including next year's tour of Cornwall. Mary was reluctant to accept this invitation at first, because she would have to leave the boys. 'What if something happens? Angus is bound to break a leg.'

He broke an arm last summer and an ankle the year before. It's only a matter of time before the other leg goes. We're all holding our breath.

'It doesn't matter,' says Eamon. 'I'm going to take some time off work. Great opportunity to get some things done in the house and garden.'

'Why can't you do that when I'm here?' says Mary. 'Do I really have to go away before you decide to take some holiday?'

'Don't complain. I've been saving my holiday for you.'

Where did Mary find him? It doesn't seem fair. Shouldn't they share some of this good nature around, marry difficult people and spread their genes more generously? But they want the best, of course, like everyone else. Why settle for Andrew when you can have Eamon?

As we come off the stage, Stuart is waiting for us. 'Lovely concert, girls,' he says.

'We're not girls,' I say. 'Can't you tell the difference between silly, empty-headed young people and mature, wise, beautiful women?'

His black hair is smothered in gel and arranged into a tangled wilderness of spikes. It doesn't look right. He's not a young man. He always seems to have a cold, which is not his fault, but he sniffs all the time. If he takes out a handkerchief, which is rare, he only dabs at his nose.

'Blow it properly,' I want to say to him. 'Otherwise you'll just go on sniffing.' But I don't say it. Honesty isn't always the best policy, according to Mary.

'They're a wonderful audience,' she says.

We're high on the music, almost dancing, fired up by the audience's reaction.

'I may have a recording contract,' says Stuart. He often says this, and it used to be exciting, but I've learnt to receive his pronouncements with scepticism. He's good, but the market for forty-something women playing duets is inevitably limited, and a concert every now and again is all we can reasonably hope for. But I like him, despite his unreasonable optimism. I approve of his ardent, all-embracing passion for music.

'Come on, Jess,' says Mary.

We return to the stage for another bow, but not another encore. If you go on too long, it all fizzles out and people start looking at their watches and sneaking out when they think no one is looking.

The audience, which is larger than usual, claps intensely. There are a few whistles and 'Bravos' from the less inhibited people who often attend concerts, but they're generally a well-behaved crowd. We bow and smile and look round at the friendly, appreciative faces. They're squeezed on to tightly packed rows of hard-backed chairs and must be longing for the chance to stand up.

As I raise my eyes towards the back of the hall, I'm surprised to catch a glimpse of a familiar face. A huge black man, his head covered with a mass of curly white hair. He looks exactly like Joshua, the homeless man from the library. I blink rapidly, glance away, then move my eyes back slowly. It still looks like him. It's not just his shape or his colour that's so familiar, but the way he holds himself, his

181

calm authority. He's wearing a dinner jacket with a bow tie, and he's accompanied by a woman of a similar age. She's slender and elegant, her grey hair tied into a loose, skimpy bun, pearls round her neck.

I lose sight of him, so I turn back to the centre of the hall and we smile and bow once more before we leave the stage.

'Let's go for a drink,' says Stuart as the audience trickles away.

We drive into the city centre and head for the bar at the Repertory Theatre. We find a table and sink down with relief.

'When are you going to get a haircut?' I say to Stuart. 'It's looking more porcupine than hedgehog.'

'Jess . . .' says Mary in a low voice, shaking her head very gently.

But Stuart doesn't mind. He laughs. 'Wait until I can't get through doorways. Then you can worry.'

'How's Sylvia?' asks Mary.

How does she do this? Carry everyone else's information in her head and find it when she needs it? I'd forgotten all about his new girlfriend.

'Ah, the divine Sylvia,' he says. 'Let's not discuss Sylvia tonight.'

I tell them about Joshua.

'Is there any reason it couldn't be him?' asks Mary.

'It just doesn't seem likely,' I say.

'Faces in a crowd,' Stuart suggests. 'Your mind plays tricks and makes them familiar so that you can cope with the quantity of people.'

Maybe he's right.

'So what happened when you phoned Andrew?'

182

asks Mary. 'What did he say?'

'Who's Andrew?' asks Stuart.

'Jess's ex-husband.'

'Why has no one mentioned him before?'

'He's irrelevant,' I say.

'He was on the local news,' says Mary. 'He climbed to the top of Waterstone's.'

I sigh and sip my drink. 'I think he did it because he could,' I say. 'A bit like Everest. You climb it because it's there.'

'But Waterstone's is always there, and most people don't attempt to climb up it.'

'Most people aren't Andrew.'

'It seems such a dangerous thing to do,' says Mary.

'I'd have thought so, but I don't know much about climbing. He's got all the equipment, he says, ropes and things like that. He bought it from a friend.'

We sit in silence for a while.

'No!' says a loud voice behind us.

'Yes,' insists another. 'I tell you it was Simon Rattle.'

'Anyway,' I say, 'there's not much I can do about it. Andrew does his own thing.'

'Do you think he'll do it again?'

Of course he will. He's bought the equipment. He's not going to waste £200. 'I hope not,' I say.

*   *   *

I drive out to Audlands the following Monday. It's late afternoon. The horse chestnuts are at their best, towering into the sky with a rustling, unstoppable vigour. The Hall shimmers in the distance, distorted by the heat, timeless as the surrounding countryside, still breathtaking, but now limping away from its days of glory, no longer able to resist natural deterioration.

Most of the serious decay is in the courtyard at the back, where you can't see it straightaway. Here, dark mould is sending out tendrils of corruption, a careless vandal with no appreciation for heritage. Window frames have rotted, causing the glass to shatter on blustery days. Rain has penetrated the upper rooms, eating away at plaster and floorboards, making many rooms uninhabitable and unsafe. When I was younger I didn't notice the rot, although it must have been well established by then. The house was committed to its inevitable path of disintegration long before my parents moved in. I accepted what was there, beetles, spiders, mould, the smell of damp. They were all part of my childhood world, constant and normal.

My father's business was sold several years ago, swallowed up by a manufacturer that supplies supermarkets all over the world. Fontaine's Crunchy Chocolate Brownies are no more. The final decline probably led to my father's stroke. And at the same time, as the money really did run out, my mother's enthusiasm for renovation faded. For the last ten years she has made no attempt to do any further work on Audlands. She was never going to win anyway. She'd had a romantic dream of opening it to the public, but as fast as she moved, damp and dry rot crept up behind her.

My mother comes to the front door and watches me park. She stands there while I climb the steps with the shopping. 'You should try going round the back,' she says. 'It might be quicker.'

'I can't get round the back, can I?' I mutter, as I put down the bags and turn to fetch the rest. 'It's too overgrown.'

The shrubbery at the side of the house is now impenetrable. The gravel path lost its gravel years ago and descended into a bog. Trees overhang the house, too low and fierce to push aside, their branches tapping urgently against the windows whenever anything stronger than a breeze ripples through them. Bushes have thrived and spread, filling every available space. The maze at the front has no entrance or exit. A Sleeping Beauty forest of formidable dimensions.

Neither of my parents can manage to garden any more and my father won't waste money on paying someone to help. I can see his point. In the days when Audlands was a great house there would have been a team of gardeners working full-time, all year round. One man doing a couple of hours a week wouldn't know where to begin.

The entrance hall hasn't changed much. It's neglected, with shabby wallpaper, but not damp. The chandelier still hangs in the centre of the ceiling, old candles still in place, cooled wax dripping over the sides, coated in decades of dust. Clouds of spider-web curtains drift down and shiver gently in the breeze from the open door.

'Did you get the Mars bars?' asks my mother.

'Of course.' Last month it was Curlywurlies. She eats them obsessively for several weeks, then suddenly declares that the ingredients have been changed. They don't taste the same any more, she says, and moves on to her next craving. I live in dread that Tesco will run out of Mars bars before she gets tired of them. 'And the apples and the

185

mangoes.' I'm currently trying to encourage healthy eating.

'I told you not to get apples, Jessica. There are plenty in the garden.'

'You can't get to the apple trees any more.'

'I bet you haven't tried, though, have you?'

My parents have retreated to four rooms in the south-east wing. They still use the big kitchen and they've made the butler's parlour, next door, into a bathroom. They had this done properly, after my father's stroke, paying bathroom fitters to do a professional job, so it's the most modern room in the house. Cream and soft green tiles on the walls, taps with sophisticated, manageable handles, a power shower.

Their bedroom looks out on to the overgrown rose garden. A white marble fireplace, carved out and filled with patterns of amber and jade, dominates the room from behind the bed. When you lie back on their duvet cover—'Country Diary' from Dorma—and look up at the ceiling, you are confronted with a gold-edged geometric design with maroon in the background. Moulded plaster figures move across an Etruscan landscape, their edges chipped and crumbling.

My parents' living room used to be the Chinese room and still has the wallpaper put up by the fifth Earl at the end of the nineteenth century. Delicately painted trees wind their way along the wall in intricate shapes, while herons sit on the branches amongst the pink cherry blossom, silhouetted against the blue background, their beaks pointing upwards. Much of the paper is faded, some patches torn away completely, but the birds and blossom still dominate the room. One wall is punctured with thousands of tiny holes, a memorial to the inaccurate darts players who were stationed here during the war. My mother has bought a cheap off-cut of beige carpet for the centre of the floor, an enormous television which is placed in the corner on its own stand, and a three-piece suite from Argos. She's abandoned all notions of authenticity.

'Argos deliver,' she says. 'The men are so nice and they'll carry everything into the right room.'

It saddens me that they've withdrawn from the drawing room and that the elegant furniture bought and restored by my mother has been abandoned. I think everything should be covered in dust-sheets, as you see in films. But there wouldn't be much point. Who would ever take the sheets off? What would they be preserving the furniture for?

'Too much cleaning, dear,' says my mother, when I try to encourage them out of their smaller rooms. 'No time for things like that.'

She's discovered the internet. The computer is set up on the kitchen table and she sits there nearly all day, wandering round the planet, exploring all those worlds of fun that she missed when she was younger, using her mind where she once would have used legs. She doesn't move around very much now—she has arthritis in both knees—so she's become overweight, taking comfort from chocolate.

My father is in a wheelchair after the stroke. You can have a sensible conversation with him, but his legs have never recovered their function. He's happy in the wheelchair. He can move himself around and sit and read the paper from cover to cover every day without my mother nagging him about things to do. Then he watches the television.

They seem contented with their routine. They don't need to talk much except at mealtimes, when my mother gazes out of the window and my father chews every mouthful twenty times with a baffling attention to detail.

'Did you cook this pork properly?' he says.

'I'm sure the lake should be dredged,' she says. 'That's where the missing statue is, mark my words.'

She's calmer than she used to be and does all her talking in chatrooms. It seems safe to let her get on with it. She probably doesn't have plans to run away with a lepidopterist from the Outer Hebrides.

I go to visit them once a week to help with the shopping. Usually my mother comes with me, but on this occasion, she chose to send me a list by email. 'I'm too busy today,' she wrote. Composing increasingly devious treasure hunt clues that no one will ever read? Learning Mandarin so she can communicate with all those potential correspondents in China?

We carry the bags of shopping into the kitchen, which is full of organised clutter. The computer is surrounded by envelopes, letters, bills, circulars, all tidily arranged into piles. A big box in the corner is reserved for recycling, and I take the contents to the tip once a month.

'Let's have some coffee,' says my mother.

'I'll put the shopping away.'

'No, no, no. You don't need to do that.' She always says this, but she doesn't mean it.

My father rolls into the kitchen in his

wheelchair. 'Hello!' he says, beaming. 'I'd forgotten you were coming.'

'I always come on a Monday.'

'Oh, is it Monday?' He hesitates, then recovers. 'A minor lapse of memory. There's nothing wrong with my mind. Still takes me less than an hour to do the *Times* crossword—only need to use the dictionary a couple of times. Keeps me sharp.'

In recent years, I've come to realise that Joel takes after my father. They share a fascination with patterns and figures. I can sympathise with them. It's a bit like the pleasure I find in scales and arpeggios. Order, symmetry, exactness.

'Some nice young men came round the other day,' says my mother.

I look up from the cupboard where I'm packing away tins of baked beans. 'Haven't you grown out of young men yet?'

My mother laughs, a clear, ringing sound that hasn't altered with age. 'Whatever makes you think that?'

'So what did they want?'

'They wanted to know if they could revive the tennis court and play on it. They were very keen. They said they would come and cut down all those bushes and nettles around the court as a form of payment, and clear the paths.'

'What a great idea. What did you say?'

'I said they were welcome to it. It would be nice to have people around again.'

I'm delighted. 'They were respectable, though, were they?'

'Oh, yes. Short hair, and only one had a tattoo. A tiny seashell on his arm—it was rather pretty, I thought. No smell of drugs.' She almost certainly knows about this. She probably didn't have access to drugs when she was a teenager, but I suspect she tried something when she was older, during some of her famous parties.

'When's Joel coming round?' asks my father. 'He owes me a game of chess.'

'I thought he was coming last Friday.'

'No, he cancelled.'

'I'll check with him,' I say. 'I'm sure he's intending to come some time this week.'

'We're neck and neck,' says my father. 'Forty-one games all.'

'I'm just going to walk round the house,' I tell them, when I've finished sorting out the shopping.

I like to wander on my own. Partly because I run out of things to say to my parents, and partly because there's something comforting about revisiting old familiar places. They've acquired a strangeness in the years since I've moved out. I know them all, but without my constant presence they've changed. I'll often just stand in one room and inspect it with adult eyes. I want to keep looking before it finally collapses.

Today, I go to the Long Gallery, which is the best-preserved of all the upstairs rooms. The powder-blue walls were never painted again after my mother's early efforts, but you can be fooled by it when you first enter. The Roman emperors remain, sneering at the passing of time. I must have skated past these Caesars thousands of times as a child, but I never once wondered who they were. They were just there: silent, permanent guardians of my solitude.

In recent years, I've found out more about them. Caligula was the one to avoid, a cruel dictator who

190

got rid of a lot of people. I've often studied his face, looking for signs of his nature. Can you tell what kind of man he was? Is there something in the bone structure, the set of the nose, the size of those blank eyes? Did his cruelty embed itself into his face, mark it and brand it so that posterity could recognise the evil, or was he born with those features, merely reflecting the genetic shape of his ancestors? What can you read from people's faces? Can you tell anything about them at all, or are we doomed to misread, misunderstand, misjudge?

I walk slowly along the wooden floor, seeing the dents and deep scratches that must have been inflicted long before my roller-skating days. I can see my younger self, skating backwards and forwards for hours, alone in my space, contented and safe. What did that version of Jessica think about? Who was she? I saw the floor then, but didn't see it. I couldn't have described any other features of the room. I was locked away in an alternative, private world, where external factors made no impression.

'Jess!'

For a moment I think I'm imagining the voice, a younger Harriet chasing me, wanting me to join in a treasure hunt.

'Mum! Jess!'

I stop and listen. Who's calling? It can't be Harriet. She's in New Zealand.

'Jess! Mum!'

It *is* Harriet. The tone, the pitch, the way she almost sings my name. I'm confused. The time between then and now has been zipped open, peeled back, and I'm seven again, lost and struggling, Harriet my only connection with the outside world.

I start to run, not believing she's there, but wanting to find her.

Harriet is waiting in the entrance hall, tall and elegant, looking at least ten years younger than she should, in a simple cotton dress that hangs beautifully and a straw hat that's exactly what our mother would have worn when we were little. 'Jess!'

'Harriet!'

She laughs, a warm, contented sound. 'I knew you would be wandering around somewhere. I saw the car.'

'What are you doing here? I thought you were on the other side of the world.' She usually lets us know in advance if she's coming home, but she's only been back a couple of times in the last few years.

Her laugh brings everything to life, makes the chandelier sparkle, clears the dust away from the corners of the marble floor, brings a shine into the mahogany of the banisters. 'I'm having a holiday.' She indicates her suitcases. 'I've got a few weeks off, so I thought I'd stay here.'

I frown. 'I don't know if there's anywhere clean enough to sleep.' Harriet hasn't stayed at Audlands for years. She usually finds a hotel.

'Oh, I don't care about that. The dust is part of our blood, isn't it? Anyway, I'd quite like to clean up a room.'

I experience a sudden thrill. It would be fun to start cleaning Audlands, make it all right again, pretend it's still alive. We could retrace our mother's work, dust and polish, possibly even do some painting.

'Darling!' Mum is standing behind us. 'You didn't tell me you were coming home.'

They embrace, Mum patting Harriet on the back, giggling with delight, Harriet unable to stop smiling.

'I'm sorry I didn't give you any notice,' says Harriet. 'It was a last-minute decision, and I just hopped on a plane.'

'There's nothing wrong, is there?' asks Mum. 'You haven't lost your job?'

'No, of course not. I just felt like a break.'

'Jessica's done the shopping. But we won't have enough food in.'

'It's all right,' says Harriet. 'I can go and get something. Jess can help.'

'Yes,' I say. 'I'm not busy this week.'

We all go into the kitchen, where my father is wheeling around looking into the cupboards to see what food has been bought. 'There's no cheese,' he mutters, then looks up. 'Harriet! Where did you come from?'

'New Zealand,' she says.

'There *is* cheese,' I tell him. 'It's on the top shelf of the fridge.'

Harriet has a successful career as an international consultant for a chain of interior designers. She stays in each country for a year or two, long enough to settle down and enjoy it, then moves on. She knows all the glamorous places in the world and she's thriving, exactly as you would expect if you'd known her as a child. She has a relaxed look, as if she's dressed without thought, run a brush through her hair at the last minute, slipped on her most comfortable shoes. Effortless, natural style. She knows everything and still gives the impression that she can read your thoughts, but nobody seems to mind very much. People always like her.

I know she has boyfriends, because she talks about them, but they change at regular intervals and no one in the family has met any of them. I find this puzzling. Is she happy with these temporary arrangements, or is she still hoping for the dream man, the great love affair? Perhaps she's had it, and it all ended in tragedy. I'd like to ask, but I can't manage that sort of question. I've found that people don't confide in me—not even my own sister. I don't seem to have that elusive, receptive manner that invites intimacy. I suspect she wouldn't tell me anyway, that there are hidden parts to her life that she would prefer to keep private.

'How's Joel?' says Harriet.

'He's fine. I'm sure he'll come and see you as soon as he knows you're back.' Joel likes Harriet. She's always been a model aunt, keeping in touch and sending thoughtful, ingenious presents from all over the world.

'Come on,' says Harriet. 'I feel as if I've been sitting on a plane for ever. Let's go for a run round the garden.'

'You can't,' I say. 'It's too overgrown.'

'It doesn't matter. Let's see how far we can get.'

'I'll make some coffee,' says my mother. 'For when you get back.'

*　　　*　　　*

When I arrive home, later that evening, Joel's music is blaring out of an open window. Our

194

neighbour, Ajinth, is outside mowing the grass. His garden is immaculate, with rigid edges to the tiny lawn and red roses, all the same variety, planted in narrow borders, exactly the same distance apart.

Ajinth is a Tamil, and he fled here with his family from Sri Lanka. They never discuss their reasons for coming. He used to be a teacher of business studies, but now he works in a factory making components for washing machines. He and his wife are tiny, determined, extremely polite, and everything they do is for their children, who have scholarships at independent schools. He spends a lot of time grumbling about the weather. 'If I had known it was so cold in England,' he always says, 'I'd have gone to Italy.'

The only thing I know of their flight here is that they handed over their life savings to an agent and had no idea where the plane was going until they were given the tickets at the airport. 'Our lives were in danger,' says Ajinth. 'We had no choice.'

I pause to say hello. He wipes the sweat off his face. 'This heat is too much.'

'It must be hotter in Sri Lanka.'

'But there you have sea breezes.'

'Make the most of it,' I say. 'It won't last.' I get out my front door key.

'Joel's in,' he says. 'We hear his music all day.'

'Oh dear, I'm sorry.'

He shrugs, happy now that he's said it. 'Doesn't bother us.'

I'm grateful for the fact that he never complains seriously. I like the veneer of politeness that helps to maintain our good relationship. 'Do you want me to cut the grass, Jess?'

I give him my best smile. 'Oh, thank you, Ajinth.

195

I'd really appreciate that.' I'm always astonished by his generosity. How can you survive everything that he has been through and still be generous? He makes me aware of my own inadequacy. I would like to do kind things for other people, but it never occurs to me until it's too late.

But Ajinth loves cutting grass, that's the difference, and he doesn't have enough of his own. He will trim the edges with a special tool, even do some weeding. He would like a bigger garden.

'Joel,' I call as I enter the narrow corridor of the hall. He can't hear because his music is too loud. He's sprawled on the sofa in the living room, fiddling with his cat models again. There are about twenty now and he's lining them up in formations, adjusting their shapes and swinging their tails around.

'So what's the new computer game going to be?' I ask. 'Cat's Whiskers? Cat's Cradle? It's a Cat's Life?'

'Hi, Mum,' he says.

'Turn the music down,' I say.

'Sorry?'

I go and turn off the CD player.

'Hey,' he says. 'I was listening to that.'

'It was too loud. Ajinth has just complained to me.'

He sits up, his face folding into sheepish embarrassment. 'Oh,' he says. 'He should have knocked on the door and told me.'

'He probably tried, but you wouldn't have heard him.'

'Sorry,' he says, trying to project sincerity into his voice, but still managing to sound unconvincing. 'You're late back.'

'Harriet's home.'

'I didn't know she was due back.'

'It was a last-minute decision.'

'When's dinner?'

I stare at him. 'I thought you were going to peel the potatoes today. You promised that you'd do something to help.'

'Did I? I must have forgotten. I've been working.' He looks up at me, an apologetic grin hovering. 'Shall I do it now?'

Joel's work is everyone else's play. I turn away irritably. 'It's all right,' I say. 'I can manage.'

'Mum—'

I stop at the tone of his voice. 'Yes?'

'I'm engaged.'

I don't hear him at first. Not properly. I'm thinking about sausages, cabbage and potatoes and my tired feet. Harriet and I have been cleaning all afternoon, moving a bed, airing the sheets. Then the words penetrate and I spin round.

'Engaged?'

He looks offended. 'There's no need to be quite so shocked. I'm allowed to if that's what I want.'

'But who to? You don't have a girlfriend.'

'How do you know I don't have a girlfriend?'

'Well—you've never brought anyone home, you've never mentioned her. Most mothers meet girlfriends before their sons decide to get married.'

'You're always so busy.'

'No I'm not. I'm here every evening, cooking dinner. You never go out.'

He looks at the floor. 'I see her during the day.'

'But you're at work during the day.'

'Well, she's at work too.'

'Oh, I see. She's an employee?'

197

He nods.

'But shouldn't you be taking her out for candle-lit romantic dinners?'

Bewilderment spreads across his face. He's like a child who's caught in a new situation and doesn't quite know the correct procedure.

I regret my cynical tone, realising with amazement that he must be serious. How can he conduct a relationship when he doesn't know the rules? 'What's her name?'

'Alice.'

Does Alice have any idea of what she's getting into?

CHAPTER FOURTEEN

I was climbing the steps to the Barber Institute with Mary when I was hit by a wave of nausea. I tried to ignore it, but the steps were starting to disintegrate in front of me and murky shadows were creeping into the edge of my vision. I grabbed Mary's arm.

'Jess, what's the matter?'

'I feel sick.' I sat down on the steps.

'Put your head between your knees,' said Mary. I did as I was told, breathing deeply but unable to fight the cloud of confusion that was slowly paralysing my mind. I sat there for some time, conscious of Mary's hand on my back, until the sensation began to recede. Slowly I lifted my head, feeling uncomfortable and foolish, and looked around. Everything was bright and sharp-edged and brittle.

'I'm sure it'll be fine,' said Mary.

It took me a few seconds to work out what she was talking about. She meant the degree results. That's why we were here.

'It's not that,' I said.

'It doesn't matter, you know,' said Mary. 'You can always do resits.'

'You think I'm going to fail, then?'

'No, of course not. I know your degree will be a good one, but I thought maybe you were worrying, and that's why I suggested—'

'I'm pregnant.'

Mary's face was static for a few moments as the information registered, and then a broad smile spread over her face. 'Jess, how wonderful.'

I studied her. The smile seemed to be genuine. 'Well, it's nice to have someone react in the way they're supposed to.'

'Surely Andrew is pleased.'

When I told him, Andrew had frozen with disbelief, then shock. I could see uncertainty on his face, then growing understanding. A tentative smile emerged, which grew and grew. 'I'm going to be a father,' he said. He seemed to grow taller, straighter, more sensible, a proud maturity seeping into him.

It's going to be all right, I thought.

'Yes,' I said. 'Andrew is delighted.'

He bought chocolates, fetched a Chinese takeaway, even made the coffee afterwards. Having a considerate husband was nice while it lasted.

'And your parents?' said Mary. 'They're going to be grandparents. They must be thrilled.'

Thrilled wasn't quite the right word.

'Who's going to support the child?' said my father. 'Andrew or the state?'

'Where will you live?' said my mother. 'You can't have a baby in that grotty little bedsit.'

She'd never mentioned before that she didn't approve of our flat.

'It's not that bad,' I said.

'It's dreadful. It's high time Andrew found you somewhere decent to live.' She still greeted Andrew with delight every time she met him. I'd had no idea that she disapproved of him in any way.

'My parents are just concerned about the financial situation,' I said to Mary. My father had never stopped worrying about Andrew's inability to earn an acceptable wage. He'd offered him a job after the wedding, but Andrew had just laughed and refused to take it seriously. My father had barely spoken to him since.

'Andrew's working at the moment, isn't he?'

'Yes, but he doesn't like it.'

He was cleaning bus shelters, and had to set off at six o'clock in the morning, ready to start before the rush hour. So I got up and made his tea, buttered his toast, poured the orange juice. He never suggested I stay in bed, even in those early days of pregnancy. He liked me to sit at the kitchen table with him while I was swaying with misery, leaping up to be sick every now and again.

'And what about Andrew's parents?' asked Mary.

I had phoned Miranda, since Andrew still wouldn't speak to her. They had been to visit a few times since the wedding, but Andrew always went out before they arrived. At least there would be something to talk about once we started a family.

'My goodness,' said Miranda. 'How in the world are you going to cope with that? It's a big responsibility, you know.'

I didn't tell her that I hadn't been able to believe it myself for some time. I'd struggled through my finals with a growing sense of disbelief, a disturbing knowledge that there was something alien inside me, a benign lodger who was already feeding off me. I could feel the stirring of a being who was nobody yet but would be somebody soon. Nausea started to murmur away inside almost immediately, adding to the unreality of the situation.

'Well,' I said, 'they're not overjoyed.' I looked down at the Barber Institute steps. I could see the accumulation of dirt from the feet of generations of music students and art lovers. A thin dusting of moss lurked in the bend of the step. 'We're going to get a council house, though. We've just had a letter.' This was a highlight in an otherwise unsettling situation.

'I thought they only gave houses to families.'

'We are a family—nearly. We've got lots of extra points now that I'm pregnant, although they wait until the baby's born.'

Mary was more dubious than me. 'I hope it's in a nice area. Some of those estates are a bit rough.'

I hadn't given a thought to the area. I was diverted by the prospect of a real home. I wanted magnolia walls and bright geometric patterns on the curtains and carpets.

'Come on,' I said, getting to my feet. 'We need to get our results.'

Several other students from our year had beaten

us to it. Michael rushed past, leaping down the steps three at a time, whooping happily.

'He got a Third,' said Geoff, following him down. 'He thought he'd fail.'

'What did you get?' asked Mary.

'A First,' he said, and walked past us with precise, measured steps, a quiet satisfaction emanating from his back.

Mary and I looked at each other.

'Creep,' I said. 'He works too hard. No time for fun.' As if I spent all my spare time having fun, as if I wasn't a married woman who went home every day to cook, wash up, do the hoovering, the washing, the ironing—

'Are you ready?' Mary asked.

'Yes.'

We walked in together and found the list on the noticeboard by the library, outside the music office. We studied it in silence.

'Congratulations,' I said.

'Congratulations,' said Mary.

Mary had a 2:1. I had a 2:2. I was filled with relief. I had been pretending to Mary earlier, trying to make myself more confident. In reality, I'd had no idea if I would even pass. The weeks before the finals had been a nightmare of nausea and worry about our changing circumstances.

'You should have had a 2:1 as well,' said Mary.

'No,' I said. 'You deserve it. I've been distracted.'

'Exams aren't that important, anyway,' said Mary. 'You're doing a far more worthwhile thing. Perpetuating the human race.'

*   *   *

Andrew was sprawled on the sofa watching *Tom and Jerry* when I got home.

'I thought you were at work,' I said.

'I've resigned.'

I sat down and tried to control my breathing. 'Why?'

He snorted with amusement as Tom the cat was flattened by a steam roller and then reinflated to his normal shape but with bent whiskers. 'They want me to do half of someone else's round while he's off sick. Don't they realise I already slog myself to death for them?'

'Would they have paid you for doing it?'

'That's not the point. Why should I put myself out for them when they only pay me slave wages?'

Because we needed the money. Because it was better for him to be out working than sitting at home watching cartoons all day. Because our child would need a role model. What if he was a boy? How would he know what men were supposed to do?

I'd intended to tell him about my degree. It didn't seem very significant in the context of our present lives, but I thought he ought to know. Now I wasn't sure what to do. He knew I'd been in to the university to get the results, so perhaps he would ask.

I told him over shepherd's pie and cauliflower. He ate slowly, picking out tiny grains of meat that he didn't like the look of. I tried two mouthfuls and felt sick again.

'I got a 2:2.'

He was too distracted to look up, engrossed in separating a thicker stalk of cabbage from the rest.

'My degree. I've got a degree.'

He kept his head down, but the movement of his knife and fork slowed. There was a blankness about him, a bleakness in the rigidity of his shoulders and bowed head.

'Great,' he said.

A barrier had been set up between us. I was qualified and he was not. My achievement diminished him, made his lack of qualifications more acute. My hand was resting on the table. His was lying by the plate, the fork balancing idly between his thumb and first finger. I wanted to reach out and touch him. I nearly did, but couldn't decide if he would like it.

He grasped the fork more firmly and went on eating. 'Shall we go and buy a cot this afternoon?' he said.

'Can we afford it?'

'Of course we can. Nothing but the best for our offspring. Made from the finest birch. Bedclothes of pure cashmere, babygros in silk.'

'But how will we pay for it?'

An easy smile transformed his face. My mood lightened. 'With buttons,' he said.

*   *   *

On the day I went into labour, three days later than my due date, Andrew had an interview with the Gas Board to get on to a training course.

'See you later,' he shouted.

'How long do you think you'll be?' I asked.

But the door banged behind him and he was gone. Five minutes later, my waters broke.

Mary took me to the hospital and stayed,

helping with the breathing exercises, offering endless encouragement and optimism like a comforting application of soothing lotion, until the baby was born.

When the midwife handed me the baby I was drained and exhausted, unable to summon the energy to appreciate him.

'It's a boy,' said the midwife.

'He's beautiful,' said Mary.

I didn't want to hold him—I didn't know how to. Mary helped me to sit up a little, raising the end of the bed behind me and arranging the pillows. It hurts, I thought. I can't sit up. I'm too tired.

The midwife put the baby gently into my arms and I looked down at him.

He was tiny, slimy, with pink mottled skin. His miniature mouth sucked in and out rhythmically, plump lips searching, knowing by instinct what he needed. He was ugly. He was beautiful.

'Oh . . .' I said.

Andrew appeared, pale and breathless. 'They wouldn't let me in,' he said. 'They made me wait outside—'

He stopped when he saw the baby.

He feels it too, I thought in amazement.

'It's a boy,' said Mary. Her cheeks were wet.

Why would anyone cry?

Andrew stood with his mouth open, disbelieving, too nervous to approach any further. His unwashed hair was plastered to his head, tangled and neglected where it reached his shoulders. A layer of grime was visible on the rim of his shirt collar. He was wearing trainers without socks. He didn't speak.

My gaze returned to the baby in my arms, pulled

by a magnetic force greater than I had ever known. Tears were spilling out of my eyes and I blinked them away. I couldn't believe he was real. I couldn't believe that I was there, holding my own child, transformed by a love so enormous, so binding that I wasn't sure if I could contain it all.

*   *   *

When I was discharged from hospital three days later, I was terrified. How could they let me out on my own, allow me to take the baby with me? Did they know what they were doing?

Joel and I came home to the new council house, a brand-new family in an unfamiliar home. I tried to follow the same hospital routines, bathing, feeding, changing nappies, putting him into his cot with the Superman duvet cover that Andrew had dashed out to buy. At the end of the first day Andrew and I crept into bed, exhausted by the newness of it all.

A piercing, agonised shriek hit the night air and we leapt into shocked action, wrenched from our dreams by the urgency of the sound. I switched on a lamp and we groped around blindly, dazzled by the light.

'Something's wrong,' said Andrew, stumbling against his bedside table and knocking over a glass of water. 'He must be ill.'

We looked down at Joel in his cot at the end of our bed. His face was a deep purple, distorted with rage and displaying far too much energy to be ill.

'Hadn't you better pick him up?' said Andrew.

Not feeling confident, I bent down and lifted him. His arms flailed wildly, the tiny wrinkled fingers stiff with protest, his whole body rigid.

'Not like that,' said Andrew. 'He'll hurt himself.'

But I couldn't contain him. He wouldn't mould himself to my shoulder. I jiggled him up and down, but this just made him more furious.

Andrew took him off me. 'Let me try.'

'Careful,' I said. 'You've got to support his head.'

The sound was so ear-splitting that you couldn't think clearly. Whenever Joel stopped to draw breath it was as if time started ticking again, a brief moment of sanity. Then he found renewed strength, and the reality shattered once more.

'I can't stand it,' said Andrew, and I could hear hysteria in his voice. 'My eardrums will burst.'

'It's all right,' I said. 'He's just hungry.'

I sat down and put him to my breast. A glorious, refreshing silence ensued as he sucked greedily. He gulped down the milk, knowing his life depended on it, and was relaxed enough afterwards to have his nappy changed. Then I put him back to bed. This was a mistake. He was a miniature monster with a colossal ego, determined to let us know he existed. He did not intend to go to sleep and wasn't prepared to be influenced by anything we wanted.

I paced up and down, holding him in my arms, but he showed no desire to sleep. Andrew took him from me and got back into bed. He laid the baby down on his chest, patting his back gently. Joel produced a giant burp and we both giggled. Then he started to settle down. His head, with its little tuft of black hair, rested on Andrew's blue and white striped pyjamas, dwarfed by the round bump of the nappy. I watched him rise and fall with Andrew's breathing. A father and son, a real-life sculpture.

'He likes you,' I whispered.

'He's my boy,' said Andrew.

It didn't last. Joel kept waking in the night, and Andrew learnt to shut out the noise. 'Wake me if he cries,' he said, but I didn't. If Andrew had a disturbed night he wouldn't get up until lunchtime, and then he was irritable and over-sensitive for the rest of the day.

So mothers hear their babies crying and fathers don't. I would sometimes wake to silence, listen to the fridge humming into the emptiness downstairs and know that Joel was about to cry. I would get up, instantly awake, anxious to catch him before he let out his first anguished scream. Andrew didn't stir. There wasn't even a break in his breathing.

Sometimes I sat alone in the dark, impenetrable night and watched Joel. He was alive, he was mine, and his crying was inevitable, his way of forcing himself into my affections, making me love him. He would never know that all his effort was unnecessary. I was smitten from the moment of his birth, bonded for life, imprisoned by this painful, torturous love that would chain me and hold me captive for ever.

All my previous experiences and beliefs were shredded and scattered into the wind. My love for Joel sliced through every subconscious barrier inside me, a laser penetrating a core that I didn't know existed. My DNA was indelibly altered, blasted into submission. I had become a different person, one whose existence I had never suspected.

I would never be able to let him near other people in case they passed on germs, destroyed his

208

innocence, severed my personal link with him. I would still be worrying about him when he was seventy and I was ninety-two. I would be walking a perpetual tightrope of love and fear for the rest of my life, never certain that he would survive.

'Put a teddy bear at the end of the bed,' said my mother. 'If he sees something familiar when he wakes up, he might not cry.'

'Check his nappy,' said the midwife. 'If he's warm and dry, he'll soon settle down.'

'Try picking him up,' said Andrew's mother. 'Babies like to be held.'

'Perhaps you need to feed him more often,' said the health visitor.

None of this advice was any use at all. Joel cried because crying was what he could do. He needed to impose himself on the world. I had no other explanation.

'Do you think there's something wrong with him?' said Andrew.

'I don't know.' How could you tell? The books said that mothers instinctively knew why their babies cry. The books were wrong.

I woke one night to hear Joel screaming as usual. I looked at the clock and it transformed itself into a face. The hands at twenty to four were a down-turned mouth, the ten and the two were eyes, winking with a wry cynicism. The face rippled and swayed, and I became convinced it was trying to talk to me. Joel was shrieking in his cot, hysterical, refusing to believe that I hadn't responded. I couldn't get up. I had no strength left.

That was the turning point. I put Joel into the second bedroom and no longer did a night feed. Maybe the neglect convinced him that he had to give an inch. Not much more, but an inch felt considerably better than nothing.

*   *   *

'You cried a lot when you were a baby,' said my mother one afternoon as we sat outside at Audlands.

Joel needed an afternoon sleep, but wouldn't cooperate. The only way to calm him down was to push the pram backwards and forwards, setting up a comfortable rhythm. His eyelids would surrender and close, his mouth moving as he dreamt of milk, but the moment the pram stopped he would be instantly alert again, drawing breath, ready for the next onslaught.

'So it's hereditary, then,' I said.

Andrew had wandered down to the lake. The statue of Artemis looked down at us with a benign smile that suggested she knew more than she was letting on. Her experience of babies must have been extensive. Two thousand years of screaming, generation after generation. The methods of dealing with them might have changed—it's unlikely anyone would emulate Herod and order the execution of all children under two now—but the sound would have been as piercing then as now. No wonder she preferred hunting. The trees rustled and the lake flashed and sparkled, reflecting the sky. It was idyllic as long as Joel didn't start crying.

'Harriet used to watch the trees through the window for hours. She loved their movement.'

I liked the idea of the natural world soothing Joel. I wanted him to look at the trees, but survival

210

was the only purpose of his existence.

'You weren't interested in that sort of thing either,' said my mother. 'You just cried.'

'You've never told me that before.'

She gazed down at the lake. 'No, I suppose you forget once you've passed that stage. And, of course, Harriet was so much easier.'

Was it possible to forget? 'How did you deal with the crying?' I asked.

'Well—it was probably a bit easier for us. The house was so big that we could put you as far away as possible where we couldn't hear you.'

She was so matter-of-fact. Hadn't it worried her as much as it worried me now? 'Do you think it did any harm?'

My mother raised an eyebrow and looked at me over her glasses. 'You seem to have survived.'

This was a good point. I was sitting next to her with my own baby, not permanently damaged, as normal as could be expected.

'There was no alternative. You didn't want to be held.'

'Joel's like that. He's worse when you pick him up.'

She nodded. 'I've noticed.'

Joel was unique, the only baby in the world who didn't like human contact. I watched other people cuddle their babies when they cried. The babies calmed down, snuggled into a shoulder, sucked a thumb or a dummy and their eyes drooped with contentment. Their crying had a purpose and once they got what they wanted they were satisfied. Why wouldn't Joel do that?

'Actually,' she said, 'you seemed much happier away from everyone else. It was the only way to get

211

you to sleep.'

I thought of that distant baby Jessica, alone in a vast empty space, surrounded by unoccupied rooms. I envied her. I wanted to go back to the comfort of that isolated place.

'I thought babies liked to be held,' I said.

She shrugged. 'I think they usually do, but it's not always necessary. It's a modern idea that you have to play with them, keep them awake until they're tired. In our day, most babies slept all day and all night.'

'And if they didn't?'

'Well, you put them to bed anyway. They got used to it in the end.'

It all sounded so straightforward. 'But Harriet was easy?'

'Harriet was a lovely baby. She slept when you put her down, she took her feed without fuss. She even smiled, right from the moment she was born. She's always liked people.'

It was strange hearing my mother talking like this. I couldn't imagine her with babies, breast-feeding, changing nappies—it didn't connect with my concept of her. She was more interested in older children. She was longing for Joel to learn to read, so she could organise treasure hunts again. I suspected that she was hoarding clues, inventing them all the time and writing them down in a little book kept just for that purpose, waiting to bring them out at the right moment. Meanwhile, she had already rescued some old toys from an upstairs room and brought them down to entice him.

Andrew sorted through the box when he returned. 'They're filthy,' he said.

They were. Cleaning had never interested my

212

mother much and the toys had travelled a long way with the whole of Audlands as a playground. Dinky cars had driven along the flags of the kitchen floor, out into the courtyard, through the old stables, down to the lake. I hadn't been interested in dolls. When I did take one with me as I wandered through the house, I usually held it by one leg while its head bumped along behind me, battered and neglected. Harriet's dolls were in better condition. She understood about clothes and hairstyles.

'Joel will like the trains when he gets older,' said Andrew.

In one of the upstairs rooms my father had an impressive railway network laid out, with stations, points and signals, hills with tunnels going through the middle. He used to spend much of his spare time up there, mending, fixing, watching the trains as they ran parallel on different tracks for a while and then went their separate ways. Their tiny motors clicked and rattled like the real thing as they swept through their miniature landscape.

'My father won't let him near them,' I said.

My mother still didn't care about dirt. She'd been down on the kitchen floor next to Joel in his bouncy chair before we came outside.

'Boo!' she said as she popped her head round the corner of the table when he wasn't expecting it.

He ignored her completely and continued with his investigation of the tyres on a yellow AA van.

'You're no good at fun,' she said, straightening up. 'Just like your mother.'

*　　　*　　　*

When Joel was six months old Andrew found a job valeting cars, so for the first time I was alone with our son all day. I started to play the piano if he cried. I thought it might calm him, and if it didn't, at least I could drown out the screaming. I crashed my way through Beethoven sonatas, the more chords the better, and Joel would finally give up. He was showing signs of intelligence—he knew when he couldn't win.

Then Andrew came home early one day while I was playing and was furious. 'I don't want my son to be brainwashed,' he said.

'I'm not brainwashing him. Why shouldn't he learn to appreciate music?'

'My parents did that. Before I was born, they decided I was going to be a genius. They had to decide between music, mathematics and chess, and they chose music.'

'Chess?'

'That's what a lot of gifted children do, according to their book. *Nurture Your Genius*, it's called, by Ronald Kowalski. Australian. That man has a lot to answer for.'

'Why would anyone go for chess? It's not very useful.'

'This is not a philosophical discussion about the merits of chess. Just stop playing the piano.'

'I can't see why it means I'm brainwashing Joel.'

'Because they played music to me. Non-stop, while I was still in the womb.'

'I didn't know that.'

'There are lots of things you don't know.'

'But how can you be sure they really did it? It's not as if you can remember.'

'I just know,' he said, his voice solemn and

214

authoritative.

'You can't have been brainwashed,' I pointed out. 'You're not a musician any more.'

'I broke free,' he said. 'Best thing I ever did.'

If he hadn't broken free he might have finished his degree, gone on playing, earned some money. 'Anyway, Joel's older. It can't do him any harm.'

'Of course it can. He will do what he wants to do, not what we force upon him.'

'But what if he doesn't want to do anything?' I was terrified he would turn out like Andrew.

'He will. He's highly intelligent. You can tell that from his eyes. He's always so alert.'

I didn't agree. I thought that Joel didn't look at things properly, that he shielded his eyes from the larger world around him and concentrated on what was in front of him. He seemed to have decided that he only needed to know his immediate surroundings, to ascertain where everything was. Nothing else was relevant.

I went on playing the piano, but only when Andrew was out and I was sure he wouldn't be coming back for some time.

We bought a car, a pale blue Reliant Robin, which we were very proud of. Because it was a three-wheeler Andrew could drive it on his motorcycle licence, so we didn't have to wait for him to pass his test. We could park in tiny spaces, and it would never rust because it was made of fibreglass.

Now we could go out for expeditions, which pleased Andrew enormously. He never liked to be at home at the weekend, doing useful things like cutting grass and putting up shelves. If it was a sunny day, we went to Arley, on the River Severn, where we could have a picnic and walk along the river. The sun soaked into us, a peaceful, calming influence, and when we drove home we would be glowing with satisfaction.

On one of these occasions, when Joel was about fifteen months old, the weather forecast was wrong and we arrived to a chilly, overcast atmosphere. Andrew and I zipped up our jackets and I put an extra blanket round Joel in his pushchair before lifting the food basket out of the boot.

'Salmon sandwiches,' I said.

'You know I hate salmon,' said Andrew, huddled up on his folding chair.

He'd eaten them last time I'd made them.

I took one for myself. 'Have some coffee,' I said, pouring it from the flask. 'It'll warm you up.'

I gave Joel a sandwich, but he threw it back at me and started to grizzle. I put it away and gave him a biscuit.

'You're spoiling him,' said Andrew. 'He should have the sandwich.'

'Does it matter?'

'What do you mean? Of course it matters. He can't just pick and choose like that.'

You do, I thought. 'He's all right. He just likes some things more than others. Like all of us.'

But Andrew wanted to make an issue of it. 'Take that biscuit away from him. Give him back the sandwich.'

I laughed. 'You try it.'

'Do it.' His voice had become tight and hard. I was conscious of a family sitting a few yards away with their picnic lunch, chatting to each other.

'Shhh . . .' I said to Andrew, indicating the family with my eyes.

216

He turned his back on them. 'Don't tell me what to do,' he said loudly.

I said nothing and ate my sandwich.

'Well?' he said.

I looked at him.

'Are you going to take the biscuit away from him, or am I?'

By now Joel was halfway though the biscuit, a pink wafer, and his face was plastered with crumbs and a pink haze. He looked almost happy. 'Well, I'm not going to take it away,' I said.

Andrew got up, went over to the pushchair and pulled the biscuit out of Joel's hand. Joel looked at him in amazement for a couple of seconds, and then let out an indignant yell that must have attracted the attention of everyone else in the area. Andrew bent down and gave him the original sandwich. Joel studied it with contempt and threw it on the grass. Andrew picked it up and shoved it into Joel's mouth.

The noise was terrible.

'Stop it, Andrew,' I said. 'Everyone's looking.'

'I don't care about everyone else,' he snarled. 'They should mind their own business.'

'But I care.'

He turned to me, the skin stretched tightly over his cheekbones, his eyes darker than usual and crackling with rage. The charming, selfish, unreliable Andrew had gone and been replaced by an adult version of Joel.

He picked up the picnic basket with all its contents, grabbed Joel's biscuit, wrenched the sandwich from my hand and walked over to the river bank. He stood for a moment then flung the whole thing into the river. I watched it from where I was sitting. The basket hit the water with a loud plop, submerged and then came up again, circling in bewilderment, until it floated lazily away in the current, sinking as it went. My half-eaten sandwich drifted off on its own, the brown of the wholemeal bread blending with the murky brown of the water.

Joel's screams rent the air around us.

'Thank you,' I said. 'I like salmon sandwiches.'

'Let's get out of here,' he said. He stalked over to the car, got in and sat behind the steering wheel, glowering out of the windscreen.

I smiled at the people next to us and pretended that everything was normal. They tried to smile back, but only succeeded in looking worried. There was nothing I could say. I lifted Joel out of the pushchair and strapped him into his car seat. He was plastered with debris from the salmon sandwich, but by this time, fortunately, he had run out of breath, so there were a few moments of peace. I picked up the blanket, shook it out and shoved it on the back seat next to Joel. Then I folded up the pushchair and put it into the boot, while Andrew stared fixedly ahead as if I wasn't there.

I got in the car. 'It's just as well we're leaving,' I said, struggling to keep my voice steady. 'It's going to rain any minute now.'

We drove in silence. The rain started, and the wipers swished backwards and forwards. A tightness filled the car, an elastic band pulled so taut that it was in danger of breaking with an appalling, terrifying snap.

After half an hour, Andrew deflated. The elastic band slackened and the air became breathable

218

again. 'Sorry,' he said. He put his left hand gently on my knee. He might have wanted me to take it, but I didn't.

'I'll buy a new picnic basket tomorrow,' he said.

An enormous tiredness settled over me.

We drove home without another word.

CHAPTER FIFTEEN

Jessica's father pushed down a corner of the business section of the *Sunday Times* and peered through the gap at her, his eyes distant and unfocused. 'You'd better wear trousers today,' he said.

Jessica stopped pouring hot water into a mug of Nescafé and tried to find a context for this piece of advice. She couldn't recall a single time in all her fourteen years when her father had discussed clothes.

'Do hurry up, Jessica,' said her mother, who was removing all the plates from the table and carrying them to the sink to wash up.

'Leave my plate,' said Jessica. 'I haven't even started my toast.'

'Your cousins will be here any minute now.'

'Why do I have to wear trousers?'

'Now, don't start being awkward, darling,' said her mother.

'We're learning to drive today,' said Harriet.

Their father lowered the side of the *Sunday Times* again. 'Not you, Harriet. You're too young.'

Harriet set down the plates she was carrying with a sharp clatter and put her hands on her hips.

Jessica watched her with admiration, wondering how she found the courage to be so challenging. 'That's not fair. Colin is allowed to.'

'Is he?' Their father looked at their mother.

'I think he might be expecting to,' she said. 'You did rather give that impression last week.'

Jessica couldn't remember any of this conversation taking place. It must have been during a meal, since this was the only time anyone ever encountered her father. But Jessica didn't often listen to the discussions going on around her. Her mind was on Brahms or harmonic progressions or whether there would be enough treacle tart for her to have seconds.

She had recently started to play the violin, because they had told her at school that she needed a second instrument if she wanted to study music in the future. She was finding it difficult to get her fingers into the right position, but she was determined to persevere and spent several hours a day on it.

'It's a good thing we live in a big house,' said her father when she first came home with the violin.

'I like listening to you playing the piano,' said her mother.

Harriet just laughed. 'It sounds awful. Couldn't you try the flute?'

But Jessica didn't care and the hours of practice were beginning to have an effect. She was no longer grinding the bow and the sound was already less painful. In the last few weeks, she had worked her way through a pile of music passed on to her by a girl who had recently given up the violin. Jessica considered that she had more or less reached Grade Four, but didn't mention this to her teacher.

She thought he might be annoyed that she had gone ahead without his guidance.

'All right, Harriet,' said her father, folding up the paper and rising from the table. 'You can have a go at driving, providing you can reach the pedals.'

'Great,' said Harriet. 'I'll wear my pink dungarees, I think. Come on, Jess.'

'I don't want to,' said Jessica.

'Get a move on,' said her father. 'They'll be here soon.'

She swallowed her last mouthful of toast without chewing properly.

'Don't be long, girls,' called their mother. 'Philip won't want to hang around.'

Philip had been nagging Jessica's father to teach him to drive since he was five years old. His first word was 'car'. His own father, a non-driving, unmechanically minded man, who preferred to play golf and watch films, was no use at all. They lived near the station and he couldn't see the need for a car. Philip's mother eventually took responsibility for their transport, learning to drive when she was thirty-five and passing her test first time. She claimed it was skill. Everyone else assumed she had bribed the examiner.

Jessica's father had three cars that he kept in the old stables, round the back of the house. There was a silver E-type Jaguar that he used for work, gliding away in executive style every morning, and there was a blue Cortina, the family car. The third was a red Mini, which he spent a great deal of time tinkering with at weekends. When the weather was good enough and he wasn't rushing off to work, muttering about takeover bids, he went out and

221

raced the Mini round the grounds of Audlands. 'It needs to be driven regularly,' he would say at dinner. 'Otherwise the engine will seize up.'

* * *

'It's not fair,' said Judy, standing with her arms folded under the dripping horse chestnut trees. 'The others aren't old enough either, but you're letting them try.'

'I'm sorry, Judy,' said Jessica's father. 'Your mother said no.'

'It's far too dangerous,' said Philip.

'It's perfectly safe, but you need to be a certain age,' said Harriet.

'Eighteen,' said Judy. 'That's what the law says. And nobody here's eighteen.'

'Seventeen actually,' said Philip.

'Well, you're only fourteen.'

It was a dreary, overcast day. Sudden sharp gusts of wind carrying flurries of drizzle tugged at them every now and again. Jessica was cold and miserable standing there, huddled into her anorak, listening to her father lecture them. She wanted to go and do some violin practice.

Before anyone was allowed to drive the car they had to try changing gear, taking it in turns and leaving the doors open so that everyone else could see. Philip was first.

'Now let's get the seat in the right place for you to reach the clutch,' said Jessica's father.

Philip wasn't waiting for advice. He found the lever, fiddled with it, and his seat shot backwards, taking everyone by surprise. Colin let out a cheer.

Jessica was waiting for her father to get irritable,

but he was still reacting with care. 'Look here, old man. Let's just take it slowly, shall we? You won't be able to control the vehicle unless the seat is in the correct position. That's it. Now, the right foot is for the brake and the accelerator. Anyone know what the accelerator is for?'

Judy giggled loudly, and Jessica felt protective of her father. How was he to know what they all knew? Besides, although she was fairly sure that she understood about the accelerator, she didn't want to say so in case she was wrong. Philip lounged back in the driving seat and refused to answer. He rolled his eyes upwards, raising an eyebrow at Colin, who sniggered.

'It's the thing that makes the car move,' said Harriet at last.

Her father nodded and smiled at her. 'Well done. Did you get that, boys?'

Philip sat up and nodded vigorously. 'Right. For going faster, as well, I think.'

'Good boy.' Jessica held her breath. He sounded like the supply teachers from school who thought they were being encouraging, but just came over as patronising. She watched as Philip and Colin exchanged glances and grinned at each other like conspirators.

Her father looked confused. 'Perhaps you'd like to share the source of your amusement with us?'

'Sorry,' said Philip. 'It was a private joke.'

They spent some time changing gears, one at a time, until they could all do it easily. The boys grew bored as soon as they had had their turns. 'When can we actually drive?' asked Philip.

'I will teach you in good time,' said Jessica's father. 'If you're not prepared to do it my way, wait until you're seventeen and pay for driving lessons.'

'All right,' said Philip. 'I was only asking.'

He and Colin wandered off to the edge of the trees while they waited. Jess watched them out of the corner of her eye as they mooched together, heads down, hands in pockets. Every now and again they scuffled in the loose earth round the base of the tree trunks, scattering dead leaves, kicking an exposed root.

Philip had grown rapidly in the last two years, and he moved with an adult confidence, his manner relaxed and controlled. He talked with a sophisticated politeness, adopting a world-weary, witty approach to life that Jessica admired.

Colin was a different build, solid and heavy, a natural rugby player with thick legs. He was a follower and imitated Philip's behaviour, good or bad. Aunt Cathy was forever shouting at them, but they always reacted with a carefully constructed indifference.

'Did you hear something?' Philip would ask Colin after one of her outbursts.

'It was nothing,' said Colin. 'Rabbits, I think.'

'Run rabbit, run rabbit, run, run, run.'

'Hop rabbit, hop rabbit, hop, hop, hop. Here comes Mr McGregor.'

Jessica's mother was no help to Cathy. She just laughed. 'Hop along, boys. It's lettuce for dinner.'

She and the boys would trade jokes so fast that no one else could keep up with them.

'Why did the rabbit cross the road?'

'Because the chicken got squashed by a passing car and someone had to fetch the eggs.'

'Because the grass was greener on the other side.'

'Why shouldn't it? There aren't any laws about which side rabbits can go.'

Cathy would get more furious, and they would all laugh harder. Jessica laughed with them, because she longed to be part of it, wanting to appreciate Philip's jokes, even if she didn't understand them. But she knew that her mother was getting it right and she was not. They were a magic circle, a privileged club where she would never be admitted.

'OK,' called her father. 'Let's get on with it. You first, Philip.'

Philip instantly stopped kicking the old conker he was using for a football and looked across. 'Am I going to drive it now?' He attempted to be nonchalant, but Jessica could hear the high-pitched note of anticipation in his voice.

'Yes. This is your chance. Come on, get a move on.'

Philip sprinted the short distance from the trees, jumped into the driving seat and slammed the door. Jessica's father was still standing outside the passenger door. 'Now watch how he does it,' he said to everyone else. 'See if you can learn from his mistakes.'

Philip had already turned on the ignition, so Jessica's father had to shout to make himself heard. 'Stand well back. We don't want to have an accident.' He climbed in and shut the door.

They watched as Philip tried to pull away, edging forward in a series of spasmodic jerks, almost stalling several times, but just managing to recover.

'Oh dear,' said Harriet. 'Daddy won't be very happy with that.'

225

'He's bringing up the clutch too quickly,' said Judy. 'It needs to be gradual.'

The car stabilised as he found a higher gear and headed down the drive, swinging wildly from side to side. The engine shrieked in protest.

'Rabbits,' yelled Colin and started to run after it, whooping with pleasure, leaping into the undergrowth on the side of the drive when the car swung too close to him. They could see Jessica's father inside, waving his hands around, warning Colin away. The car bounced in and out of the potholes, with Philip clearly struggling to change gear. It disappeared as it turned the corner and headed for the gates at the far end of the drive.

Once the car was out of sight, the sound of the engine stopped abruptly.

'Do you think he's crashed it?' said Harriet.

'No,' said Judy. 'They're just turning round.'

She was right. In a few seconds the car reappeared, slithering around like a drunken caterpillar. Philip had still not managed to work out how to change gear smoothly and steer the car at the same time.

Jessica, Harriet and Judy scattered in a panic as the Mini headed directly towards them and ploughed into the grass on the side of the drive. It skidded to an abrupt halt, leaving a long trail of mud in its wake.

Philip emerged from the car with a great cry of delight. 'I did it! I did it!'

Jessica's father climbed out in a more leisurely fashion and strode over to where the girls were standing. He looked pale and Jessica could see a fat drop of sweat sliding down his nose. Colin raced back up and joined them, panting, his breath visible in the chilly air. 'Well done!' he shouted.

'Over here, Philip,' said Jessica's father.

Philip joined the others and they stood in a semicircle, facing the Mini. Philip seemed to have grown taller and wider, and he was glowing with pride at his achievement. A smile kept sneaking on to his face. He would catch it as it threatened to take over, making himself serious for a few seconds until it crept up on him again.

Jessica's father walked up and down in front of them without speaking, taking about five strides, then swinging on his left heel and turning round, ready to pace back again. A rim of mud was accumulating on his left shoe. The children watched in silence, aware that he was not pleased, uncertain of what he expected from them.

'Is the brake on the right or the left?' he demanded, coming to an abrupt halt in front of Philip.

'Middle,' said Philip.

'And how many times did we go over that before we got in the car?'

Philip looked thoughtful. 'I would guess about five times,' he said eventually. 'No, six.'

Jessica's father put his face close to Philip's and stared into his eyes. For all his bravado, Philip couldn't hold the gaze. His eyes shifted away to the side.

'Ten times,' said Jessica's father with absolute conviction. 'I deliberately said it ten times. I counted them.' He stopped and faced Colin. 'Which pedal do you use for the brake?'

'Ten,' said Colin, looking pleased with himself.

'Middle,' said Harriet.

Her father scowled. 'I was asking Colin, not

you.'

'Sorry.' She sank back into line.

He relaxed. 'Right. It is imperative that everyone here understands where the brake is. Why do you think that would be the case?'

Harriet put her hand up.

'Harriet?'

'So that we can stop the car.'

'Yes! Because if we want to drive a car, what is the most important thing that we need to know?'

'How to stop it,' said Colin.

Jessica's father nodded. 'Good lad,' he said. 'OK, Jessica. Your turn.'

Jessica froze. She studied the ground and pretended that she hadn't heard him. She could feel the heat rising in her head, pressure building up, a band tightening round her temples.

'Come on, Jessica.' Her father turned towards the car, which appeared to be embedded firmly and permanently in the grass.

'No,' she said. 'I don't really want to.'

'Don't be absurd,' he said.

Jessica hesitated and then followed him, hating to turn her back on the others. She could feel their eyes on her, seeing through her skin, observing her imperfect blood whizzing through enlarged veins. In her mind her body was swelling, too enormous, too awkward to walk normally. Every movement was magnified a hundred times and she bounced with a jarring lack of rhythm every time she took a step.

'Can't Colin go next?' she asked, but her voice didn't come out as she intended and she only produced a breathless squeak, which her father ignored.

'Wait there,' he said to her as he walked over the grass and climbed into the car. He turned on the ignition and revved up the engine, the warm, powerful sound echoing along the drive, challenging the chill of the hostile wind. He reversed the car off the grass in one dramatic sweep and manoeuvred it until it was facing in the direction of the gates. Then he got out, leaving the door open. 'Get in,' he told Jessica and walked round to the passenger side.

She climbed in and sat looking at the steering wheel.

'Shut the door, dummy,' called Colin from the edge of the drive.

Blushing, she leaned for the door, but the handle was too far away and she couldn't reach it. She had to stand up and pull it closer before getting back in. Then she shut the door. It slammed harshly and enclosed her in the small space with her father.

'Right,' he said. 'We're heading for the gates. We should have time to get up to fourth gear, and then you brake.' He leaned out of the window and raised his voice. 'Which pedal do you need for the brake, Philip?'

Philip pretended he hadn't heard.

'Middle,' called Colin.

'Good man.'

Jessica touched the steering wheel. Philip had been here only a few minutes ago, letting the same wheel slide through his hands. She grasped it more firmly, feeling its smooth texture, conscious of its latent power.

'Turn the ignition on.'

She turned the key and the engine roared

instantly into life.

'Clutch down, into first gear. Ready with the accelerator. Rev her up a bit. Now lift the clutch ... gently ...'

And they were off. Slowly, slowly, but under control. Very smooth. *Legatissimo*.

'Good girl,' said her father in her ear. 'Now clutch down, into second, ease it up again.'

It was extraordinary. She could do it. The drive was being swallowed up behind them as they cruised towards the gates, sliding easily into fourth gear. Now it was *Allegro*.

'We're going to slow down now. Foot on the brake—gently, gently ...'

It worked, a long, gradual *rallentando* with a *diminuendo*, until the engine faded into almost silence and they were stationary, facing the gates. Her father looked unusually pleased. 'Well done, Jessica,' he said.

They both got out, and then he turned the car round. 'OK, let's see if you can do it as well on the way back.'

She drove back, elated, conscious of the speed of the car and the vibration of the engine. She concentrated on the clutch and the gear changes, feeling the forward movement, confident that small adjustments of the steering wheel would keep her on the drive.

She glanced across at her father, and he turned to smile at her with a generosity that she had never seen directed at her before.

She looked forward again and froze.

'Look out!' shouted her father.

Philip was directly in front of her with his back to the car, bending over and waggling his bottom at them. His face appeared between his legs, with his tongue stuck out, so close that she could see the distortion that came from being upside down. The plumpness of his cheeks hanging down, making his eyes small and squashed. The holes of his nose pointing upwards and his blond hair flopping like a ragged curtain of straw.

Time slowed and stretched as she tried to work out what to do. She couldn't turn to the right, because Harriet, Judy and Colin were standing there, mesmerised into an appalled audience. She had to turn to the left, although the trees came closer to the road on that side. But before she could act, her father leaned over and grabbed the steering wheel. Jessica slammed her foot on to the brake, still aware that it mustn't be too hard in case they went through the windscreen.

They swung to the left and plunged into the grass, sweeping aside mud and fallen leaves for some distance. A loud bang reverberated through the body of the car and Jessica had an impression of Philip flying past the side window.

She and her father were thrown forward, then back against their seats. There was a moment of silence while they struggled to breathe, then they leapt out of the car simultaneously, racing towards the body lying in the undergrowth behind them. Colin, Judy and Harriet were running up the drive, Judy shrieking, 'Philip, Philip!'

Jessica arrived there first, having run faster than she had ever run in her life. She bent over his still body, and suddenly didn't want to touch him. She searched anxiously for blood, but couldn't see any. She sank down beside him, wondering what to do.

Her father arrived. 'Philip, old man, are you

badly hurt?' Jessica looked up at him and, with a painful flash of insight, saw that he didn't know what to do either.

The others ran up. Tears were pouring down Judy's cheeks, her nose running messily. Harriet was the one who acted with presence of mind. She grabbed Philip's body and pulled him over. 'He's dead,' she cried. 'He must be. He's not breathing.'

But he was breathing. His chest moved slightly, then faster and faster until he started to shake.

'Shock,' said Jessica's father.

It wasn't shock. It was laughter, and it burst out miraculously, great hoots of raucous laughter, ringing out around them. They watched him, bewildered, nobody able to respond.

'Fooled you,' he said, between hysterical gasps. 'You thought you'd got me, didn't you, Jess?'

Jessica had thought this. Now she didn't know how to behave. Relief, apologies, embarrassment? She remained sitting, staring at him, unable to move.

Harriet was furious. She grabbed Philip's jacket and started pulling it from side to side, rocking his body, making his head roll backwards and forwards. 'How dare you? How stupid can you get? I thought you were dead!'

He finally calmed down. 'I bet you're glad to see I'm not, though, aren't you, Harriet? And I bet Jess is, too. She could have been done for manslaughter.'

Jessica sat on the ground beside Philip, hunched into a frozen crouch, conscious of the fact that she couldn't feel anything. Everything around her seemed unusually still, and although she could hear Harriet shouting she couldn't make sense of

232

what was going on. She could feel drizzle falling on the top of her head, and she was aware that her foot was bent awkwardly underneath her and was losing sensation.

Her father started to react. He grabbed Philip by one arm and pulled him into a sitting position. 'I cannot believe your behaviour. What did you hope to gain from it? Suppose Jessica hadn't been as good a driver as she was and she had really run you down? What would your mother have said?'

But Philip seemed unwilling or unable to take any of it seriously. He was laughing again, gulping for air, howling with mirth, and Colin caught it from him, because he started to laugh as well. They both sat there in the long grass shaking with giggles.

'When you hit the car with your fist,' stammered Colin. 'It was brilliant—'

'Lunch is ready!'

Connie had appeared at the entrance to Audlands. She was wearing a green Crimplene dress with a little white collar and huge buttons down the front and knee-length cream boots. She looked about eighteen years old, with her long plait and pale, almost white lipstick.

She saw them all crouched on the grass, and when they didn't move, descended the steps and came over to see what was going on. She didn't fit into the scene. A sunny smile in the midst of a funeral, a nursery rhyme wandering by mistake into Verdi's *Requiem*.

'Didn't you hear?' she said. Then she saw Philip sitting on the ground. 'Is everything all right? Is Philip ill?'

'No,' said Jessica's father, getting up. 'Philip

233

isn't ill. He's a complete idiot, and if he ever, ever does that again I shall no longer allow him on to my property.'

He went over to the Mini, shut the doors and locked them. Then he turned his back on all of them and walked towards the house.

'Philip,' said Connie, bending over him. 'Are you all right?'

Philip grinned at her. 'I'm fine, Auntie Connie.'

She ruffled his blond hair. 'Whatever's the matter with your uncle?'

As they walked back towards the house Harriet started to explain all the details in a shrill, urgent voice. Philip accompanied Judy. She was recovering rapidly, dancing alongside him as he chatted to her. Colin ran ahead. 'Rabbits!' he shouted.

Jessica stayed where she was, watching them climb the steps to the front door. She was still shaking, but she couldn't work out what had shocked her more. The belief that Philip was dead, or the realisation that her father, who should have been the adult, the authority, had been paralysed with fear.

CHAPTER SIXTEEN

'So did everyone have a go at the driving?' asked Connie, smiling at Roland while she handed him the mint sauce. She had understood from Harriet's rushed account that something had gone wrong, but the details were not at all clear. The Royal Worcester gravy boat shone in the dim electric light and serving spoons clinked against china. Everything was under control and civilised. 'It wasn't the best weather for it, was it?'

'No,' said Roland.

'A bit slippery underfoot, or under the tyres, I imagine.'

'Yes.'

For a while, nobody said anything and concentrated on eating. The food was not quite as hot as it should have been, because Connie always insisted on Sunday lunch in the dining room and it was a long way to carry everything from the kitchen. She'd asked Roland to make a fire, and weak flames flickered, moderately enthusiastic, between the two half-naked Greek maidens with protruding stomachs who supported the fireplace. Connie liked real fires. They reminded her of mellow autumn mists and the nights drawing in. Roland thought electric fires were easier, but she was adamant. 'A real fire is cosy, more natural, warmer.'

'Messier,' said Roland. 'You have to clear it out afterwards.' But he did it. To please her.

There were nine people grouped round the centre of the long mahogany table which Connie had found at the back of one of the stables when they first moved to Audlands. She had spent hours polishing this table, convinced it was a Hepplewhite, but hadn't managed to eliminate the scratches.

Cathy's husband, Charles, who was an accountant, was dining with them today. He was a quiet man who moved with great care, making sure his elbows were always in the right place, his feet lined up exactly, his hands still and contained. He

235

didn't fit in well with the Fontaines.

'How was the driving, Philip?' he asked.

'I was brilliant,' said Philip.

'Rabbits,' said Colin with contempt. And they both dissolved into giggles.

'Boys,' said Cathy, her dangling amber earrings shivering with indignation. 'Manners. People don't know what you're laughing about.'

'I trust you didn't run anyone over,' said Connie.

'No,' said Colin, 'but Jess did.'

'I didn't,' said Jessica. 'It wasn't my fault.'

Connie stopped eating. 'Does that mean you did run someone over?'

There was a moment of silence and then the boys burst out laughing. 'So what happened?' asked Connie, smiling and waiting.

'I've already explained it, Mummy,' said Harriet. 'Philip was just messing around, that's all.'

Roland looked up, frowning. 'I wouldn't call it messing around,' he said. 'I'd call it behaving like an idiot.'

'Philip,' said Cathy, 'have you been annoying Uncle Roland again?'

'I still don't get how you did it,' said Harriet. 'One minute you were standing there in front of the car and the next minute you were somewhere else completely.'

'I'm an athlete,' said Philip. 'I can jump. Very high and very fast.'

'How did you get on, Jessica?' asked Connie.

Roland's expression softened. 'Jessica was superb. An absolute natural.'

A tiny, secret smile crept its way into Jessica's eyes and almost to her lips. She put her head down quickly, her face flushed.

236

'Goodness,' said Connie. 'We've found something you can do, Jessica.'

'Don't underestimate her,' said Roland, getting up.

'Don't you want any pudding?' said Connie. 'It's apple and blackberry crumble. Your favourite.'

'What makes you think it's my favourite? I eat it because it's there. We get it at least four times a week,' he said to Cathy, who was always transparently delighted when he attacked Connie.

'That's a lie,' said Connie.

'I'm off to watch the cricket,' he said. 'I shall savour the last remnants of civilisation.'

He left the room, picking up an apple from the sideboard as he went past.

'Well,' said Connie. 'What a lot of nonsense he talks when we have visitors.'

'I'm glad to hear he's not always like that,' said Cathy, lifting her fork to her mouth.

'You mustn't take him seriously,' said Connie. 'He doesn't mean it.'

'Jess was brilliant,' said Harriet. 'She changed gear really smoothly, and you should have seen her emergency stop.'

Jessica kept her head down.

'Philip changed gear smoothly too,' said Colin, 'but he was experimenting a bit. You know, seeing what the car could do.'

'Oh yes?' said Harriet. 'I thought he couldn't control it.'

'You're just jealous,' said Judy, 'because you didn't have a go.'

*   *   *

237

After lunch, Jessica went to her room and settled herself on a stool, hugging her knees and studying the old fir tree outside her window. Clusters of needles hung limply, in sympathy with the grey, drizzled mist. Its spindly trunk was bent with age, and the branches were thin and sparse. The tree reflected the weather. Violent winds would send it into a paroxysm of fury, yet branches never came off and the needles remained firmly in place. It accepted rain stoically, drooping with the weight of the water, but willing to spring back up at the first opportunity, and in a heatwave the needles remained green and sharp in contrast with the surrounding brown grass.

Jessica put a record on and concentrated on the Brandenburg concertos. The chuntering Baroque semiquavers were in tune with a movement inside her that she didn't understand. Agitation, a hammering of thoughts too fast for her to grasp. She kept hearing her father's words: *Jessica was superb*.

Eventually, she settled on her bed with *The Grapes of Wrath*. She was working her way through Steinbeck, having read *Of Mice and Men* for school. She ignored the untidiness of her room, and curled up on the blue candlewick bedspread. Above her, nymphs flitted across the painted ceiling, depicting the four seasons. She'd spent much of her childhood lying on her back, unable to sleep, watching each nymph roll back the curtains of spring, summer, autumn, winter. She liked winter best. Snow, icicles, white fur wrapped round the nymph's shapely shoulders, while the rest of her body remained exposed to the elements.

There was a knock on the door.

238

For a moment she thought she'd imagined it. Then it came again. She jumped to her feet, confused, and turned off the record player. Her parents never came near the room and Harriet was playing table tennis with Judy. She could hear their voices, shrill and determined in the distance as they argued about points.

Jessica tried to say 'Come in', but her voice wouldn't work properly, so she went to the door and opened it.

Philip was outside.

She stared at him.

'Can I come in?' he said.

She didn't know what to say. She couldn't understand why he was there. She was only conscious of a desperate need not to let him see the untidiness of her room.

But he didn't wait for an answer, stepping forward so she was forced to move back. He walked to the middle of the room and looked around with amusement. 'My mother would describe this as the aftermath of Hiroshima,' he said.

She found the courage to look at him. 'I was going to do it this afternoon.'

'I thought you'd have a four-poster bed.'

'Don't be silly,' she said, and allowed herself a small giggle.

He smiled at her and sat down on the edge of her bed, his long legs stretched out in front of him. 'Lucky you,' he said. 'You couldn't swing a cat in my room.'

He sounded friendly and relaxed, and Jessica started to breathe more easily. 'I know your bedroom. We used to play Monopoly there.'

'You're right. I seem to remember Colin always won. We must do it again. We had some good times, didn't we?'

Did they? Mostly they had argued about money, or accused each other of cheating, or had tantrums when they landed on Mayfair and lost all their money.

She didn't know what to do with herself. Philip was leaning back and testing the bounce of the bed. She tried to fold her arms, which were swinging down as if they were too long and getting in the way, but then she felt too formal and let them hang loose again.

'You need a new mattress,' he said. 'Can't you sit down? You make me feel crowded.'

The stool was too far away, over by the window, and there was nowhere else to sit except on the bed. So she sat down next to him, rigidly upright with her hands placed on her knees, and stared ahead, not wanting to turn towards him.

'Come on, Jess,' he said in a gentle voice that she remembered vividly. It came from the time when they'd played tennis two years ago, when he'd comforted the injured Judy. 'You're always having a go at me. Why can't we be friends?'

'It wasn't my fault that I nearly ran you over,' she said.

'I've come to apologise.'

She was so surprised that she turned to look at him. She'd never heard Philip apologise for anything.

'I shouldn't have done it. I thought it would give us all a good laugh.'

'No, you shouldn't have done it.'

'See? You're always wanting to score points.

240

Why can't you just relax a bit and stop wanting to make everything my fault?'

She didn't know how to reply to this. Did he really blame her for his unpleasantness? She'd tried to be nice to him. She still liked him, his suntanned legs, his clear, finely carved features, his blond hair. She could feel herself trembling at his proximity on the bed. She could smell him, see the hairs curling on his arms, hear his breathing.

He picked up her book. '*The Grapes of Wrath*? They tried to make us read this at school, but I thought it was boring. Shakespeare was better. More action, more blood, more death.' He laughed, and she laughed nervously with him.

He put out an arm and rested it on her shoulders. 'Come on, Jess, relax. We're cousins, we've known each other for years. We should be able to get on.'

'We do get on,' she said, but it was breathed so softly that he couldn't hear her.

'What did you say?'

'Nothing,' she said.

'Yes you did. Come on, tell me.' He leaned over, placing his ear in front of her mouth, and she could see its whorls, a dash of white downy hair on the outer edge, a trace of wax further in. She pulled away and they both fell backwards on to the bed. He laughed softly, moving towards her. She struggled to get up, but he pushed her down again, and then he was trying to tickle her, his hands groping round her stomach, his fingers rough and intrusive. She pushed him away. He lay back for a minute, looking at the ceiling. 'Don't you like being tickled?' he asked in a puzzled voice.

'No.' She raised herself on to her elbow, but he

241

pulled at her arm so that it collapsed, and she fell down next to him again. She could smell his heat, his breathing, his sweat. They were sour and primitive, choking her.

Then, suddenly he was on top of her again, his mouth against hers, trying to kiss her. She was confused, paralysed with fear. His kiss was clumsy but strong, his face pressing down against hers, his tongue forcing its way into her mouth. She could taste his saliva, feel his teeth grating against hers, and she couldn't breathe. His weight was slowly suffocating her and she began to sink down into the bed, knowing she had no defence against his strength.

Then, just as suddenly, he broke away and rolled to the side of the bed, breathing heavily. She didn't move, didn't give any reaction. He propped himself on one arm and started to stroke her head.

'Your hair is beautiful, Jess,' he said, picking up her plait and using it to wipe sweat away from his face. She could see the black mass of her own hair as if it didn't belong to her. It glistened with the grease of his sweat and, deep inside, her stomach curled up with disgust. She tried to remain completely still, as if she was no longer alive. The smell of him was overwhelming and frightening.

'Come on, let's have another kiss.' He bent over her again, his hand moving towards her mouth, turning her face towards him.

A taste of sickness rose in her throat. 'No,' she said, struggling to get up. 'No.' She could feel panic giving her strength and she pushed his hand away. 'Get off!'

'Jess—'

She jabbed at his arm with her fingernails,

taking him by surprise so that he fell back, giving her the chance to try and stand up.

But he grabbed her, pulling her down again with a lazy, effortless strength. 'Don't ever do that to me again, Jess.' His voice was calm and quiet. 'I go out of my way to offer you something good and you reject it. You've just been leading me on, haven't you?'

His smell became hotter. A layer of sweat shone across his cheeks, his brow, his nose. He took her left hand and held it tightly. She tried to sit up, but he yanked her arm backwards, away from her and she couldn't get her balance.

'Oh, look,' he said. 'Fingers.'

She didn't understand what he was doing. He started to pull each finger in turn. 'Do you know the rhyme about the pigs? Or better still, rabbits. "This little rabbit went to market, this little rabbit stayed at home."' He was pulling at each of her fingers in turn. ' "This little rabbit ate roast beef, this little rabbit had none, and this little rabbit . . ."'

He was holding her little finger.

'This little rabbit went wee, wee, weee . . .'

He was pulling it backwards, further and further.

'Aah!' She cried out with the pain.

'All the way home.'

It snapped.

He got up, straightened his shirt and turned towards the door. 'Don't tease me again, Jess,' he said. 'I don't like it. If you can't be friendly, keep out of my way.'

And he left the room.

*   *   *

Later in the afternoon, after Cathy and the children had left, Connie returned to her upholstery project with a sigh of relief. She'd been attending classes at the local adult education centre, and had four reproduction Chippendale chairs that she wanted to restore. She had measured out the material—maroon and cream stripes—and was poised to cut when Jessica came into the room.

'Could we talk later, darling? I'm so worried I'll cut this material wrong, and then I'll have to start all over again. There's barely enough for all four chairs.'

'I've hurt my finger.'

'Have you, dear? You know where the plasters are. Oh, there may not be any left. Your father had the last one the other day when he tried talking to that stray cat. He really should be more careful. I know we don't have rabies in this country, but even so.'

Jessica didn't go away.

'Well, run along, darling. I must concentrate.'

Jessica put her hand out. 'Look.'

Connie looked and shrieked. The little finger on Jessica's left hand was jutting out at an awkward angle, dark, swollen and bruised. Connie stood up and grabbed her hand. Jessica drew in her breath sharply.

'Good heavens, Jessica, how in the world did you do that?'

Jessica looked at the floor. 'I don't know.'

'You don't know?' Her mother grabbed her hand and examined the finger in more detail. 'How

244

can you possibly not know?'

'It must have been when I fell over down by the lake.'

'When did you fall over?'

'After lunch.'

Irrational fury swept through Connie. 'Why didn't you tell me at the time? How am I supposed to help when I have no idea what's going on?'

Jessica looked past her, out of the window, her face tight and pale, revealing nothing.

'Well, you'll have to have it X-rayed. I'll get your father to take you in the car.'

At the hospital they confirmed it was broken and decided eventually that they would have to operate to set the bone back into the right position. They kept her in overnight.

Connie suspected it was something to do with the driving episode. 'What really happened?' she asked Roland when he had returned from the hospital.

'I've no idea,' he said. 'She was fine when we came in for lunch.'

'Are you sure?'

'I think we'd have noticed. She wouldn't have been able to manipulate a knife and fork.'

'Did you actually look at her?'

'Did you?'

'But she can't have done it by falling over, can she?'

He shrugged. 'Who knows? You can't tell with these teenagers. They're always up to something and don't tell you.'

'I still don't really understand what went wrong with the driving. You were so angry when you came in.'

'Was I? I can't remember.'

Connie struggled to keep her temper. 'For goodness' sake, Roland, it was only this morning, and you were furious.'

'No,' he said. 'I don't get furious. I'm even-tempered. They admire me for that at work. That's why we're so successful.'

Connie sat down and turned on the television. She was so irritated with Roland that she couldn't speak. She sat watching the news, jiggling her leg up and down, not taking anything in. She hated not being kept informed about things.

Suddenly, she felt Roland's hand on her leg. 'Look,' he said. 'It was nothing. Philip stood in front of the car when Jessica drove back. It was a stupid joke. We thought she'd run him down.'

She stopped jiggling and put her hand over his, stroking his fingers lightly. They were smooth and pale, coated by a sparse layer of silky hair. The hands of a man who didn't do manual work. 'But she didn't run him down?'

'What do you think?'

'So how did she break the finger?'

He sighed and withdrew his hand. 'I have no idea.'

'She needs that finger, Roland. For the music.'

He picked up the paper and turned to the crossword. 'Mmm,' he said.

*   *   *

Jessica spent an anxious four weeks not knowing if the injury would affect her violin and piano playing. She practised right-hand scales and arpeggios, worked out difficult chords in some

246

Chopin preludes, read her way through Steinbeck.

Her finger healed properly, although it was several weeks more before her playing was back to its original level. She stayed up late every night, making up for lost time.

Whenever Philip came to Audlands she retired to her bedroom and moved the bed across the door. He never came to find her again.

CHAPTER SEVENTEEN

'It can't have been Joshua at the concert,' says Isolde. 'He's homeless. How could he possibly afford to dress up in a dinner jacket and go to expensive concerts?' She's sitting behind the library counter, handing over piles of books for me to replace on the shelves. We're talking in low, confidential voices. 'It was probably someone who just looked like him.'

'No,' I say. 'It was him.'

'And why would he have a woman with him?'

'Why shouldn't he?'

'How did you manage to see him at all, Jess? You're not normally that observant.'

'I'm improving,' I say.

Mrs Jenkins, who comes in every Wednesday morning at half past ten precisely to select three large-print romantic novels, shuffles up behind me to get the books stamped. She's holding *Jebb Thursday's Return*, *The Rhythm of the Tide* and *Amelia's Secret*. Gripping the desk for support, she drops the three books in front of Isolde. Her hands have an alarming tremble, fluttering in perpetual

247

motion as she waits for the books to be stamped. I look at her flimsy hair, the blue-spotted veins standing out on the back of her hands, her thin mouth, and wonder what kind of satisfaction she gains from these books. Does she see herself as the heroine, falling passionately into her lover's arms?

'There's no need to take all day,' says Mrs Jenkins.

'Well, the good news is,' says Isolde, stamping the books cheerfully, 'it'll all be done in thirty seconds.'

Maybe something inside Mrs Jenkins is still only twenty years old, and she forgets the wrinkles and the deterioration by not looking into a mirror. Maybe she remains young and tender in her mind, waiting for the right man to appear. Maybe it's just nostalgia.

I have never understood nostalgia. Gilded youth. The best years of your life. To be young is to be alive. What is there in a young person's life that is more desirable than maturity? The awkwardness, the not knowing, the cringing shame of getting things wrong? I like being older. My mind works better now.

'I can't see why this library needs two librarians,' says Mrs Jenkins.

I help put the books in her bag, avoiding her gaze.

Isolde smiles at her. 'Jessica's only part-time. It's not as bad as it looks.'

Mrs Jenkins's face remains hard and inflexible as she limps out of the library on her swollen feet. The books swing in a string bag hanging from the side of her walking frame. Her son waits for her in his car round the corner.

Isolde refuses to watch her exit. 'That's what my work's all about,' she says. 'Bringing a ray of sunshine into the life of lonely, unhappy people. Teaching them to smile.'

'Are you reading *Pollyanna*?' I say.

'Ask Joshua about the concert when he comes in,' she says. 'That should clear it up.'

I don't want to ask him. 'What if I've got it wrong?'

'Then he'll say so.'

'But he might think I'm implying that he should be attending concerts. Especially mine.'

'Watch for clues,' she says. 'See if he betrays any signs of being a classical music lover. Does he hum *Eine Kleine Nachtmusik* every now and again? Does he tap his fingers rhythmically as if he's hearing a tune in his head?'

A few minutes later Joshua ambles past us, treading softly on his down-at-heel trainers. He nods at me, giving no sign that our exchange of glances means anything more than usual. He heads for the computers.

*   *   *

At lunchtime, I hover by the entrance before leaving. Isolde joins me.

'What's the matter?' she says. 'Don't you want to go home?'

'No,' I say. 'Joel's girlfriend is coming for supper and I don't want to think about what to cook.'

'Joel has a girlfriend?'

'Didn't I tell you?' I know I haven't told her. I've been trying to see how long I can hold out without letting on. It's a test. I want to believe that I can

249

resist Isolde's curiosity, but the excitement is too great. 'Fiancée, actually.'

Her eyes widen. 'Jess! This is wonderful.'

It might be wonderful, but I'm not allowing myself to think about the implications. I would like to consider the pleasure of going home to an empty house, the airy sensation of space, freedom from the obligation to cook every day, but it seems unwise to contemplate it yet. Alice might be unsuitable. 'Well—we'll have to see.'

'What's she like?'

'I've no idea. This is the first time he's brought her home.'

'Joel is engaged and you haven't met her?'

I laugh. 'That's Joel for you.'

'Make a curry. Everybody eats curry.'

I've been thinking that myself, but for some reason it doesn't feel right. I'd be sending the wrong message. Too easy, too predictable. 'No, I'd prefer to do some kind of casserole.' I don't want Alice to think I lack imagination.

'Good idea. You can make some salad, get some French bread and it's ready in no time. They'll love it.'

How does she know? She has no more information about Alice than I have, and she's never even met Joel. 'Thanks for the advice,' I say.

But she doesn't want to let me go. 'Did you ask Joshua?'

I shake my head. 'He seems too unapproachable.'

'But that's ridiculous. How are we ever going to find out if it was him? I'd really like to know if he's a closet music lover and what other concerts he goes to.'

'He must be a man of taste,' I say. 'He picks his concerts with discernment.'

'I still don't know how he could afford it.'

'We don't know he's homeless. He's never actually said so.'

'But he looks as if he is,' she says. You can tell from the clothes.'

'Maybe he has two sets of clothes. One for concerts, one for every day.'

'It seems a bit unbalanced.'

I stop trying to guess and head for Marks & Spencer's.

*   *   *

After preparing the lamb casserole, I leave it simmering in the oven and go to the piano. I select Schumann's 'Of Strange Lands and Peoples', and wait for a few seconds to prepare the atmosphere internally before placing my hands on the keys and starting to play. Strange lands. Places we can explore alone, the private land of the mind. I once saw a concert on television, when the Russian pianist, Horowitz, came out of retirement to give a concert in Moscow. He hunched over the piano, his fingers gnarled and bent and he played 'Traumerie', also from *Scenes from Childhood*. Dreams. The music is easy to play, nothing technically demanding, no frenetic semiquavers, no crashing climaxes, just a straightforward tune accompanied by chords. But while he played, the camera focused on the audience. They were motionless, as if they were all holding their breath. Nobody coughed, not even a hand fluttered. A single tear rolled down the face of an old man. The power of music. Simple, quiet, moving.

I wait for a while after I've finished, listening to the last echoes, the tune still in my mind, then get up reluctantly to clean the house. I'm vacuuming with unaccustomed zeal when I see a taxi pull up outside the house.

They're early. I can't entertain them for a couple of hours until supper's ready. My mind races through possible activities to pass the time— Scrabble, Monopoly, three-handed whist—when Harriet steps down out of the taxi. I try to make myself invisible by standing back a few paces from the window, and watch her. She talks to the driver for a while, laughing with abandon, gesticulating with such animation that I can only assume she's telling him some long anecdote about her life. The driver seems to be talking with equal enthusiasm. They look as if they've known each other for ever. How does she do it? If I take a taxi, the driver can't understand my directions unless I show him on the *A–Z*.

Harriet runs down the garden path and I go to open the front door.

'Jess!' she cries. 'Are you going to be in for the next hour? Can I visit you?'

'You know you don't have to ask.'

She runs back to the taxi and pays him. He's still grinning while he drives off.

'I'll make some coffee,' I say when she returns.

As we stand in the kitchen side by side, looking out over my small back garden, it feels as if we hardly know each other. We're not connected in the way that sisters should be, even though we're related. Harriet has never been here before. She wouldn't come when I was married because she

252

didn't want to meet Andrew. We never discussed it. She just avoided him. And since he left, she's always been so busy, only returning briefly, rushing around her social circle in the area, renewing her friendship with Audlands. I'm pleased to see her now she's here, but we're almost strangers.

'How are you getting on at Audlands?' I ask. 'Running out of things to do?'

'I tried to get Mum and Dad to go out for the day—you know, to Warwick or somewhere like that—but they won't do it.'

'Well, they can't get around very well.'

'I was going to pay for a taxi.'

'What? All the way to Warwick?'

'It's not that unreasonable. I can afford it. They could afford it themselves if they wanted to. Taxi drivers like days out. It gives them a break from their dull routines.'

It seems painfully extravagant to me.

'The house is lovely,' she says after a while. 'It's so stylish.'

I'm proud of my home. I've spent a lot of time and money on it, planning meticulously, so every inch of space is used in the best possible way. 'Thank you,' I say. I'm not sure if she means it, or if she's just being encouraging. 'I've done it all myself.'

'Didn't Dad help?'

'Dad?' I look at her in surprise. 'He's no good with décor. That's Mum's department.'

'No, I meant financially.'

'No, of course not!' I'm alarmed by the question. I'm not accustomed to discussing financial matters with anyone.

'Did you refuse?'

'He never offered.'

'And you didn't ask for help?'

'Would you?'

She doesn't reply.

The kettle boils and I pour hot water into the mugs. 'You'll notice that you can walk through my garden,' I say.

Our attempt to penetrate the garden at Audlands two days ago was not successful. We ploughed our way through overgrown grass and weeds for a while, but the rhododendrons were too rampant, the brambles too wild, and we eventually admitted defeat.

She sighs. 'Do you think Mum and Dad are safe there?'

'Oh, I'm sure they're fine.' I don't mention my worries about ceilings falling in. It feels disloyal.

Harriet gazes out of the window at the houses opposite. 'I think they should sell it and find somewhere more suitable.'

'Leave Audlands?'

'Why not? It's hardly a practical place for them to live.'

I couldn't bear the thought of not being able to go back home any more. It's always been the centre of my life, the starting point of my existence. Harriet and I were born in the four-poster bed in the bedroom looking out over the lake. The bed's still there, although my parents don't use it any more because they can't get it downstairs. The royal blue drapes still hang from the frame, rich and vibrant, scattered with red peonies, maroon chrysanthemums, orange poppies. I can't imagine how my mother persuaded my father to pay for the material. Even with the passing of time and the accumulation of dust the bed has managed to retain its grandeur and dignity. I often go up there and sit on the edge, enjoying the solitude of the unoccupied room.

I've never really left Audlands. I have a permanent place in the silent, ancient conversations that are written into its walls and it has imprinted itself indelibly into my mind, a living, constant presence. I know every inch of the house, every new crack in the floorboards, every hole in the wall where the plaster has abandoned hope and disintegrated. I know where the wallpaper's falling off, where the mice have invaded.

'Why should they leave?' I say.

'Look at them. They're falling apart themselves. Why stay in such a crumbling wreck?'

It's not a wreck. 'It just needs a bit of work. If some of the windows were replaced, it would all dry out and settle down.'

'Where would you start? It's like the Forth Bridge—never-ending. It always was. They couldn't possibly afford the kind of renovation that it needs. They should be living in a modern bungalow with central heating, gas cooker, dishwasher—'

'They've got a dishwasher.' They call it a washing-up machine. They're very proud of it.

'You know what I mean.'

'But they're not that old. Mum gets around all right. She's got years to go. They're independent.'

'That's not the point. They need more security.'

I don't want to talk about it. I take our coffee into the living room and clear a place on the table. The plasticine cats are taking over. They're everywhere, ready to leap off surfaces and surprise you. Sitting upright with ears pricked, preparing to pounce, stretching up the side of a pile of books on their hind legs. Their tails are arranged in every conceivable position—precisely vertical with a kink at the tip, slinking along behind, curling seductively. There's something vaguely human about them, which I hadn't noticed before. One of them has an angry face, another looks bewildered. The latest ones seem to be carrying something in their paws. Weapons?

'What's all this?' asks Harriet.

'They're Joel's. He's naming them after composers. This is Rimsky-Korsakov. That's Handel. It's something to do with a new computer game.'

She nods and sits down, looking round the room but not commenting. 'How's his work going?'

I don't know. He doesn't discuss it. 'Fine,' I say.

'He must be making a lot of money.'

'Do you think so? He doesn't talk about it.'

'I've seen his games in Australia. You don't go international unless you're making a fortune.'

'Australia?' I thought he pottered around on the computer at his office with a few other nerdish people, all playing games together. I'd assumed they made up a few games and sold them locally.

'Oh, Jess, you're as hopeless as ever. When are you going to step into the real world?'

I'm offended. 'I work in the real world. I've been married into it, had a child, divorced.' The only thing Harriet has done is work.

She picks up a cat and examines it. 'This is very good. I never saw Joel as an artist.'

'It must be a bit quiet at Audlands,' I say. 'A

256

contrast with your normal exciting life.'

'You don't know anything about my life,' she said.

Is she inviting me to ask more about it, or is she telling me to mind my own business? Would it be thoughtful and considerate to ask, or would it be prying?

'I'm expecting Joel and his fiancée for supper,' I say.

She stares at me. 'You didn't tell me he was engaged.'

'I've only just found out.'

'What's she like?'

I really wish Joel had brought her home earlier. 'I don't know. I've never met her.'

Harriet opens her eyes wide and starts to laugh. 'I don't know how you survive, I really don't. Do you realise most people would demand to see the girlfriend as soon as they know there's anyone interested in their son? They wouldn't wait until they're engaged.'

'That assumes they know the girlfriend exists.'

She stops laughing. 'Sorry, Jess. He's hopeless, isn't he?'

'Would you like to see the garden?' I ask.

Outside, under the white lilac, admiring the heathers round the miniature pond, we relax again. 'You've done a brilliant job,' she says.

'Mary gave me a lot of cuttings from her garden,' I say. 'It's taken a few years for everything to get established.'

Her eyes slip past me and I can see she's worrying about the houses that overlook my garden. 'It's not a problem,' I say. 'People don't go into their bedrooms much during the day.'

'Do you ever wonder what happened to Philip?' she says.

Philip? I shiver. 'You mean Philip and Colin? Our cousins?'

She nods.

'No. Never.'

'I met him. In Saudi Arabia.'

'Really?' Of course he would be in Saudi Arabia, or San Francisco or Sydney. All those exotic places where Harriet goes. He would be rich and successful, like her, well able to afford to travel, whether for work or for pleasure.

'Yes. It was so strange. We happened to be in the same hotel.'

Five-star, unadulterated luxury. Flowers in the bedroom. A maid folding back the sheet every night and putting a chocolate on the pillow. An Olympic swimming pool where Philip could show off.

'I didn't recognise him at first. He approached me. He was completely different.'

Tanned, fit, thriving on a healthy diet.

'He has rather a nice life—'

'Mum!'

Joel and Alice have arrived, earlier than I expected and they've let themselves in. I jump up, embarrassed that I wasn't watching out for them. 'They're here,' I say.

'Great,' says Harriet. 'I was hoping to meet her.'

They step out through the patio door. Joel looks different, less edgy than usual, grinning in a way I've never seen before. 'Hello, Mum,' he says.

Alice is black.

This is the first thing I see, and it shocks me because I'm not expecting it. I realise immediately

258

that it doesn't matter, but then I'm terrified that I might have let my surprise show.

'Hello,' I say, trying to make my smile as welcoming as possible. 'I'm Jessica.' I think she's African, but I'm not sure, and I don't know if it's all right to ask that sort of thing.

'It's so lovely to meet you at last,' she says, as if we've been missing each other for weeks. Her hair is arranged in an elaborate concoction of geometric shapes, and it's difficult not to stare at it. Bits of hair stand upright, stretched against a system of combs, giving the effect of open fans. 'Three Little Maids from School'. She's Yum-Yum. 'Joel!' says Harriet, and throws her arms round him. He tolerates this, but refuses to reciprocate.

'Harriet is Joel's aunt,' I explain to Alice once we have all drawn apart. 'We don't see her very often.'

She nods. 'He's told me about Harriet. And Audlands. I'm dying to see Audlands.'

He manages to communicate with her, then.

Alice turns out to be rather impressive. She has plenty to say, giggles a lot, and teases Joel in a way that I wouldn't dare. What does she see in him? Harriet stays for supper and is a useful companion, sharing jokes with Alice, taking control in quiet moments, while I produce the food.

After the casserole, which everyone eats with enthusiasm, I go and fetch the lemon meringue pie—the height of my culinary skills. I pause in the doorway, watching the three of them at the table. Harriet is describing a client in Los Angeles.

'She looks like a stick of celery,' she says. 'Tall, ridiculously thin, with a green tinge to her skin. Nothing useful to say, either. Just as you'd expect

259

from someone who only eats celery.'

Harriet is flushed from the wine or the company. Her movements are lively and animated, exactly as she used to be when she was a child. She's always believed that people want to listen to her. She knows she can entertain them effortlessly and enjoys being the centre of attention.

Alice is leaning forward, a faint smile on her lips, a veneer of sweat making her face glow. She doesn't appear to be overawed by Harriet's exotic lifestyle, and she's ready to laugh whenever the occasion arises. Not a hair has moved on her head, which now reminds me of the top of a wedding cake. She seems comfortable and at home, easy in the presence of Joel, whom she cajoles with endless good nature. She's teaching him to be civilised.

Joel is talking more than usual, gradually coming to life, a puppet who's testing to see if he can manage without strings. He's smiling, laughing, openly adoring of Alice.

The phone rings. 'It's all right,' I say. 'I'll get it.'

They barely pause in their conversation, as if they haven't even heard the ring.

I put the pie down on the table and go into the hall to answer it.

'Hello?'

'Mrs Courtenay?'

'Yes?'

'West Midlands Police. Birmingham Central.'

Something must have happened. There's been an accident.

'We have a Mr Courtenay here, who says you're his closest relative. He seems to think you'll come and take him home.'

260

I breathe a sigh of relief. 'We're divorced,' I say. 'I'm not related to him.'

The policeman's voice is very patient. 'He's explained that, Mrs Courtenay, but he says you are the only person with a connection to him.'

I don't have a connection. He's misleading them. 'What's he done?'

'He's been climbing up the House of Fraser, madam, and playing the violin at the top. Bach, I believe.'

CHAPTER EIGHTEEN

Joel's Year 2 teacher, Mrs Helston, peered at me through her abundant fringe, her eyes big and blue like a child's, while I perched on one of the children's chairs, feeling enormous. Above us, imperfectly painted pirates brandishing cutlasses glared down. 'Shiver my timbers', it said underneath. We were leafing through Joel's worksheets.

'He really must learn to be more tidy,' she said.

This seemed a minor complaint to me. 'Surely content is more important than presentation at this age.'

'You might like to have a look at other children's work, Mrs Courtenay. I think you'd be surprised.'

I'd seen their work. It was pinned up on boards all round the classroom. 'My Pets', by Donna Bakewell. 'Our trip to the Black Country Museum', by Helen MacPherson. I couldn't find anything by Joel.

261

'But he's only six.'

She looked at me gravely. She was wearing a frilly mauve blouse with a low neckline, revealing a glimpse of provocative lace. Copper-brown curls hung down the sides of her cheeks, partially controlled by a glittery pink hair-band. Why couldn't my son have a grown-up teacher?

'All the children in my class are six,' she said.

'Or seven.'

She acknowledged this with a brief nod. 'Have you tried helping him with his writing at home, Mrs Courtenay?'

Of course I had. We sat down together every evening and worked on reading, maths, handwriting. His letters were a bit wonky, but I thought he was doing well until I saw the other children's work. I couldn't believe their neatness. It seemed so unnecessary.

'Oh, what a good idea.' I didn't want Mrs Helston to know that he practised at home and still wasn't very good. It would reinforce her low opinion of him.

She smiled, her face pleased with her rightness. 'Well, could I suggest a little bit every day? I'm sure we'd soon see the difference.'

'He understands everything, though, doesn't he?' She must have known my son was a gifted child, capable of highly intelligent conversation. He'd been an adult from birth, serious, thoughtful, his mind logical and analytical.

'It's difficult to know what he understands when he can't accurately record it on paper,' said Mrs Helston.

How could she fail to see his originality of thought? Didn't she ever talk to the children?

'What about his reading?'

'Yes,' she acknowledged. 'His reading is coming on nicely.'

'And his maths?'

'Well—again, it's difficult to know, since he can't form the numbers properly.'

But he could. We'd worked on them at home. I could read his figures, so why couldn't she? He liked maths. 'He's very good at mental arithmetic,' I said.

'Is he? That will be useful.'

She didn't know. That's what she meant. 'He knows his tables up to ten.'

A faint frown drifted across her face. 'It's not necessary to go that far ahead, Mrs Courtenay. We will come to all these things in due course. Your time would be better spent helping him with his writing.'

'But surely we should be filling his mind with exciting things, stimulating him.'

'Oh, I think he gets plenty of stimulation here. You need have no worries on that account.'

I sat back. I wanted to tell her all about Joel, how he worked out the exact number of minutes allocated to playtime every day, the hours he spent in school, the days of holiday in a year. How he played chess with his grandfather and sometimes beat him, how he always knew who had which card in Happy Families, how he had worked out a method of cheating in Snakes and Ladders. You couldn't fool Joel. He was a very smart boy.

But I couldn't convey this to Mrs Helston. 'He's doing all right,' she said. 'Nice and average. Just help him with his writing and he'll be fine.'

She was wearing three-inch heels as usual,

although Joel told me she changed into flat shoes when they did PE or Music and Movement. Thank goodness for that. She couldn't walk in them properly. Her toes pointed inwards and she bent her knees to keep her balance. She looked ridiculous. But she saw me as more ridiculous. I had unreasonable expectations. I thought my child was better than all the others.

But he was.

'He is still quite immature,' she said.

I almost let my mouth drop open to gape at her. Joel, immature? He could discuss concepts like personal space, self-control, excellence. 'In what way?' I asked. 'I always find him very mature.'

She crossed her legs. She didn't understand about intelligence. 'He doesn't mix well.'

'How do you mean?'

'He doesn't play.'

'He plays at home,' I said.

'With other children?'

'Well—no. He plays with me. And his father.'

'That wasn't quite what I meant, Mrs Courtenay. He doesn't mix with the other children or join in their playground games. He doesn't play football.'

So that's what it was all about. 'We're not very interested in football in our family.'

She leaned forward. 'Perhaps you should encourage him to take an interest, then, Mrs Courtenay. Find some out-of-school activities. He needs that contact with his peers. Could you invite some of his classmates round every now and again, give him the chance to learn how to behave like them?'

Now I was insulted. 'I think he behaves well

already. He's always very polite.'

'We have problems with his behaviour here,' she said.

I stared at her. She hadn't mentioned this before. 'In what way?'

'He doesn't cooperate. If I ask all the children to line up, he'll ignore me and carry on with what he's doing.'

'But he's probably just interested in what he's doing.'

'And if he's playing with something, he won't share it. He hits children who try to take it away from him.'

Quite right. Why should they take his toys away? 'Perhaps they should learn to share with him.'

She sighed. 'We've had complaints.'

'Who from?'

'Other parents.'

I was appalled. We'd been talking for five minutes about Joel's work, about what they were covering in class this year, and she had only just got around to mentioning this. 'Are you telling me he's violent?'

She tried to look compassionate. 'No, not really. He simply doesn't have the social skills of most children of his age. They will develop, I'm sure. But perhaps you could talk to him about the hitting, Mrs Courtenay. Children do need to learn to think of others.'

I didn't believe her. I couldn't imagine Joel hitting anyone. But I nodded anyway, determined to give her the impression that everything was under control.

'And it would be a good idea to get a hearing test. That might explain why he doesn't respond when I ask him to do something.'

He wasn't deaf. He could hear sounds that I couldn't. 'Mummy, can you open the window for that trapped fly? It's upstairs on the landing window.' Or that noise he kept asking about when lying in bed. I couldn't hear anything. He eventually announced that it was the sound of next door's television, coming up through the floor and the walls. And he was upset by sudden loud sounds. They hurt, he said, and he would hold his hands over his ears, screwing up his eyes in pain if a low-flying aeroplane went over, or a dog barked close by.

'I don't think he's deaf. He just concentrates very hard and shuts out extraneous sounds.'

'Nevertheless, it's good to check these things out, Mrs Courtenay.'

Why did she keep using my name? It was as if she thought I would pay more attention to her, that it gave her more gravitas.

She stood up and held out her hand. It seemed unnecessarily formal, until I realised that it was her way of terminating the conversation. My ten minutes were up. 'I'm sure we'll resolve all these little problems,' she said and smiled, her mouth glistening with pink lipstick.

They aren't Joel's problems, I wanted to say. They're yours. He just doesn't fit into your way of thinking. 'Thank you,' I said and smiled back.

*   *   *

I knew Joel was an unusual child, but I liked the way that he thought about things. He approached life as if it was a puzzle to be teased apart and

266

analysed. He ignored some events as if they'd never happened, but worried away at others.

'Can we write to Captain Kirk? I want to know how the transporter works.'

'We can't. He doesn't really exist.'

'You don't know that for certain.'

'It's just a story. Like reading a book, but on the television.'

'It might be real.'

'I don't think so. Everyone knows it's made up by writers and actors.'

'The *Starship Enterprise* can travel through time, so if they were in the future they could come back to our time and tell someone about their adventures. Then that person could write all the television stories.'

'Yes—that's a possibility, I suppose.'

'I think that's what they did.'

'It's unlikely—'

'See. There really is a Captain Kirk and a Spock, but not yet.'

'Have you cleaned your teeth?'

Joel had started to talk very early, bypassing simple words and leaping straight into fully formed sentences. Andrew found him much easier to deal with at this stage, providing he didn't have to take part in any arguments about food. If Joel refused to eat sprouts or potatoes or gravy, Andrew would simply pick up his plate from the table and go to eat in the living room, where he could watch television at the same time. I didn't mind. If he stayed, he became as unreasonable as Joel and everything would be my fault.

Andrew was working on the assembly line at Longbridge at this point, making Metros, changing from day to night shifts every fortnight, so for a few brief months we had money coming in. It would have been wonderful if he hadn't developed a passion for motorcycles at the same time. He bought a second-hand Yamaha, which continually went wrong, so every spare penny went on new parts.

'What do you think of this?' he said one day, coming in after a ride on his bike. He was glowing with pleasure and his cheerfulness brought a brief holiday spirit into the house, a wave of relief washing over the tension that lay tightly packed beneath the surface.

The purpose of my existence was to be a passive reflection of Andrew and Joel. If I absorbed their emotions I could deliver them back, refined and enlarged, waxed and polished. If they were happy, I was happy.

Andrew was unwrapping a leather jacket, black with red trim. I put my hand out and felt the soft, supple leather. Expensive. 'It's lovely.'

'There's a new shop in Halesowen. They've got some great bargains.'

I didn't want to ask about the price because we would end up arguing about money. 'How much?'

'Jess, stop worrying. We're fine. I have a good job, I can afford it. Twenty per cent off—I couldn't believe it. I've been needing a decent jacket for ages.'

Twenty per cent off a lot of money still leaves a lot of money. I thought of the gas bill, the television licence, the milkman. The sleeves on my winter coat were beginning to fray. Joel would need new shoes soon, and I would probably have to ask my mother to help, as always. I was determined that he would grow up with straight feet even if his trousers were passed on by neighbours and his shirts came from jumble sales. Andrew was elated by his bargain, the quality of the leather. He prowled around the house, agile and energised, itching to do something.

'Let's go for a ride,' he said. 'We could go up to the Lickey Hills. There's not much traffic around at the moment.'

'There isn't time. I have to fetch Joel from school in half an hour.'

'Oh, yes. I forgot that.'

We'd had a child for six years and Andrew still had to be reminded that he existed. Self-sacrifice was not a word that meant anything to him.

*   *   *

When Joel was seven, we went on holiday for the first time to Cornwall, with a tent borrowed from a neighbour. But we didn't adapt easily to camping. We spent several days circling aimlessly in our newly-acquired, faltering Volvo, unable to find anything to do in the rain. Meals were difficult, since Andrew found food boring if he had anything more than once a week and our cooking facilities were severely limited. Joel was terrified of spiders and beetles, and spent much of the time shrieking.

'Don't worry, we'll find it,' I would say, desperate to calm him before Andrew lost his patience.

I rarely found anything but pretended I had, producing a black speck and throwing it into the grass, away from the tent.

'How do you know it won't come back?'

'It won't. I've given it a good talking to.'

'That's it, then,' said Andrew. 'If your mother commands, the world obeys.'

We pottered together on the edge of the sea, collecting seaweed and dead crabs, until Joel discovered the joy of digging. He was so quiet one day that I dozed off on the blanket. I woke up with a jerk, shocked to find that Andrew was also asleep. Joel was nowhere to be seen.

'Joel!' I called, fear making my voice tight and high-pitched. I could already see the headlines. *Neglected child drowns. Parents sleep while boy dies.*

Joel's head popped up from nowhere. 'Yes?'

He'd dug a hole, big enough to hide in.

'Look,' I said to Andrew, who was waking up beside me. 'He's dug a hole.'

'So?' said Andrew. 'What's the big deal about a hole?'

'That's it,' I said. 'It's big.'

'I bet I could dig a bigger one.'

'I bet you can't.'

They littered the beach with holes, digging and digging as the light faded, long after everyone else had gone home. It was a competition for the deepest, the widest, the nearest to the cliffs, the nearest to the sea without being washed away.

We drove home from the holiday exhausted but pleased with ourselves. We'd done a normal thing, gone on holiday and survived. There was sand all over the car, our trainers were stiff with salt and our feet were covered with little cuts from shells and shingle, but I felt we'd achieved something, made progress.

*   *   *

Andrew left the job at Longbridge after six months. He gave it up to be an insurance agent, collecting premiums from clients in their homes. He told me he was good with old ladies and middle-aged couples, his main customers. He flashed his charming smile and told them jokes. They didn't get his jokes, he said, which I knew to be elaborate and confusing, but they laughed anyway, because they were polite. As long as he was only there for ten minutes, they liked him. 'This is right for me,' he said. 'A job for life.'

Austin-Rover hadn't suited him. 'It's the night shifts,' he said. 'I can't sleep properly during the day.'

I was disappointed. I'd enjoyed having the bed to myself, reading before turning off the light, breathing into the empty air of the bedroom, knowing that I didn't have to share it with anyone and that I could have the duvet to myself all night.

The insurance job lasted about three months. It had too much flexibility for Andrew. He could do his collections when he wanted to, wait for the right mood, as long as he covered the round once a month. He started to stay in bed later and later before going out. When he did go out, he had to come home afterwards and balance the figures.

'I'm not keen on maths,' he said. 'It was my worst subject at school.'

He spent hours at the kitchen table, his tight, brittle frustration spreading outwards as he attempted to add up columns of figures and arrived at different answers every time. The calculator didn't help.

'Stupid thing doesn't work,' he said. 'It misses

271

out the decimal points.'

He spent much of the time gazing into space. 'The numbers are taking me over,' he said. 'I have nightmares about them. Make me a cup of tea, Jess.'

'Give it time,' I said. 'You'll get used to them.'

But he wouldn't give it time. 'They're after world domination. Massed armies marching through my mind, waving flags, goose-stepping their way to victory.'

'Don't surrender,' I said.

He gave up the job.

He didn't work at all for some time and we lived on income support. He wouldn't get up until lunchtime and stopped looking after himself. While the rest of the country cut its hair, smartened up and put on suits, Andrew's hair grew long and wild. He hardly ever washed it and grease spread downwards through the blond curls until they became dark and matted. Intervals between baths stretched into weeks. He started to put on weight.

'You could get a job,' he said to me as he lounged on the sofa one evening, watching *Neighbours*.

This was unexpected. He'd always wanted me to be at home, cooking, looking after him. He had never acknowledged my degree. 'What about Joel?'

'He's not a baby any more. Lots of mothers work when their children go to school.'

'But who would pick him up from school? What about the holidays?'

'You could get a real job, something professional, earn decent money. You're the one with the qualifications.'

'What would you do all day?'

'I was thinking of starting a business.'

'Doing what?'

'I haven't decided yet.'

No, of course not. 'And you'd look after Joel at the same time?'

He didn't answer immediately. 'I don't see why not. I'm capable of walking to the school and back. It's easy enough to fit that round self-employment.'

'What kind of self-employment?'

'I had lots of ideas when I was at school. If I'd followed them up, I'd be a millionaire by now.'

'So you had alternatives to violin playing?'

He shrugged. 'Obviously.'

He didn't have an alternative. He'd told me ages ago that when he was a teenager, he was only aware of what he didn't want to do. But I didn't believe that either. I was certain he'd always expected to play the violin. It wasn't until he reached university that the possibility of escaping his mother's ambitions occurred to him.

'You could always teach the violin,' I said.

He sat up and stared at me, his eyes heavy and red-rimmed. 'And how do you propose that I should do that, with no violin?'

'Couldn't you use mine for the time being?'

'A cheap, mean, student violin? Are you serious? It would be like putting on a sack when you've worn smooth cotton shirts, eating penny chews when you've tasted oysters, drinking vinegar when you've been used to Chardonnay—'

Stop him, I thought, or he'll go on for ever. 'Have you considered asking your mother for the violin back?'

He turned the television off. 'I cannot believe you just said that. My relationship with my mother is not up for negotiation. You know as well as I do that she's responsible for the sorry state in which we find ourselves—'

'I don't think that's quite fair.'

His eyes stopped moving and his face stiffened. 'You don't know what you're talking about.'

'No,' I said, forcing my voice to sound warm and easy. 'You're right.'

A dark, vicious coldness settled around us. 'You know my mother. How can you possibly imagine that I'm making it up?'

'No, I'm sorry. I shouldn't have said that.'

'But you meant it.'

He turned the television back on and sat watching it, silent and bitter. Breathing with an effort, relieved that he was not going to turn the situation into a full-blown argument, I crept out to make a cup of tea. A peace offering. It wouldn't work and he would brood for days, draining my energy, but the resentment would finally melt away if I was careful and made no more wrong moves.

Anyway, he was right to reject teaching. All those potential violin pupils had been saved from a fate worse than death.

*   *   *

The possibility of finding a job for me eventually resurfaced.

'You're wasting your degree, Jess,' said Andrew, one evening. 'You should work.'

'But would you look after Joel?'

'I've told you I will.'

274

'And what if you find a job that you want? What then?'

'Well, obviously, I'd take it.'

'So if I was working full-time, I'd just have to give it up at a moment's notice?'

'That would only be right. I should be the breadwinner. That's what husbands are supposed to do, you know.'

'But how could I have any commitment to a job that I might not be able to keep?'

'Don't be ridiculous, Jess. You're just twisting my words.'

'What about the housework? Are you going to do the cleaning?'

He smiled. 'What do you think?'

I knew what I thought, but it wouldn't be wise to say it. 'Would you cook the evening meal for when I came home?'

'Jess, Jess, you know I can't cook.'

'You could learn.'

'Why would I need to when I have such a capable wife?'

I didn't say anything for a while. The television flickered through *Coronation Street* and *EastEnders*. We sat back and stared at the screen like an ordinary married couple. Joel was upstairs making lists of prime numbers, his latest obsession.

'Well?' said Andrew.

I knew I would end up doing everything. Even if he said he would do things, he wouldn't. If he started a business, he would become distracted, forget to fetch Joel from school, leave him on his own for hours. I couldn't trust him.

I swallowed. 'No,' I said.

'Thanks a lot,' said Andrew. He went into the

hall, put on his motorcycle gear and went out, slamming the front door behind him. I could hear him roaring up our street and on to the nearby main road, opening up the throttle, driving too fast.

Even after he had left, his anger filled every space in the house, forcing its way into the backs of cupboards, behind the cooker, under my fingernails.

*   *   *

'Perhaps Andrew's right and you should go out to work,' said Mary one day. I had brought Joel round to her flat after school and we were sitting on her balcony, looking at wedding brochures. Eamon had just proposed and they were planning the wedding for next year.

Mary was so clear-sighted about everything. It was always accepted that she and Eamon would get married. They had been going out for years, not living together, but living in each other's pockets anyway, and there was a steady predictability about their lives that was very attractive. They wanted to give the relationship time to develop, to be sure they were doing the right thing. I could have told them they were doing the right thing from the first moment I saw them together, but I don't suppose my opinion would have carried much weight.

Joel was sitting on the floor next to us, absorbed in a geometry set I'd just bought him.

'I can't believe you just said that,' I said.

'Why not? I've seen lots of women flourish once they've started working.'

'They're not married to Andrew,' I said and

276

then wished I hadn't. I didn't like disloyalty. 'I mean,' I added hastily, 'some men are rather good at cooking and cleaning and managing the children, and some men aren't. Andrew's one of those men who isn't.'

'Yes,' said Mary.

I looked up at her sharply. She never criticised, that was her great skill. But her face was blank. She didn't seem to be implying anything.

'I'd be worried that he'd forget to fetch Joel from school. He's a bit absent-minded,' I said.

'Find a morning job,' she said. 'Then it won't matter.'

'But what about holiday times?'

'Find something that's connected to schools,' she said. 'Then you can be at home in the holidays.'

I pointed at a frothy wedding dress with a plunging neckline and a full, sweeping skirt. 'I could just see you in that,' I said.

She screwed up her face. 'I think not.' She liked simplicity. 'You know, it's possible you would enjoy working. It might make you feel better.'

'But I feel fine,' I said.

She hesitated. 'You look worn out, Jess. Always exhausted.'

I was amazed. There was too much to do to worry about things like that. 'Then how could I possibly go out to work?'

'It requires a different kind of energy. You'd be doing something you wanted to do.'

I already do what I want to do, I tried to say, but I stopped before I'd started. Did I? I hadn't thought about it for so long that I had no idea what I wanted to do. 'What would happen if Joel was ill?'

She smiled. 'I'm sure I could help out in an emergency. And there's always your mother. She'd be delighted to have him.'

Delighted didn't seem to be quite the right word. It was one thing to offer the occasional treasure hunt and quite another to give up her aerobics class, Italian cooking lessons or jogging sessions to babysit. And Joel wasn't the right kind of child for her. He didn't like fun.

*　　　*　　　*

Andrew brought the subject up again at supper a few days later. 'So? Have you thought about it?'

'What?' I was dishing out mashed potatoes.

'I don't want any potatoes,' said Joel, watching me.

'Well, you have to have them,' I said.

'The job,' said Andrew. 'Are you going to look for work as we discussed?'

I needed longer to think about it. I didn't want to commit myself without a lot of thought. 'No,' I said.

He didn't speak to me for a fortnight. The atmosphere grew and grew, a monstrous balloon that kept on expanding beyond all reasonable expectation. It took over the house, sucking the air out, making it difficult to breathe. Andrew normally filled a lot of space with words, rambling conversation, theories, calculations. Now there was no talking, no intimacy, no jokes. When Joel spoke to me, I had to force myself to reply. It was as if I had lost the habit, as if my brain had wound down and needed to be cranked up, a mechanical clock which had ticked itself to a complete standstill.

'Come on, Andrew,' I said one evening as we sat watching *Coronation Street*. 'We can't go on like this.'

'Like what?'

'Not talking. We have to communicate.'

'You're the one who's not communicating. You have the power to make our lives easier and you're not using it.'

I thought of Mary's offer to babysit.

He got up and went out. The motorcycle roared off again. He'd either knock someone over soon, or kill himself. I wondered how it would feel to be a widow.

'Mummy,' said Joel. 'Can I watch *Star Trek*?'

I let him stay up past his bedtime and we watched the television together. I needed to wash the dishes, but it seemed such an effort.

I should have appreciated the silence. But this silence was poisonous, like mustard gas, infiltrating everything. Even the space inside me was invaded and contaminated.

Then the final reminder came for the electric bill.

*   *   *

I enrolled on a part-time course for librarians, so I only had to worry about Joel for half the time.

Mary was right. I enjoyed the fact that I could go out, close the front door behind me and start thinking again after seven years of stagnation. It was difficult, because my mind was loose and weak, unaccustomed to exercise. I was invigorated by the fresh air, conscious that I was coming back to life.

Thin threads of knowledge started to feel their way through abandoned corridors.

While I was out, Andrew learnt to communicate with Joel. They talked to each other, watched *The Flintstones*, Bugs Bunny, *Roadrunner*, sprawled out on the chairs in the lounge, oblivious to anything else.

I paused outside the door on one occasion and listened to their conversation.

'So,' said Andrew. 'You've got the chance to be a bionic man. But you can only have one bit. Which would you go for? Arms, legs, eyes?'

Joel didn't answer straightaway, and I wondered if he was ignoring his father. Then he started to talk, his voice thoughtful and hesitant. 'Legs would be useful. You'd never get tired. You could run at seventy miles per hour along the M5.'

'They wouldn't let you,' said Andrew. 'No number plate.'

'You could buy one,' suggested Joel.

'No tax or insurance. You'd never get away with it.'

'OK, then,' said Joel. 'If you had the arms, you could shoplift so fast no one would see you.'

'Or do a hundred press-ups in a minute,' said Andrew.

'Big deal,' said Joel.

Another long pause. I could just see Joel through a crack in the door. He was sitting up, untidy hair swirling across his face, his eyes looking unseeingly into the distance. 'There's not a lot you could do with arms. You'd be brilliant at semaphore, but it would be too fast for anyone to read.'

'You could lift cars,' said Andrew. 'Overturn them if people annoy you.'

'But without the legs,' said Joel, 'you couldn't run away fast enough. They'd catch you and put you in prison.'

'Good point.'

'If you had the eyes, you could read a whole book in a minute.'

'No you couldn't,' said Andrew. 'You wouldn't be able to turn the pages in time.'

They stopped talking. A companionable silence.

'If you'd got the hands,' said Andrew after a while, 'you could play the piano like your mother.'

For some reason they found this hilariously funny, doubling up with laughter for a good two minutes.

'It doesn't really work, does it,' said Joel. 'You need everything to be bionic.'

'That's the answer,' said Andrew. 'It's got to be all or nothing.'

A surge of pride was spreading through me. Father and son. There was a connection. They thought the same way. They would feed each other, teach each other to be more human, and become normal. Joel was gifted like Andrew, but music was not for him. He would go in another direction, be a scientist, change the world. He could already reason like an adult. And Andrew would find a job, save our family.

'Jess!' called Andrew. 'When's dinner ready?'

CHAPTER NINETEEN

Andrew is waiting for me in the reception area of the police station. It's a dismal place—four plastic chairs screwed to the floor and an old lady limping round the room. She has a Top Shop bag in one hand and a walking-stick in the other. Enormous round glasses balance on the end of her nose and almost meet the line of red lipstick that she has applied over-generously.

A policeman stands behind the desk, leaning on his elbow, sorting through papers. 'Go away, Annie,' he says. 'They've got a bed for you in the hostel.'

She doesn't reply and carries on circling, a dangerous glint in her eye, her route erratic and unsteady.

Andrew has positioned himself at the side of the chairs, close enough to the wall to prevent Annie from walking behind him, but far enough away to avoid touching it. He would not have considered sitting down, not wanting to be contaminated by the association with crime or someone else's grubbiness which would be so much more offensive than his own. He's wearing Lycra leggings, shiny electric blue, and a red and black striped T-shirt. Circles of rope and metal clips are attached to a belt round his waist. A rucksack clings to his back, a monstrous orange growth, and he's holding his violin case.

'Jess!' The twenty-year-old student leaps out with youthful enthusiasm, unsettling me until I remember where we are.

'Have they charged you with anything?' I ask.

He continues to look delighted to see me, and it's obvious that I'm not going to get much sensible information out of him. 'No. They said they will next time.'

'But there isn't going to be a next time, is there?'

He doesn't reply.

The policeman behind the desk looks up and winks at me. 'You'll have to keep him under control, love.' His voice has a hint of humour just below the surface.

'When you discover the world of Bach,' says Andrew, 'you will realise that there's another dimension to life, a greatness that you can never touch in your mundane world of restrictions and intimidation.'

'Andrew!'

The policeman's face settles into a predesigned network of weary wrinkles. 'We get all sorts here,' he says to me, his tone light and unthreatening. 'I just put them behind me when I get in my car and listen to Beethoven string quartets on my way home.'

'Let's get out of here,' says Andrew. 'He doesn't know what he's talking about.'

'Thank you,' I say to the policeman as we head for the door.

He nods amiably. 'We aim to please.' He returns to his paperwork.

Does he really listen to Beethoven?

Annie starts to sing in an unexpectedly clear soprano. 'There'll be bluebirds over, The white cliffs of—where were they again?'

'Couldn't you have gone back on the bus?' I say as we walk to the car.

'I could have done, but I didn't want them to feel they'd wasted their time. They almost certainly think I'm not safe to be let out on my own.'

I sigh, irritated that I've been summoned unnecessarily. 'In other words, you wanted a lift home.'

'They wouldn't breathalyse me. I wanted them to, because I've never done it before and I thought it would be an interesting experience, but they said I hadn't been in charge of a vehicle so it wasn't necessary.'

'What could they have charged you with?'

He shrugs. 'Breach of the peace, danger to the public. They'd think of something.'

We reach the car and he puts his rucksack into the boot, but holds on to the violin as he climbs into the front seat.

'How did you get all that up to the top of House of Fraser?' I ask.

'I didn't. I've got everything I need on my belt—the rope, the nuts, the krabs. I left the rucksack at the bottom and put the violin case on my back.'

'Weren't you worried someone would steal the rucksack?'

'Yes, but there was nothing I could do about it. And nobody did. All the potential thieves are probably Bach enthusiasts and decided to enjoy the concert instead.'

I try to visualise the practical details. 'Where did you put the case when you played the violin? Was there room to put it down on the roof?'

'It was fine. I was playing to the gods up there, Jess.'

The gods? Since when has Andrew been interested in gods?

'The sound just soars up into the sky. You'd think it would get lost, wouldn't you? But it doesn't. It echoes round you, comes back at you, surrounds you. Even the sparrows stopped to listen. I reckon they'll be diverting aeroplanes soon, once they know I'm doing a concert.'

'Did you practise before you went up there?' Did he take the violin out of its case, wind up the bow, put it on the A string, pull it, hear that amazing sound for the first time in years?

He hesitates. 'I tuned it,' he says.

'Wouldn't it have been easier to play it on the street? Then people might have given money and you could have benefited from it.'

'Jess, Jess, you're missing the point. It's the climbing. The challenge, the sense that you're the only person in the world doing it. The playing was just the icing, a bit of fun.'

'So playing didn't feel like a chore, something you'd been forced into?'

He doesn't reply and I breathe in, taste the freshness and freedom of the air. I'm safe. I've grown up and walked beyond the role that Andrew created for me. Maybe the walk is more of a run, less controlled than I would like, but at least I can keep running, more or less certain that he can't catch me.

Does he still carry all that rage round with him, the symbiotic relationship that keeps him going? He feeds off the anger, the anger feeds off him. It can't have been defeated, but taking away the need for responsibility from him seems to have loosened its grip. Maybe he should never have had a family and that was the mistake we all made, tying him down, expecting him to honour his obligations, believing that he was capable of such accountability.

'So what next?' I say. 'The Rotunda? Or off to London for Westminster Abbey?'

'You can't climb every building,' he says. 'The Rotunda is just blank concrete—nowhere to get a

285

foothold.'

'Well, that's a relief.'

'On the other hand, it might be worth going up in the lift and abseiling down. I've been thinking about that.'

'There's always the Bull Ring. I've seen people walking on the glass roof.'

'No point in me doing it, then, if someone else has got there before me.'

I'm still interested in the violin playing. 'Why did you decide to play Bach?'

'It's unaccompanied. I didn't think I could persuade an accompanist to join me. The piano would have presented a slight problem.'

'You weren't able to leave the violin in its case, then? You wanted to play it.'

'You said that, not me.'

I'm right, though. Within a few days of his mother returning the violin he has taken it out, tuned it, carried it to the top of House of Fraser and played it. He's more closely linked to the violin than he will admit.

'I'll drop you off at your flat, then I must get back. I've left Harriet at home with Joel and his fiancée.'

'Harriet's home?'

'Yes, for the time being. And your son's engaged.'

He doesn't comment.

'She's called Alice. She seems very nice, although her hair's a bit odd. She works for him.'

When I pull up outside his block of flats, we have to manoeuvre round a large BMW clumsily parked by the entrance. Andrew studies it. 'You can't leave a car like that here at this time of night.

286

It's an open invitation.'

He opens the car door. 'Thanks, Jess. I owe you one.'

I don't want him to owe me anything. 'Just find another hobby, Andrew. I can't keep coming out to rescue you. I have my own life to live.'

The door of the BMW opens and someone steps out. Andrew turns and stops, half in and half out of his door, frozen into an unnatural crouch.

'Andrew!'

I don't recognise the voice immediately. It's barely louder than a whisper, but intense and penetrating. I turn round and find that his mother is standing behind us. I wonder if I could avoid her and just drive off, but Andrew is in the way, giving no sign that he will move.

I climb out and walk round to meet her. She hasn't changed much, her iron-grey hair still cropped close to the skull, the drooping eyelids lower than ever. 'Miranda—' I say and stop. There's something wrong.

'Jessica—'

I go over and take her by the arm. She's breathing heavily and for the first time I can see in her a human frailty. 'Andrew—your father . . .' she says.

With a rush of guilt, I remember the liver cancer that Andrew told me about a fortnight ago. I've been distracted, my attention focused on Joel and Alice and Andrew's activities, and I haven't given enough thought to his father.

'Has he died?' says Andrew, straightening up.

'No, not yet. But he only has a short time left, they think. I want you to come and see him before he goes, Andrew.'

We're a small, isolated group on the pavement, enclosed by the open door of my car. A street lamp shines down on us from a few yards away, orange light distorting all the natural colours, and the heavy beat of someone's music thumps out from a nearby flat. Cars swish past with no idea of what's going on. A sharp crack of wind tugs at us and the cold of the night air starts to penetrate. Andrew looks past his mother towards his block of flats. Miranda shivers, her lean, bony body unprotected. She looks exhausted, the sockets round her eyes deep and unnatural, as if she hasn't slept for days.

We're bound together. Not voluntarily but inevitably. We have a common history. It's written all over us, seeping out of our pores, bringing us together however little we might want it. Even Andrew is affected, I can see. In normal circumstances he would have walked off. I could imagine his voice. 'Sorry, not my problem.'

But it doesn't happen.

'Is Donald at home?' I ask.

'No, he's in the Queen Elizabeth.'

'Should we go there now?'

'Yes,' she says.

'OK,' I say. 'Shall I drive?'

I wonder if Miranda will protest, fuss about the BMW, but she doesn't. She sighs with relief, as if she's been waiting for someone else to take charge. I immediately regret it, because I don't want the responsibility. But who else will do it? Not Andrew, who would be incapable even if he hadn't got a communication problem with his parents. 'Go and get changed,' I say to Andrew. 'You can't go dressed like that. I'm just going to phone Joel.'

He gets his rucksack out of the boot and

disappears into the block of flats. Miranda locks up her car and gets into my front passenger seat. She knows her place. Her dignity and sense of importance have not diminished with the difficult circumstances.

Joel answers the phone straightaway. 'Where have you been?'

'Are Alice and Harriet still there?'

'No, I've just taken them home. You've been ages.'

He's exaggerating. All I've done is fetch Andrew and take him back to his flat. 'Joel, you need to go to the QE. Grandpa is dying.'

'How do you know that?'

'Grandma was here, waiting for Dad when we got back.'

There's a pause while Joel takes in the information. 'OK,' he says. 'Will Dad be there?'

'Yes,' I say.

He doesn't reply.

'We'll see you there, then.'

'OK.' He rings off.

*   *   *

Donald is in a single room, wired up to all sorts of machines and he isn't even conscious. 'His family are at his bedside', they say on the news if someone is dying. So this is what they mean. I wonder why we're all here. What does it achieve? Will he even know we've come, that his estranged son has made the effort and is sitting obediently by the bed like the rest of us? Does Donald know that he can safely drift off into the unknown because his son has returned and is sharing his last silent hours, breathing into the same air?

Joel walks in after about twenty minutes. I smile at him and indicate the chair next to me. Miranda gets up and gives him a kiss. 'Joel,' she says. 'Thank you for coming.'

He smiles, a soft, shy smile, and sits down. 'Hi, Dad,' he says.

Andrew has been studying the floor, but now he lifts his head. 'Hello,' he says. 'Long time no see.'

I breathe more easily. They're not going to collide. They've both braked in time and come to rest side by side.

We don't talk much. It's difficult. There are too many spaces between us, too many years which should have been filled with conversations, arguments, reconciliations. Instead, everyone has retreated, built great edifices of protection that can't be scaled, concrete surfaces that can't be climbed. Nowhere to fix the rope. I don't care about Andrew and Miranda, but I would like Joel to see the pointlessness of it before he grows hard and impenetrable. I don't want him to become a shadow of Andrew. 'Andrew's been learning to climb,' I say to Miranda.

She nods. 'I was told that he was on the television.'

A nurse comes in to check the monitors. She smiles at us. 'You can get drinks from the machine at the end of the corridor,' she says.

'Thank you, dear,' says Miranda. 'They're all so nice,' she adds when the nurse has gone, as if she wasn't expecting kindness.

What if he doesn't die? Will we sit here for two days, three days, unable to speak, forced to endure each other's company indefinitely? Will Joel decide he needs to go to work? Will I? Is there anywhere we can lie down and sleep for a bit, or will we just have to doze here in our seats?

Donald opens his eyes. Miranda leans forward and takes his hand. 'Donald, we're all here. Andrew and Jessica and Joel. Just say whatever you want. Anything at all.'

It's difficult to tell if he can understand. He stares in front of him, moves his eyes and then shuts them again. His lips move, as if he's trying to speak, but no sound comes out.

Miranda leans forward and puts her ear to his mouth. 'I can hear you. Say it again.'

She wants a deathbed confession, a declaration of love. She believes he can summon the remains of his consciousness, gather the failing traces of his self and breathe a last message.

He sinks back into inactivity. There are tears in Miranda's eyes. She's spent most of her life in charge, making decisions, treating Donald with a barely disguised irritation and all the time she must have loved him. They've had so many years together, getting on each other's nerves, sharing the disappointment of their son, perhaps not even thinking about love. But you couldn't live with someone for so long and not have feeling for them. There's a linking of roots, of history, an intricate tangling that's impossible to unpick.

I watch them and admire it. I have no equivalent. No one to love except Joel, and I can't keep him. He will belong to Alice soon, if all goes well. But even as I appreciate Donald and Miranda's relationship, I have no sense of loss for myself. I don't mind the absence of love. For me comfort lies in solitude, in not having to think of

291

anyone else.

Twenty-five minutes later, Donald dies.

* * *

'I'll drive you home, Grandma,' says Joel.

'But I've left the BMW outside your father's flat,' she says. Her skin is papery pale, her eyes shrunk into their sockets, dull and worn out. She looks like an old lady.

'I don't think you should drive,' I say.

'I'll come round tomorrow,' says Joel, 'and we'll fetch the car then. He hesitates for a moment and half-looks at Andrew.

'Ring me,' says Andrew.

'OK,' says Joel. 'But if I leave a message, ring me back.'

'OK,' says Andrew.

I drive Andrew back to his flat. He's more upset than I expected, bearing in mind that he hadn't spoken to his father for over twenty years. It occurs to me that some of his recent actions may have been prompted by his father's illness. Perhaps that's why he contacted me after so many years, why he's taken up climbing, started playing the violin. He's caught a glimpse of himself, his own mortality. Has he seen his own failures too?

We travel in silence, too exhausted to speak. When we arrive outside Andrew's flat I park on the side of the kerb, but he doesn't get out.

'Wake up, Andrew. Time to go home.'

'There's no point in going to bed,' he says. 'I've got to be up in an hour for work.'

I'm about to suggest that they might let him off for the day if they understand the circumstances when I remember that he doesn't need any help with excuses. It wouldn't be sensible to offer him any new ideas. 'Well, at least you've got time to have a shower and a decent breakfast.'

He still doesn't move.

'Off you go, Andrew.'

'Jess—can't we get back together again?'

I look out of the window. I don't want this conversation.

'They were closer than you realised, weren't they?' he says. 'I suppose when you live with someone for a long time you just get used to them, and we didn't give each other enough time. If I'd stayed longer it would probably have worked itself out.'

No, it wouldn't. He isn't Donald. 'Your father was a good-natured man—'

'Yes, he was. It wasn't him I had problems with, it was her.'

'Maybe you should have stayed in contact for his sake.'

'But she was impossible.'

'Lots of parents are impossible. Most people manage something.'

'I couldn't do it. I hated her.'

'You could have pretended. If you act it out long enough, you start to believe it.' Pretence gives you room to get round obstacles without touching them, the space to observe that there are other sides to people, not just the abrasive, challenging attitude that you can't cope with. You have to view people from new angles, see where the light falls, discover which edges have been worn down and softened with time. Otherwise you get so caught up in the negatives you can't see anything else.

'So—couldn't you pretend? If we got back together?'

'No.'

He gets out of the car. 'See you,' he says and turns away. His cheeks look wet in the glistening orange of the street lamp, but it might be a trick of the light. I watch him as he goes to the entrance and opens the door. He doesn't turn round.

*   *   *

My intention was to offer Miranda some practical help, but I should have known it wouldn't be necessary. She's brisk and organised, and within three days her house is immaculate, with no evidence of any emotional upheaval.

'In a way, it's a relief,' she says as we drink coffee together in the living room, overlooking the garden. Three giant birds sculpted out of the yew hedge lean towards us with a fixed melancholy, as if they know what has happened. 'He'd been ill for so long, and the last few months were very difficult.'

'You should have let me know,' I say.

'He didn't want to alarm anyone until he knew he was near the end. He sorted out all the paperwork and everything's under control. He was a good husband.' She pauses. 'We've had to get a gardener,' she says. 'Donald did love his topiary and I can't neglect it.'

I want to say that I'm sorry I hadn't realised he was so ill, that he was a good man, but I'm worried I'll use the wrong words. Everything sounds like a cliché.

We sit for a while without talking.

294

'So how do you think Andrew is managing these days?' she says at last.

How do I know? I don't see him often enough. 'Well,' I say, 'I think he's upset by his father's death.'

'They never had anything to say to each other,' she says. 'Donald was not one to be involved, you know. He let me do whatever I thought was right, and then he backed me. I don't think he and Andrew had a close relationship, which I regret now. I should have done more to encourage it.'

'I doubt if anything you did would have made any difference.'

'No, probably not.'

I look round her room. It's very calm, without pattern or clutter, nothing to indicate that anyone lives here. There's just one picture over the fireplace. They're proud of the fact that it's an original, an oil painting of a country scene, a path through a woodland leading to a stile and a distant meadow. I imagine Miranda and Donald walking round art galleries on holiday, politely admiring the modern works, privately hating them, not seeing the point. They would be looking for something they could identify with, a landscape, trees, the sea, everything painted exactly as it appeared.

'I wish Andrew had continued with his violin playing,' she says. 'It was the only thing he could do. He should have gone into teaching, if nothing else.'

I take my eyes from the picture. 'Do you really see him as a teacher?'

She smiles, a thin, vague smile. 'No, you're probably right.'

A flash of understanding passes between us. We both know Andrew, we're saying. There's no point in being unrealistic about this.

'Did you play music to him every day before he was born?' I ask.

'When did he tell you that?'

'Years ago. He thinks he was brainwashed.'

She hesitates. 'Do you know, I can't remember. I suppose I might have done. You're like that when you have a child, aren't you? You want everything for him, you know he's the brightest, the most talented, the best . . .'

I feel exactly the same about Joel. I always believed he was brilliant, and couldn't understand why no one else noticed.

'It's to do with security, I think,' she says. 'You want to know they have the skills to look after themselves and won't live in poverty. You want to give them the means to be happy.'

I'd wanted Joel to go to university, but he'd refused. 'Mum, I can earn my own living now,' he said. 'I don't need qualifications.' He was right, but I didn't feel confident about it at the time.

'You do your best,' she says. 'That's all you can do. It's only later that you wonder if you did the right thing. And who can decide if it was right or not? You can't go backwards and have another go.'

'In the end they do what they want to do anyway, don't they?'

She looks directly into my eyes and I have to turn away. 'I'm sorry he was such a bad husband,' she says.

'He wasn't that bad,' I say. 'We managed all right for a while.' I still can't bring myself to criticise him to anyone else because it would be an acknowledgement of my own stupidity. I should never have married him, and to confront the truth of my weakness would be to peer too far into the distance, just beyond my stretched fingertips.

'You're too generous, Jessica. You always were.'

How odd that she interprets my cowardice as generosity.

'It was partly my fault,' she says. 'And partly his nature.'

I'm embarrassed, not wanting to think about it. 'Andrew is Andrew,' I say. 'I don't think anyone is responsible for that.'

She gets up and goes to open a drawer in a table. She brings back a photograph album. 'Have you seen these?' she says.

I assume I've seen them before—the records of Andrew's achievements. Andrew in a concert at the age of seven, part of an orchestra, smaller than the other children, Andrew in the National Youth Orchestra, Andrew performing his first solo at nine, Andrew doing his recital for the semi-finals of Young Musician of the Year.

But these are not the photographs of Andrew's success. They're ordinary photographs, the rejects that didn't make it to the official albums because they were slightly blurred, or someone's thumb obscured a corner, or Andrew was being difficult and not smiling adorably. I'm moved that she's kept them. Here he is as a baby, his face screwed up into a fierce scream, a toddler having a tantrum, scowling, pulling faces, a typical naughty little boy. You can see his character developing, the unwillingness to cooperate, but he's still somehow likeable, a boy with a future, a boy who will grow up to be sensible, have a proper job, look after a

297

family.

'My brother was like him,' she says. 'He was very difficult too.'

'I didn't know you had a brother.'

'No. We never talked about him. He destroyed my mother. He dropped out of school when he was seventeen and disappeared until he turned up, seven years later, an alcoholic, and stole half my mother's jewellery. He was found dead at the age of twenty-five in a derelict house only a few miles from home.' She pauses. 'I was determined that Andrew wouldn't turn out like him.'

I suddenly see a vulnerable Miranda, a caring mother who wanted the best for her child. Just like me. She had been determined that he would live a productive life, with a skill, that he wouldn't turn her into a replica of her own mother. And it hadn't worked. 'I'm sorry,' I say.

There is a local paper on her coffee table, open at page two. The headline is written in bold capitals. 'FIDDLER ON THE ROOF,' it says.

CHAPTER TWENTY

'Jess! Can you type a letter to Mrs Flannel-face, Fungus-infested Forster before you go out? The miserable old skinflint still hasn't paid up.' Unusually for half past eight in the morning, Andrew had dragged himself out of bed to shout down to me. He stood at the top of the stairs in the same blue and white striped pyjamas that were new when Joel was born. Eight years later they were disintegrating, the material muslin-thin and transparent, the stripes fading into each other. Pyjamas were not high on my list of priorities.

'I can't,' I called up. 'We're already late for school.'

'It'll only take ten seconds.'

'He's been late twice this week and Mrs Lewis isn't very nice about it. He gets into trouble.'

There was a sulky silence at the top of the stairs and I felt guilty. We needed the money. Maybe it was possible to fit it in.

But Joel was still sitting at the computer. 'Come on, Joel. We really have to go.'

He ignored me.

'Please, Joel. Turn it off, this minute.'

He tapped away, his fingers moving so fast that it was impossible to see what he was doing. Neither Andrew nor I had taught him how to use it. He simply sat there and worked things out for himself. I'd watched him. He would press keys just to find out what happened, and get excited by the chain of events that he had set off. The screen was filling with figures, symbols, meaningless threads of letters that could have been the work of an eight-year-old genius or complete nonsense.

'You know what Mrs Lewis is like.'

He stopped then and looked round at me, his face pinched and tight. 'I don't want to go to school.'

I sighed and sat down next to him. 'I know. But you have to.'

'Why?'

'It's the law.'

He turned back to the computer. 'So let them put me in prison. It can't be worse than Mrs Lewis.'

299

'Unfortunately, it's not you that goes to prison. It's me. Or it's a fine, which we can't afford.'

'How much?'

'I don't know. Thousands, I imagine.'

He didn't reply. His fingers continued to fly over the keyboard. I decided that it was time to get annoyed. 'Enough, Joel. You have to finish right now.'

He never paid any attention to my threats. To him, my voice was equivalent to a wasp buzzing at the window, a drill out in the road, an aeroplane flying past in the distance. But today, self-preservation influenced him. He knew he would be in trouble at school if he was late. 'I'm just coming. Stop going on.'

'Don't be rude,' I said, to satisfy myself. My attempts at discipline were always met with complete disdain. Stop pretending, his silence seemed to imply. You don't mean it.

'You'd have had time to write that letter if you'd done it when I asked you,' shouted Andrew from upstairs.

'Sorry. I've been getting Joel ready for school. I'll write it this afternoon.'

I smiled at Joel, to show that there was no real animosity between his father and me, but he rarely showed much interest in Andrew's outbursts. He had the ability to withdraw, shut out external trivialities and reach total absorption in whatever he was doing. We were only the enablers, the ones who gave him access to the computer. He reminded me of myself as a child, the way I managed to play the piano while everyone else got on with things.

I tried to pretend that we weren't hurrying,

knowing that Joel would automatically resist if he thought I was being anxious. But once we had made it out of the house he trailed one step behind me, reluctance muffling his movements. It was late February, bright and cold, a silver dusting of frost glittering on the pavement. Normally, Joel would have been interested in this. 'I don't like Mrs Lewis,' he said, his voice thin and whining.

'No, neither do I. But you've put up with her for six months now. Only another six to go.'

'Five. There's no school in August.'

'Good point. And we've still got the Easter holidays to come—plus two half terms. That takes it down to about four months. There is hope that you might survive.'

'I bet Luke Skywalker didn't have to go to school.'

This was his *Star Wars* period. We'd videoed the films from the television and watched them at least twice a week. He could quote the scripts word for word, and frequently did so. Andrew and I could probably have reproduced the whole thing by then as well. If Joel managed to find someone to play *Star Wars* with him at school, someone who was willing to follow directions, then he could almost be described as happy.

'Luke Skywalker still had to learn things, even if he didn't go to school. That's what Obi-Wan Kenobi was for. He taught him.'

'Well, I want a teacher like that. At least he was learning something useful.'

'Most of your stuff is useful. You just can't see it at the time.'

'Yeah—like I'm really going to need to know how to write poetry. What rhymes with snow?

Crow, no, although, so? It's too easy. She should make us write about icicles. At least everyone would have to think a bit harder.'

'The only word to rhyme with icicle is bicycle. It's a bit limiting.'

'OK then, snowman. You could have go van or slow tan.'

He was managing to keep up with me now, his short legs moving twice as fast as mine. He was wearing a navy hat with robins round the rim, which he pulled firmly down over his ears. Other boys were too cool for hats, too aware of the potential for mockery. Not Joel. He was concerned about warm ears.

'Maybe thinking about snow will send you on a voyage of discovery and you'll be a great inventor of new technology—the next generation of fridges, freezers, skating rinks—'

'Blow fan, no pan—'

We were now in sight of the school, and he stuck his hands in his pockets, his face closed. We were just in time. The children were still lined up in the playground, waiting to go in.

'Run,' I said.

He sighed. I sympathised with his lack of interest in physical activity. How many times had I endured class hockey matches, playing left back on the winning side because they wanted me out of the way, my hands numb with cold, goose pimples clustering on my white, unweathered legs? All I ever wanted was the chance to go back indoors and sit down.

'Go man,' I said.

He glanced up with a quick, appreciative smile, then hurried over to join his class.

302

He ran without putting his heels down, his limbs somehow disconnected, like a puppet with tangled strings. He moved heavily, legs bending at the wrong moment, elbows swinging without rhythm, his whole body out of alignment.

I watched him enter the school gate and had to turn away. He appeared so vulnerable, so far away from the boyhood club that he couldn't embrace. No wonder he had no friends, never became part of a gang. It didn't bother him. He was oblivious to taunts, to the intense desire to conform that drove most children. He was only affected by the teachers who had the power to control him.

I was now worried about being late at the library. Walter, my boss, was never sympathetic. He was an unlikeable man with a love of correctness, a need for everything to be in the right place at the right time. He wrote short stories and had had some poetry published, which meant that he felt able to criticise modern literature with authority. He was contemptuous of women writers. Martin Amis was his idol. Head and shoulders above the competition, he told us with biting conviction.

'Late again, Jessica,' he said as I pushed through the front door of the library and skidded to a halt in front of him. I glanced at the clock above the desk. 9.03. 'You're being petty,' I said, and smiled to soften my words.

'Look after the minutes and the hours will look after themselves.'

'That's meant to be money,' I said. 'Pennies and pounds.'

But he had already returned to his lists, so I took off my coat and settled down without another

303

word.

*   *   *

Andrew was self-employed during this period, and my days had become frenetic. If I was late home at the end of the morning, lunch would be delayed and the whole day wasted. I needed to help him get started long before I had to fetch Joel from school. Otherwise, he would give up for the day. 'It's not worth it. I'll have a good go tomorrow.'

He was advertising himself as an odd job man, doing all the heavy, difficult jobs, like putting up curtain rails or operating a hired carpet-cleaning machine. He could lift things, go to a garden centre to buy garden ornaments, transfer them from the car and put them into position, even cut the grass if that's what people wanted.

Oddjobkins was the name of the business, and we'd had cards printed advertising his services. There was a nice little cartoon on the front—a man bent double with a door on his back. He was pushing a wheelbarrow in front of him at the same time as polishing the floor with his feet, which were wrapped in dusters. We'd walked the streets of Harborne, Edgbaston and Moseley, knocking on doors or putting cards through letter-boxes, seeking little old ladies, busy professional people who had no spare time, single mothers with daughters. I just hoped that nobody would ask him to put together a flat-pack wardrobe. We'd done one for our bedroom last year and I didn't want to repeat the experience.

Our search for work had gone well at first, and there were several jobs that needed doing immediately, but it had died down a bit in the last couple of weeks. The trouble was, once you'd cleared out the gutters, saved the bookshelves from collapse and constructed the new desk from MFI, that was it. They didn't need you any more.

So we intended to go out again that afternoon, looking for people, telling everyone how much they needed help.

When I arrived home, he was still in his pyjamas.

'Will you be ready in time?' I tried to keep my voice light and unaccusing.

He didn't move from the sofa, where he was sorting through his *Beano* collection. 'No rush,' he said.

'But there is a rush.'

'We haven't had lunch yet.'

'I'm just about to get it ready. Why don't you dress while I do us a sandwich?'

I left him on the sofa, hiding my irritation, because I knew that if he picked up the slightest hint of criticism, the day would be lost. While I was buttering the bread I listened for movement, desperate for him to get up, to show some energy and initiative.

But he shuffled into the kitchen in his dressing-gown and sat down at the table, the skin on his face loose and blurred round the edges.

'What?' he said to me.

'Nothing.'

'You're moaning.'

'I haven't said a word.'

'You don't have to.'

We sat together eating jam sandwiches, sipping coffee, not speaking. The air between us reverberated with unspoken resentment, pulled

305

and stretched by each of us in turn, while I tried to pretend everything was all right. He needed to work. We needed the money.

'It's not working out, is it?' he suddenly said, stretching his arms above his head and puncturing the atmosphere in one easy movement. He looked cartoonishly long, almost elegant, tipping his seat backwards, balancing on two legs. I had a moment of panic, imagining that the chair would give way and he would collapse into a broken heap on the floor, never able to work again.

'What isn't working out?'

He swung back into an upright position. 'The job. I'm not going to earn enough to live on.'

'I don't see why not. It's early days yet.'

'It's unsustainable. Either the entire known world wants work done at the same time, in which case I can't do it all anyway, or we go for weeks while people change their own light bulbs and buy pre-constructed furniture from Laura Ashley at vast expense.'

'It hasn't been weeks. You've got to give it a chance. If we go out this afternoon, we're bound to find something.'

He leant over the table towards me. All that stretching seemed to have realigned his bones, squeezed out the surplus air between them. They shrank back together, miserable and reduced. He sighed. 'It all seems so pointless. I'm just not cut out for this sort of thing.'

'We've had all those cards printed. And what are we supposed to live on?'

He looked across at me, his eyes dull and hard. 'It's all right for you. You have a nice comfortable job. You don't have to go into horrible houses and talk to strange people who think you're just a labourer.'

But he was just a labourer, an odd-job man. He didn't have any skills except playing the violin, and since he wouldn't do that he had to earn a living in some other way.

'Most of them are nice people,' I said. 'They're generous. Mrs Fellows paid you an extra five pounds.'

'I've been thinking about that. I reckon she made a mistake and it wasn't a tip at all. She just confused a ten pound note with a five pound note. Fairly typical. She's a bit batty.'

'So should you take it back?'

'Don't be stupid.'

He studied the table and chased some crumbs around with a thumb. 'I can't go on like this. I can't cope.'

I clutched my sandwich too tightly. The bread resisted, changed texture, lost its elasticity. 'What do you mean?'

He gestured round the kitchen. 'This—the pointless work, the bills, the house, Joel . . .'

I put down the mangled sandwich and licked the jam off my fingers. 'But Joel's your son.'

He shrugged. 'I hate this dump. I hate my life. I want to do something worthwhile, not sit here in an old council house with nothing in front of me.'

I felt betrayed. I'd worked very hard on our home. I'd bought curtain material from the market, hauled it home on the bus and sewn it together in the evenings once Joel was in bed. I'd bought second-hand furniture, stripped it down, revived the wood, re-covered the chairs. I'd found lamps in discount shops, lightshades in clearance sales, cheap wallpaper in bargain boxes. 'It's a nice house.'

'No it's not. Look around you, Jess. It's all so small, so petty, so cheap. Is this it? Is this what we're doomed to for the next twenty, thirty years of our life? I don't know about you, but I can't bear it.'

I started to rub my hands together. I could feel the rough texture of my fingertips, the dryness of the skin, the coldness of the knuckles. What was he saying? That he wanted to give it all up, emigrate? 'Why don't you go back to university and qualify? Get a job that interests you? There are lots of things you could do.'

'Like what? Work in a boring library? Teach kids like Joel's vile contemporaries? Sell washing machines all day, be nice to tedious people? No way.'

'So what do you want to do?'

And at that point, I saw the truth. He didn't want to do anything. Nothing gave him any sense of purpose or interest. He always thought there was something enthralling around the next corner, but couldn't be bothered to walk far enough to find out. I felt a surge of sympathy for him. What do you do if you can't smell the ground coffee beans, taste the chocolate fudge ice-cream, feel the heat from the sun on a spring morning? Where do you go next?

'It's the end of the road, Jess.'

'What road?'

He didn't reply. The house was getting gradually colder. We had turned the heating down because Joel wasn't at home, and the winter temperature crept in from the frost-bound garden, seeping

308

under the kitchen door, chilling my fingers, my toes, my nose.

'You're just feeling low,' I said, forcing my voice to be calm and reassuring. 'Maybe you should go to the doctor's. Depression makes people feel like that.' But if that were true, then he must have been born depressed.

He laughed, but it was just a rise and fall of wordless noise. Ha-ha, as you read in books. Unfeeling, unnatural. There was no laughter in his laughter. 'I don't think so. I'm just telling you the reality.'

I couldn't work out what had led to all this. One minute we were eating jam sandwiches, drinking coffee, talking about work and the next minute everything was hopeless.

'I don't understand what you want.'

'No, that's the trouble. You don't understand much, do you?'

'That's not fair. I work very hard to understand you.'

He looked at me with contempt. 'Quite. My point exactly. You work very hard at it. It doesn't come naturally, does it?'

But if you don't understand people, what can you do? Surely it's better to make an effort, to pretend, to work at it? There must be something to be gained from trying.

Was it so unreasonable to expect him to keep a job? A last vestige of indignation fired up inside me. He had a family to support.

Then I was crushed by the hopelessness of it all. Could you force someone into a role that didn't fit them? Make them dress up when they had trouble identifying themselves in normal clothes? Was it

309

reasonable? Andrew wasn't a typical man. I'd been expecting something impossible.

'We've reached the point of no return, haven't we?' he said.

'What does that mean?'

'I think maybe we should separate for a bit. Have a bit of breathing space.'

I stared at him. One minute he was complaining about his job, the next he was contemplating divorce. What was the link? 'I don't think that at all,' I said.

His mouth stretched into the shape of a smile. 'Poor Jess. You can't see the obvious, can you?'

I should have been angry, but I couldn't summon the energy. We'd slipped into a soap opera, resorting to a standard script. People didn't really talk like this. It was all a game, a story, a made-up nonsense.

'But—what about Joel?' That was a cliché too, echoing hundreds of television dramas. But how else do you say it?

'He won't mind. He'll be better off without me.'

'Don't say that. You get on all right with him.'

Andrew laughed again, a nasty, empty laugh. 'Ask Joel what he thinks about it. He'll be glad to see me go.'

'That's not true.'

'How would you know?'

I looked out of the window. The sun was already low in the sky, blindingly bright as it hovered above the roofs opposite, highlighting everything in its path with unforgiving severity. It was a distorting light, transforming cars and people into cartoons, painting eccentric shadows, harsh and demanding.

'Look,' I said, trying to keep my voice steady. 'If

310

you don't like working for yourself, don't do it. We can find something else. We can sort things out.'

He stood up, knocking the table, causing the coffee to slosh over the side of the mugs. 'I don't think so.'

What was he going to do? Would he sweep out of the house in a grand gesture, or would he take time and pack all his stuff? Almost everything frivolous in the house belonged to him. All our spare money had been spent keeping him happy—hi-fi, tapes, videos, watches, cameras. An attempt to engage his attention, foster some enthusiasm for a brief period, both of us pretending that he could be pleased, that he could find some fulfilment in ownership. And it was all pointless. He didn't know how to be happy. He had a momentary flash of pleasure in the chase, and then it was all gone. Getting married, having a child, it all followed the inevitable path. Boring, unnecessary, tedious. It was miraculous that he had stayed married for so long.

'I'll be upstairs,' he said and left the kitchen.

I sat at the table for a long time, growing colder, unable to move. I didn't know what he was intending to do. I couldn't say, 'Are you leaving us?' in case that gave the impression that I was in favour of the idea. I couldn't say 'Where will you go?' because his interpretation might be that I accepted the situation. I felt trapped by my inability to react.

I could hear him moving around upstairs. Was he packing, or was he just returning to bed?

After a long wait, I went up to the bedroom. He'd emptied the drawers and was arranging his clothes in piles on the bed. White shirts, blue

311

shirts, T-shirts, jeans, smart trousers.

'Look,' I said, keeping my voice calm and gentle. 'Surely we can work this out.'

He was folding shirts as if they were new, doing up the buttons, lining up the collars. 'We've been trying for years.'

'But—we've been all right. We've managed. I know it hasn't been easy, but we've coped. Everybody has difficulties. It's not particularly unusual. You just have to stick at it, and everything comes out all right in the end.'

'You think I haven't stuck at it? You think I've enjoyed sitting around in this hovel with you moaning all the time and Joel refusing to listen to me?'

'But we've had some good times. It hasn't all been bad.'

He stopped for a moment and met my eyes. I found his direct gaze more uncomfortable than his refusal to look at me. 'When? I don't remember them.'

I could feel tears forming. 'Lots of times.'

'Name them.'

'You know—' Tears were pouring out, but I brushed them aside with my hand. 'We've had lots of nice trips out, we've worked on the house, had meals with friends—'

'What friends?'

'Well, Mary and Eamon—'

'Your friends, not mine.'

I was choking on the tears now. 'Andrew, come on. You don't really mean it.'

'Oh, you think I'm lying, do you?'

'But where would you go?'

He shrugged. 'Don't worry about me. I have

places to go.'

He didn't have any friends he could stay with. He couldn't ask his parents, since he didn't speak to them. He could hardly expect my parents to give him a room at Audlands, although it wouldn't amaze me if he asked. Had he rented a bedsit somewhere?

'Did you plan this?' I asked. My tears dried up as I grasped the implied calculation behind his actions.

But he turned back to his packing. 'Isn't it time you went to fetch Joel?'

It wasn't. It was an hour early. But I left anyway and went to Mary's.

CHAPTER TWENTY-ONE

Mary and I sat on opposite sides of her kitchen table. I could smell the heat of the water as she poured from the teapot, steam rising with gentle delicacy into the air. A milk jug and a sugar bowl stood by in a state of futile readiness. Mary enjoyed the full ritual of tea-making, even though few visitors took sugar any more.

'He can't mean it,' she said.

'I think he does.' I stirred non-existent sugar with a teaspoon. Nothing felt real. It was as if I was living in the middle of a bizarre dream. Now that I was sitting here, safe and comfortable with Mary, I couldn't get the feel of the dream right. It sounded tame and unthreatening.

'But he loves you.'

How would she know? 'That was ages ago,' I

said. 'People change.'

'No,' she said. 'Nobody stops loving someone just like that. The love just follows a different pattern.'

I wasn't sure she was right about this. Did Andrew ever love me? Did he even know what love was? 'You'd think he'd consider Joel, wouldn't you? I mean, he's only eight.'

'It's always hard for children,' she said.

I sipped the tea and it washed through me, a temporary placebo. Mary's kitchen was bright and warm. I didn't want to move.

Mary leaned over and rubbed my arm. She liked to punctuate her thoughts with touch, although she knew I preferred not to. It didn't seem to me that you needed physical contact to show affection or understanding for someone. Surely the tone of your voice had that effect. But Mary wanted more than words. As if she couldn't function without touching people, as if they weren't real to her if she couldn't feel them. An insecurity, maybe? A lack of belief in what people said?

'It'll be all right, Jess, you'll see. He's just going through a difficult patch.'

'You said that last time, when he refused to speak to me for a fortnight after he didn't get the arts administrator job.'

'Well, I was right, wasn't I? He talked to you in the end.'

I looked past her, my eyes filling with tears again. 'It's different this time. He's still speaking to me, and he was packing when I left.'

'But where would he go?'

'I have no idea. But he seems to have a plan.'

Mary was as surprised as me that he had chosen

314

this moment to give up. She couldn't understand why Andrew would reject our house or his new business. She loved the idea of Oddjobkins and had already found several jobs for him, insisting on paying the full amount, refusing to accept discounts. 'What does he really want, do you think?'

'Nothing. Well—everything, I suppose, but when he gets it he doesn't want it. He can't accept that he may not be rich one day, that he's never likely to have enough money to take up sailing as a hobby, go skiing or travel round the world. He's always been like that. Right from when we very first knew him. I just didn't understand it then.'

I thought I could see tears in Mary's eyes. 'Oh, Jess,' she said softly, and it was obvious she knew what I was talking about. She must have struggled with Andrew over the years, but she had never spoken about it.

'Have you considered . . .' she said hesitantly and stopped.

'What?'

'Well—that maybe things would be easier if he did go?' She started to move the teapot over to the sink, fetching a cloth to wipe the table. She kept her eyes lowered.

I didn't know what to say or think. I'd never allowed my thoughts to go in this direction. I believed in loyalty. 'I've got to pick up Joel,' I said. 'I'm late.'

'I'll take you in the car.'

'What time's your first lesson?'

She taught the piano at home in the early evenings, so I was grateful I'd been able to catch her before she started.

'It's an easy day. Really. Three children from the same family are on holiday.'

'OK. Thank you.'

'Look, I'll leave the boys next door and we'll come round later. Perhaps Eamon could talk to Andrew if he's still there. They get on well, don't they?'

I nodded. I didn't like to tell her that Andrew was scathing about Eamon. 'Typical lawyer, thinks he's right whatever he does. He's got too much money. It makes him complacent.' I'd always assumed Andrew was jealous. Eamon was a little pompous, but he was likeable and easy-going and he was very good to Mary. No man is perfect.

'Joel's teachers don't understand him,' I said as we drove to school.

'But he's so intelligent,' said Mary.

'Yes, but not in a conventional way, so they don't get it.'

If Andrew leaves, I kept thinking, I could go home to silence.

*   *   *

'How was your day?' I asked Joel as we walked home.

'Fine,' he said.

I felt I should be talking to him, but I couldn't think of anything to say. He stomped along, eyes fixed on the ground. It was difficult to know if he even realised I was there.

Should I tell him about his father's intentions? It seemed a good idea to prepare him, but at the same time I couldn't be sure that Andrew wouldn't change his mind. 'Daddy might be going away for a

316

while,' I said at last.

'Oh,' said Joel.

What did he feel for his father? There wasn't much evidence of love in Joel. He didn't like kisses or hugs and he was much happier on his own than with us. But children's love for parents didn't necessarily manifest itself in any physical way. It was more an automatic dependence, a built-in feeling that didn't need to be put into words. Something he'd only recognise if it was taken away.

So did Andrew love Joel? I'd always thought that he did. He was so proud of him when he was a baby, and there had been good times when they'd managed to talk on the same wavelength. But he didn't show it in any obvious way either. Did he understand love, or was there an absence there, a disability, that meant he didn't know how to do it or even recognise there was something missing? Did he only love for what he got in return? Attention from me, conversation from Joel, admiration from onlookers.

The cold air was beginning to chill my fingertips inside my gloves. I needed to change the subject of the conversation with myself.

'Did you do maths today?'

'Yes.'

'How did it go?'

'Fine.'

'Was Mrs Lewis pleased with you?'

'No, of course not. She never is.'

I gave up.

The car was outside the house when we arrived home, so Andrew was still there. I raced down the front path, leaving Joel behind, and opened the front door.

317

'Hello!' I called in a pretend-cheerful voice. 'We're back.'

Andrew was in the living room, putting his comics into piles. 'You were a long time,' he said, as I walked in.

'Yes, I was a bit early, so I went to see Mary on my way,' I said, relieved that he was talking normally and his earlier mood had lightened. I sat down on the sofa next to a pile of comics. They were well-thumbed and ragged, the original garish colours faded to an antique softness. Andrew looked up, saw me touch them, and moved them out of my reach.

'Would you like a cup of tea?' I said.

'Great.'

I made the tea and brought it through to the living room.

'Thanks,' he said.

The day slipped deeper into its atmosphere of dreamlike unreality. Andrew never said thank you. It wasn't part of his vocabulary. 'You're not really leaving, are you?'

'Yes,' he said.

I thought of Mary coming round with Eamon later. 'Are you going to have some supper with us first?'

He nodded. 'OK.'

Joel came into the living room with two ginger biscuits on a saucer and saw the piles of comics. 'Cool,' he said. 'Beryl the Peril.'

I looked at Andrew over his head. 'Are you going to tell him, then?' I asked. 'Or shall I?'

'In my own time,' said Andrew.

'Tell me what?' said Joel.

'Daddy's going away,' I said.

Joel sighed. 'You said that before.'

'So you've already told him,' said Andrew.

'No, not really. I just said you might be going away for a bit. That's all.'

'You're not taking the comics, are you?' said Joel.

'Yes,' said Andrew. 'I am. What are you going to do about it?'

'I'll scream,' said Joel. 'Until I'm sick.'

'I'd better get out of the way, then.'

Joel picked up a comic and settled down on the sofa reading it. He chuckled to himself every now and again. I went out into the kitchen to prepare supper.

*   *   *

I made some coffee after we'd eaten. Andrew sat at the table, gazing out of the window into the darkness, as if it was an ordinary day. You could just see the edge of the garden in the light from the house. He doesn't mean it, I thought. He's not really going. He's just trying to make a point.

'You'll have to move the camellia once it's flowered,' he said. 'You've planted it in the wrong place. The early morning sun will kill off the flowers.'

'You could do it,' I said, although he wouldn't have done it in normal circumstances. He never got round to these things.

'I won't be here,' he said.

Joel had left the table and was playing with the computer in the living room. 'Look,' I said in a low voice. 'You don't have to do this. We can work it out.'

'I don't think so.'

'Andrew—think of Joel.'

'He doesn't need me. He doesn't need you either. You must have noticed that.'

'He doesn't realise he needs us, but he does. All children need their parents. We're his security, his safety—'

'Tautology,' he said. 'Security and safety are the same thing.'

'Please,' I said. 'Stop playing with words. You know what I mean.'

He put down his mug of coffee and looked at me directly, pushing his head forward so that I could see into his eyes. 'I told you,' he said. 'I'm going.'

He was too close. I could smell his unwashed hair, see the individual strands of his eyebrows, the sheen of coffee on his lips.

The doorbell rang.

I started to push my chair back, expecting Mary and Eamon but he grabbed my arms so that I couldn't move. I was pinned against the table, leaning forward at an uncomfortable angle, the pressure from his fingers digging into my skin. 'I've had enough,' he said. 'You've nagged me for ten years. You think you know me, but you don't. You can't penetrate beyond what you see. You're blind, Jess and you don't even know it.'

The doorbell rang again.

A thin whimper came from nowhere, confusing me until I realised it was coming out of my mouth. 'The door,' I whispered. 'There's someone at the door.'

'They can wait. We're talking.'

'I think we should answer it,' I said. The concept of not opening the door when there was someone

320

outside was too difficult for me, impossible to accept. But at the same time, I didn't want Mary and Eamon to find us like this. Mary knew that Andrew was leaving, but she'd never seen him as he was now. This Andrew was a stranger, a secret, frightening alter ego that I didn't want anyone to know about. I was ashamed of him.

The doorbell rang for a third time. I could hear the letter box rattling. 'Jess! Andrew! Are you there?' It was Eamon.

'You asked him to come, didn't you?' said Andrew in a slow, hard voice.

I shook my head, denying it to myself. I didn't know they were coming. I knew nothing about it. It was as much a surprise to me as it was to Andrew. 'No,' I whispered. 'No.'

He let go of my arms and jumped up. I wanted Mary and Eamon to go away as well. This was private, between me and Andrew. But I wiped away the tears with the back of my hand and stood up. I breathed in and out, and composed my face so that it would appear as if nothing was the matter, then I followed Andrew into the hall and watched him open the door.

Eamon's shoulder was just visible in the doorway, with Mary's concerned face behind, lit up by the porch light.

'Andrew!' he exclaimed with a theatrical over-friendliness as he stepped forward to come in.

Andrew shut the door.

'Andrew!' I said, unable to believe what he'd done. 'You can't do that.'

He turned to me. 'I can do anything I want.' His face was expressionless.

'No, you can't,' I said.

'Try me.'

'Come on, Andrew,' I said, struggling to prevent my voice from shaking. I had to reach inside him, force him to switch into a different way of thinking. 'We ought to let them in. They'll wonder what on earth's going on.'

'Let's give them a treat,' he said.

There was a vase on the hall table, one that my mother had given me a few years ago. She had bought it at an auction, along with some tulip vases for Audlands. It was Wedgwood, beautifully shaped, turquoise, with a gold rim.

Andrew picked it up.

'Careful,' I said, concentrating on calmness. 'It's quite valuable, I think.'

'Yes,' he said and threw it at the front door. It hit with a spectacular crash and shattered, tiny sharp slivers flying out in all directions.

I couldn't prevent myself from crying out, but immediately regretted the sound. It was too dramatic. He was only playing, acting out a part without meaning it. It wasn't a good idea to play along with him, to pretend it was serious.

I swallowed and tested my voice. It was thick and unnatural, but I managed to speak without crying. 'Now look what you've done. The mess.'

'Jess!' It was Mary's urgent voice from outside. 'Are you all right?'

'Mum?' Joel came out of the living room, frowning. We had finally succeeded in diverting his concentration from the computer. 'What's happened?'

'It's nothing,' I said, making myself smile. 'Just an accident. Go back to the computer. I'll clear it up, don't worry.'

Andrew was standing by the door, legs apart, arms hanging loosely by his sides, panting slightly. He looked triumphant, as if he'd just blasted his way into the enemy's headquarters and lobbed a grenade amongst them. The position didn't suit him. He was too thin for a hero, his face not rugged enough.

'Jess!' Now it was Eamon calling. 'Open the door!'

Joel turned his back on us and went back into the living room.

'We'll have to let them in,' I said in a low voice. 'We'll tell them it was an accident.'

'Why?' he said. 'Why not tell them the truth? That I'm a sadistic monster who's about to kill you.'

I made myself smile. 'Don't be silly,' I said. 'There's no need to be melodramatic.'

'I've told you before. Don't call me silly.'

'Jess! Jess!' I could hear Mary starting to panic and I felt sorry for her.

'It's all right,' I called. 'Everything's fine.'

'Andrew!' It was Eamon this time, speaking in a calmer voice. 'Could you let us in, old man? It's rather cold out here and you've got us a bit worried.'

Andrew's face was completely blank. No emotion, no embarrassment, no anger, no compassion.

'I'm coming,' I called, making my voice as cheerful as possible, desperate to pretend there was nothing wrong. 'Won't be a second.'

I walked past Andrew to the door and put my hand on the catch but he clamped his hand over my wrist. 'Don't touch that door,' he said. 'If I want to let them in, I'll do it, not you.'

I tried to push past him, but he grabbed my other arm. 'Do as you're told!' He pulled me back and then threw me against the wall. My back rammed into the corner of the hall table and I yelped with pain. I struggled to keep my balance, but my feet were in the wrong place and I could feel myself falling over.

Mary was screaming in the distance. 'Jess! Jess!'

I could hear Joel's raised voice, urgent and annoyed. 'Why doesn't anyone let them in?'

My knees and hands jolted on to the floor. Someone—Joel, it must have been, was squeezing past me to the door. Andrew was shouting. 'You never know when to stop, do you? When to give it a rest? On and on and on, driving me mad!'

It was difficult to work out what happened next. The front door flew open and there was a sudden confusion of people, feet, shoes, raised voices. Mary appeared beside me, but her head was turned away. 'Eamon!' she yelled.

Andrew and Eamon were fighting, grappling with each other like schoolboys in a playground. But they were so much bigger, and there was no room in our hall for this kind of thing. It was like watching a film but more real. There was no sense that they were acting, that they would stop at a word from a director and have another go. It was an ugly, muffled battle of strength, almost silent except for subdued grunts of pain.

'Stop it!' I shouted. 'Andrew! Get off him.'

I could see Joel standing by the half-open door, his jaw dropped, his eyes round with amazement. Andrew and Eamon parted briefly and I thought they were going to stop, but Andrew lurched forward, grabbed Eamon's shoulders and flung him against the banisters. The wood splintered with a shriek of protest and Eamon slumped to the floor.

Everything stopped. Mary and I were holding our breath, Andrew was bent over, gasping for air, while Eamon's chest rose and fell, shuddering with the effort of breathing. A silent tableau, everyone frozen in confusion, the pause button pressed on the video.

Then Andrew straightened up. 'For goodness' sake,' he said. 'This is no way to carry on.'

He bent down and offered his hand to Eamon, who was half-sitting, half-lying at the bottom of the stairs, a broken banister resting on his shoulder, his left leg bent underneath him at an odd angle. 'I don't think I can get up,' he said. 'I might have broken something.'

Mary rushed to his side. 'Don't move,' she said. 'I'll phone for an ambulance.'

'No need,' said Andrew. 'I can run him to Casualty in the car.'

I pulled myself up, aching with the effort. 'We should look at it first,' I said. 'It might not be broken.'

Mary, Andrew and I managed to half-carry Eamon into the living room and laid him on the sofa. He was very pale and a thin layer of sweat shone on his cheeks. He was trying not to complain, but his leg hung limp and twisted and we could see that he was in considerable pain.

'I'm ringing for an ambulance,' said Mary and went into the hall to the telephone.

She came back quickly. 'They'll be here in a few minutes,' she said and burst into tears.

I put my arm round her and steered her towards a chair. 'I'm so sorry, Mary,' I said. 'Sit down here.' I fetched her a glass of water, which she sipped slowly.

'Sorry,' she said. 'I suddenly felt a bit faint.'

I looked across at Joel, who had returned to the computer. He was tapping away, his eyes glued to the screen, oblivious to what was going on around him.

'I can't come with you to the hospital,' I said to Mary. 'I'll have to stay with Joel.'

Andrew was backing away from all of us. I don't know if he was physically moving, or if it was just his manner, but he didn't seem to be in the room any more, or even in the house. He was far away, on another planet.

An unfamiliar anger swept through me. How could he do this? In front of his own son? The Wedgwood vase had been worth a lot of money. Mary and Eamon were my friends.

'I think you'd better go,' I said in a clear, strong voice.

But he may have left before I said it.

*   *   *

Eamon's ankle was broken in several places and he had to have pins inserted. He stayed in hospital for a fortnight, then needed crutches for the next three months. He didn't make any attempt to press charges against Andrew for assault, which was decent of him considering he was a lawyer. I went to see him in hospital several times, wanting to apologise, but he wouldn't discuss it.

Carry on as normal, he seemed to be saying.

Let's not make a meal out of it. It's just one of those things.

A decent man. A man who could have taught Andrew a thing or two, if only Andrew had been there to be taught. But he wasn't. He had gone. I was left with Joel, most of the furniture and rent arrears on the house. No car, not enough money to pay the gas bill. And no prospect of maintenance, since Andrew was unlikely to earn a reasonable income.

Joel never spoke of the incident. He acted as if it hadn't happened.

Andrew turned up after a couple of months to claim his right to see Joel, so they went out every other Saturday. They wandered round the Science Museum together, sat in McDonald's or went to the cinema. I often wondered what they talked about.

CHAPTER TWENTY-TWO

The oak floorboards in the Long Gallery dip and creak, then spring back into shape as Harriet and I make our way through the dust. The air is dry, warmed by the sun from the southwest-facing windows. The heels on Harriet's sandals click with a confident, authoritative rhythm.

'I used to skate up and down here,' I say. 'When I was about seven.'

'Yes, I remember.'

'I didn't realise anyone knew I was here.'

Her face softens with amusement. 'There were lots of things you didn't realise.'

As we reach the end of the gallery we peer through the tall, multi-paned window. I pull a tissue out of my cardigan pocket and wipe the clouded glass, but my efforts are only partially successful, as much of the grime is on the outside. We lean forward to see past the muddled branches of overgrown larches and beeches, searching for a glimpse of the lake. Distant water glints in the sunlight and it's just possible to see the skeleton roots of trees, the tracery of their ancient bones exposed by erosion as unprotected topsoil tumbles into the silted water. Canada geese have taken over tenancy of the lake during the last few years and they seem content with the privacy of their exclusive home, pottering around the water's edge, gliding through the water, multiplying.

'Look.' Harriet points at an overgrown area of dandelions and cornflowers, hedge parsley and nettles. 'You can't see the clock tower any more.'

'Or even the statue of Artemis.'

'It's difficult to imagine we once played football there with the cousins, isn't it? I used to practise for hours on my own, determined to beat Philip, but it never seemed to make any difference.'

'I don't know why you bothered,' I say. 'It was always going to be a lost cause.'

I visualise myself curled up on the window seat, watching through a corner of the window, my head low in case they thought I was spying, even though they couldn't possibly have seen me. I was so apart then, so unconnected, with no concept of other people. What was the defining experience that wrenched me out of that dreamlike existence and dropped me into the coldness of reality? It must have been the discovery of love that did it. For

Andrew or Joel. Was it worth it? Wouldn't it have been easier to stay where I was?

A sudden thump in the distance interrupts my thoughts. 'What was that?' says Harriet.

There are more thumps, a regular beat, the thwack of balls against rackets. 'Tennis,' I say. 'Mum said that someone from the village wanted to renovate the tennis court. She was quite keen— you know, young men coming and going.'

'Of course, I'd forgotten. She did tell me. Can we see them?'

We move along to another window. 'Here,' I say. A man in jeans, shoulder-length hair held back by a band round his forehead, bounds into our line of vision, racket outstretched, his trim body focused into a formidable strength and energy.

Harriet watches closely. 'We ought to go and join in,' she says.

'Not me. They look far too good.'

The man crosses the court, out of our line of vision.

Another figure comes into view and swings his arm back with controlled expertise. We can hear the ball hitting the centre of his racket with a satisfying crack. 'I wonder which one has the tattoo.'

Harriet raises an eyebrow. 'Tattoos?'

'Apparently one of them has a tattoo on his arm. A little seashell. Very discreet, Mum thought.'

'Hmm. Not a good idea to put into her head. If she was a bit more mobile, she'd probably go and get one for herself.'

We wander back through the patches of sunlight, stopping to examine the busts of Caesars. Their faces have been eroded by time and careless ownership, but they still demand attention, regarding us with the same mixture of pride and contempt that they would have held for their subjects.

'They could be sold,' says Harriet. 'They must be worth something, even in this state.'

'No!'

She stops and studies my face, smiling gently. As usual, she slips into the role of older sister. She believes she's wiser, more experienced than me, and I believe it too. 'Everything changes, Jess,' she says. Her tone is heavier than her words, as if she wants to convey something more serious, without actually saying it.

'What do you mean?'

Light from the window catches the side of her face. Natural shadows form in the curves of her cheekbones, down the side of her nose, round the contours of her perfectly formed lips. I find it difficult not to stare at her. I've always known she was attractive. I hadn't realised until now that she was beautiful.

'It's just common sense,' she says. 'People are always so afraid of the future, of new things, as if there's some automatic, intrinsic merit in age. They're obsessed with preserving old houses, old languages, old customs. Why? Why is progress an enemy?'

We stop in front of Caesar Augustus. The one who did the census, who announced the decree that led everyone back home and Joseph and Mary to Bethlehem. Something about the shape of his head, the way his hair curls, reminds me of someone, but I can't think who. 'Perhaps the past is comfortable because you know what happened.

The uncertainty of the future makes it more alarming,' I say.

She puts a finger out and strokes Octavius' nose. 'I find it exhilarating.'

The tip of his nose is missing. Was he once dropped, or did a stray cricket ball come hurtling through the air? 'You're home for longer this time,' I say after a while. 'Is everything all right?'

She doesn't look at me, and her finger goes on stroking the damaged nose. 'Of course. They owe me a lot of holiday, so I thought I'd take it all in one go. I wanted the chance to relax properly, to forget work for a while.'

'Do you achieve that by coming back to Audlands? Living in the shadow of old things?'

A brief smile hovers round the corners of her mouth, then fades. 'I needed time to think.'

I find that I'm holding my breath, waiting for information. I let it out a bit at a time, hoping she won't hear me, struggling to formulate the right question.

She speaks before me. 'You know, this statue reminds me of someone.'

'I was thinking exactly the same thing.'

'Philip.'

I examine the statue again in surprise. He's a man with a belief in himself, an easy over-confidence. 'Yes,' I say. 'You're right. There's a definite arrogance there.'

She doesn't react to this, but I have the feeling she isn't pleased. 'I told you I met him,' she says.

'Yes. What's he doing now?' I try to make my enquiry breezy, as if I'm only casually interested.

'Not at all what you'd expect. He's a professional diver.'

'Is he rich?'

'No, I don't think so.'

This is difficult to believe. 'I thought he'd be a corporate lawyer or an accountant, something like that, earning pots of money.' He wasn't the type to follow his instincts and do something for the love of it.

'You didn't like him, did you?'

I can feel a shudder rippling through my body, but I don't want her to see it. 'Did you?'

'Yes, he was fun. I liked it when the cousins came over—we always had great games.'

'I wasn't much good at them though, was I?'

She doesn't seem to be listening. Her eyes are watching the tennis players as they dart in and out of sight.

I sit down on the window seat, and after a few seconds Harriet joins me. 'Do you remember the country dancing?' she asks.

There had been a period when our mother abandoned treasure hunts in favour of barn dances. The Dashing White Sergeant, the Gay Gordons, the Cumberland Square Eight. The dances took place regularly for a while, once a fortnight on Saturday afternoons, and most of the village came at first. Our mother had come across an old man called Bert, who worked in a museum somewhere and knew all the moves. He would stand in front of the main fireplace and bellow directions in a huge voice that mushroomed out from his tiny, shrivelled body.

After a few weeks, the pleasure of the dancing started to fizzle. Some of the children became too much of a nuisance, skidding up and down on the wooden floor, getting under the feet of the adults, and the record player kept breaking down. Eventually people drifted away and the Long Gallery sank back to its solitude, happier with antiquity than the heated enthusiasm of younger generations.

'It was a good idea,' I say. 'Like most of Mum's ideas.'

'Maybe, although I think lots of people felt patronised.'

'Really?' How had Harriet picked that up at such a young age?

'Well, it's obvious, isn't it? There was Mum, all airy and generous, extending the hand of bounty to the villagers. It was bound to fail.'

'So why did they come in the first place?'

'Curiosity, I imagine.'

'Didn't they like her?'

'What do you think?' says Harriet. 'Most of them were out all day, working long hours to pay the mortgage, while Mum swanned around Audlands collecting antiques, buying statues, organising treasure hunts for the deprived children of the neighbourhood. She didn't stand a chance, did she?'

'I wonder why she liked the treasure hunts so much?' I say. 'She was quite obsessed.'

'Maybe she needed the intellectual stimulation.'

'Of course. "It's not very cosy if you're looking for pillows, You'd have much more fun playing Wind in the—"'

'Tricky,' says Harriet.

'Intellectual stimulation isn't exactly the right expression somehow.'

'I used to find her so embarrassing,' says Harriet. 'The way she came and talked to all my

333

friends as if she was one of us. Her clothes . . .'

Harriet embarrassed? 'You hid it well,' I say.

There's a mirror opposite us, edged with swirls of leaves and Greek urns, black where the gold leaf has worn away. I study our reflection without moving my head, wanting to see us as strangers, people who don't believe they're being watched. We don't look alike—it would be difficult to identify us as sisters. You can't see our parents in either of us. And yet there is something—the angle of our heads, tipping very slightly to the right, an almost imperceptible slant to the eyebrows, an inability to relax the muscles round the mouth. None of it would show up in a photograph. It's the way we take up space, the way the air is disturbed around us.

'I got to know Philip really well while we were in Saudi Arabia,' says Harriet.

I turn to look at her. 'What do you mean, really well?'

A faint blush is creeping up her cheeks. 'I mean really well.'

I can't believe what she's saying. 'Philip? We're talking about Philip?'

'There's no need to be quite so amazed,' she says.

'But he's our cousin.'

'So? It's not illegal. First cousins are allowed to marry.'

My sister and Philip? Philip the bully, the arrogant sadist, with Harriet, who is elegant and charming, who knows about people, who wears white dresses and hats?

'Well, say something.' Her voice is tight and nervous.

'I don't know what to say.' I need time. I'd rather not think about them together. I can't.

'So what's the problem?'

'But—Philip? He's—'

'What?'

'Well—he's not your sort of person . . .' How do I know that? I know nothing about her tastes, her friends, her lifestyle.

'I told you he's changed. He's a different person.'

'You're not going to marry him?'

'Why shouldn't I if I want to?'

She is going to marry him.

'Anyway, I can't,' she says. 'He's already married.'

'And you're the other woman?'

'No, not really. They don't live together. Not for about five years now.'

'So why aren't they divorced?'

'It's complicated.'

'Isn't it always?'

I've spent years trying not to think about him. I thought all that embarrassment and fear had gone, but I was wrong. It was just lying dormant, a rash waiting to break out at the first available opportunity.

'Is that why you've come home for a bit?' I ask.

She nods, holding out her fingers and inspecting the delicately painted pearl nails. 'I needed time to think it over.'

'Harriet, he's not nice.'

'You're wrong. He's kind and considerate.'

'Not as I remember him,' I say.

'You only knew him as a boy. People change when they grow up, they mellow. Anyway, he

335

wasn't that bad. Just a bit of a show-off.'

'He was nasty.' I don't want to believe that he's changed. You must be able to link the child to the adult. It's a natural process—each stage leads to the next. If he's being kind and considerate, how does she know he's not pretending, acting out the part that she's looking for? Is he simply reflecting her wishes?

She looks up. 'In what way was he nasty?'

I shake my head. 'I don't want to talk about it.'

Her eyes are clear and direct. 'You know, Jess, you've never wanted to talk about unpleasant things. Maybe you should.'

I turn away from her and look up the Long Gallery. 'Actually,' I say, 'this room was made for barn dances.'

'We should do it again,' says Harriet, jumping up suddenly. 'Have a dance, invite the whole village.'

She skips up the gallery, snapping her fingers, heels clicking. I can see that she's used to dancing, her body swinging and swaying in time to an invisible beat.

'Careful!' I call, getting to my feet and stumbling after her, worrying that she'll trip on an uneven edge of wood. I'm the musical one, I know all about rhythm, but I'm not streamlined. I don't have her grace, and I've never been able to summon that kind of physical energy. Watching her, I just feel tired. She's still a young woman, preserved by her lifestyle, her high earnings, her ability to enjoy herself and, above all, her friendly nature.

'You're so boring, Jess,' she shouts, her laughter ringing upwards and bouncing back down from the ornate carved ceiling. 'How can you not enjoy this wonderful room?'

'I do enjoy it,' I call. 'Why should you assume that I don't?'

'No reason.' She turns and skips back to me. 'Let's persuade Mum to have another party. A last party.'

'Why a last one?'

'Before they leave.' She stops and gestures wildly with her arms. 'Come on, Jess. Just look at the garden, the lake, the rotting windows, the holes in the floor. It's going to fall down.'

'Nonsense. It's been here for over two hundred years. Why would it fall down now?'

'Because nobody's looking after it any more.'

It's so easy to be fooled by the sunshine, the shafts of benign light that cast a warm glow on the oak floor, bleaching the powder-blue walls, reflecting back from the mirrors. In reality, the wallpaper is coming away, the floor is uneven where damp has penetrated and the Caesars are grey with dirt.

'However could we have a party with the house in this condition?'

She grins. 'We could tell everyone it's a falling down party, a farewell party.'

'We can't do that without telling Mum and Dad.'

'Oh, they won't mind.' They might not mind if she says it. They would if it came from me. She's already inventing explanations. 'We could just say it's a chance to explore the old building, give it back a brief glory. I bet people would come.'

The idea is appealing. 'Why not?' I say.

She looks delighted. 'Let's go and see what Dad thinks.'

No need to ask Mum. She'll be thrilled.

337

As we walk back, Harriet links arms with me. I find it awkward as we negotiate the doors, but I let her stay there. It obviously pleases her.

'You know, keeping secrets hidden away does you no good,' she says. 'They become too big, more likely to eat away at you as you get older.'

'That's good, coming from you,' I say, wondering if this is a reference to Andrew.

She reacts with genuine surprise. 'Whatever do you mean? I've just told you about Philip.'

You haven't told me anything, I think. Only hinted. 'People put too much emphasis on discussing their feelings,' I say. 'In the end, they shape their emotions into whatever they think the other person wants to hear.'

The view I want to have of Philip is the one I have from all those years ago. It's an image that hovers in the background of my life, a statue hanging over the lawn, fully formed and permanent. If I have to challenge that image, let it crumble a little, it's a threat to the memories which have formed me. Why should I think of him with kindness or forgiveness? What could I tell Harriet about him? That he pinched me occasionally, that he tried to kiss me? Is that it?

But it's more than that. More even than the broken finger. It's the way he was. The way he hovered over me when he wasn't there. I don't want to acknowledge the fact that I once found him attractive or that he was the monster creeping around my bedroom when I woke up from nightmares. This is not something I want to share with anyone, let alone my sister.

To talk about it, to let him be changed, would be like a betrayal of the girl I was then. I don't want to see him as he is now. He is forever the ogre in my past.

*   *   *

My mother is less enthusiastic about the idea of a barn dance than we were expecting. 'Well, it's a nice idea,' she says. 'But I don't think my knees are really up to it any more. And Audlands isn't looking as good as it should these days.'

'It's missing your magic touch,' says Harriet. 'But we don't need to open up as much as we used to. Just a few rooms downstairs and the Long Gallery.'

'Is it safe?' says my father from behind his newspaper. 'They can sue you nowadays, you know.'

'I'm not sure I'm mobile enough to clean the Long Gallery,' says my mother. 'It's awfully big.'

'You don't have to be mobile,' says Harriet. 'Jess and I are going to do it. We'll get some help from Joel and that fiancée of his. Alice.'

'Have I met Alice?' asks my mother, knowing she hasn't.

'He's going to bring her over,' I say. 'There's been a lot going on recently. Joel's grandfather died, you know.'

'I'm his grandfather,' says my father.

'Not you,' I say. 'His other grandfather. Andrew's father.' I don't like to name Andrew in their presence. It's like a one-second power cut. The lights flicker and the clocks don't stop, but you know something's happened.

'Really?' says my father, rolling his wheelchair towards us, no longer pretending to read the

339

paper. 'He was younger than me, wasn't he?'

I don't know. 'Oh, you're a good ten years older than him,' I say.

'Hmm,' he says. 'So I'm living on borrowed time.' He opens up the paper again. 'Are you going to make us some coffee, Harriet? I like that Colombian stuff you bought.'

'Fair Trade,' says my mother. 'Such a good idea.'

'So shall we do it?' says Harriet.

'Make coffee? Yes, of course.'

'The barn dance?'

'Why not?' says my father. 'It'll liven things up for a while.'

'Absolutely,' says Harriet. 'We could even try the candles again.'

'No, I don't think so,' he says. 'You wouldn't get away with that today. Health and Safety. What if there's an accident?'

'Why would there be an accident?' says my mother. 'We've had lots of parties in the past. We didn't have accidents then.'

'But we might have done,' he says. 'They could so easily have turned into disasters.'

'We used to have such fun,' says my mother. 'Do you remember the Saturday afternoon dances? They went on for years. People were so upset when it all stopped. But I couldn't go on with it. It was too exhausting to organise.'

'Why don't you do a treasure hunt?' I say. 'For the children. It would keep them out the way of the dancing.'

'Oh, I don't know,' she says, but something about her changes. She rummages in a drawer on the side of her desk. 'Actually, I might already have some clues we could use. I write them down occasionally, when the inspiration moves me.'

CHAPTER TWENTY-THREE

Isolde puts her head round the side of the tiny kitchenette that borders our office. 'I've put the kettle on,' she says. Her hair is less exuberant than usual, its bounce drooping into a faded tiredness, reflecting the fact that we're at the end of a long week.

'Great,' I say and return to the estate agent's website on my computer screen. 'I'm going to have to ask Joshua about this. I can't seem to find it.'

She peers over my shoulder. 'Are you thinking of moving?'

'No, not me, Joel . . . Ah! Here it is.'

The screen opens up and we're confronted with a three-storey Victorian house. The photograph shows the front and side, both generously proportioned, with tall bay windows on the two lower floors. Sections of roof peak at different levels, with dormer windows built snugly into the eaves. A converted barn separated from the main part of the house contains a double garage.

Isolde stares at it. 'Are you serious? Joel wants to buy that?'

I'm embarrassed by her reaction. 'He says they might as well start where they intend to end up. Then they won't have to go through the hassle of moving again.'

'How many children are they expecting to have?'

I laugh. Joel with children? Surely not. 'He doesn't discuss things like that with me.'

341

Isolde studies the picture on the screen. 'It's enormous.'

'That's what I said.'

'And?'

'He says it will be easy to fill the space, once he starts.'

'But—can he afford it?'

I swivel my chair round and face her. 'Isolde, he's rich. Apparently, his computer games are selling all over the world. Harriet's seen them in Australia.'

'Really?'

I nod. 'I didn't fully appreciate the significance of this until he showed me the house.'

'What's he worth?'

'He won't tell me, but it's a lot.'

'So he's risen from the poverty of his childhood to riches and success. From shivering, frost-bitten, bare knees to designer trousers.'

'He only ever wears jeans,' I say.

'Armani jeans then.'

'Do Armani make jeans?'

'It's a triumph of the human spirit.'

'We weren't that poor,' I say. 'I did manage to keep the central heating going.'

The kettle hisses with its unique series of unpredictable explosions, and she goes to switch it off before the lid shoots into the air. Steam billows out and clouds the windows of our office. I remove my jacket from the other chair so that Isolde can sit down and push a pile of gardening books out of the way to make room for the coffee. She brings over the mugs and positions them on two damaged copies of *Goldfinger*. Both books have been anonymously censored, with several pages torn out. I imagine an unknown reader at home, either watching righteously as the pages burn up on an open fire, or reading the sex scenes over and over again.

'How much rent does he pay you?' asks Isolde.

I regret showing her the house. I should have known that she'd start asking why Joel still lived with me, why he wasn't taking me on exotic holidays. 'It's his money,' I say. 'Not mine.'

I don't tell her that I have to remind him every week. That sometimes he's two or three weeks in arrears. He's not mean, just forgetful, a typical young man who's never had to take his responsibilities seriously until now. It's nothing to do with him trying to take advantage. 'It's probably not that easy to get hold of the money—I imagine it's all tied up in some way.'

'Although he can produce enough to buy this mansion.'

'It's not a mansion. It's a large house.'

'That's only by your standards.'

'It's not the same as Audlands,' I say. 'Joel isn't in that league.'

'Alice is no fool, is she?'

'She didn't realise he had all this money.'

'How do you know?'

'Because I was there when he showed her some houses on the internet. She was flabbergasted. They nearly had a row about it when she realised he could afford them.'

*　　　*　　　*

In fact, she hadn't believed him. He had to access all his bank statements on the computer before she

343

would accept his claims. Her expression had changed from astonishment to bewilderment to worry.

'But I didn't want to marry a millionaire,' she said, her face mobile with confusion. 'I just thought you were an ordinary person with your own business.'

'I am,' he smiled.

'But the money changes things.'

'Why?'

'Because people with money become selfish and hard and inconsiderate.'

'But wouldn't I be like that already if it was going to happen?'

'Perhaps you are,' she said.

'Then why did you agree to marry me?'

She frowned. 'I don't know. Now I'm seeing you in a different light.'

'I can give the money away, if it makes you feel better. Although it's a bit of a problem trying to stop more of the stuff coming in. I don't do very much to make it happen.'

No, I thought, looking round my living room which was now overflowing with plasticine cats. It doesn't require much effort. You just sit around and play.

'I need to think about it,' she said.

They were sitting side by side at the computer desk and I could see their fingers brush against each other on the keyboard, a tiny rub of skin, so brief it almost didn't happen. Their faces turned towards each other very slightly, their eyes sliding sideways and making contact. Joel's legs were under the desk and Alice's were folded up on her chair, but even though they didn't quite touch they were intimately close, rays of invisible attraction linking them through the air.

I'd been talking to them, leaning over the computer to see the house when I saw their connection. There was something so sensual about their proximity that I felt as if I'd been hit by a violent gust of wind. All the breath was sucked out of me.

'Right,' I said. 'I'll—' They didn't even notice that I was there. I backed away and went into the kitchen.

My son, I thought, has grown up. Where did he discover this sensitivity? How did he learn it? Not from his father, surely? Not from me. I hadn't taught him anything. As far as I knew, he hadn't had any friends at school who could have instructed him. Did he talk to his work colleagues? Had he been fooling me all this time, pretending that he didn't know how to feel, when all the time he was learning it, studying books about love, observing others, practising in front of a mirror?

I was appalled, amazed and exhilarated. Joel had formed a real relationship with someone who appreciated him for what he was, not what he possessed. She wasn't interested in his skills or his resources. She wasn't fooled by his status. He was doing what he enjoyed doing and he was good at it, earning money at the same time. There was no thwarted genius in the background, threatening to destabilise the whole thing.

I'd never thought this would happen. I'd feared that he would spend the rest of his life living on my sofa, taking over my house, feeding off my energy.

My nerdish, unsociable son had become a man.

'So is he going to share some of this good fortune with you?' says Isolde.

I don't want to discuss this with her. 'Why should he?'

'Well, if he paid off your mortgage, you could retire.'

'But I don't want to retire. I like working.'

'Really?'

'So do you. You like interacting with people. You'd be bored stiff if you didn't come here.'

She laughs. 'Don't you believe it. There are all sorts of things I want which I can't have because I can't afford them.'

What I want from Joel is his space, the place at home that he occupies, the air he displaces. I long for solitude, the peace that comes from no obligations, the ability to be as I want to be with nobody else around. I want silence. 'I'll just be happy if he gets married and they go and live wherever they want to.'

'No, you won't. You wouldn't like them to emigrate to Australia.'

'Why not?'

She stares at me, her eyes wide and her eyebrows almost touching her hairline. 'Come on, Jess. If they have grandchildren, you'd never see them except for your annual fortnight in December. That wouldn't do at all.'

Isolde isn't married, hasn't had a boyfriend for ages, and is too old to have children now, so there's no chance of grandchildren. It's never occurred to me that she might have wanted them, despite her protestations, that she would rather not be lying

346

alone in bed every night, finishing off the book of the day. It's as if a door has opened, just a tiny crack, and I've caught a glimpse inside, almost by mistake, seen a world that she dreams about, even though she pretends that she doesn't. Why haven't I ever questioned her version of her life? I just assumed that she was where she wanted to be.

'You're right,' I say. 'I should be more realistic.' But she's wrong. A fortnight once a year would suit me very well.

The clock on top of the filing cabinet buzzes slightly as it approaches nine o'clock. It knows our opening times better than we do.

'I bet Joshua is out there now,' she says. 'Itching to get in and look at houses. He'd get on well with your Joel. You should put them in touch.'

'What a good idea. They could swap information about room sizes and loft space or utility rooms.'

'Or secrets. Have you asked Joshua about the concert yet?'

I shake my head. 'It's too long ago. It would sound odd if I asked him now. He'd wonder why I hadn't mentioned it before.'

'We're all wondering that.'

Including myself. I don't know why I can't ask him. But it's as if I've caught him out in a lie and I don't want to trap him with my knowledge. He must know that I know, since I looked directly at him. Yet somehow, by neither of us saying anything, we've created a conspiracy, a desire to protect each other. I can't break the silence, and neither can he.

'I'll unlock the doors,' I say.

Joshua and Luke come in together, shuffling

like old men, Luke so close to Joshua's heels that it's a wonder he doesn't trip him up. Joshua acknowledges us with a dip of his head. His clothes are as threadbare and ill-fitting as ever. Luke stares at the floor and pretends we're not there. We watch them go into the computer room.

'I don't trust Luke,' whispers Isolde, into my ear.

I turn to her in surprise. 'What do you mean?'

'Things have started to go missing.'

I check over my shoulder to see if they're safely out of earshot. 'Like what?'

'CDs, videos, floppy disks. Just a few every week.'

'How do you know it's him?'

'I don't. It's just a feeling. I've been watching and there's something odd about him.'

'Are you reading Miss Marple?'

She looks offended. 'No, of course not. P.D. James. Inspector Dalgleish. He's a sophisticated man. He writes poetry.'

*   *   *

I park the car on my front drive and turn the engine off. Before I close the window I hear a woman's voice, high-pitched and furious. Fragments of her words reach me. 'Self-righteous . . . arrogant . . . opinionated . . . crossed your mind you could be wrong?'

I shut the window and get out, not sure where the sound's coming from. The voice is vaguely familiar, but not easily identifiable because of its fury. I open the back door of my car and lean in for the Tesco bags. I'm cooking tonight for Joel and Alice. She's started to come round quite often

348

now, and the three of us have a meal together. Occasionally they arrive before I've finished preparing it and Alice will sit in the kitchen with me, chopping parsley and crushing garlic. Even Joel join us, lays the table, cleans the surfaces as we finish preparing the food, conducting a conversation with Alice all the time. I like the cosiness of it all. It's how real families are supposed to be.

'I don't know how you do it,' I said to her last week. 'I've never been able to get him to lift a finger.'

'He needs to be told,' she said. 'He doesn't think of things unless you tell him, but he's fine then. He's a good employer, well liked. He analyses a lot, reads books about what makes employees happy.'

What a difference a generation makes. I couldn't imagine Andrew trying to please people. 'He doesn't do it for me,' I said. 'He expects me to wait on him most of the time.'

She smiles. 'You're not authoritative enough. And anyway, you're his mother. That's what mothers are for.'

Alice lives at home with her parents, a brother and three younger sisters. She knows how to get on with people.

As I pick up the Tesco bags, a door opens noisily and I can hear heels clicking towards me. As they get closer, someone pushes the open car door against me and I fall back into the car.

'Oh, I'm sorry,' says Alice's voice. 'I didn't realise you were there.'

I struggle to get out and organise myself. 'Alice—are you all right?'

She looks the same, but there's a wildness around her eyes, a tightness that restricts the movement of her mouth. Her hair, normally so carefully arranged, has lost its perfection and developed angry wisps.

She doesn't smile. 'I'm fine. Thank you for asking.'

She turns away from me and walks down the street. I stare at her disappearing figure. 'Alice!' I call. 'What about supper? Are you coming back?'

But she doesn't respond. The air around me is dangerous, threatening, loaded with anger. I shut the car door, lock it and carry the bags to the front door, expecting it to be open. It isn't, so I press the doorbell.

Nothing happens. I ring again. Still no reply. 'Joel!' I call. 'Let me in.'

In the end I put the bags down, fumble in my pockets, find the key and let myself in.

The house feels wrong. Nothing's out of place, nothing's been disturbed, but I know immediately that the situation is serious. I go into the living room and find Joel sitting on the sofa with his legs stretched out in front of him and his arms folded, staring into space.

'Well, thanks for letting me in.'

He doesn't reply.

'What's been going on?'

The cats are on the move. They've been swept off the surfaces and are lying in piles on the floor. I step on some of them as I enter the room, and have to take off my shoe to scrape away the plasticine. I examine the mangled remnants in my hand. 'Sorry,' I say. 'I didn't realise they were there.'

They're all over the floor, their tails tangled, their paws bent and broken, their faces squashed into flat expressionless shapes. I grab a handful of them, but it's impossible to sort them out. They're melting into a mindless dough, losing their character, slipping back into non-existence.

I pick up a large, smooth ball of plasticine, still warm from handling, the result of someone rubbing the cats together, rolling them around until they disappear into a general mass. The final humiliation, total absorption into an anonymous whole.

'Have you been arguing about the cats?' I ask.

He doesn't reply.

I go into the kitchen, trying to decide if I should be sympathetic or angry. The plasticine is going to get trodden into the carpet. Who's going to clean it up?

I start preparing the meal, although if Alice doesn't come back, what's the point of the coriander and the spinach? I chop anyway, put the frying pan on the stove, heat the oil, cut up pieces of chicken and start to brown the onions. The actions are familiar and soothing.

She'll come back. She's bound to. All engaged couples row. It's normal. They'll make it up. Just leave it to them.

I hear the front door bang. 'That'll be Alice,' I call.

After a few moments of silence, I go to investigate.

Joel has gone. There's no one in the house except me, so why am I bothering to cook something I don't want to eat? I turn off the gas and sit down at the table. The smell of the heated oil drifts past me and fades into early staleness.

I sit for a long time, unable to summon the energy to move, a cloud of misery hovering above me. Everything about Joel and Alice is just right. It can't stop now. But Alice's shouting and Joel's moody refusal to respond have reminded me of my years with Andrew. The tension, the heavy atmosphere. The anger. I can't go back there, can't even allow myself to think about it. It's too much.

I should go out myself before it gets dark, before I become a permanent statue and never move again. I could go to Mary's, or Audlands, where Harriet and my parents would be sympathetic, even go and visit Isolde.

But I don't want to speak to any of them. I don't want them to know there's anything wrong. They'd only blame Joel and I don't want them to. It's too private.

After a long time, I force myself to move. I put on my coat, go out of the front door, lock it behind me and get into my car. I've decided that I should eat out. I drive for a while, park and walk along the street, examining the restaurants, pretending to read menus. But they're daunting and I'm not hungry.

I end up in McDonald's, sitting in a corner with a Filet-O-Fish and an apple pie. I'm too easily defeated. When Andrew was living with us, when Joel was young, I didn't spend time feeling sorry for myself like this. If things went wrong, I picked myself up, took a deep breath and carried on. I collect up all the debris on the tray, but I don't want to leave. It's comfortable here, surrounded by other people but not connected to them. There are several groups of children supervised by a single adult, one or two families with both parents, and a few people on their own, reading a paper or gazing ahead into nothing. At a table next to me, an elderly woman sits opposite a teenage girl. They're eating their Big Macs, with salad and fries, in separate worlds, not exchanging a look or a word.

The door swings open and two young men come in. They're both about sixteen, dressed in black, almost identical, with thin, gaunt faces and rows of tiny rings dripping from their pierced ears, eyebrows and noses. They stand at the entrance and look around.

One of them is Luke.

I'm not sure if he's seen me and I can't decide if I should wave to attract his attention. But then they step forward, pushing past tables and chairs, knocking against other customers.

'Hey!' shouts a woman with two young children. 'Watch what you're doing.' She's wearing round glasses and her eyes are big and distorted through the lenses.

Luke stops and stares at her. Then he goes over and places his face about two inches in front of hers. 'Yeah? What're you going to do about it?'

Her face sets into a porcelain mask, her eyes filmy and immobile behind the glasses, but her hands are scrabbling frantically, pushing her two young children away from her to safety. She doesn't reply.

He straightens up, lifts the side of his nose with contempt and joins his friend at the counter.

'Can I help you?' says the young man who has been serving. He looks about twelve, despite a gossamer-thin ginger moustache which slouches along his top lip. It's meant to be a mark of maturity, but it doesn't work. It adds to the impression that he's pretending.

Luke's companion leans over the counter and grabs the young man's shirt. 'Damien, eh?' he reads from the name badge.

Damien nods, but can't speak.

'Put him down, Adam,' says Luke. 'He can't serve us if you do his face in.'

'Yeah,' says Adam, letting go. 'I'll have a double quarter-pounder meal—large.'

'Same for me,' says Luke.

They stand and watch while Damien hurries to fill their order. I can see the ineffectual moustache twitching, his hands trembling as he collects the right containers and puts them into bags. I know what he's thinking. Get it right and they'll leave. Nothing'll go wrong if I can do this quickly.

Luke and Adam turn to survey the room while they wait. The children stare back at them, fascinated by the power of their presence, but the adults keep their heads down, eating earnestly, pretending that everything is normal. A skinny lad close to me is murmuring to his girlfriend, and it sounds as if he is being reassuring, but I can hear his words. 'Just give me thirty seconds with them. I'll teach them a thing or two. Who do they think they are?"

The girlfriend doesn't respond. She's holding an apricot tart, picking at the edges of the pastry and putting tiny crumbs into her mouth, but then forgetting to swallow.

I lower my eyes. I don't want Luke to recognise me.

'That's £8.58,' says Damien.

Luke puts his head back and laughs. 'Get real,

man,' he says, picking up the paper bags.

I rise to my feet. I didn't mean to do this, I didn't expect to do it, but an overwhelming sense of injustice takes hold of me and compels me to act. This is Luke. I know him. I see him almost every day of my life. Why should we all be intimidated by a boy of sixteen, just because he has pierced ears?

They've started to walk towards the door, kicking the tables on their way past.

'Luke!' I call loudly into the hushed room.

Heads lift, jaws stop moving. I'm aware that everyone's eyes are on me.

He stops.

I step out from my table and advance towards them.

Luke turns and recognition flares up in his eyes.

'What's going on?' I say, sounding like a teacher.

He's hovering between anger and uncertainty.

'You haven't paid,' I say.

I can feel the silence around us as everyone holds their breath, astonished at my recklessness, afraid of the consequences.

Nothing happens.

'It's £8.58,' I say.

There's a moment—I see it in the way he moves his head—when blind fury threatens to burst out of him into a terrifying explosion. We're balanced on the edge of a precipice.

'What would Joshua think?' I ask in a reasonable voice.

Nobody moves. At the centre of the universe, my gaze is locked into Luke's and I'm invincible. I can stand here for ever, longer than he can. I've been trained by decades of stoicism for this moment.

I see the exact moment when he knows he can't win, when his eyes start to slither away from me.

'OK, OK,' he says. 'There's no need to be like that.' He digs into his pocket and produces a ten pound note. He walks back to the counter, swaggering with the effort to maintain his self-esteem. 'Keep the change,' he says and heads back towards the door.

A small boy of about six comes out of the toilets. He crosses in front of Luke and Adam, sees them and freezes, his mouth open in surprise, his small, clear eyes crushed with uncertainty.

'Mum—' he starts, and his voice disintegrates into a thin wail.

'Jamie!' His mum leaps up from a table on the other side of the room, a large, round woman bulging out of faded jeans and a yellow T-shirt which says 'I'm Yours, Johnny Depp'.

Tension returns to the room as Adam bends down towards the child.

I try to shout, 'No!' but my voice has given up. I can't manage two crises.

Adam picks up the child and removes him from his path. 'Have a good day, kid,' he says and hands him one of his fries.

Then they're gone, the doors swinging behind them. I stand in the middle of the room, my legs trembling, not sure what to do. Everyone starts talking in unnaturally loud voices.

A girl comes over to me from the counter. Her name is Jody, it says on her badge. 'You were brilliant,' she says.

'Thank you,' I say.

'Can I get you a drink—on the house?'

'Coffee,' I say. 'That would be nice.' I walk stiffly back to my table.

Damien is leaning on the counter, wiping sweat away from his forehead with a paper serviette.

'Should we call the police?' asks a voice behind him from the kitchen.

'Nah,' says Damien. 'They won't do anything.'

I can't believe what I've just done. Was I crazy? Where did the anger come from that drove me to stand up? How did my will prove to be stronger than Luke's?

A warmth is spreading through me, an extraordinary sense of satisfaction.

Jody brings me the coffee. 'Anything else?' she says. 'You can have anything you want. No charge.'

'No thanks,' I say.

I don't need anything.

CHAPTER TWENTY-FOUR

I wake early and open my eyes to see a stream of sun rippling across the ceiling. It flickers like water as it negotiates a pathway through the branches of the rowan tree in my front garden, round the edge of my curtains and into the bedroom.

There's something different about me this morning.

The world feels benign, generous even, and for once I'm part of it. I pull a curtain back. The sky is crystal clean, enamelled with a blue so intense that it hurts my eyes. If I don't sit up, I can't see the windows of the houses opposite and they can't see

357

me. It's Saturday morning, only seven o'clock. Ajinth, next door, starts his car and drives off. He does weekend shifts.

Then I remember. I'm not the same person as I was yesterday morning.

There's nothing physically different about me. I haven't recovered from a migraine, achieved a dramatic loss of weight, had a broken leg miraculously healed. I've changed inside. There's something new that wasn't there before. Yesterday I got out of my seat, stood up and challenged two threatening young men. Bullies. I didn't let them hold us to ransom.

It's a pleasure to stretch, to feel awake and alert, to step into the patches of sun on my bedroom carpet. Yesterday, I had to force myself awake and drag myself to the bathroom, my eyes sandy and reluctant to open. Today I have an inner energy. I imagine myself to be like Harriet, who always looks as if she's leapt out of bed with enthusiasm and run a couple of miles or swum fifty lengths before a healthy breakfast.

Out on the landing I hesitate, disorientated by Joel's open bedroom door. He never forgets to shut it. Privacy is important to him. I tiptoe to the doorway, wondering whether to peer in. Perhaps he was too upset last night, too distracted to follow his usual routines. I put my head round the door.

The bedroom is empty, the bed undisturbed.

I go downstairs in my dressing-gown, not sure whether I should worry. Maybe he followed Alice and made it up with her. Would he do that? Would he give in so easily? And if so, why didn't he come home afterwards?

Perhaps he went out for a walk last night and

358

was mugged. He could be lying in a coma in a hospital, waiting to be identified.

I potter in the kitchen, preparing breakfast, my earlier energy draining away. I put on the radio, clatter the dishes on the table, sing to myself. Why not? There's no one to disturb.

I should ring him. I need to know where he is.

He'll be fine. He's an adult.

Things are not normal. He was upset by his row with Alice.

I go into the living room, tiptoe through the piles of plasticine until I reach the sofa, and dial his mobile.

He answers immediately. 'Hello, Mum.'

'Where are you?'

'At the office.'

'But it's Saturday morning.'

'Just something I wanted to sort out.'

He must have been there all night, but he's not going to say so. Too embarrassed to come home, or just engrossed in his work? 'Well, don't forget you're sanding the Long Gallery floor today. They're delivering the sander at 8.30.'

'I know, Mum. I can manage my own affairs.'

'Except with Alice, it seems.'

'Mum . . .' I can hear him making an effort, forcing his voice to be patient. 'I'll be there.' He rings off.

I start to pick up handfuls of twisted cats, determined not to let yesterday's black mood surface again. My intention is to dispose of the ones smashed beyond repair and rescue the more identifiable ones, so I try to be careful, erring on the generous side. But it takes too long as I dither over each individual cat, trying to assess the extent

359

of its damage. In the end I find myself shoving most of them into the bags, ruthless as I abandon them to mass oblivion, only saving a handful of perfect specimens which I place on the coffee table. If he wants to be fussy, he should have stayed and cleared up for himself. He can always make them again.

Did the cats feature in the argument between Alice and Joel, or were they just a convenient weapon when things got out of control? Do the cats matter or are they the central issue of a profound disagreement?

I do the best I can, then return to the kitchen for breakfast. I said I'd be at Audlands as early as possible. There's just time for half an hour's practice before leaving. Mary and I have a concert in three weeks' time, the week after the barn dance, and I need to get my speed up in the Moskovsky Dances.

*   *   *

I turn into the drive at Audlands and brake, allowing myself a few seconds to admire the view. From this distance, the house remains untouched by time, solemn and dignified. My mother could still be painting walls, planning grand schemes, the baby Jessica could be screaming in an isolated bedroom, Harriet and my cousins could be chasing each other through the maze of unoccupied rooms.

A car horn stirs me and I look in my mirror. Mary and Eamon, who have offered to come and help with the big clean-up, have pulled into the drive and stopped behind me. I raise my hand, smiling, and they return the wave. I can see Angus and Tim bouncing around in the back seat.

We park next to each other in front of the steps. The boys jump out almost before the car has stopped and race up to the house. The front door has been propped open to let in the morning sun and wedges of dust hang in the hall, illuminated by a shaft of sunshine.

My mother limps into view. 'Jessica! Mary! Eamon!' she says, as if it's a total surprise. 'How lovely to see you.'

'Has the sander arrived?' I ask.

'Yes. Harriet's dealt with it. She and Joel are in the Long Gallery, working out how to operate it. It's a bit noisy for me, I'm afraid.'

Joel must have taken a taxi to get here before me. There hasn't been time for him to catch a bus and walk from the bus stop.

'Who's in charge?' asks Eamon.

'Oh,' says my mother, thrown by the concept of anyone being in charge but keen to take on the responsibility. 'Me, I suppose.'

Eamon and Mary are unloading equipment from the boot of their car—scrubbing brushes, buckets, paintbrushes, white spirit. They're dressed in identical faded jeans and over-large T-shirts. The boys have already disappeared. I can hear them racing through rooms in the distance, whooping with joy. It's ages since they've been here.

'Are they all right?' asks Mary, looking anxiously at my mother.

'Oh yes, dear. As long as they don't go upstairs. The floors aren't safe.'

'I'll go and tell them,' says Mary, following the direction of their shouts.

361

My father glides up in his wheelchair. 'Healthy pair of boys,' he says with envious approval. 'They nearly knocked me over.'

'Sorry,' says Eamon.

'No need to apologise. They might as well make use of all this space.'

'But they must be careful,' says Mary.

'We're using the drawing room, the library, the dining room and the stairs up to the Long Gallery,' he says. 'I think that's all we need to worry about. We'll keep the doors to the other rooms firmly closed.'

'I'll print out some notices,' says my mother. 'KEEP OUT, in a very big font.'

'Are the stairs and the Long Gallery safe?' asks Eamon.

'The left branch of the staircase is all right,' says my mother. 'We'll block off the other side with rope. And the rain doesn't seem to have got into the Long Gallery, although there are a few damp patches. It just needs cleaning.'

'Where shall we start?' Eamon asks my father, forgetting that my mother has claimed overall responsibility.

The two men head for the drawing room. My father likes Eamon. They discuss money and legal matters and business and more money. 'These EU directives are going to strangle small businesses,' I can hear my father saying as they disappear through the doorway.

I find Mary staring up at the chandelier. 'I can't wait to get my hands on that,' she says.

'I'm going to find Joel,' I say to my mother. 'What time did he arrive?'

She laughs. 'Incredibly early. About eight, I

362

think. He's just had breakfast with us.'

So the three of them have sat down together in the kitchen over cornflakes and toast. I wonder what they talked about. Treasure hunts? Cats? Weddings?

I climb the stairs and hesitate at the door of the Long Gallery, shocked by the violent, bone-shaking noise of the sander. Joel is at the far end, moving the machine slowly over a small area, his face set into a fierce concentration. Swirls of sawdust dance through the air, a fine mist of wood particles, soaring up into the ceiling and settling on the arched network of plaster cornices. There's no sign of Harriet. Joel looks up and sees me. He stops and turns the machine off, removing his goggles and ear muffs. He always does these things properly—he would never cheat on safety regulations.

'Hello,' I say, walking towards him and trying to brush away the dust, which is flowing round me like water. 'We'll have to open a window.'

'They're stuck,' he says. 'I've already tried.'

He wipes sweat from his face with a shirt sleeve—blue and white stripes, substantial, quality cotton. He's wearing the same clothes as last night, not ideal for serious physical work. His hand is still trembling from the vibration of the sander. 'It's heavy work.'

'Why do you think we asked you to do it?'

I kneel on a window seat and fiddle with the catch on a pair of casement windows. It's stiff and rusty, reluctant to submit. 'This used to open. It must be possible.'

'Careful.'

The handle moves a fraction and resists, so I

apply a bit more force. The window groans, then flies open and I nearly fall through. 'There,' I say, struggling to keep my balance. 'That's better.'

We move along the room, loosening all the catches until most of the windows are open and the sawdust starts to drift out into the summer air.

It's not much cooler, though. We sit down on the window seat and the sweet heaviness of a nearby honeysuckle wafts in.

Joel straightens his legs. He shuts his eyes, breathing deeply, and the lines of fatigue on his pale, unshaven face relax slightly. I experience an unexpected urge to stroke his cheek, something he has not allowed me to do since he was a baby.

'So what was it all about?' I say.

'What?'

'Alice. The fuss last night.'

He doesn't reply.

'Did you spend the night in your office?'

'She didn't like the cats,' he says.

'What's wrong with them?'

'Nothing really.'

'So you argued about nothing.'

'It's not the cats exactly.'

'But you just said it was,' I say.

'It's the guns.'

'Ah.'

'All computer games need some violence. That's what gives them tension.'

'Alice doesn't approve?'

'No. She thought it was a game for children when she first saw the cats.'

'So did I.'

He sighs and moves his head towards the window, positioning his face so that he can catch some of the light breeze. 'Children like fighting too, you know.'

'You don't have to follow trends. You could set them.'

'That's what Alice said.'

Good for Alice. 'Couldn't you use the cats in a different context?'

'What do you think I've been doing all night?'

He raises his arms above his head and stretches out in a straight line, lifting his back away from the seat. His body seems excessively long. It could be Andrew sitting here beside me, the same build, the same shape, the same wiry strength. But it's not Andrew, it's Joel, and he's listened to Alice and compromised. I can hear a bird singing outside, light fragmented snatches of melody, repeated over and over again. I feel light and refreshed, as if I've just woken up from a deep sleep.

'It's a huge job,' he says. 'We'll have to rewrite the whole story.'

'Have you told Alice this?'

'No, not yet.'

'Well, don't you think you should?'

'Obviously. I can't afford to lose her.'

'I should think not.'

'She's my best programmer.'

I stare at him, bewildered. I've assumed that Alice is the secretary, the one who organises, makes telephone calls, types the letters. It's never occurred to me that she's highly skilled, as indispensable to the company as she is to him personally. 'But what about your relationship?'

He pulls himself into an upright position. 'Stop worrying about it, Mum. I know what I'm doing. We'll sort it out.'

He gets up and goes over to the sander. I hear a series of clicks, a whine, and the machine roars into life again. Is it that easy? Does he simply turn things on and off by casually flicking a switch? How does he know Alice will accept his willingness to change course? How forgiving is she?

I don't understand the casual nature of their relationship, the way they can argue with such vehemence and then recover. The balance of power between them is much more evenly distributed than it was in my marriage. Andrew was always too frightening, on the verge of violence, his toes hanging over the edge while he swayed dangerously in the wind of his anger.

Arguing with Joel is safer. He is unexpectedly becoming the son I always wanted to believe in. Please come back, Alice. All is forgiven.

I stand up. The statues of the Caesars are now disguised and softened by a benign layer of dust. I'm looking forward to cleaning them, but now is not the time. Joel sees me and switches the sander off again.

'Harriet's in the drawing room, I think,' he says.

I look at the work he's already done. 'Are you going to do the whole floor?' I ask.

'No, of course not—it would take all week. Just the uneven bits.'

He's enjoying himself, I realise, in control of the machine, doing something useful. 'You remind me of Mr Spock,' I say. 'Funny ears.'

'Mr Spock had pointed ears,' he says. 'Not fluffy.'

'You don't look like him anyway,' I say. 'Your eyebrows are round.'

'Is Dad coming to the barn dance?' he asks.

I'm surprised by this. 'I don't know. I hadn't intended to invite him. It would be easier if he didn't.'

He nods. 'Quite.'

'Have you rung him?'

He gazes past me, his eyes blank. I can't tell if he's trying to remember if he's phoned, or refusing to think about it. I'm just about to say something else when he opens his mouth. 'He hasn't spoken to me for about five years, you know.'

'What was it all about?' I've wanted to ask for ages, but our level of communication has always been too limited, restricted to our individual opinions on washing-up, peeling potatoes, cooking. We have meticulously set up boundaries, placed a net between ourselves and regarded each other from opposite sides of the court. It's too hard trying to form questions when you know there will be no answers. It's like trying to play a game when your opponent never returns the ball. Today, we seem to have lowered that net and I don't want to lose the opportunity.

He doesn't answer for a while. 'The funny thing is, I'm not quite sure.'

'I don't believe that. How can you fall out with someone and refuse to speak to them for years when you have no idea what it's about?'

'Well—he wasn't very nice a lot of the time.'

'We all know that.'

'Sometimes he was OK.'

'That's the way most people are. Sometimes OK, sometimes not.'

'Well—Dad's OK was considerably lower down the scale than most people's.'

Right at the bottom, I'd say. 'But it must have

367

been more than that.'

'He's so selfish. He doesn't think of anyone except himself.'

An interesting observation from Joel, who expects me to cook his meals and iron his shirts, who gets engaged without telling me he has a girlfriend. 'So what actually happened?'

'He let me down. I went to his flat at the right time and he wasn't there—again. I was fed up and left a note saying if he wanted to speak to me again he could phone, because I wasn't going out of my way for him any more.'

'And he didn't?'

'No, never.'

So. Five years of non-communication because of nothing, because someone didn't phone, because of an unwillingness to compromise. Two equally stubborn men who've never heard of conciliation, who don't have the skills to sort things out. Once the silence starts, nobody knows how to break it and it goes on and on, building up, gaining significance in its own right long after the original disagreement slips out of sight. Andrew needs careful managing, but so does Joel. And neither of them is capable of managing the other.

'This is absurd. Surely you can bypass it all and speak to him?'

'Why?'

It's a valid question. What would Joel gain from a relationship with Andrew? Is it worth the effort? 'He's your father.'

'So?' He pulls the goggles down over his eyes.

'He's the only one you've got. He didn't speak to his own father for years and years, but I think he regrets it now that it's too late. You can invite him to come to the barn dance if you want to.'

'I have to get on, Mum. There's a lot to do.'

Why did I make that offer? I want to move away from Andrew, not towards him.

Joel turns on the sander again and I leave him to it, going back to the kitchen. My mother is preparing a trayful of drinks.

'You'll have to carry this tray, Jess. I'll only drop it.'

She's looking younger, moving with a greater ease than usual, almost bouncing. 'What do you think of this clue?' she says. 'If music be the food of love, play on—'

It seems a bit obvious. 'I thought the Music Room was going to be shut off.'

My father manoeuvres his wheelchair round the kitchen, collecting paint charts, energised and cheerful. 'About time the Hall had a makeover,' he says. 'Jessica, I might have to send you out for more paint. I've got Eamon doing the drawing-room walls, but there may not be enough. It's a big area—difficult to estimate.'

'Do you remember the tennis players?' asks my mother. I nod. 'They're going to come and cut the grass below the Long Gallery. Then, if it's a nice evening, we can all go outside to cool off after the dancing.' She fills the last mug with tea. 'Such nice young men. Did I tell you one of them was in a car accident? He has a scar from his shoulder to his navel.'

However did she find that out? 'What about the dances?' I say. 'Who's going to call out the steps?'

'I'm doing it,' says my father. 'No problem. Your mother has printed the details off the internet. Just a question of having a loud enough voice.'

369

My father taking part in the proceedings? He always refused to contribute anything except champagne and Crunchy Chocolate Brownies to my mother's parties. Too busy, too preoccupied, too concerned about Bakewell tarts and lemon sponges. Now that he has nothing else to do except read the paper and watch the television he must feel the need for action.

'Here you are,' says my mother. 'You take the tray.'

There are seven mugs of tea, two glasses of squash and a tray of homemade cookies. 'You've been cooking,' I say.

'There's no need to be so surprised. I know how to cook. If you remember, I managed to produce three meals a day for us and rustled up enough to feed an army when your cousins came.'

'I wasn't implying that you couldn't cook. I just haven't seen you doing it recently.'

'I've started to make cakes for the boys.'

'Boys?'

'The tennis club. They like it if I produce refreshments.'

I rather think that she likes it too. I pick up the tray and put it straight back down again. 'It's too heavy. I'll have to do it in two halves.'

'But they'll get cold.'

'No they won't.' I take off two mugs and the glasses and pick it up again. 'I'll be back in no time.'

Harriet and Mary are in the hall. Harriet is pulling off wallpaper while Mary stands on a ladder and dusts the chandelier. I put the tray down on the hall table and watch Harriet. The wallpaper is piling up on the floor at her feet. 'Do

370

we have to be so extreme?'

'I don't see why not. I'm good at wallpapering and we've already got the paper.'

'It seems to be coming off incredibly easily.'

'This is Mum's old work. She papered over the original paint.'

Rolls of fresh wallpaper have been stacked in a corner—dusty pink roses loosely sketched on to a pale cream background. Laura Ashley. Pretty, but not quite authentic Georgian. Above the picture rail, the ceiling rises into a high dome. No one is going to be able to paint up there. Tackling the bit we can reach seems to be the most sensible course of action.

Mary climbs down from the ladder and picks up a cup of coffee. 'I'll take this in to Eamon. Nice-looking biscuits.'

'There's some juice in the kitchen for the boys. Do you know where they are?'

'No, but I'll find them. Better not let them loose on the biscuits before everyone else has had a chance.'

Harriet takes a mug of coffee. She kicks the rejected wallpaper into a pile and looks up at the half-cleaned chandelier. 'It sparkles. I'd forgotten that.'

The crystals are gently swaying in the almost imperceptible air currents set up by our movements. Diamond points of lights dance on the surrounding walls. 'Mum called it a lustre,' I say.

She nods. 'Do you think we should light the candles again?'

'Wouldn't it be dangerous?'

'I can't see why. They're a long way from the ground. It's not as if we're going to fill the whole house with candles this time.'

'I hope not. It was so difficult keeping them alight.'

'I seem to remember that lighting them all in the first place was the problem.'

All I remember is the magic. The transformation of our everyday world into a parallel, make-believe fairy story where anything could happen.

A car drives up outside. Harriet and I look through the open door.

'It must be the tennis players,' I say. 'Mum's asked them to cut some of the grass out the back.'

'Goodness. Do they know what they're taking on? They'd need several hundred sheep for that.'

A man gets out of the back seat and leans through the front window to talk to the driver. He hands over money. Why would the tennis players use a taxi? Surely they have cars. The man is tall, deeply tanned, dressed casually in an open-necked shirt and jeans. He lifts a travelling bag out of the back seat with an easy strength, moving comfortably, fit and controlled. His hair is unusually blond, almost white, as if it's been bleached by the sun. He looks towards us. His eyes are in shadow, but there is a penetrating quality to his gaze, a genial familiarity that for some reason confuses me.

He raises an arm in greeting, and then Harriet is running down the steps, her pink T-shirt bubbling up behind her, a lightness in her step that makes her flirtatious and girlish.

'Philip!' she cries and throws herself into his arms.

CHAPTER TWENTY-FIVE

Philip.

When Harriet calls his name, the assorted parts of him—his hair, his nose and his shoulders—drift together into a faded, dog-eared photograph and I know it's him.

Am I embarrassed, fascinated or furious? I should feel all these things, but I don't. It's so long since he was last at Audlands that his footprints have faded, there's no lingering trace of him in the dust, no echo of his voice. But he's still there inside me, exerting his malicious influence even after all this time.

He and Harriet hug, their arms tight round each other, each face resting on the other's shoulder. Their bodies slot together neatly, impossibly close, a controlled entanglement.

People embrace like this all the time nowadays. You see them at the station, outside restaurants, in the middle of the street. Fathers and sons, mothers and daughters, brothers and sisters, people who haven't seen each other for ages, people who meet every day, casual acquaintances. I know it doesn't necessarily mean anything.

The taxi driver turns his car round, skidding in the gravel, and sets off down the drive, swerving to miss the worst of the potholes. He's driving too fast. I can hear the squeal as he applies his brakes, the thumps and rattles as he miscalculates and bounces in and out of the holes.

Harriet and Philip draw apart and Philip bends down to pick up his travel holdall. He turns round and sees me.

'Jess!' he calls and springs up the steps, the bag in his hand.

I edge backwards, unwilling to be drawn into a hug like Harriet's, but he doesn't offer one and I experience an irrational disappointment. 'How are you?' he says.

'Great,' I say. 'And you?'

'Great.'

Mary has come up behind me and is studying Philip with interest.

'Mary,' I say, 'this is Philip, our long-lost cousin. Philip, this is Mary. She's helping us to clean up Audlands for the barn dance next week.'

They shake hands with a solemn formality.

'What's this about a barn dance?' he says, turning to Harriet. She smiles in a knowing, flirtatious way that irritates me. As if there's some great secret that only certain people know about and she will share it with him if he's nice to her. Despite the fact that almost everyone we know has already been invited, and several we don't.

'I'll tell you all about it if you're patient,' she says.

My father wheels himself into the hall with two rolls of wallpaper on his lap. He stops when he sees Philip and adjusts the angle of his head so that he can examine him through the correct part of his bifocals. 'Do I know you?'

'Yes,' says Harriet. 'You do.'

He hovers, frowning, without taking his eyes off Philip's face. 'You don't have much luggage, so you can't have come from abroad—people don't travel light any more. Too much money, too many things to buy.'

'Look at his face,' says Harriet. 'Can't you see?'

I don't like guessing games. It's embarrassing when people get it wrong. 'It's Philip,' I say. 'Your nephew.'

Harriet flashes me a look of resentment. 'I wanted him to guess.'

'It's not necessary,' I say. I can sense Philip looking at me.

'Philip!' says my father, and he seems genuinely pleased. 'So what have you been up to, old man? Haven't heard anything of you for years.'

'I'm in Bahrain at the moment,' says Philip. 'Diving.'

'Living the good life, then. I might have known it.'

'Absolutely.'

'Philip!' My mother has appeared and recognises him immediately.

'Connie!' he says and they manage an embrace too, although the enthusiasm is generated more by my mother than Philip. He doesn't mould to her in quite the same way as he did with Harriet.

'Where have you been all these years?' she says as they part. A faint wash of pink lights up her face with a girlish innocence.

'I'm a diver,' he says again. 'I work in the Middle East.'

'Isn't that a bit dangerous?'

He laughs, a comfortable, intimate chuckle that involves all of us and draws us in. 'Do you mean the diving or the Middle East?'

She looks uncertain. 'What do you dive for? Wrecks and things?'

'Sometimes. I clear barnacles, snagged propellers, things like that. Fairly routine stuff.

And I get to stay in nice hotels, paid for by my clients.'

'Goodness,' she says. 'I thought you'd be a businessman, making millions before you were thirty.'

He smiles and a fleeting memory of the fifteen-year-old Philip flashes out. Knowing, confident, cheeky. 'I was,' he says. 'But then it became boring.'

I don't believe him. There has to be more to it than that.

'I'm sorry to turn up out of the blue,' he says, 'but I was rather hoping you could put me up for a few nights.'

'Great idea,' says my father.

My mother's more uncertain. 'But where?'

'It's all right,' says Harriet. 'I'll find somewhere. There are plenty of beds and we're not short of rooms, are we?'

'No, I suppose not,' says my mother. 'You'd better start airing a bed, open some windows, wash some sheets and things.'

Sunshine is streaming into the hall through the open door. 'Nowhere is going to be damp,' says Harriet.

'I wouldn't be so sure,' says my mother.

'Come on,' says Harriet to Philip. 'Let's go and see what we can do. Can you carry on stripping the wallpaper, Jess?'

'Another pair of hands,' says my mother with pleasure. 'We need everyone we can get.'

'Great,' I say. That's one pair of hands less, I think. He'll stop Harriet working.

Philip and Harriet go up the stairs together. 'Didn't you say the upstairs floors weren't safe?'

376

asks Mary.

'They're all right if you know what you're doing,' says Harriet over her shoulder.

They disappear round the corner of the stairs.

'Fancy Philip turning up,' says my mother. 'How extraordinary.'

'Something not quite right there,' says my father. 'He was set for a big career, the last thing I knew.'

'You always said he wasn't very disciplined. Maybe he didn't like sticking to the rules.'

'Cathy's kept it all rather quiet.' My father turns away with an expression of gentle satisfaction.

I grasp a loose edge of wallpaper and pull. It comes away easily, a long strip ripping off as if it's only been held up by a gossamer thread of paste. This is easy, I think. It'll be done in no time.

*　　　*　　　*

It's difficult to concentrate in the library after the weekend. I watch Joshua in front of his computer screen, tapping keys, jotting down notes on a piece of paper beside him on the desk.

I don't know what to think about Philip. I don't want to think about him at all, but he's there, insistent, intruding on my privacy.

'I wonder what's happened to Luke,' says Isolde.

'Ah,' I say. 'He may not be coming again.'

She looks up from the notes she's making, her eyes large and instantly interested. 'What do you mean?'

I tell her about my confrontation with him in McDonald's.

'You must have been crazy,' she says. 'It could so

377

easily have turned nasty.'

I nod. 'I don't know what came over me.'

'I've always thought there's something not right about him.'

'But I had an advantage over everyone else—I knew him.'

'Seeing someone in the library every day doesn't mean you know how he behaves elsewhere. He could be taking homeless girls back to his flat and burying them under the floorboards for all you know.'

'You're getting carried away.'

'Why? How do you know? You only see the face that he chooses to present to you.'

'Like Joshua.'

'Yes, like Joshua.'

At eleven o'clock, Luke walks in. He nods at me and Isolde in his usual way and goes to sit down at the computer next to Joshua. I stare at him, but he gives no indication that he's the same young man who tried to steal a couple of double quarter-pounder meals.

Isolde raises her eyebrows at me. I can tell she's already doubting my story. Perhaps it wasn't him at all and I challenged a complete stranger.

Joshua and Luke prepare to leave at the end of the morning, just before me. As they walk past the counter where I'm tidying up, Luke raises his eyes from the floor and looks directly into my face. Is he trying to tell me that he doesn't bear any grudges, or that he will get me later? How can you tell?

I leave five minutes later and set off along the High Street to do some shopping. Joshua is just ahead. I hesitate, not wanting to give the impression that I'm following him, but after a few seconds he stops abruptly and turns round.

'Hello,' I say, intending to walk straight past.

'I enjoyed the concert last month,' he says.

'Oh,' I say, taken by surprise. 'Thank you. I hadn't expected to see you there.'

Unexpectedly, he puts his head back, his huge, white-haired, walnut-coloured head, and starts to laugh. It's not a small laugh. It's a great, belly-shaking laugh that goes on and on, getting louder and louder. Everyone round us turns to look. Two middle-aged women in earnest conversation pause, their mouths half-open with the desire to express their opinions but unable to continue; a man talking into his mobile phone takes it away from his ear and scowls; a toddler in a pushchair takes his thumb out of his mouth and stares at us with round, startled eyes.

'Stop,' I say. 'I don't know what you're laughing about.'

He calms down, wiping his eyes, the laughter blending back into the everyday sounds around us. Conversations resume. People walk faster to make up for lost time.

'I thought you were never going to mention the concert,' says Joshua.

It doesn't seem that funny. 'I was waiting for you to say something.'

He moves to the side of the pavement, easy with the flow of people round him, letting them weave past. We're in front of a fruit shop. An elderly woman in a straw hat with a hole in the brim reaches past us for a melon and a bunch of grapes. I watch her slip two plums into her red and white plastic bag.

'Do you often go to concerts?' I ask.

379

'Occasionally. I like music.'

'With your wife?'

He nods. 'She likes music too.'

So. The elegant woman who wears pearls is definitely his wife, and they must live together somewhere.

The smell of warm, savoury croissants wafts out of the French café.

'I like your little secret,' he says.

'Secret?'

'You are a librarian by day, a concert pianist by night.'

'Well . . .' I say. 'Not exactly a concert pianist. More like half of a double act.'

'Exactly,' he says. 'A cleverly hidden talent.'

I feel as if he's making me more important than I really am, and that I should protest. But I can't think of anything to say that sounds convincing.

'Well, I must be off,' he says.

'Wait,' I say. 'I just want to know—'

He watches me, his eyes still and patient.

'Why do you come to the library every day? Isolde and I—we've often wondered.'

He opens his mouth and I have an uncomfortable feeling he's going to start laughing again. But a slow gravity settles over him. 'I like libraries,' he says. 'They're good places.'

That's it? He comes because he likes it?

'I'm so glad we finally managed to communicate,' he says, offering his hand to shake.

His skin is warm, leathery and reassuring and he grips my hand with authority.

'Would you like to come to a barn dance?' I say.

He looks surprised. 'Where?'

'Audlands Hall. It's just outside Birmingham.

Towards Bromsgrove. I grew up there—my parents might be leaving soon and my sister and I wanted a last chance to have a party. We're inviting everybody. Absolutely everybody.'

He frowns, and then his face clears. 'I know Audlands Hall. I once drove down the drive to have a peep. An impressive place.'

I remember Andrew's parents telling me how they went down the drive to look. It seems that half the world has been there without my knowledge. 'It's not so impressive when you go inside. It's falling down.'

He studies me thoughtfully. 'So you are a member of the aristocracy.'

It's my turn to laugh. 'No. My parents bought it when I was a baby. They made a lot of money from selling cakes. Crunchy Chocolate Brownies.'

His eyes gleam. 'I remember Crunchy Chocolate Brownies. I thought I'd discovered paradise when I first came to England.'

'There you are, then. You helped fund our acquisition of Audlands Hall.'

He nods. 'I'm proud to have been such an essential part of British heritage.'

'You're welcome to come to the barn dance. It's on Saturday week. Bring your wife.'

'I will come,' he says. 'With pleasure.' Then he's gone. I wait for a few seconds, smelling the punnets of strawberries without seeing them. I thought he was the mystery man, the one with the secret, when all the time he was thinking the same about me. And there was no secret. Isolde and I were simply wrong. You can talk about something endlessly, sketch the outline, construct the tower in your mind, when in reality there's nothing there.

381

No foundations or bricks or mortar. A folly of the imagination.

*   *   *

I'm back home preparing a late lunch when the phone rings and I pick it up.

'Jessica, it's Alice.'

'Alice!' I say, thrilled to hear her voice, but terrified she's rung to say she's never coming back.

'I'm round the corner,' she says. 'I left my purse somewhere in your living room on Wednesday. Can I come and pick it up?'

'Are you sure? I haven't seen it.'

'Yes, I'm sure.'

'I'll go and have a look.'

But she arrives at the door almost as soon as I've put the receiver down.

'That was quick,' I say, letting her in.

'I was only round the corner. I thought I'd better ring before turning up.'

I can't cope with the suspense. 'Is everything all right?' I say.

'Everything's fine,' she says.

I'm not sure if she's fully understood my question. 'So are you speaking to Joel?'

She smiles. 'Oh, yes. It's all sorted.'

Sunshine penetrates the frosted window of the front door and lights up the hall, bringing an unaccustomed depth and height to the tiny space. The coats hanging at the bottom of the stairs have acquired a soft, easy-going appearance in their capacity as casual onlookers. 'Would you like a cup of coffee?' I say.

'I'd love one if you have time.'

382

She follows me into the kitchen. 'I thought I might never see you again,' I say, concentrating on filling the kettle so that I don't have to meet her eyes.

'Why ever not?'

'I thought perhaps you'd split up with Joel.' It sounds naïve and foolish, and I wish I hadn't said it.

She laughs, an uninhibited sound. 'But why would we split up? We're getting married.'

I take two mugs out of the cupboard and place a teaspoon of coffee in each one. 'Sometimes people call off weddings,' I say carefully. 'It's not unreasonable. You don't have to go through with something just because everyone else expects it.'

'I know that,' she says. 'But we've made our decision and I would never do anything I didn't want to.'

I turn to study her face. She possesses an extraordinary certainty, a self-belief that radiates towards me and makes me believe in her too. I discover that I've been holding my breath, so I let it out slowly and quietly.

'We have to have rows occasionally,' she says. 'Otherwise he gets too full of himself.'

Rows can serve a purpose? They didn't used to feel like that with Andrew.

We carry our cups of coffee through to the living room.

'You've cleared up,' she says.

'Well, I could hardly leave the room in that state. The plasticine would have been trodden into the carpet.'

'Sorry,' she says. 'But it was very satisfying, squeezing the cats up into balls.'

383

'And throwing them?'

She laughs again. 'Oh yes.'

'Actually, I don't mind at all. They've been around for too long.' I want to ask her how she could have been so sure that he would make concessions. 'Joel stayed out all night. He went into the office.'

'He told me. I wasn't surprised.'

'Really?'

'Don't forget we've worked together for three years now. We've had arguments before. He just takes time to admit I'm right.'

I experience a stab of jealousy. He never admits anything to me, and I'm his mother. 'I don't know how you manage it. He's never been able to see that he's in the wrong.'

There's a long pause. Alice looks past me, through the window, studying the garden with a strange intensity. She seems reluctant to speak, as if she wants to say something but doesn't know how to put it into words. I let the silence stretch, unsure what she wants me to do.

She turns back to me. 'You know he has Asperger's, don't you?' she says at last.

I stare at her.

'Asperger's Syndrome. It's a form of autism.'

I put my coffee down on the table. The cup gleams, electric blue, shiny with an artificial brightness that wasn't there a second ago. The sides of the furniture seem oddly hostile, hard-edged. 'Are we talking about Joel?'

She nods, her head moving up and down with an unnatural slowness. 'I recognised it in him straightaway—my brother has it too, you see. It's the way they both deal with social situations, their

384

difficulty in interpreting other people.'

'I don't understand—' I say.

'Have you heard of Asperger's?'

'Of course I have. The whole world talks about it nowadays.' Their conversations are chattering in my ears, arguing, discussing, informing. I can hardly hear my own voice, let alone Alice's.

She pauses. 'I'm sorry, Jessica. I didn't mean to upset you.'

'I'm not upset.' But I still can't quite grasp what she's trying to say. Is she telling me my son is autistic?

Alice speaks slowly. 'I know what a shock it must be to you. When we found out, my parents couldn't accept it either. But actually, in the end, it was an enormous relief, because everything suddenly made sense. It was so much easier once they realised that his behaviour wasn't their fault.'

My mind is racing through volumes of half-remembered information, newspaper articles, radio documentaries, televisions chat shows. Other people's children. 'But Joel went to an ordinary school. He earns a living. If what you say is true, surely he couldn't do all of that?'

Alice takes a sip of her own coffee. I see the liquid flow into her mouth, the movement in her neck as she swallows. 'Well—there's an autistic spectrum. The severe ones are at the far end, but some people, like Joel and my brother, are just hovering on the edge. They can go either way—it just depends on how much help they get.'

'You mean they can get better?'

She leans back on the sofa, more relaxed than she was at first, sure of her own knowledge. 'Not exactly—it never completely goes away, but it can improve, especially if you work with their obsessions. My brother used to spend all his time taking things apart and now he's studying engineering at Cambridge. He's not quite up to the same social life as everyone else, but he copes.'

I try to imagine her clever brother, fiddling with the insides of a television, slicing through a cable to see how it worked. Joel was just as inquisitive, but he preferred to press keys on computers instead. 'Isn't there a danger you start thinking that everyone who's a bit different has something wrong with them?'

'It's not to do with having something wrong. You have to see it as a condition, rather than an illness. It means they live in an alternative world, a strange land that runs parallel to everyone else's. They're often very creative—they ask the questions that nobody else even thinks of.'

A strange land. These words have an immediate impact on me. They describe Joel's world exactly, his remoteness, his unawareness of others. When you talk to him, you always feel that something is missing, that you've lost a key point in the translation. No wonder he prefers to operate in his computer language, obsessively creating fantasy places where he has control over any threatening and unpredictable characters. It must provide him with security in an otherwise uncertain existence.

She's right, she must be right. The more I think about it, the more obvious it becomes. All those times when I was summoned to the school because he was being disruptive, when he refused to wear anything except his blue trousers, when he turned away from me as if I wasn't there. I'd always assumed it was my inability to manage him properly, the trauma of living with Andrew's unpredictability. It had never occurred to me that there might be an alternative explanation.

There's a roaring in my ears, a waterfall of immense proportions. Powerful and terrifying, but at the same time a release of pressure that has been steadily building up for years. It's a shock, but a liberating one. 'Are you absolutely certain about this?'

She leans over to touch a tail on one of Joel's cats, easing it upright and putting a tiny curl in the end. 'I suspect my family is more expert than the experts. When you've lived with it for so long, you sense things, and it's easier to recognise them in others. I can lend you some books if you'd like to find out more about it.'

'No, it's all right. I can look in the library.' I want to do this myself, not have it fed to me by someone else, even if that someone is Alice. There must be volumes of information waiting to be discovered. A vast panorama of knowledge out there that I've only seen from the edges. 'What causes it? Where does it come from?'

'I don't think anyone really knows, but it often runs in families. Apparently, people start remembering reclusive grandfathers or eccentric great-aunts.' She looks at me steadily.

Andrew, I think. He's the explanation. Like father like son. Their conversations about superhuman powers, their shared fascination with comics and cartoons. I've been unfair to Andrew, I realise with a jolt. None of it was his fault. He had a condition and I didn't know.

'Have you talked about it to Joel?' I ask.

'Well—I've dropped hints. I thought he might

387

identify with my brother when he met him, but he's not seeing it. I don't think it's deliberate, he's just not very perceptive. Obviously. Then I thought perhaps I ought to talk to you first, in case you knew more than you were letting on.'

'No,' I say. 'I didn't know. I'm not very perceptive either, I'm afraid.'

She smiles. 'But you might prefer to be the one to tell him about it. You've known him a lot longer than I have.'

I don't know him at all. I hardly ever manage to persuade him to have a sensible conversation. Alice is the one who's already crossed the frontier and entered the strange land. 'I think it would be better coming from you.'

'OK,' she says. 'I rather think it won't be easy to convince him, so you'll probably need to back me up later on.'

'Do you think it would be worth going to see someone—I mean, shouldn't he consult an expert? So we can be absolutely sure.'

'Possibly—let's see how he feels about it."

'Could they help him? Guidance, or therapy, or something?'

'I don't know that he needs any help. You've done most of the hard work already.'

'Me? What have I done?'

'Look at him. He manages his life, he runs a successful business, he's about to get married. You've always supported him and communicated with him. That's the best therapy he's ever going to get.'

I'm embarrassed. It doesn't feel as if I've done anything useful, more as if I've failed right from the beginning, not even recognising the problem.

I've just muddled through. I get up and start pulling cushions off the chair.

'What are you doing?' she says.

'Your purse. It must be here somewhere.'

'It's on top of the mantelpiece,' she says. 'Behind the pink vase.'

She's right. I don't know why I didn't see it before. 'Will you be late for work?'

She shrugs. 'Doesn't matter. The boss hasn't been in for most of the week. He's off renovating ancient houses for dances.'

I smile. 'Oh, yes. I should be there myself.'

She stands up. 'I'm sorry if I've delayed you.'

'No—it's all right. I'm so glad you've told me.' I feel slightly off-key, as if I'm out of tune with my surroundings, not certain how to proceed.

She buttons up her coat.

'You must be a glutton for punishment,' I say. 'First your brother and now Joel. I'd have thought you'd be wanting a break.'

She picks up a plasticine cat that's still intact—Scarlatti, I think—and places it in the palm of her hand, studying it from several angles. 'I suppose I'm comfortable with Joel. I'll always know where I stand with him. He'll never lie to me or be disloyal. He doesn't know how to. And I can bring out the best in him.'

She's like Mary. She needs someone to mother, to look after, to guide. That's what fulfils her. 'You already do that,' I say.

We walk to the front door. She puts her arms round me and kisses my cheek. I let her do it. We have a new connection, a secret, special knowledge. 'I need to think about all this,' I say.

I wonder if she left her purse on purpose.

389

Every day when I've finished my work at the library, I sit down at a computer and go on to the internet, finding out, learning, trying to reconcile my new knowledge with the image I have of Joel. He is undergoing a transformation, losing his blurred outline, beginning to make sense. It's as if I only ever half knew him. There were so many promises to teachers that I would talk to him about his behaviour, so many futile conversations that he never contributed to, so many tantrums. Remembering him in his isolated, alien world, I wonder that he has survived at all. Why didn't anyone see this earlier? Why didn't I see it? Things could have been so much easier.

And yet his life has been much more successful than his father's. I've been thinking a lot about Andrew, trying to work out what went wrong. I know his mother tried as hard as I did. There was that one moment, in the concert, when he was finely balanced at the centre of a crucial tightrope, and something made him fall off. Did Miranda push too hard? Would it have been better to let him follow his own inclinations, create cartoons of his own, perhaps, explore his own personal country? Maybe the music was a mistake right from the beginning, forcing him towards a world where he never felt at home, driving him down a dual carriageway in the wrong direction.

Perhaps if I'd been more tolerant, more understanding—

Guilt about Joel, guilt about Andrew.

*   *   *

At Audlands, I often clean on my own while Harriet and Philip go out for meals and explore places that they remember. My parents seem happy with this arrangement. They're pleased to have Harriet at home for a while, but they find it a strain having to make conversation. They've got used to their isolation, their silence.

I don't intrude on them. When I arrive, I call hello through the kitchen door and my mother looks up from her internet activities to reply. A newspaper rustles as my father labours at the *Times* crossword, a dictionary and a thesaurus at his side. I leave them to it and carry on.

Once the sawdust has been cleared away from the Long Gallery and the floorboards are varnished, I start on the statues. Tiberius gets the privilege of being first. The surface dirt comes off immediately, but there are older, ingrained marks that need more attention. Wondering if I'm breaking some unwritten rule of restoration, I use a nailbrush and Tesco's cream cleaner. After some intense scrubbing, I wipe a cloth over the statue and Tiberius emerges, fresh and innocent, sparkling with resurrected glee.

'Well, hello,' I say, pleased with my achievement. 'Even your wife would recognise you now.'

He stares back with his blank stone eyes.

'You don't fool me. Vanity is important to you. I can tell from the hairstyle.'

'Jess!'

I nearly drop the cloth. Philip has come up behind me. A shudder runs through me, an

391

unsteadiness in my legs. I don't want to talk to him on his own.

'Where's Harriet?' I ask, turning slowly.

'Gone for a bath—if the hot water ever gets there. The heating system's a bit temperamental, isn't it?'

'It does work. The water's got miles of pipes to get through to reach the bathroom, that's all. You just have to run it for ten minutes.'

'I'll bear that in mind.'

He sits down on a window seat. I carry my bowl of dirty water to Octavius and start work on him, pretending I'm alone.

'Talk to me, Jess.'

'Why?' I don't want to. I want him to go away.

'You're my cousin. We were friends once.'

'Were we? I don't remember.'

'I loved coming to Audlands—tennis, boating, driving your dad's car. We were all friends then,' he says.

Has he forgotten? 'No, we weren't. You played with Colin and Harriet and Judy. Not me.'

'You joined in sometimes.'

I scrub until a dirty grey scum covers Octavius' head, pooling into the eye sockets, the crevices above his lips. Bending down, I rinse out the cloth and wipe it over again. He looks good. Not perfect, but there was never any chance of that with his broken nose.

'Why won't you talk?' asks Philip.

I take a breath. 'You weren't very nice to me.'

There. I've said it. The words have been rolling round in my head for days, but I'm still impressed that I can say them.

'Wasn't I?' He sounds so amazed that I turn

392

round to look at him, suspecting secret laughter, but what I see is a blank expression.

I meet his eyes. 'Don't you remember?'

He shakes his head. 'No. What did I do?'

How to be specific? He laughed at me, poked me, whispered nasty things in my ear, fired tennis balls at me. It doesn't sound bad enough. 'You broke my little finger.' I don't want to say anything about the other events in my bedroom.

He looks bewildered. 'I don't remember that. How did it happen?'

'It didn't just happen. You did it. You took my finger and bent it up until it snapped.'

He stares at me. His face has aged well. He's retained much of his boyish charm, but it's balanced with an air of experience and wisdom. 'Are you sure you're not talking about Colin? I was far too nice to do something like that. Still am.' His expression softens and his smile is generous and open. I'm a nice chap, he's saying. You have to like me.

'It wasn't Colin.' I return to Octavius, manipulating the nailbrush in his ears. Up and down, round the complex networks of stone tissue.

'Well,' he says after a while. 'If it was me, I'm sorry. I can't believe I did something like that on purpose.'

'It was you,' I say. 'And you did it on purpose.'

It's hard to maintain the role of accuser in the absence of any resistance. It makes me feel harsh and confrontational. But I must hold on to my certainty. There's an injury inside me that was never addressed, never sewn up, never put in a splint. The after-effects have been throbbing for decades, aching and sour, affecting everything I've

393

done since. I should attack him with rage, try to inflict the same injuries on him. But it requires so much energy. I drag myself to a window seat.

He's watching. 'Are you all right?'

'I'm fine.'

'The statues look good.'

'Yes.'

'Harriet says you still play the piano—give concerts.'

'What about you?' I say. 'Why aren't you an accountant?'

He sighs. 'Well—I got myself into a bit of trouble.'

Ah, now we're getting somewhere. 'What kind of trouble?'

'You know how it is when people have too much money and nothing to spend it on—always looking for something more exciting.'

'No, I don't know.'

'Well—one day it all blew up.'

I wait but he doesn't expand on this. 'In what way?'

'I got caught. Six months' suspended sentence.'

'Oh.' I'm shocked. 'But what exactly did you do?'

'It's complicated—these financial affairs always are. It's debatable whether the police should have taken it so far.'

'So you lost the job?'

'Yes. And the luxury apartment, the car, the lot.'

I don't feel any pleasure or victory—just a flat sense of disillusionment. I'm irritated that he hasn't remained nasty and I can't hate him as much as I would like to. With a few off-hand words he's wiped out the comfort of resentment that I've been

394

carrying around with me, the incidental music that I didn't even notice was there. His failure humanises him, turns him into a victim, someone I have to feel compassion for.

'So what did you do? Go back home?'

He smiles. 'To Mummy and Daddy? No way. I tagged along with some friends, took a course in diving and ended up going abroad. Best thing I ever did. I was fed up with a life that was created for me by everyone else.'

Is this true? Was he simply the product of everyone's expectations? It's possible, I suppose. It wasn't his fault that he was good-looking, clever, a sportsman. Once you've reached the goals that everyone else aims for, it can't be easy to ignore them all and reject the rewards that are unattainable to most people.

'Does Harriet know about all this?'

'Oh, yes—well, maybe not the details. I think I told her I gave up the job and followed my dreams. Something along those lines.'

'Shouldn't you tell her the truth?'

'I don't think so. She doesn't really want details.'

Aren't they supposed to have a close relationship? Isn't this why he's here? Surely they shouldn't have secrets from each other?

'And you're married?'

'No, not really.'

I get back up and move my bowl to Caligula. The water's dark and murky and needs changing, but Caligula's going to have to put up with it. I start scrubbing with tight, angry strokes. 'What's that supposed to mean?' I say.

He remains sitting. 'It's just a game, Jess. Harriet knows that.'

'And you don't think you're being a bit dishonest?'

'Harriet knows what's going on. She likes the idea of uncertainty. I spotted that in her straightaway. She was bored, tired of predictability, and I gave her what she wanted.'

I don't like the way he's talking about Harriet. 'What are you doing here, then?'

He pauses. 'I wanted to meet you again, Jess, resolve a few things.'

'You came to see me?' I'm so surprised I turn to look at him.

His eyes have narrowed with concentration, as if he's fighting some inner conflict, preparing himself to make a confession. 'Did you know that I had a crush on you?' he says after a few seconds.

What's he talking about? He ruined me, destroyed my confidence, sent me down a fractured pathway which redesigned itself into the crazy paving that led to Andrew. 'I think you're remembering it all in a distorted way,' I say.

'Or you are.'

'I don't think so. I was afraid of you.'

He looks genuinely astonished, and I see that something has left him: the razor-sharp blade that used to be able to slice through everything in front of him. That's why he can't recognise my portrait of him. He can't remember the way he was, can't recapture his old magnetism, because he's forgotten that it ever existed. He's still attractive, and he knows it, but his power is weaker. The vicious edge has been rubbed down, blunted and rendered ineffective by the damp salt air that hangs between then and now.

I should be pleased about this. But the fact that

he can't remember his old self takes away the impact of my discovery. I'm not entirely convinced that the cruelty doesn't lurk somewhere still, gathering strength, prepared to emerge again when the circumstances are right. You can't tell with people. You never really know what they are thinking.

'So do you have any intentions for Harriet?' I ask.

He looks surprised. 'Whatever made you think that?'

And there it is. The lack of empathy. The inability to recognise that he has misled Harriet. While they've been playing their grown-up games, she's responded to him emotionally and he's just been enjoying himself.

'Don't you think you're being irresponsible?' I say.

'No, just realistic.'

I want to grab him by the ears and batter his head against the marble fireplace behind us. I've never experienced this kind of anger before. It's as if I've just discovered I've been driving a Mini instead of a Ferrari. 'You're messing with Harriet,' I say. 'How do you know she thinks it's a game? Have you asked her? Maybe she takes it all more seriously.'

He stands up and walks over, studying my face with a disconcerting earnestness. 'You've changed, Jess,' he says.

'Well, that's hardly surprising. It's twenty-five years since you last saw me.'

'No, you've changed inside. You would never have challenged me like that years ago.'

Of course I've changed. I've loved someone

misguidedly, had a baby, taken that baby by the hand and helped him develop into an adult. I've been exposed to the elements. The walls were bound to crumble. The windows have been smashed by the wind, the rain has swept in to do its damage.

'You've lost the indifference that I always admired. You were the castle with walls that no one could scale, the unassailable fortress. That's what I liked about you.'

He seems to be talking about Joel. He was the difficult, impenetrable child, the unassailable fortress.

It often runs in families, Alice said.

Maybe the weather had to break down the walls. Maybe light and air needed a chance to penetrate and illuminate an interior that was too dark, too remote, too far away from human contact.

I stare at Philip, but he's no longer there. I'm seeing something new, my own life transformed by the removal of a filter, a different Jessica, someone I have never seen before.

It's me, I realise with sudden clarity. It wasn't Andrew who passed it on, it was me. I'm the one with the condition, the infinite space that separates me from the rest of the world.

I've spent all these years groping my way along in a bewildered silence, almost blind to everything except my own limited perceptions. I've been travelling without a compass or even a friendly hand at my elbow to guide me. I've lost my way, wandered in circles, never understood how you can use the stars to navigate.

And now, finally, after all this time, the dense fog is parting, drifting away and I can see where I am. I'm on a narrow pathway that leads out of the strange land. I'm about to cross the border, show my passport and step into the real world, blinking at its brightness.

A seven-year-old Jessica skates past me, her plaits swaying from side to side, her whole body absorbed by the rhythm. No wonder Harriet started to look elsewhere for friends, no wonder their mother gave up trying to communicate with her. That other Jessica was unreachable.

Music must have helped me to wake up. Something indefinable that dripped down inside, an imperceptible erosion over decades. A slow *crescendo, poco a poco*. Little by little. And then the shock of Andrew, not gradual, but *sforzando*, suddenly loud, explosive, blasting his way in without subtlety. How could I resist him when I had no defences, no ability to assess other people?

I don't need to feel guilty any more. The disability wasn't his, it was mine. He could have helped me, eased me more gently into the real world, but he didn't.

But maybe he did, by giving me Joel. The other defining experience of my life. The revelation that I could love a child, the discovery that everything was in place but hidden, waiting for the signal to emerge.

'Jess?'

I look at Philip as if I've never known him.

'Are you all right?' he says. 'Did I say something?'

'No,' I say. 'Nothing.' He's told me everything, but now he seems an irrelevance, a speck of dust that I can brush aside. I need to make an effort to be polite. 'How long are you staying?' I ask.

'Oh . . .' He looks vague. 'I'll wait for the barn dance, if it's all right with you.'

'You can do whatever you want,' I say, taking the bowl of water to the open window.

I pour it out and watch it slosh into the bushes, grey with dirt, leaving a patch of foamy scum on the leaves of the laurel.

CHAPTER TWENTY-SIX

The doors and windows of Audlands have been thrown open so that warm, aromatic air fills every room. Honeysuckle, roses, clematis—their rampant, unpruned blooms wrestle for space alongside the house. Petals scatter as each flower dies, pushed out of the way by the next one. Survival of the fittest. Explosions of young, fresh scent rise on the wafting currents of evening. There's a hum vibrating through Audlands, a sense of resurrected life, of empty corridors and abandoned rooms stirring and starting to breathe again. Dust has been disturbed and blown away, at least downstairs, and cobwebs have been banished to the garden. Spiders still lurk in corners, peering out with resentful, rheumy eyes, plotting their return, the restarting of the internal machines in their silken web factories. It's the country house of my childhood again, a magical place where people wander in and out of rooms, infecting the air with their vitality. Bursts of laughter rise sporadically and drift away again, snatches of human melody dissipating in the high open spaces below the ornate ceilings.

Everyone has dressed according to his or her interpretation of the event. Some women are wearing cotton dresses with full skirts, petticoats and ruffles, while their partners leap around in jeans and lumberjack shirts. They've come for the dancing, the fun, the *Oklahoma* atmosphere. Others are more formal: evening gowns, black tie, aiming for sophistication but slightly ironic. And others have dressed as a compromise, smart but casual, rejecting ostentation, ready to dance and enjoy themselves, but not prepared to fully embrace the American pioneer theme.

I stand by the front door with my parents and Harriet, greeting everyone, smiling, smiling, aware that this bright burning of energy might be Audland's last stand.

The tennis club arrive together, a group of five young men in kilts, and their girlfriends.

'It's a barn dance,' I say. 'Not a Scottish dance.'

'My point exactly,' says one of them. 'But do you think they'd listen to me?'

'Jessica, Harriet,' says my mother, glowing with pleasure, proud that she knows them. 'This is the tennis club.' She doesn't notice that she's only acknowledged the men. The girlfriends hover on the side, ungreeted.

'Do they have names?' I ask.

'Ben, Will, Scott, Joe and—' She stops and looks embarrassed.

A man in blue and green tartan steps forward and holds out his hand. 'Hugo,' he says. A gold chain, thin and delicate, links both sides of his waistcoat. One end is attached to a round, intricately decorated watch, which can be seen peeping out of its pocket.

'How could you forget Hugo?' I ask my mother.

Her smile is wide and girlish. 'I didn't forget you, Hugo,' she says. 'You know how it is—so many people, so much to think about.'

He bows, old-fashioned but convincing. 'I completely understand, Connie,' he says.

My mother has salvaged a shimmering maroon evening dress from the back of a wardrobe, but it doesn't quite fit any more. She's not as streamlined as she used to be. She's swept her hair into a chignon, a mixture of grey and the old honey, wisps escaping and fizzing out round her head, almost swamping a fake diamond tiara. Her face and arms glint with sprayed-on glitter. She must have been into a shop for teenage girls and spent many happy hours sorting through the acres of sparkle. It wouldn't surprise me if she'd also bought fairy wings and stowed them away in her wardrobe for a future occasion.

'I often hear you playing in the distance,' says my father, holding out his hand for the tennis players. 'I'd join in, but . . .' He gestures at his wheelchair.

'We could always try a handicapped game,' suggests Ben.

My father grins, without mentioning that he didn't play tennis before being confined to a wheelchair and probably couldn't hit the ball anyway. He's unusually relaxed, but nevertheless keeps a wary eye on the chandelier.

The candles shiver and tremble above the visitors, but they won't have any serious impact until the sun goes down. It's still early evening and the normal entrance hall gloom is illuminated by shafts of light from the open door and the quick movements and chatter of the guests.

My neighbour Ajinth arrives with his family: his tiny wife, who always laughs when she talks to me, giggling as if we share some special secret; their teenage girls, who tower above them, strong and athletic, gleaming with health, a combination of reserved English politeness and Tamil beauty. Ajinth offers my mother a covered bowl. 'Our contribution to the refreshments,' he says with a small bow.

'Oh,' says my mother, confused. 'Thank you so much.' She hands the bowl to my father, who hands it to Harriet, who puts it on the table with the glasses and champagne.

Stuart, our agent, follows them in, his hair even wider, even springier than usual. 'Hi, Jess,' he says. He sniffs.

'Would you like a paper hankie?' I ask.

He grins. 'Careful,' he says. 'Mary will hear you.'

Mary comes up behind me. She's opted for the American barn dance look. Her dress is red with white polka dots, pulled in at the waist and flaring out to the knees with dozens of petticoats underneath. She has a big red bow in her hair. She looks hilarious, but delights in the shrieks of laughter that she arouses in everyone else.

'Shall we start the food?' she says.

As a gift to my parents she and Eamon have paid for caterers, so Harriet and I have not been forced to heat up hundreds of frozen sausage rolls and vol-au-vents. My mother's concept of party food has not become more educated with time.

'I don't see why not,' I say. 'Most people seem to have arrived.'

After a few minutes, waiters appear and

circulate through the downstairs rooms with trays of food. Voices become subdued as people start to eat.

Joshua arrives, immaculate in a dinner jacket, accompanied by his wife, who's wearing a necklace of glowing, multi-coloured beads and matching earrings.

'Jessica,' he says, holding his wife's arm. 'This is Mayowa.'

He says it with quiet pride, as if he's offering me his most precious possession and knows I'll be impressed. I am moved by his sincerity, his delight in her, the way he presents her as a well-loved companion.

'Joshua has spoken about you,' I say.

'He's talked about me in the library?' she says. 'Where you are not supposed to talk?'

'Well . . .' I say and then she starts to laugh, a rich warm laugh that ties her to Joshua. 'I'm glad you could come,' I say.

'So am I,' says Joshua. 'I've been looking forward to seeing inside Audlands Hall.'

'Well, now's your chance. Before it all falls down.'

The musicians in the Long Gallery are tuning, bows moving easily, strings sliding comfortably into place. I glance at Harriet and we exchange private smiles. I can see a similar anticipation in my mother's face too.

'You'd better go, Roland,' she says. 'They'll be needing you to give directions.'

'Yes, of course,' he says and propels himself away. An importance glows out of him, a pleasure at being wanted, a belief that nothing can go ahead without him. The four men from his old factory who've been delegated to get him upstairs with the wheelchair are waiting at the bottom of the stairs. My mother has been admiring them for some time.

'Shall we go up now?' says Harriet. 'I want to join in.'

'I should think so,' says my mother. 'Everyone seems to be here.'

The cars are parked neatly on either side of the drive in the overgrown grass, all facing the same direction, diagonally parallel to each other. How orderly people are when they have to organise themselves.

In the Long Gallery, people are starting to pair up for the Virginia Reel. My father is using a microphone.

'Can we have five or six couples in each set? There's room for several sets. Just grab a stranger if you don't have someone to dance with. Anyone will do.'

'Take your partners!' yells someone in an American accent.

Some people are hovering along the walls, nervous, never having been to a barn dance before. Others pour on to the floor immediately, eager and willing to do whatever's asked of them. Harriet and Philip leap up, hand in hand, forming one of the first sets. Isolde is there too, her auburn hair piled up on her head in an elaborate confection of curls and ringlets, and she's found herself a tennis player, half her age but romantic in his kilt. Her face is flushed and soft, her eyes shining, a solitary emerald on the end of a gold chain hanging round her neck.

The music starts.

'Bow!' shouts my father as the first chord hangs

on the air.

Some bow, some curtsey, others stare round in bewilderment, watching everyone else.

'Face your partners! Join hands in a long line, four steps forward, four steps back—'

What more can my father ask for? It sounds exhausting, but he has a sound system and everyone's attempting to obey his instructions. He must feel as if he's back at work, in charge of several factories, making decisions, manoeuvring teams of people, churning out Crunchy Chocolate Brownies.

Men shuffle in the wrong direction, unwilling to hold hands with their partners. Mrs Thompson, my mother's cleaner, bumps into everyone and dissolves into high-pitched giggles. 'Sorry,' I can hear. 'Sorry.' Their arms are up in the air, forming an arch, while oddly matched couples link arms and skip under the arch, heads bowed to get through, high heels skidding on the wood, heavy flat shoes solid and safe. Middle-aged men walk through the steps, young women skip, self-conscious, unknowingly abandoning themselves to the beat of the music. Children dart between them. Couples take a wrong turn. Shouts from everyone. 'No, you go left . . . You have to split up . . . You've got to go the other way.' They're running in a panic, trying to catch up with themselves. A giant circle as everyone joins hands and walks round, smiling faces, panting, sweating, everyone good-natured.

My mother's dancing with Hugo. She's walking rhythmically, with a bounce, not quite skipping. She must be aware of her arthritic knees, but there isn't much evidence of them. I suspect she's

406

overdosed on painkillers.

'Will you do the next dance with me?' Alice is at my side, shouting into my ear. 'Joel's hopeless. He won't join in.'

'We'll see about that,' I say and turn to see him with a glass of wine in his hand, studying the dancing couples with an expression of bewilderment on his face. My newly understood son. Does he know yet? Has Alice talked to him? Does he believe her?

Alice is moving with the music, unable to keep still, her body somehow murmuring and rolling in sympathy with the beat.

'I don't know how you put up with him,' I say.

'Joel's Joel,' she says. 'You just have to know how to manage him and then he's fine.'

Mary and Eamon skip past, each of them partnering one of their boys. Eamon is walking the steps, but Mary's skipping, her face alive with joy.

'You know,' says Alice. 'You really have done a brilliant job with Joel.'

'Have I? I don't know what I did.'

'You loved him,' she said.

'Back in position!' shouts my father. 'Make sure you're opposite your partner. Step towards each other. Now backwards.'

They start all over again. There's hysterical laughter as people bump into each other, go the wrong way, stand helplessly. The floor bounces under their weight, the wood bowing and springing back up.

The milkman is surprisingly nimble. He's dancing with the lady who delivers potatoes once a week. 'Yah-hee!' he yells, and there's an echo from enthusiasts on the other side of the room. They've done this before, I can tell.

Alice's hair is set into hundreds of tiny plaits that hang down and end in beads. They tinkle and click whenever she moves her head. She's so much more certain than I was at her age, so capable. She has natural, instinctive skills, an ability to read people and manage them. She's never had to peer through fog or translate from a foreign language to make sense of the world.

I look across at Joel, who's droopy and awkward in jeans and an open-necked shirt. He's watching the dancing with fascination, tapping his foot. 'I think he might be enjoying himself,' I say to Alice, smiling at her with affection.

*   *   *

We stop for a break, spilling out down the stairs and into the garden, where more refreshments are being served. The tennis players have cleared a large area during the last fortnight, cutting back bushes, trimming the grass and scattering new gravel to differentiate between the paths and the lawns. The statue of Artemis is visible again, looking down on us with barely concealed superiority, her smile patronising and tolerant. They're all children, she's thinking. Nothing changes.

The sun is low in the sky, casting shadows across the scene. Tendrils of light thread through the branches of trees and reach the windows, slanting into the music room and library with a dazzling intensity.

Waiters hover discreetly with trays of food and drink. A subdued exhaustion settles while everyone cools down and breathing returns to normal. A group of young people attempt to negotiate the old path to the lake.

Joshua is talking to my mother. 'Are you thinking of selling?'

'No, of course not. I've been here all my adult life. It's my home.'

'It's idyllic.'

'We've worked so hard on it over the years.'

'But your home becomes so empty once your children leave, doesn't it?'

'Do you have children?'

'Oh yes. Five.'

'Goodness. However did you cope?'

'My wife must take the credit,' he says. 'She is a paragon.'

My mother's face reflects a dilemma. She can't decide whether to laugh or be impressed. In the end she gives way to a wild giggle, and pops a miniature pizza topped with Parma ham and an olive into her mouth. Her eyes are on Ben and Will, who are jumping around on the edge of the lawn, trying to reach the lowest branch of a sycamore tree. Grown men with the energy of ten-year-olds.

'We really must start the treasure hunt,' she says. 'It'll be dark soon.'

Harriet and Philip are standing side by side in the shadow of Artemis, squinting up at her through the setting sun. He's casually dressed and has a piece of straw sticking out of the side of his hair, held in place by a knot of string. This is his concession to the barn dance ethos. She's as elegant as ever, shining, laughing, attempting to remove the piece of straw every time he turns his head away.

'You look silly,' she says.

'I am silly. The whole thing is silly.'

'But fun.'

'Yes. What do you reckon she's thinking?' He points to Artemis.

'The same as always, I suspect. Nobody here is as beautiful as she is. It's a matter of principle.'

This is the cue for him to give Harriet a compliment, I realise, and I watch his mouth open, ready to follow the rules, when I'm grabbed from behind. I turn to find Joel breathing heavily, as if he's been running.

'What's the matter?'

'It's Dad.'

Resentment floods through me. I'd forgotten that I'd told Joel he could invite him. 'What's he up to?'

Joel's face is grim and annoyed. 'Climbing again.'

I might have known it. 'Where is it this time?' Probably the top of the Post Office Tower and they want me to go and persuade him to come back down.

'Here. Audlands.'

I would have preferred the Post Office Tower. I follow Joel back through the house. As we pass my mother, she grabs my arm. 'Jessica, what about the treasure hunt?'

'It's all right,' I say. 'We'll start it when I get back. I just need to sort something out.'

'But it'll get too dark.'

'Why don't you get it going now? Harriet will help.'

The musicians are going back upstairs,

410

expecting to continue. 'Tell Dad to start the dancing again,' I say to my mother. I don't want people to be diverted by Andrew, or give him the attention that he craves.

Vibrant opening chords echo through the house as we descend the front steps. A small group of people has gathered in the drive between the parked cars, looking back towards Audlands, past the pillars, over the arch of the porch and up to the second-storey windows. Mary and Eamon are among them, and I would like to tell them to let me deal with it. I don't want them to have to cope with the embarrassment of meeting Andrew after all these years.

I join them, looking upwards, shading my eyes against the red glow of the setting sun. A figure is working his way up the outside of the building, his long, bony legs accentuated by electric blue leggings. He's wearing the same black and red T-shirt he wore when he climbed the House of Fraser, and a canvas-covered violin case sticks out at an awkward angle from his back. A cross between a participant in the Tour de France and Dennis the Menace.

'Who is it?' says someone.

'Must be one of those Fathers for Justice people. They're all a bit nutty, I think.'

'What's he carrying?'

'No idea.'

'Who's he meant to be? He doesn't really look like Batman.'

He's reached the top of the second floor, just below the edge of the roof, and is clinging to the moulded plasterwork, his feet wedged between the edges of a window recess. I can't see how he's

411

going to get past the overlapping stucco ridge, which sticks out some way above him, decorated with clusters of rosettes and a variety of animals. He grasps the wing of a griffin to balance himself and I catch my breath. Doesn't he realise how easily it could break?

A group of children comes racing out from the hallway and stops in the entrance. They seem to be searching for something. They stand and study the front of the house.

One of them reads the words on a scrap of paper: ' "Face the front, count four to the right, I'm in the crack behind, out of sight." '

They hesitate, counting, then dash over to the fourth pillar and scramble round it.

'Here it is!' shouts a boy.

'What does it say?'

He removes a piece of paper from a hole at the back of the pillar and unfolds it. They jostle against each other, trying to read it.

' "Mary, Mary, quite contrary—" '

'What's that supposed to mean?'

I consider shouting up and telling Andrew to come down immediately, but I don't think he'll take any notice.

'He's such a worry,' says Mary.

'He's better doing this than bashing up his family,' says Eamon.

There's a brief moment when Andrew seems to be hanging from one hand only, and I can hear everyone round me draw in their breath. But he must be bluffing, because he swings one leg over the balustrade, then the other, and rolls on to the flat part of the roof. He jumps to his feet and raises his arms in triumph, then leans over and pats the swirling mane of a lion's head.

The treasure hunters are oblivious to the drama going on above them. 'There aren't any silver bells or cockle shells.'

'What about the pretty maids all in a row?'

'Girls?'

'No, stupid. Flowers.'

'Do you think the roof's safe?' asks Mary.

I shrug. 'Who knows? I shouldn't have thought so.'

Andrew twists an arm and removes the violin case from his back. The barn dance is gathering momentum in the distance. A frenetic hoedown is blasting out, accompanied by yells of excitement as more and more people lose their inhibitions. They're mellowed by the wine, exhilarated by the exercise, loosened by the wildness of the music.

Andrew removes his violin from the case and starts to tune.

'I know!' says Will, one of the tennis players, who seems to have allied himself with the children rather than the adults. 'We planted some dahlias by the fountain!'

They disappear back into the house, chattering with enthusiasm.

'We won't be able to hear the violin with the barn dance going on,' says Mary worriedly. 'He's going to be annoyed.'

But she's wrong. As soon as Andrew starts to play, the sound expands and travels, filling the air around us. It must be the quality of the violin. Perhaps those old masters from Cremona— Stradivarius, Guarnerius, Amati—had this in mind when they mixed their mysterious potions and painted their violins with a varnish that's never been matched since. Perhaps they knew that their instruments would be used in the open air, and made them for just this kind of occasion—mad musicians playing on the roof of a stately home.

I can see why it has to be Bach. The chords add deep, rich supporting harmony that echoes through the background and reaches us on the ground. The sound is exquisite, the way it always was, the reason that I married Andrew. It's so long since I've heard him play that I've forgotten the impact he can have. He weaves magic, stirs a unique passage through the atmosphere, moves the universe a few millimetres. Bach's melodies soar out and wrap their sinewy fingers around us. I can't move. Mary and Eamon are silent at my side. This is what Andrew was made for, the reason he exists, the purpose of his life. Without the music he is nothing. With it, he is in absolute command.

I was wrong to think that Miranda shouldn't have led him to the music. I should have taken her side, stepped into the opposite camp and tried to persuade Andrew to keep playing. Without the music, he shut down and ceased to function at full capacity. There must have been a self-destructive circuit inside him. I should never have let him press the switch.

When I was a student, did I love the man or the music? The man, I used to think. The music, I think now. My emotions were too new then, too overwhelming for me to sort out. I was a child adrift in an adult world.

Starlings drift along thermals and come to investigate. He was right. Even the birds know that something special is happening.

A strange rumble creeps into the background. I

barely notice it at first—the distant clatter of a lorry maybe, a Boeing 747 crossing our space on its way to Canada, a murmur of summer thunder? But it grows until we can't ignore it. I've never heard anything like it before. A sound of creaking, groaning, ripping. We stare at each other in bewilderment.

'The roof's falling in!' says someone.

But it isn't. Andrew is still there. Nothing is happening. The hoedown stops in the distance, and the shrieks of pleasure seem to have taken on an edge of hysteria.

I turn and run back up the steps into the house, Joel beside me, Mary and Eamon following. People are pouring down the stairs from the Long Gallery.

I recognise the milkman and grab his arm. He stops, causing the people behind him to bump into each other. 'What's happening?' I shout as he recovers his balance.

He stands solidly, flexes his shoulders and makes it clear that he isn't panicking. 'The floor's collapsing.'

The floor? The beautiful oak floor that we spent so much time restoring? Joel and I look at each other. We must have done something stupid, dislodged the joists, not fixed the boards firmly enough. 'Is anyone hurt?'

The milkman considers. 'I'm not sure. Let's just say I didn't see any injuries.'

By the time we reach the Long Gallery, most people have managed to retreat into the main part of the house or down the smaller staircase into the garden. The musicians are edging round the side of the room, holding their instruments up to protect them. The second violin player is taking the lead, testing each floorboard before stepping on it.

'Just follow me,' he is saying. 'Step in exactly the same place.'

'It's all right for you,' says the cello player, wrapping his arms round his cello. 'There's no substance to your instrument.'

The strain of two hundred years of pounding feet has proved too much for the floor and mankind has imprinted his indelible mark on nature, defeated the strength of oak. Several floorboards have split in the middle and then risen at both ends. Jagged holes have appeared between them, as if they had some hidden agreement to surrender at the same time, and they offer a glimpse into a black cavernous emptiness below.

Joel and I stand side by side and stare. 'Well,' he says after a while. 'So much for Audlands.'

'I can't believe that nobody has fallen through.' My mouth has gone dry and my voice sounds unnaturally thick as I realise how close we have been to a major disaster. They'd have gone straight down to the ground floor.

The tennis players have taken charge and are guiding people to the stairs. A tall woman is standing on the landing, leaning against a waist-high Dresden vase, whimpering and clutching the ripped skirt of her bottle-green dress. She's trying to wrap it round the top of her legs but without much success, and an expanse of white, wrinkled flesh gleams out. A waiter offers her a glass of wine, which she grabs and drinks greedily. Another middle-aged woman is limping down the stairs, helped along by a solicitous Stuart. She's smiling at something he's saying. In the passageway, one or two people have sat down on the floor, looking dazed, but there's no sign of blood.

Joel approaches an elderly man, who's taking deep breaths with his eyes shut. 'Are you all right?'

He snaps his eyes open and grins, removing ten years from his face. 'Fine,' he says. 'What an adventure!'

'Angus! Tim!' Mary's voice rises up behind me, tinged with hysteria.

'It's all right,' says Eamon, cool and organised. 'All the children were doing the treasure hunt. They weren't even in here.'

'I'd still be a lot happier if I could see them.'

I experience a sense of just-missed horror as I imagine small children sliding down planks of wood into the rooms below.

Eamon appears at my side. 'A few people are suffering from shock, but that seems to be all. Just cuts and bruises as far as I can tell.'

My father's wheeling himself round the upstairs corridor and landing, looking efficient and in control. He'll be thinking about the legal repercussions soon—being taken to court, huge financial settlements. 'You'd better let my father know there are no casualties.'

There's a gradual lightening of tension as the confusion lifts and everyone begins to work out what's happened. Not a bomb, not an earthquake, not even the roof falling in. I can even hear people laughing.

'I said you shouldn't be dancing,' says a voice from downstairs. 'Now look what you've done.'

'Well,' says another voice. 'I thought I'd seen everything.'

'I don't see why a few bits of wood should spoil the fun.'

'I thought you had to join the army or go abroad for real action.'

'I can't understand it,' says my mother. 'It's been here for hundreds of years and these places were built to last.'

Eamon is bending down by the doorway, examining a piece of broken wood. He stands up. 'Death-watch beetle,' he says. 'Riddled with it.'

So tiny creatures have been our secret companions for years, nibbling their way through acres of wood, burrowing onwards, ticking with order and habit, while we made plans that didn't include their presence. How clever they are. The ultimate weapon. With a slow, insidious shuffle through time they have the means to undermine security, wreck fortunes, destroy empires.

'But we didn't see any beetles when we sanded the floor,' I say.

'Did you do the entire floor?'

'Well, no, just the bits that had swollen, where the rain had got in.'

'It all happens beneath the surface, out of sight. The joists, I imagine. You mustn't let anyone in there again.'

Downstairs, the musicians have set themselves up in the drawing room and started to play again— the Dashing White Sergeant. I can hear feet moving, hands clapping the beat. Nobody seems to think they should give up and go home just because there have been a few minutes of unscheduled events.

'Is the downstairs floor safe?' I ask Eamon.

'Not sure,' he says. 'It might be better to

418

persuade them to go out into the garden.'

'Can you find someone to lift my father down? Otherwise he'll be stuck up here on his own.'

I turn and almost bump into Joel. 'Mum! I've phoned for an ambulance!' He's white and trembling, his hair dark with sweat.

'We don't need an ambulance,' I say. 'Nobody's seriously hurt.'

'No,' he says, 'no, no.'

What's he talking about? 'Joel,' I say, putting a hand on his arm. 'It's all right. It wasn't a real disaster.'

'It's Dad,' he says.

He turns and runs back down the stairs to the entrance hall. I sigh and follow him. Why can't Andrew just leave us to get on with our own lives without trying to take the limelight all the time? Presumably he's faked a heart attack, or broken his leg on a loose tile. No doubt he wants us to send for the fire brigade as well, to get him down in one piece.

It's nearly dark at the front. The sun has set and although there's still light in the western sky, it's not managing to penetrate past the bulk of Audlands. The parked cars are ghostlike in the failing light, and Joel leads us to something lying on top of a silver Astra. A heap of clothes, bright against the metallic paint. Electric blue. Red and black.

As I stumble towards the car, I catch my foot on a piece of wood. How can a floorboard from the Long Gallery be out here? I pick it up and stare at the curved, reddish brown, splintered wood with jagged edges. There's half an f-hole carved into one side.

419

'He fell,' says Joel.

It's Andrew, his body contorted, scrunched and lifeless. I'm holding part of his violin, the violin that was so expensive that his parents had to take out a long-term loan to pay for it.

Shadows from the house engulf us. Starlings have started to twitter in the horse chestnuts. The Virginia Reel is playing in the distance, far away in another world. A swallow swoops down, close to our heads, then soars up into the darkening sky.

CHAPTER TWENTY-SEVEN

Every morning before I leave for the library, I wander through my home and let the empty space wrap itself around me. Joel has been gone for a year now and I like to go into his old bedroom and breathe deeply, appreciating the stillness, the lack of his presence. He's left behind his childhood furniture—the small, masculine wardrobe, his desk and the bed, which is now covered with a bright poppy-spattered quilt-cover. I've removed his cork noticeboard, taken down the posters of the Horsehead Nebula and Battlestar Galactica, and painted the walls apple white. It's ready to be used as a spare bedroom, but I'm fooling myself. I'll never invite anyone to stay. I have too great a desire for silence.

The walls of my house are crowded with bookcases, china and pictures, while the floors collect half-sorted volumes of music and mounds of junk mail waiting to be recycled. I have no problem with being surrounded by objects. They don't threaten or encroach on me. It's the air I want. The breathing space.

Downstairs, the plasticine cats have long disappeared. Alice tells me they're marketing the new game specifically for families who want non-violent games for their children. Joel has decided to specialise in that area. I'm delighted that he listened to Alice, weighed up her arguments and adapted. They've received a lot of media interest, but it seems to me that his success is far less important than his willingness to listen. His Great Leap Forward.

My kitchen is pristine, the surfaces sparkling with lack of use. No more washing-up lying around waiting for Joel's delayed good intentions. I only cook once a week, when he and Alice come on Friday evenings. Otherwise, I have ready-meals without additives from Marks & Spencer's or bread and cheese and salad. My diet is perfectly healthy. All those years of cooking for Andrew, then Joel, have worn me out and I've lost interest. Braised kale bores me, I don't care about Malaysian chicken or crushed peas and mozzarella on toast with pecorino. I've wasted too much of my life cobbling together the inadequate contents of the fridge, consulting *Meals on a Budget*, or *How to Use Leftovers*, extending small amounts of meat with pastry or extra potatoes. The kind of meal that nobody wants today. Shepherd's pie, liver and bacon, heart stew.

I spend more of my time at the piano now that there are fewer distractions. I play for pleasure, working my way through Beethoven sonatas, Schumann's *Scenes from Childhood*, Mendelssohn's *Songs without Words*. I have begun to appreciate Bach's Preludes and Fugues, discovering in myself a new ability to appreciate the clear, mathematical counterpoint. There's a simplicity and depth in them that helps me breathe comfortably. It's like fresh, easy air blowing in from the sea, cool and invigorating.

I've woken up. It's been a gradual process over many, many years, but I know what I'm doing now. I'm no longer drifting in the rocky wake of someone else. I haven't completely abandoned that strange land, once removed from the world like a distant cousin, but I can cross over when I want to, knowing where I am, how to behave.

I'm learning to unravel the riddle of other people. When I was a child I hardly noticed their existence, the treasure hunt that went on without me. As a teenager I began to realise there were clues, but I couldn't find them. In my years with Joel and Andrew I could read the clues, but they didn't make sense. Now, finally, with my new understanding, I'm getting there. The treasure of perception is just around the corner.

I observe Joel and Alice closely when they come, never quite believing that it's all working and they're still getting on. It seems too good to be true. They often disagree, but they've established a pattern of behaviour to deal with conflict and it never flares out of control. Alice does most of the communicating.

'How's the business going?' I say.

'Fine,' says Joel.

Alice rolls her eyes. 'We might have a contract in South Africa,' she says.

'That sounds like a lot of extra work.'

'Yes,' says Joel.

'Maybe,' says Alice, 'but we're about to open a new office in Australia and they'll handle most of it.'

'Thanks for the information, Joel,' I say.

'Blood out of a stone,' says Alice. 'He'll be saying it's fine when the Arctic melts and we're all under six feet of water.'

Joel sighs. 'It usually is fine,' he says.

'But most people want more information,' she says, irritation creeping into her voice.

'Anyway,' I say, 'I like to know what's going on.'

Alice smiles at me. 'I bet you didn't know anything until I came along.'

'Exactly.'

'I think you did the right thing when you got rid of the grass in your garden,' says Joel, looking out of the window. 'It takes me hours to cut ours.'

'That's because you chose to buy a house with acres of lawn. Surely you could afford a gardener?'

'He loves doing it himself,' says Alice. 'He can't wait for the weekend when he can get on the mower and drive up and down in endless straight lines.'

He looks at her, raises an eyebrow and tries to suppress the smile that's creeping across his face.

They've wriggled themselves into a position that suits both of them. In public Alice is in charge, organising the conversation, nudging, manoeuvring, shoving gently. In reality, Joel is in control. She knows it and he knows that she knows it, so he doesn't mind her pretending to other people. They are like two pieces of machinery that don't quite match, but which can be rubbed down, oiled and manipulated until they fit together, each losing some edges, snuggling up against each other, adjusting until they run smoothly.

I've watched Joel look at Alice from the other side of the room, his face soft and secretly delighted. I can't imagine that Andrew ever looked at me like that. Joel's genes must be more diluted than Andrew's. Something made it through from past generations. He's fortunate that he has an obsession for computers because he's been able to channel the ability into a practical way of making money. Earning a living has never been a problem. And, unlike Andrew, he's not static. He learns as he goes along.

Alice has taught him how to be generous, a previously underdeveloped aspect of his personality. He brings me flowers every now and again.

'Here,' he says, waving a bunch of daisies and pink carnations at me. He hasn't yet mastered the art of doing it graciously. 'We got them from a flower stall just off the motorway. There's a lay-by, so it's easy to park.'

'Thank you. How lovely.' I'm still taken by surprise—it's not easy accepting gifts when you haven't had much practice.

Alice is changing us bit by bit. We're watching her movements so that we can copy her steps. We proceed with a certain hesitancy, but at least we're both willing.

When they come for supper, she throws her arms round me with enthusiasm. An extraordinary warmth pours out of her, both emotional and physical, which passes over to me, a deep heat that penetrates my skin, relaxes muscles, soothes spidery, taut nerves. I can tolerate it.

I have learnt to love Alice in a quiet, satisfying

way.

But I don't need her. I don't need anyone. I'm still the baby who didn't want to be held, who was happy in an isolated corner somewhere upstairs in Audlands, out of earshot. I'm most comfortable without too much emotion. Whenever I step out into the wide avenue of normality I'm cleverly disguised, a skilled impostor. I've spent all my life attempting to put on the same clothes as everyone else, keep up with the fashion, but it was never going to work because I'm the wrong shape. And it doesn't matter. That's what fills me with secret delight when I wake in the early morning and feel the warmth of my bed, see the promise of a new day creep past the edge of my curtains, hear the raindrops spattering against my window, or the wind rattling the drainpipe on the front of the house. I don't have to pretend any more.

I wonder if Alice saw through me. I prefer to think not. I've had years of practice in the art of deception. I just didn't know I was doing it.

I want to hear the echo of nothing for miles around. I want to be the only person who can disturb the air when I walk through my house. I can feel it parting to let me through, closing up again behind me. The silence soaks into my mind, an invisible medicine that drips down, melting hardened arteries, easing its way into neglected and forgotten places.

Apparently, loneliness is a twenty-first-century disease which leads to alcoholism, drug-taking, depression, suicides. It's better to be married if you want to live longer. I defy all of this research. I thrive on the emptiness of my house.

Andrew landed on his head and broke his back, dying instantly, according to the doctors.

There weren't many of us at the funeral. Joel, Alice, Harriet, Mary and Andrew's mother. A representative from the council turned up at the last minute. 'The streets of Northfield will miss him,' he said. 'He cleaned with an unusual enthusiasm.'

'It wouldn't have lasted,' I said. 'His enthusiasm always turned to boredom in the end.'

Mary cried. I was more moved by her reaction than by Andrew's death. I couldn't produce any tears for him.

'He never found what he wanted, did he?' said Mary.

'He didn't know what he wanted,' I said. 'He wouldn't have recognised it if it had come up behind him in the street and tapped him on the shoulder.'

'I knew he was like that from the first time I met him,' said Harriet. She doesn't remember her flirtatious behaviour, her silent approval, her thumbs-up sign. 'It's a pity you didn't have any other boyfriends—you'd have seen through him in seconds,' she said.

'He died amongst friends,' said the man taking the service. 'Doing what he loved most—climbing.' I wondered who'd given him that information.

Miranda stood by her car after the service and talked to me for a while. She seemed to have acquired a calm resignation. 'His whole life was a disaster, really.'

But I'd heard him play Bach on the roof of

426

Audlands. 'How could anyone play the violin like that and be a failure?'

She looked past me. The gates of the crematorium opened on to a complex system of five converging roads. Drivers hesitated to pull out, looking left and right several times as if they were watching a match at Wimbledon.

'It was such a struggle to get him to do anything,' she says. 'You can't help wondering what it was all for.'

After he died, Miranda and I went back to his flat to sort out his things and we found nothing there except mirrors. We could see ourselves on every wall, reflected by the mirrors. Was his lack of identity so great that he could only believe he existed if he could see himself all the time?

There wasn't even a television. It was a small, empty bedsit with very little food in the fridge, no books, nothing except the climbing equipment that he hadn't needed for his ascent of Audlands. I opened a few drawers and cupboards and found them almost empty. A handful of unpaid bills sat on the table.

'How odd,' I said. 'He used to like television. And where are the comics?'

I turned round and found Miranda sitting on the bed with tears spilling out over her bony, shrivelled cheeks. 'What did he do all day when he wasn't working?' she said.

'I suppose he went out.'

'But he didn't have any friends.'

'We don't actually know that. Perhaps someone will turn up.'

He needed people, even if they irritated him. Without them he didn't exist.

427

I sat down next to her, but couldn't decide if she would like me to put an arm round her shoulders so I didn't. We sat side by side for some time until she sighed and slipped back into her capable mode. She didn't wipe away the tears—they dried on her cheeks.

'He must have sold the comics to buy the climbing equipment. It was only a matter of time before the violin went too.'

We both knew no friends would ever appear. Other people only existed as a backdrop to his life and he had never appreciated this. In the last few months, nostalgia had bathed our marriage in a rosy, unrealistic light, which led him to believe that we should get back together again. He wanted human contact, conversation, someone to moan at. He was undermined by the bleak chill of loneliness.

Even though he denied it, I suspect he started to spend all his spare time playing the violin once his mother had returned it. The sound he made when he stood on the roof of Audlands was too powerful, too assured to be a half-remembered technique from twenty-six years ago. He must have been practising. For hours. Preparing his concerts in the air.

Did he fall, or did he jump?

He'd looked secure up there on the roof of Audlands when we left, and there was no way of knowing what really happened. I have tried to imagine his reasoning. He was performing for an audience, which always made him happy. But the audience disappeared when the floor collapsed in the Long Gallery. He was up there on his own, playing to no one. He wanted to be the centre of attention, but he became a neglected sideshow as the main event happened elsewhere. Did that tip him over the edge, metaphorically and physically? Did he throw himself over in a typical theatrical gesture, so that he could imprint himself on my consciousness for the rest of my life? But how disappointing to fly through the air unwatched, without the collective intake of shocked breath. Perhaps it was a momentary decision as he was hit by a wave of despair, suddenly confronted by his own hopelessness and lack of purpose.

Or did he simply try to peer over the edge to see where we had all gone and lose his balance?

I have discussed the possibility of depression with Miranda. It seems the most likely explanation for his behaviour, but why didn't any of us ever consider it? Maybe because he was always like that. Can you be born with depression? Is there a magic pill somewhere that might have improved him, drawn back a curtain and revealed a window so that he could look outwards instead of inwards?

I have to remind myself that there were some good times. He made an effort occasionally.

'I want to treat you, Jess. We'll dine out today. Caviar, ocean salmon, crème brûlée. Only the best.'

'How will we pay for it?'

'Buttons.'

He was witty, I suppose, clever with words, able to read a situation and recognise other people's weaknesses.

'Steady there, Eamon. You almost sounded natural for a second. Mustn't let the hot air out too quickly, eh? Global warming and all that.'

Funny to the rest of us. Not to Eamon.

Perhaps I should be grateful to him after all, for the shock to my system. At least he woke me up long enough to recognise what I didn't want.

*　　　*　　　*

I stand in front of my bedroom mirror, trying to decide what to wear. I don't want to look old, but I shouldn't try to be young and frivolous either. I settle for a skirt and jumper. Sensible, mature, unobtrusive.

The doorbell rings and I run downstairs. A courier stands there with a large bouquet of flowers. 'Have you got the right house?' I ask.

'Jessica Courtenay?' he says.

I nod and take them. There's a card inside. 'Congratulations!' it says. 'Love, Mary.' How does she always know the right thing to do?

I've phoned my parents, but I'm not picking them up today. My father's wheelchair is heavy and cumbersome, and I usually manage to inflict some major damage on myself or the car whenever I try to get it into the boot.

My parents moved about three months ago. The death-watch beetles forced the decision upon them. Once you think of all those creatures ticking away throughout the building, time becomes more significant. You can hear the seconds passing, linking up, becoming minutes, hours, days, expanding into years of munching and crumbling.

They sold the estate to a consortium. I think there are plans to turn it into a country club—stocking the lake with salmon, breeding pheasants. The new owners must know about the beetles, but I'm not convinced they appreciate the extent of the problem.

My parents found a nice bungalow in Bromsgrove. They like the solid concrete floors, the certainty that the building will hold up, remain constant.

Every now and again, when I'm passing, I drive into the entrance of Audlands—just to check. It still takes your breath away. The house is undefeated, indestructible, an ultimate survivor, like Artemis. It looks as if another hundred years couldn't touch it, even though you know there's a fatal disease eating its way through the interior.

My father wheels himself round his new home, grumbling about the lack of space, the cramped doorways, the heat.

'The central heating is ridiculous. Can't bear it,' he says to me. 'Such a waste of money.'

'But you can afford it.'

My mother, on the other hand, loves the heating. She has one of the bedrooms as a study and sits with her computer for hours, no longer needing to leap up and do something to keep warm. She's lost interest in décor and furnishings.

'The colour's fine,' she said when I asked about the grey walls in the lounge. 'Doesn't matter. I'm hardly ever in there. Did you know they do treasure hunts in cars now? You can get the clues off the internet.'

'Yes, I've heard that.'

'There are dozens of websites that cover local areas. We must try one. You could do the driving, couldn't you?'

'We'd have to find someone else to join in.'

'Mind you, I think my clues are better.'

It still upsets her that they never finished the

431

treasure hunt at the barn dance. 'If only Andrew could have waited a bit. Well—I mean, poor dear, I know he didn't mean to—But they were so close.'

She produced the treasure a few days later. An enormous box of chocolates with a picture of Chatsworth on the front. Better than the token prizes of my childhood. The evening before Harriet left, back to her job abroad and Philip, the three of us sat down together in front of *Coronation Street* and ate our way through the chocolates. It was a satisfying, companionable evening and my father's contempt didn't touch us.

'Disgusting,' he said. 'Why would anyone want to eat that much?'

'You built your fortune on chocolate,' said Harriet.

He picked up his book of Sudoku. He gets through the daily crossword too quickly now and needs more of a challenge. 'Not much use when the floors give way underneath you,' he said.

Philip left two days after the funeral. He shook my hand before he went. 'Goodbye, Jess,' he said. 'I'm glad we were able to meet up again and get a few things sorted out.'

Did we? I couldn't think of anything to say.

'I'm sorry if I was unkind when we were younger,' he said, unexpectedly. 'I don't think I would behave like that now.'

'I wouldn't give you the chance,' I said, and smiled.

He smiled back, open, friendly, without rancour.

Harriet drove him to the airport in my car and came home dry-eyed, wanting to know if I'd go for a trip to Warwick Castle with her. If she wants to be private, that's fine with me.

'It was odd seeing Philip at Audlands again,' she said.

'It would be. He hadn't been back for years.'

'He was like a brother to us once, wasn't he?'

I'm not sure. I don't know enough about brothers. 'Will you keep in contact with him?' I asked.

'Probably,' she said.

'He's not as he seems,' I said.

A gentle smile hovered on her lips. 'Don't worry, Jess,' she said. 'I'm grown up. I can handle my life.'

*   *   *

I wait downstairs in the reception area, clutching a little giraffe that I found in Marks & Spencer's. There was only one left on the shelf, and he was watching me with large eyes, his head on one side. I want him, I thought.

I watch the clock. Just before two Joel appears beside me, grey-faced and unshaven. 'Did you get any sleep?' I ask.

He shrugs. 'About an hour,' he says and grins, his whole face lighting up in a way that I've never seen before. 'How's it feel, Grandma?'

The word is shocking and amplifies the ambivalence that's been steadily growing inside me for the last eight hours, since Joel phoned me at six o'clock this morning. Delight that I have a grandson, and fear that I'll be drawn out of the purity of the spaces I've set up around me. I have a sense of imminent invasion.

'Wonderful,' I say.

They'll keep asking me to babysit, I keep

433

thinking. Other people will want to share my air.

'You should see him,' he keeps saying. 'He's unbelievable.'

'If you don't mind,' I say. 'I prefer Granny to Grandma.'

On the dot of two, we move with the crowd towards the lifts. 'Let's take the stairs,' says Joel. 'It's quicker.'

Alice is half-lying, half-sitting, beaming, glowing with a rich, inner warmth.

'He's gorgeous,' she says when I give her the giraffe. She shakes him so that his head wobbles up and down, while the big eyes keep staring at her.

'When are your parents coming?' I ask.

'Not for an hour yet. I've had a long talk with Mum on the phone. They're waiting for my sister to arrive. She's driving up from Gloucester.'

The baby is in a cot at the end of the bed. I lean over and look at him. 'He's not black,' I say, disappointed. I'd envisaged a baby with vibrant glossy skin, but he has a light tan with a matt finish. His delicate head is facing upwards, gently blurred with sleep. His cheeks flutter in and out as he sucks in his sleep.

'He'll get darker,' says Alice. 'They're always lighter when they're born. Do you want to pick him up?'

'But he's asleep.'

'He won't mind,' she says. 'He hardly ever cries.'

I look at him in awe. A baby that doesn't cry? Surely not.

Alice gets up and limps round the bed. Leaning over, she puts a hand under his head and lifts him, her face open with tenderness. She places him in my arms. It's a long time since I held a baby. I'm

434

not sure if I can remember how to do it. He wakes and looks up at me, his eyes black and direct. Newborn babies can't really see, I say to myself, but it's difficult to believe as I look into those soft, knowing eyes. He blows a bubble and drops peacefully back to sleep. His eyelids are moist and translucent, flickering with baby dreams.

There's music in the background. Semiquavers, *pianissimo*, just a whisper, growing with controlled impatience, gathering strength. *Crescendo, poco a poco.*

I've spent my whole life plodding a weary path to where I am now. I've arrived at a place where I can breathe easily. Alone, surrounded by space, my hair blowing in the wind. I don't want to surrender it for the tangled world of other people.

Now that space is being folded up without my permission, tied with a neat knot, sent spiralling away by a stronger, more urgent gale.

But there's nothing I can do to save myself.

A flurry of machine-like semiquavers, falling over each other, climbing, growing, growing. The crash of huge chords in the bass and a glorious melody bursting out in a tumultuous exuberance.

I fall in love all over again.

ACKNOWLEDGEMENTS

I would like to thank the following:

My writing group—Chris, Pauline, Jeff, Gina, Margaret and Dorothy—for their continuing willingness to read through and comment in detail.

Laura Longrigg for being such a good agent and emailing so frequently and cheerfully.

The Gateleys for the use of their upstairs room and the view of their wonderful garden.

Carole Welch, Ruth Tross, Henry Jeffreys and everyone else at Sceptre for all their help and advice.

CHIVERS LARGE PRINT
-direct-